I0645356

OUT OF TIME

The Great Library Series by Laurie Graves

Maya and the Book of Everything (Book One)

Library Lost (Book Two)

Also by Laurie Graves
Tales from the Other Green Door (Podcast)

The Other Green Door Podcast is available at
Hinterlandspress.com/podcast.

OUT OF TIME

Laurie Graves

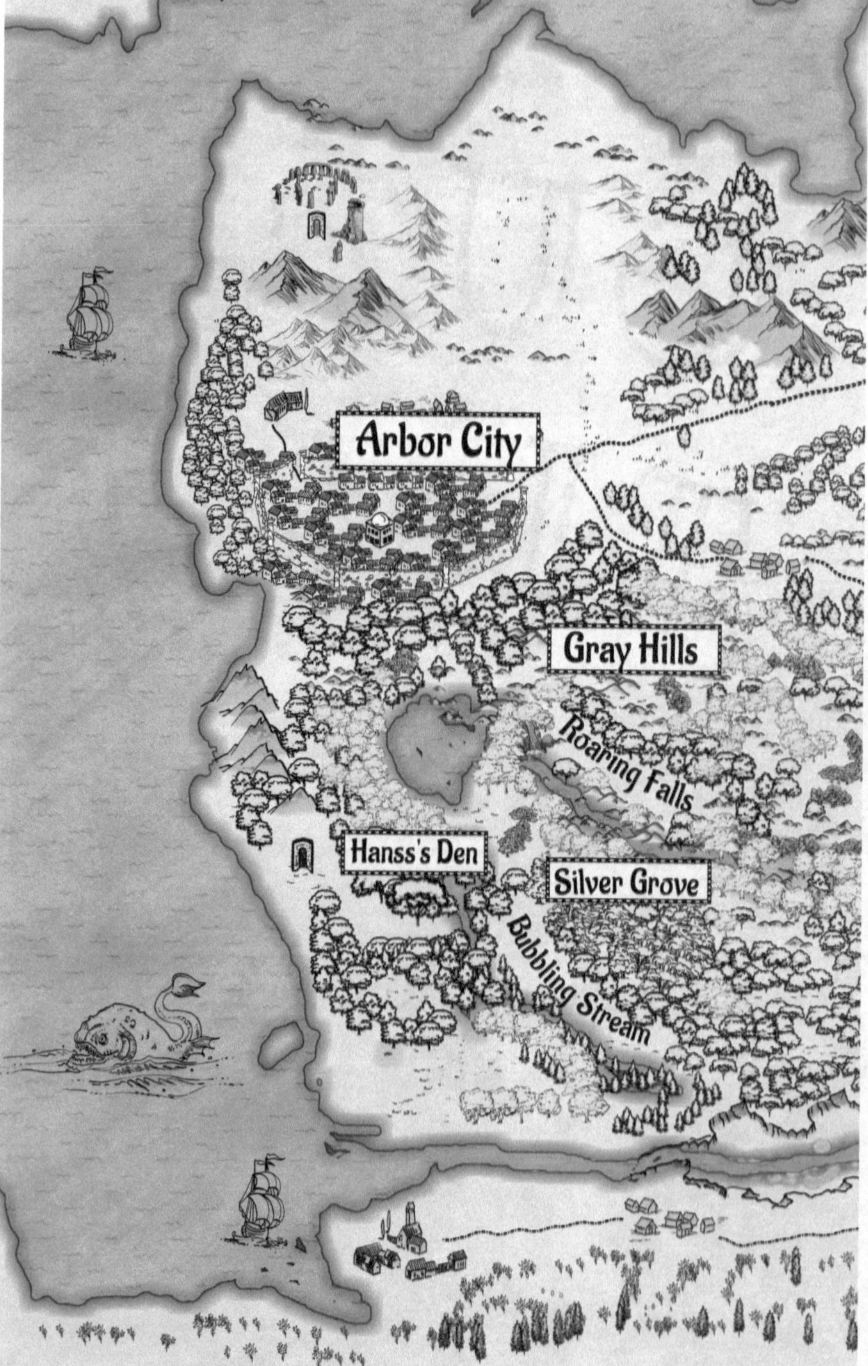

Arbor City
Gray Hills
Roaring Falls
Hanss's Den
Silver Grove
Bubbling Stream

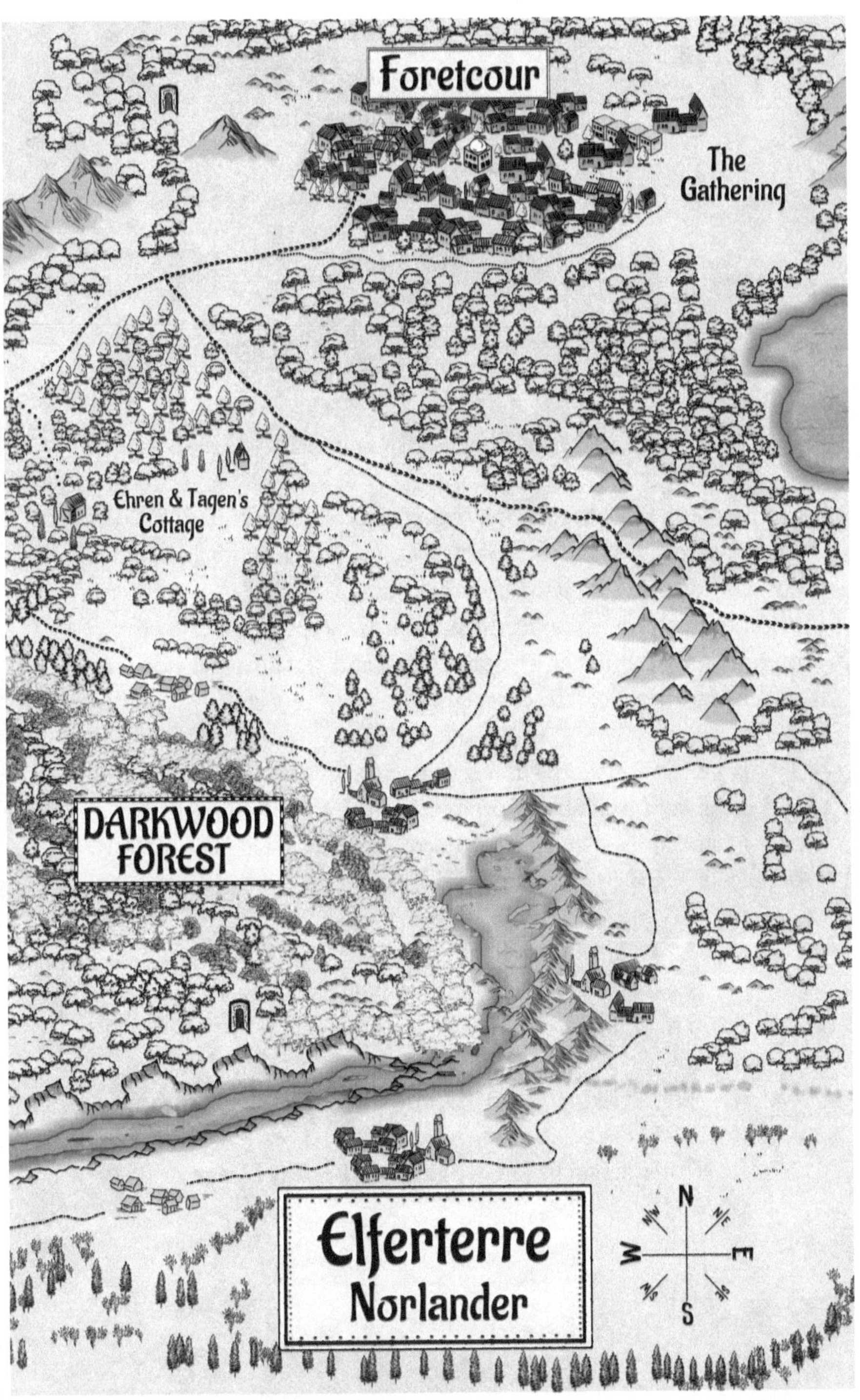

Foretcour
The Gathering
Ehren & Tagen's Cottage
DARKWOOD FOREST
Elferterre
Norlander
N
NE
E
SE
S
SW
W
NW

Published by
Hinterlands Press, Winthrop, Maine
hinterlandspress.com

Copyright©2020 by Laurie Graves
All rights reserved.

ISBN: 978-0-9978453-6-5

Library of Congress Control Number: 2020921589

No part of this publication may be reproduced, distributed, or transmitted in any form or by any means, including photocopying, recording, or other electronic or mechanical methods, without the prior written permission of the publisher, except in the case of brief quotations embodied in critical reviews and certain other noncommercial uses permitted by copyright law.

This is a work of fiction. Names, characters, businesses, places, events, and incidents are either the products of the author's imagination or used in a fictitious manner. Any resemblance to actual persons, living or dead, or actual events is purely coincidental.

Hanss on the Run illustration by Clif Graves
(based on *A Maine Coon cat in the snow of Canada* by tomitheos)

Map of Norlander by Clif Graves

Cover design by James T. Egan of Bookfly Design

In memory of my father, Ronald James Meunier
who showed me that my heart's home was in
County Tolkien

Special thanks to Deirdre Graves, Shannon Mulkeen, and
Mike Mulkeen, whose generosity, constructive criticism, and
unflagging support helped shape this book.

1: Stranger in a Strange City

Maya fell to her knees as she watched her younger self and her mother go into the corner store. All around her were sights, smells, and sounds that Maya knew well—the tall brownstones, the dusty sidewalk, the clanking of a garbage truck. But everything felt off-kilter to her, as though the city street were on a slant, and what was familiar looked unfamiliar. Swallowing, Maya felt horribly sick, and for a moment she was afraid she was going to throw up on the sidewalk. Maya swallowed again and again. "No, no, no," she said to herself, and gradually her stomach settled down. Blinking, Maya looked up and down the street. The sidewalk was empty, and no one had noticed her. But for how long?

Next to the store, there was a brownstone with a large stoop. Not wanting to be seen by anyone going in and out of the store—especially her mother—Maya stumbled to the far side of the stoop, hiding in its shadow behind a row of garbage cans.

Sitting hunched up, with her face on her knees, Maya shivered, thinking about Cinnial, the Office, Bigly, and the devices he had used on her. Maya started to cry as she remembered the pain, the way the devices had dug deep into her brain, how she had held out until blood had come from her nose and ears, and how two trolls had to drag her back to her cell. Her head still ached. Her mouth was dry, and it was hard to swallow.

But she hadn't betrayed the Great Library or Black Mountain or Jeam or Captain Creb or anyone else. Gradually, Maya stopped crying, and taking deep breaths to calm herself, she leaned against the stoop.

"Tomorrow and tomorrow and tomorrow," Bigly had leered at her. "Eventually, I'll get what I need."

Wiping the tears from her face, Maya smiled a little. "Take that, Bigly. If I'm not there, then you can't torture me." Maya's smile broadened, and she thought, "I wish I could see Bigly's face when he finds out I'm gone." Picturing the troll's furious expression, Maya even laughed. It was a shaky one but a laugh all the same, and suddenly Maya was struck by what she had done. On her own, without assistance from a Book of Everything or a special acorn, she had escaped from Bigly and the Office and had returned to Earth. Well, maybe not exactly on her own. Time had helped, and her mother had, too. But the energy and the will had come from within herself, and Maya trembled, thinking about the implications.

"They knew I might be able to do this," Maya said to herself. "Sydda, the Great Library's Book of Everything, and even Ariel. They were counting on it." Maya sighed. "It was all part of the plan."

Still, part of the plan or not, Maya felt proud, triumphant even, and for a little while she simply sat and smiled. Gradually, she realized how thirsty and hungry she was, and Maya stood on shaky legs. She had no money, but remembering what her younger self had done, Maya knew where she might find some if she was lucky. Slowly, Maya made her way around the stoop and peeked cautiously into the small store. Maya was relieved to see that the store was empty, that her younger self and her mother were gone.

Mr. Hopper, the owner, sat behind the counter, and he smiled in his pleasant way at her when she came into the store. Maya smiled back at him before going to the aisle with the chips and the snacks. All those years ago, her mother had told Maya that because it was her birthday, she could choose anything she wanted, and briefly, Maya had considered getting a big bag of potato chips, her father's favorite snack. Standing before the chips, Maya had deliberated with herself, weighing the pros and cons of potato chips—which she could share later with her father—versus Peanut M & M's. But the Peanut M & M's had won, as they always did, and when Maya had rushed to the front to get her candy, she left behind the little red pocketbook with the gold handles, her birthday present from Mémère. Her mother, distracted by the jumble of colors in the store, hadn't noticed.

And there it was—the little red pocketbook with the gold handles—sitting next to a bag of chips. Mr. Hopper, waiting on another customer who had just come in, didn't see Maya remove some of the money and put the pocketbook into one of the roomy pockets of the gray trousers that Chance had given her.

Maya thought, "Sorry, young Maya, but I need this money."

Maya grimaced a little, remembering how, as a six year old, she had howled with grief when she had realized she had lost her birthday pocketbook and money. That day there had been no new castle for her ponies. Lily had patiently let Maya cry until she had worn herself out, going from sobs to hiccups.

But then Maya's dry throat and rumbling stomach brought her back to her present condition, reminding her how thirsty and hungry she was. Maya bought two bottles of cold tea, a bag of potato chips, and some Peanut M & M's.

"After all," Maya thought. "It's my birthday. But am I six, or am I sixteen?" Maya shook her head at this silly thought, but she did feel disoriented, as though she were being stretched between her past and her present.

After paying for the tea and the food, Maya said, "Thank you, Mr. Hopper."

The old man squinted at her. "You know my name. Do I know you?"

Maya shook her head. "No. I'm here visiting family, and they told me your name."

Mr. Hopper said, "Well, then. Welcome to New York."

"I've heard it's a great city."

"It sure is," came the cheerful reply. "The greatest."

Maya left. Outside the store, she gulped down one of the bottles of tea and then wished she hadn't. The cold drink gave her cramps, and Maya stood with her eyes closed until the pain went away. Then shuffling like an old person with bad knees, Maya walked slowly one street over to the small park with the swings, a park she had often played in. All the benches were full with mothers and nannies who were watching various children. Maya settled under a tree, and looking up, she noticed the way the sun streamed through the branches. She munched some chips, ate M & M's, and drank tea. Never had food or drink tasted as good, and Maya sat in a sort of dream under the tree, watching the pattern of light on the leaves and listening to the children laugh and shriek.

"Maya! Is that you?"

At first Maya didn't respond. She continued eating and staring at the leaves. Who would be talking to her? There must be another Maya in the park.

"Maya!" a familiar voice called. "I know that's you even though your hair is the wrong color."

"You were told her hair would be blonde," a man said patiently.

"Even so, I wasn't prepared."

Shaking her head, Maya looked around. Maybe somebody was talking to her. Not far away stood a tiny woman in bright clothes and a taller man with dark hair. They were both holding books, which they put in their back pockets.

Maya blinked at them and blinked again. "Alani? Alexander?"

"Maya!" Alani cried joyfully, rushing over to Maya and hugging her. "I knew it! I knew you'd make it."

"What are you doing here?" Maya asked.

"Looking for you," Alani answered.

"Looking for me?"

Alexander crouched beside Alani. "For you. We've come to bring you home."

"Home?" Maya felt like a fool for parroting Alexander, but her sluggish mind couldn't take in the fact that Alani and Alexander were both on Earth, in New York City, looking for her.

Alani stared at Maya's peaked face. "Can you walk?"

"Not too well. I've come a long way. Without a Book."

Alani squeezed her arm. "We know. And it took a lot out of you. Of course it did."

Alexander, too, was studying Maya's face. "We had better take a taxi. I don't think she can handle the subway."

"Right," Alani replied briskly. "The League will have to cover the cost."

"They will," Alexander said. "They'll be thrilled that Maya made it here."

Maya sighed. "It wasn't easy."

Alani gave Maya another hug. "I'm sure it wasn't. Oh, Maya! We have a lot to talk about."

"But not right now," Alexander said firmly. "Maya needs to rest first."

A while later, Maya was in a taxi, sitting between Alani and Alexander. Maya drooped with fatigue, and Alani whispered, "Rest your head on my shoulder."

Maya slid down, leaning against Alani's strong little shoulder. She dozed as they crossed the Brooklyn Bridge and only woke up when the taxi stopped in front of a brick six-story apartment building in Bay Ridge.

"Is she going to be all right?" the taxi driver asked as Alexander paid him.

"She'll be all right," Alexander replied. "She needs to rest. She's come a long way."

"She doesn't look so good."

"She'll be all right," Alexander repeated as they got out of the cab.

The taxi left. Alani put her arm around Maya to steady her. "Our apartment's on the fourth floor. But there's an elevator. You won't have to walk."

"I could have carried her," Alexander said.

Maya grinned a little. "That wouldn't be embarrassing."

Alexander grinned back. "Lucky for you there's an elevator."

"Lucky for you, too," Alani pointed out. "Maya's small, but she's not that small. You would have been huffing and puffing by the time you got to our floor."

The elevator had a heavy wooden outer door, which opened to a traditional elevator with a sliding metal door. As Maya went into the elevator, she smelled curry and other spices coming from the apartments on the first floor. Even though it smelled good, Maya knew her stomach couldn't handle spicy food. Not yet.

On the fourth floor, Alexander and Alani's apartment was small and clean. There was a galley kitchen with a round table at the end, a good-sized living room, a bathroom, and two bedrooms, one of which had been prepared for Maya. In that room were a twin bed with a blue comforter, a bureau, a nightstand with a lamp and a clock, a desk, and even a bookshelf filled with books. On the wall above the bed were two framed pictures of nautilus shells.

"This is all for me?" Maya asked, blinking back tears as she thought about where she had come from—that dark, dank cell in the Office.

"For you," Alani answered gently. "We were hoping you'd make it."

"We were counting on it," Alexander added firmly.

Alani kissed Maya on the cheek. "Get some rest. There are pajamas in the bureau. And other clothes, too. I'll be checking on you, and later I'll bring in some tea and toast for you."

"Okay," Maya said, walking slowly into the room and closing the door. She took off the gray shirt and trousers and laid them on the chair. She found some pajamas—black leggings and a top with red polka dots—put them on, and gratefully slid between the cool clean sheets.

Maya slept until Alani brought in some toast and tea as she had promised. But Maya didn't say much, and Alani, sitting on the side of the bed as Maya ate and drank, didn't press her.

For two days, Maya slept on and off, only getting up to go to the bathroom or to get something to eat. One day, Alexander was gone. "Where is he?" Maya asked, sitting at the round table in the kitchen as she ate some cereal. Alani sat down across from her.

"He's at work."

"Where does Alexander work?" Maya asked in surprise.

"He's working at the Brooklyn Public Library, not far from here, and I do, too. The League of Librarians has a presence there. We both wanted to do something useful while we were waiting for you, and after all, we're librarians. Tomorrow, I'll be working, but Alexander will be here."

On the evening of the second day, Maya was ready to talk and to eat something more substantial than toast and cereal. She came out of her bedroom to find Alani and Alexander both reading in the living room. Alexander was sprawled across the couch, and Alani sat in a small chair that looked as though it had been made especially for her.

Sitting up, Alexander put his book aside and peered at Maya. "You're looking better."

Alani said, "Not nearly as peaked. Would you like something to eat besides toast and cereal?"

Maya smiled. "I would."

"Chinese food?" Alani asked hopefully. "There's a little takeout place around the corner."

Alexander rolled his eyes. "Alani's obsessed with Chinese food."

Maya laughed. "I love Chinese food, too. Sounds great."

Alani stared triumphantly at her husband. "Ha!"

"Ha!" Alexander said back, and he was smiling.

It wasn't long before they were all sitting around the glass table in the kitchen. From outside, Maya could hear people calling and cars starting and stopping. This street was much busier than the one in Manhattan where she lived with her parents, but Maya liked it as she felt the rhythm of the neighborhood and the families who walked by on the sidewalk below the apartment. Everyday people as her mémère might have called them.

At first Maya, Alani, and Alexander didn't talk and instead concentrated on their food—crispy tofu with vegetables, rice, and dumplings.

Maya laughed when she saw the message in her fortune cookie: *You have traveled a long ways.*

"You sure have," Alani said. Then she asked gently, "Maya, are you ready to tell us about what happened in Mortmain?"

"Yes, but first tell me about the Great Library. Has Cinnial...?" Maya didn't finish the question.

Alexander answered sadly, "Caxton's green Book finally fell and gave Cinnial the information he wanted. But we had been preparing for that day, and there was enough time to evacuate the Great Library. Astrid, Sydda's wife, took the Great Library's Book to a planet called Pamant, which is on the edge of a galaxy far away from the Great Library. Only Sydda, Ebeneezer, Mortimer, and Ichabod stayed behind."

"Are they dead?" Maya asked.

Alani blinked as her eyes filled with tears. "They are dead."

Alexander said, "The goings-on at the Great Library are blocked from us now that Cinnial is in charge. But it wasn't blocked when Cinnial murdered them all. Our Books told us when Sydda and the others were killed." He stopped, and all three were sad and silent as they thought about the four librarians who had stayed with the Great Library until the end.

Bowing her head in grief and out of respect for Sydda, Maya thought, "I bet Sydda knew he was going to die." Maya looked up. "What about Viola, Simon, Rosalind, Sebastian, Evangeline?" Here Maya's breath caught. "And Mémère?"

"All fine," Alexander answered. "You might like to know that Andy and a spy named Diana are with them. They used Earth's Book of Everything to get to Caxton. And Chet is their prisoner. Mémère saved the day by hitting Chet over the head with a branch when he was attacking them. Viola used Earth's Book of Everything to take the children to the Forest of Arden, where they are safe."

"Wow!" Maya said, feeling proud of her grandmother and relieved that bringing Mémère to Caxton had been the right thing to do.

Alani patted Maya's arm. "You are your grandmother's granddaughter."

For a while nobody said anything, and Alexander was the first to speak. "Tell us what happened to you."

Maya took a deep breath. Where to begin? She decided to start with Julian. "You know about Julian and how he lost his memory?" Alani winced at hearing Julian's name, and Alexander nodded. "Well, he got it back, but he's different now. Still loyal to Cinnial but a little softer." Maya hesitated. "Julian brought me to Cinnial, but I think he felt bad about it."

"Julian's part isn't over," Alexander said. "Not by a long shot."

"Let's hope he redeems himself after all that he's done," Alani muttered. Then she leaned forward. "Tell us about Mortmain. None of us even knows what it looks like."

Maya told Alani and Alexander about the dark city with its tall buildings and with streets that always seemed to be in shadow. She told them about the troll Bigly, about his homely face and tiny feet.

"But I met some good trolls," Maya added quickly. "I'll tell you more about them later."

"And what about Cinnial?" Alexander asked.

Maya answered, "I didn't expect him to be so good looking. But inside, he isn't good. Not at all. He only thinks about himself, about what he wants. Nothing else matters to him, except maybe Julian. And Cinnial is still mad that his Apprentice Book was rejected at the Great Library. I think he always will be."

"Fair is foul, and foul is fair," Alexander said.

Surprised, Maya asked, "Where did you learn that? It's from *Macbeth*."

Alexander replied, "When I knew I would be coming to Earth, I read some Shakespeare. He had Earth's Book of Everything for a while. Did you know that?"

Maya shook her head. "No, but it makes so much sense."

"Never mind about Shakespeare," Alani said impatiently. "Tell us what happened in Mortmain."

Maya continued with her story, from her confrontation with Cinnial to her escape from Bigly to meeting Chance, who told her to go to Black Mountain. Smiling, she described Jeam and Captain Creb. "They helped me even though it was dangerous for them. I'll never forget those two. They showed me that not all trolls are bad."

Alexander said, "A good lesson to learn and remember."

"Yes," Maya answered, but the expression on her face was serious.

"You found Black Mountain?" Alexander asked gently.

"I found it. Did you know there was a Book of Everything there?"

"Sydda told us," Alexander answered.

Maya shook her head. "He never told me. Sydda hardly told me anything. If it hadn't been for Ariel, I don't think Sydda would have told me that the Great Library's Book of Everything wanted me to go to Mortmain."

Alani looked sad. "I know."

"Their overall goals are good," Alexander said quickly. "But the Books do plot, and it's not always good for those involved."

"Yeah," Maya replied, taking a deep breath, and she was silent for a few moments as she thought about Bigly and the Office.

Alani squeezed her hand. "Maya, I'm sorry."

Maya frowned, and Alexander asked, "What happened at Black Mountain?"

Maya answered, "I told everyone that Cinnial planned to take over the Great Library. They didn't know. Their Book hadn't told them."

"I bet that stirred things up," Alexander said.

"It sure did."

Alani laughed. "That might be one of the reasons that Chance sent you there. To stir things up."

Maya's smile faded. "But I didn't stay at Black Mountain for long. I got an image of Ariel, still alive but in bad shape. I knew I had to go back to Mortmain to save Ariel. But I didn't succeed." In a rush, Maya finished the story, ending with being thrown in a dark cell in the Office, being tortured by Bigly, and being rescued, in a way, by her mother. And Time.

Maya rubbed her tired eyes. "Mom saved my life."

"It all came together," Alani marveled. "You, your mother, and Time."

"But what if it hadn't?" Maya asked. "What then?"

Alexander hesitated before speaking. "There are others. But Sydda said you were the one who had come the farthest. That's why he sent us here. To help you in case you made it. He and the Great Library's Book foresaw the possibility that you would come to this time and place if you could escape from Bigly. However, it wasn't a sure thing. Not at all. But Alani and I came here to hope and to wait."

Maya thought, "Of course there are others. I should have known they wouldn't depend on one kid from Earth." Aloud she asked in a weary voice, "What now?"

On the coffee table in front of Alani and Alexander there were two books—one red and one black. Maya knew right away that these were the two Apprentice Books that Alani and Alexander had made and that these were the same Books the pair had had when they found Maya in the park. Leaning forward, Alani and Alexander opened the Books.

"Time to stop moping," the red Book said. "You have more work to do."

"You're going to theater camp," the black Book put in. "You're going to be in a play, and you're going to look for someone called the Accumulator."

2: An Unexpected Find

Maya stared at the black Book. "Theater camp? What the heck! I need to rescue Ariel and the Great Library. I don't have time for theater camp."

Alexander's Book answered patiently, "Ariel is fine. We would know if something happened. We are all connected, and there's nothing Cinnial can do about that. He might be able to block us from Mortmain, but he can't disconnect us unless one of us is destroyed, the way his team did with Caxton's green Book. We knew right away when the green Book went down."

"But what if they decide to destroy Ariel?" Maya asked in alarm.

Alexander's Book replied, "Nobody will care about an Apprentice Book now that Cinnial has taken the Great Library."

Alani's Book sniffed. "We're always underappreciated."

Maya was beginning to realize how useful it was to be small and underappreciated. And unnoticed. "Who's the Accumulator?"

Alexander's Book answered, "We don't know that much about him. Somehow he's always on the edge of what we can see. Out of focus, if you will. However, the Accumulator has a legendary collection of odd and useful things. We think he might have something that will help you. Or know where you can get it."

"How will I find him?" Maya asked.

"He will probably find you," Alani's Book replied. "From what we know, the Accumulator always has an eye out."

Maya's response was crisp. "Looking for odd and useful things. That would be me, wouldn't it?"

They all laughed, but it was a rueful laugh because they knew that Maya was more than a little right about herself and her potential appeal to the Accumulator.

After they stopped laughing, Maya said, "But theater camp? It seems so..."

"Trivial?" Alani's Book finished. "Not at all. You will come across something important because of theater camp."

"Like what?" Maya asked.

"We can't tell you too much," Alani's Book said in a guarded voice.

"We want you to make your own choices," Alexander's Book added.

Maya shook her head. "All right, all right."

"Besides," Alani's Book put in, "you know what a ham you are. Theater camp will be perfect. It's at a place called the Little Bard Theater, not far from the Brooklyn Academy of Music. Also, the Accumulator has been spotted in that area. We think he lives or works nearby."

Alexander's Book said, "You have been signed up as Anne Page. We thought it would be best if you didn't use your real name."

Maya waited for the Books to explain more, but they didn't. "What are they getting me into?" Maya wondered, knowing it was useless to ask the evasive Books any more questions.

The next day Maya watched kids her age enter the Little Bard Theater. After all she had been through, Maya should have felt confident about going into a theater in Brooklyn with kids her own age whom she had never met. Instead, Maya felt shy—self-conscious, even—and mostly it was because of the clothes she was wearing, baggy pants and a tunic top, all in eye-popping red, purple, and white with little black zigzags. Rummaging through the bureau drawers that morning, Maya had discovered that the rest of the clothes were also bright with bold patterns—exactly what Alani herself would have worn—and Maya had felt a sort of panic as she put on the pants and top. Styles came and went, but Maya was certain that when she was six, teenagers hadn't dressed like this.

But Alani had looked delighted when Maya, wearing the pants and top, came out of her bedroom. "Oh, you look cute. And even though you are blonde now, those bright colors are so becoming on you."

"I've always looked good in bright colors," Maya managed to say, not wanting to hurt Alani's feelings.

However, as Maya was leaving, Alexander had slipped her some money while Alani was in the bathroom. Raising his eyebrows, Alexander didn't say a word, and neither did Maya. She took the money, put it in her new wallet—purple with red hearts—and slid it into her backpack, which to Maya's relief was black with the logo of the Brooklyn Public Library on it. It had been a gift from Alexander as was the phone in the outside zipper pocket. As soon as theater camp ended for the day, Maya planned to buy new clothes.

Chin up, Maya went into the Little Bard Theater, a small building with a box office in front lined with long glass windows. Though the house wasn't large, Maya felt her spirits lift as she stood at the back of the theater and stared at the rows of seats and the stage—not big but with room enough for most plays. The Little Bard Theater had a spirit of expectation that Maya felt in even the humblest theaters—a place for the gathering of actors and story and audience—and there was no other space, not even the cinema, that gave her the same feeling.

Most of the kids were at the front of the theater in seats by the stage, but Maya and a few others stood in the back.

"Come on down!" a familiar voice boomed. "And let's get started."

Startled, Maya took a step back. She would have known who was speaking even if her eyes had been closed. But Maya's eyes were open, and she saw her father—tall, handsome, and with dark curly hair—stand up and beckon to the stragglers in the back, which included his daughter. Except he didn't know this. A woman with red hair got up and stood beside Maya's father. She smiled and beckoned more gently. "Professor Hammond is right. Come on. Don't be shy."

"Inga Peterson," Maya muttered to herself. "I can't believe the Books sent me here, where my father would be with the woman he left Mom for."

Right then and there Maya nearly rushed out of the theater. One foot, wearing a red sparkly sneaker, was poised to pivot so that she could march out and never come back. But then Maya thought about the long journey she had been on—from the South End in Waterville, Maine, where she had met Andy, to the Forest of Arden to the Great Library to Mortmain. The Books had had a purpose in wanting her to go to these places, and Maya sensed that this theater had a purpose, too. Once again, the Books hadn't told her everything she needed to know, but that didn't mean Maya shouldn't be at the Little Bard Theater with her father and Inga Peterson.

Therefore, Maya didn't leave. In her ridiculous outfit—an ensemble, as Mémère would have called it—she marched grimly down the aisle. With her arms folded, Maya stood in front of her father and Inga.

"What play are we doing?" Maya demanded, growing angrier and angrier as she stared at the two of them and thought about how they would hurt her and her mother. But Maya had faced Cinnial, and she would face her father and Inga.

For a while, nobody said anything. The other kids stared at her, too astounded to even snicker at her clothes. Flushing, Inga blinked at Maya, and her father frowned as though trying to remember where he had seen this fiery girl before.

Finally, with a glint in his eyes, her father answered, "*A Midsummer Night's Dream.* Does that meet with your approval?"

Inga laughed nervously, and some of the kids did, too. Maya swallowed. She had seen that look in her father's eyes many times, and Maya realized what would come next if she kept pushing. Her father would bellow at her. She would bellow back and then would be asked to leave. Maya saw this possibility in a flash and knew that she had come too far to risk it all by fighting with her father.

Maya swallowed again and for once backed down. "Good play," she said weakly.

Her father nodded curtly. "Right. And what is your name?"

Maya almost blurted out her real name but then caught herself. "Anne Page."

"Anne Page, huh? Well, go sit down so that we can begin."

Most of the kids were sitting in the first row, but Maya sat by herself in the second row apart from the others. Despite feeling flustered after the encounter with her father, Maya thought about how *A Midsummer Night's Dream* was a perfect play for high school students. It was set in a magical forest with feuding fairies; it had four young lovers who were sent into a tailspin by the trickster Puck; it had Bottom, a man whose head was turned into a donkey's head; after which Bottom, with the donkey's head, became the love object of the fairy queen, who had been put under a spell by her conniving husband.

"But I hope I get a small part," Maya thought. "I'm short. Maybe one of the fairy queen's attendants. Peaseblossom would be perfect for me."

Inga began, "My name is Inga Peterson, and this is Professor Giles Hammond from NYU. He teaches Shakespeare, and he's generously agreed to help with theater camp this year. Today we're going to read through the play, and we'll do it again tomorrow. We'll switch it up as we go along so that we can get a sense of who's best for which part. We'll be going downstairs where we can all sit around big tables."

"Let's go, buckaroos," Giles boomed in a deep voice, motioning for them to follow him.

Everyone laughed—even Maya. She thought wistfully about how much she had missed her father. "If only I could tell him everything that's happened. If only I could tell him who I really am."

They went downstairs into a large basement with tiny windows. The basement had been divided into rooms—an office, a wardrobe room, restrooms—but to the side was an open space with two conference tables set end to end and plenty of chairs for everybody.

Sitting at the farthest end of the table away from her father and Inga, Maya found herself next to a boy who had shiny black hair and a short, straight nose. He grinned impishly at her, and Maya grinned back. "There's Puck," Maya thought. The boy on the other side of Puck was tall and had a quiet, watchful presence. He was slim, had reddish-brown hair, hazel eyes that glinted with humor, and, as

Maya would discover, a mobile face and voice that allowed him to take on almost any character.

As Maya stared at him, she thought in a flash, "He's the one." Then Maya shook her head. Where had that thought come from? The one for what? The last thing she needed was to become attached to someone from another time. Maya had done that before with Andy, and she didn't want to do it again.

Sensing Maya's gaze, the boy stared quizzically back at Maya as though he too felt something but didn't know exactly what it was. On the other side of him sat a tall girl with long blonde hair and an imperious expression. Frowning, she regarded Maya and put her hand on the boy's arm. Reluctantly, the boy turned away from Maya.

"All right," Inga said briskly. "Before we begin, I want you to introduce yourselves and tell us where you're from. Anne Page, you made a memorable entrance. Let's begin with you."

Maya stood and said in her best stage voice, "As you all know, my name is Anne Page." Then she added impulsively, "I'm from East Vassalboro, Maine, but right now I'm staying with friends in Bay Ridge."

Maya's father did a double take. "East Vassalboro?"

"That's right. Not too far from the library."

Her father shook his head. "What a strange coincidence! My in-laws live in East Vassalboro, and they're not far from the library either."

"Strange indeed," Maya murmured as she sat down. She had certainly given her father something to think about.

"That's a hard act to follow." Inga tipped her head to one side, considering Maya. "But let's continue on clockwise from Anne."

The boy with the impish face stood up. "I'm Jay Valdez, and I'm from Williamsburg."

Around the table, kids introduced themselves. Maya learned that the imperious girl was Lexie Norton. The boy with the hazel eyes was Will Henley. The rest of the names passed over Maya in a blur, but she knew that as the weeks went by, she would learn their names.

Leaning on the table, Maya rested her face against her hand and thought, "When this is over, I hope I know how to travel to the Great Library without a Book. But first I have to find the Accumulator. How am I going to do that?"

The room was silent, and Maya realized everyone was staring at her.

"Anne Page," Inga said, and Maya could tell by the tone of Inga's voice that this wasn't the first time her name had been called.

Maya sat up straight. "Sorry!"

"Would you start by reading Hermia's part?" Maya saw her father glance at Inga with a look that asked, "Are you sure you want to start with this pain in the ass?" But Inga smiled. "And Will Henley, would you read Lysander? As I mentioned before, we'll mix it up throughout the reading, both today and tomorrow."

The rest of the parts were assigned, books were passed out, and the play haltingly began.

Maya felt an even stronger connection with Will as they read their lines, and it seemed as though they were the only two in the room. The connection was there as the play progressed, and other kids read.

When that day's session was over, Maya jumped from her seat, rushed up the stairs, and left the theater. She didn't want to talk to anyone, especially Will. Or her father or Inga. All Maya wanted to do was get something to eat and drink.

Not far from the Little Bard Theater was a bakery and café called The Other Green Door. True to its name, there was a dark green door on the front. Inside, the café had a dim, mysterious feel. Next to each wooden booth by the wall there were windows nearly obscured by hanging ferns. Light filtered in through the green plants, barely illuminating the walls that were covered with honey-colored wood. Even the lights were gentle, adding a soft glow over everything. To complete the sense of otherworldliness, all the servers were slim and ethereal, and for a moment Maya wondered if she had stepped into another dimension. But no, the café was definitely on Earth. However there was something distant about the servers, something that rebuffed Maya as she considered them, and Maya couldn't read them the way she could read most people. The same was true for the cook, who occasionally came to the pass-through between the kitchen and the café to ring a chiming bell with a carved wooden handle to let the servers know an order was ready. Maya caught a glimpse of the cook's face, and with her high cheekbones and lovely dark face, she fit right in with the servers. Briefly, the woman considered Maya before turning back into the kitchen.

Despite the unusual atmosphere of the café, Maya immediately felt at home as she slipped into the one empty booth, and Maya knew she would be coming to The Other Green Door as often as she could. As Maya ran her hand along the fern hanging by the window, she sensed someone standing by the table. Turning, she expected to see one of the elven-looking servers, but instead Will Henley stared down at her, and he was alone.

Maya jumped. "I didn't expect to see you here."

Will smiled, but it was a tentative smile, and Maya could sense that even though he was not normally awkward around girls, Will was unsure about her. "May I sit here? All the other booths are full."

No, Maya wanted to answer, but instead she said, "Go ahead."

Will sat across from her, and for a while neither of them spoke. They both looked at their menus, and it didn't take Maya long to realize that the food served here was all vegetarian. Instead of turkey sandwiches and BLTs, there were rice and noodle bowls as well as whole-grain bread with toppings such as hummus, white beans, and walnut pâté.

Will glanced up from his menu. "Quite a selection, huh?"

Maya stared into his hazel eyes. "The food looks delicious," she said faintly, and Will grinned at her.

Their server, tall, slender, and dazzlingly handsome, stood by the table. He said, "Along with all kinds of delectable baked goods, we have sweet potato fries. Perfect for an afternoon snack."

"I've had them before, and they're good," Will said. "Want to share a large order?"

"Sure," Maya agreed and then silently berated herself. What in the world had made her agree to share an order of sweet potato fries with a boy she had recently met? It indicated that she at least wanted to be friends with Will. But between trying to find the Accumulator and figuring out how to get to the Great Library on her own, Maya felt as though she didn't have time for a new friend, boy or girl.

Maya turned to the server. "What do you have to drink?"

The server answered quickly, "Our specialty is chamomile iced tea, and it is especially delicious. Some customers come here just for that tea." Then he grinned. "And for our pastries and fries, too, of course."

Maya said, "I'll have a chamomile iced tea. Will, do you want one, too?" A little bemused, Will nodded. "Good," Maya continued. "And put everything on my check."

After the server left, Will said, "Though she be but little, she is fierce."

Despite her good intentions, Maya laughed. Then she caught herself and asked earnestly, "Will, why are you here?" Fidgeting, Will shrugged, and Maya sighed. "Look, I'm not going to be around long. Only for the play. Then I'll be leaving New York City."

"That's all right. I just wanted to get to know you. We're going to get the parts of Hermia and Lysander. You know we are." Without boasting, Will might have truthfully added, "We were the best of everyone there, except for Jay and maybe Lexie." But he didn't.

Maya grimaced. "I know."

For the first time, Will frowned. "Don't you want the part? I know I want to play Lysander."

"I would think you would want to play Bottom," Maya replied tartly. "That way you can be stroked and kissed by the fairy queen. Lexie Norton, that girl you were sitting next to, is going to get that part. You're going out with her, aren't you?"

Will actually flushed a little. "Kind of. Not really. Only a few times."

"Uh-huh."

"It's not serious!"

"For Lexie it is. I could tell by the way she looked at you."

Will blinked at Maya. "How old are you?"

"Sixteen going on forty," Maya answered. They both laughed, and the tension between them went away.

As Maya regarded the way Will's eyes crinkled when he smiled, she thought, "Oh, no." Then Maya noticed another thing: Will could see, and it was almost as strong with him as it was with her.

3: The Course of True Love

When Maya got back to the apartment in Bay Ridge, both Alani and Alexander were there, and they only had to glance at her face before asking simultaneously, "What's wrong?"

"You could have told me," Maya said, setting her bag down and plopping into a chair in the living room.

Alani sat in her small chair, and Alexander sat on the couch. "Told you what?" Alani asked.

"That my father and Inga Peterson would be running theater camp. Inga is the woman Dad left Mom for."

There was a long silence, and Maya could see they were as shocked as she had been. "You didn't know." Maya wearily leaned back in the chair. "The Books didn't tell you."

Alani and Alexander shook their heads. "Maya, I'm sorry," Alexander said. "You know how the Books are."

Maya ran a hand through her blonde curls. "I sure do. They only tell us what they think we need to know."

"Do you want to talk to them?" Alani asked. "They're in our bedroom. I can go get them."

Maya replied, "No, what's the use? That's how they are. We're like game pieces on a board to them."

"Except the game is deadly," Alexander said.

Maya sighed. "I know. And we're all part of it. Especially me."

Alani frowned. "Still, it wasn't right. They should have told you."

Alexander nodded. "They probably thought Maya wouldn't go if she knew who would be there."

"True," Alani said. "Nevertheless. Maya, you don't have to go back if you don't want to. I bet we can find the Accumulator some other way."

"No, I'll go back. Whenever the Books send me somewhere, it's always for a good reason." Maya didn't mention that there was another reason she wanted to go back—to see Will.

Maya tried to brush Will away from her thoughts as she ate the delicious macaroni and cheese Alexander had made for dinner, and as they took a walk afterwards to the Italian bakery, where they got gelato for dessert. But somehow Maya kept picturing Will's face and the way his hazel eyes crinkled around the edges when he smiled. Then there was his ability to see. Now that Maya had had her eyes peeled, it seemed that she was drawn to people who could see—Viola, Jeam, and now Will. This made a weird kind of sense, but it was more than a little disconcerting. And Maya had a hunch that her relationship with Will was going to be more than a summer romance. "Which I don't want anyway," Maya thought, realizing ruefully that this was both true and untrue. Then, "Poor Will! What do the Books have in store for him?"

When they got back from their walk, Maya was tempted to ask the Apprentice Books about Will, but instead she brushed her teeth and went to bed. Maya sensed it had something to do with the Accumulator. "I'll find out soon enough," she said to herself, settling into bed. "And so will he."

The next day at the Little Bard Theater, in the basement at the tables, most of the kids sat where they had the previous day, and Maya took the empty seat next to Jay. As soon as Maya sat down, Jay asked in a saucy voice, "What? No many-colored pantsuit?"

Embarrassed, Maya laughed. "Not today." She had used some of the money Alexander had given her to buy two pairs of jeans and some plain tops. "It's dusty at the theater," Maya had told Alani that morning. "I don't want to get those pretty clothes dirty. I'll save them for special." Alani didn't say anything, but Maya could tell she was disappointed that Maya was wearing jeans and a black v-neck shirt instead of one of the bright outfits in the bureau.

"I still have my red sneakers," Maya said, lifting one of her legs to show Jay. Somehow those red sparkly sneakers reminded Maya of Dorothy's ruby slippers, and they seemed lucky to her.

"Excellent! That was some entrance you made yesterday. And you're going to get the part of Hermia."

Shrugging, Maya regarded Jay and his mischievous face. "You'd be a great Puck."

Jay grinned. "I hope so."

Maya could feel Will staring at her, but she didn't look at him. "No," she said to herself. "No."

"Here they come," Jay whispered as Inga and Maya's father walked down the stairs and over to the table. There was still a friendly distance between them, and Maya realized that their relationship hadn't started yet, that it would take a few years of working together before they would discover that they were in love. But this summer would be the beginning. Perhaps even worse, Maya could see that her father and Inga were a good pair. Conversation came easy to both of them, and they loved Shakespeare, literature, and theater. "Inga goes with Dad better than Mom does," Maya thought, and she felt a pain in her chest as though she were being squeezed.

"Are you all right?" Jay asked.

Maya was unable to speak. A tear slid down her cheek, and she brushed it away quickly, hoping Jay wouldn't notice.

But Jay had noticed. "Do you know them?" he whispered.

"Yeah, but they don't know me."

"How?"

"It's complicated."

"Okay." Jay looked as though he wanted to ask more questions, but he didn't.

For the rest of the afternoon, there were no more surprises. They read through the play, and Inga did assign the role of Peaseblossom to Maya, but she also had Maya take Hermia's part again.

"Great," Maya thought, and she briefly considered reading the lines in a monotone, but somehow she couldn't do it. Instead, Maya was crisp and funny, and when she came to the part where Hermia fought with her friend Helena, everyone except Lexie laughed and clapped.

"All right," Inga said when they had finished reading the play. "I think both Professor Hammond and I have a fair idea about who will be best for which role. But we'll talk it over and let you know to-morrow." She smiled. "You kids were great today. It's going to be a fabulous production."

Maya's father pretended to scratch a nonexistent beard. "Not too bad, young actors."

Everybody laughed, even Maya, but she stopped when she saw Will smiling at her. Quickly, she stood up and gathered her things.

"Where are you going, young actor?" Jay asked.

"I don't know," Maya said.

"Want to go to The Other Green Door for a drink and some sweet potato fries?"

"Okay," Maya answered quickly, thinking that maybe if she left with Jay, Will wouldn't follow her to the café.

But they had barely settled down in a booth when the door opened, and in came Will. He pretended to be surprised to see them, and Jay waved him over. "Come join us."

Smiling sheepishly, Will slid in beside Jay. "Sweet potato fries?"

"Of course," Jay said. "It's a woo-woo place, but their sweet potato fries are the best. And the chamomile tea that the servers al-ways push isn't too bad, either."

"The fries were good yesterday. Right, Will?" Maya asked tartly.

Will actually blushed. "Yeah, they were."

"Oh, ho!" Jay laughed. "So this is where you came yesterday when you gave Lexie the slip."

Will frowned. "I wouldn't exactly put it that way."

Maya asked, "Do you two know each other?"

"Yup," Jay replied. "We go to the same school and are in the same class. So is Lexie. We've even been in school plays together. Will's good, almost as good as you are, Anne."

"Thanks a lot," Will replied, but he was grinning, and Maya could tell that he and Jay were friends.

Turning, Maya glanced out the window. Through the fern fronds, she could see a frowning face peering at them. Startled, Maya gave a low shriek, and Will and Jay looked at the face.

Will tried to smile. "Lexie."

"Busted," Jay whispered, but he motioned for Lexie to come in. Maya thought, "Oh, great."

"We don't have much choice," Jay said softly as if reading Maya's thoughts. "Here we all are. No place to hide."

The door opened with what seemed like a bang. Even the servers paused to stare at the angry girl striding toward the booth with Maya, Jay, and Will.

"Let me out," Jay said in a low voice. "I'll sit next to Anne."

Will sprang out of his seat, and as Jay slid in beside Maya, Lexie was at their booth.

"Hi, Lexie." Will's voice came out a note higher than it usually was.

Lexie's voice, on the other hand, was deep with anger. "Will, why did you run off when I was in the bathroom? You did that yesterday, too."

Despite the scene they were making, Maya bit her lip, trying not to smile as she thought about how ridiculous the whole situation was. Here she was, trying to find the Accumulator so that she could defeat Cinnial and rescue Ariel, and she was caught in a teenage love triangle.

"Sit down, Lexie. Join us. We're going to have sweet potato fries," Jay said. "And chamomile tea."

Will scooted back in, and regal and stiff, Lexie sat next to him. She glared at Maya. "Do you think this is funny?"

"A little," Maya admitted, trying to swallow her laughter, and beside her, Jay watched in fascination. Will, on the other hand, looked stiff and remote.

"Who the hell are you?" Lexie asked, her lovely face red with anger.

"Oh, just a kid from Maine," Maya answered in a pert voice, knowing that she shouldn't goad Lexie. But somehow, Maya couldn't resist. From the time she had started preschool, Maya had known arrogant girls like Lexie who never questioned whether or not they should be in charge. Even at four and five, they had bossed everyone around, said whatever mean thing came into their heads, and decided who was cool enough to join their exclusive groups. Whoever was excluded wasn't even worth considering, except for a cruel put-down. Maya had been excluded again and again and had often come home crying. Her mother had held her and had finally given Maya some of the best advice she'd ever gotten. "There are other girls in your class. Make friends with them." And that was how Maya had become friends with Leah and Danielle. Once that had happened, Maya never again tried to be friends with the queen bees, as Mémère called them.

"Just a kid from Maine," Lexie mimicked in a high voice. "Is that where the stupid outfit you wore yesterday came from?" She snickered. "Is that what people wear in Maine?"

Maya felt her cheeks flush, knowing she was going to say things she shouldn't, and the words came out cool and precise. "Sure, Lexie, that's how we dress in Maine. You would know, wouldn't you? Because you've been everywhere and have seen everything. You freaking know it all." Maya ended with something she had heard Mémère say many times. "Maybe that's why you think you can fart higher than the fire."

Jay's laugh came out in a bark, and grinning, Will turned his head away from Lexie.

Clutching the table, Lexie leaned forward. "You little shit! Who do you think you are?"

Maya was raging mad, but she continued in her precise voice, "I think I'm a way better actress than you'll ever be, even though you think you're so great. While you'll probably be kissing an ass in the play, I'll most likely be kissing Will. And let's be honest, Will wants to kiss me way more than he wants to kiss you. With your personality, who can blame him?" An image of Lexie—in her sixties and with a wrinkled neck and face—came to Maya. She leaned forward. "Looks only go so far, Lexie. When you're sixty, what will you have?"

Lexie sat back abruptly as though she had been slapped. Without saying a word, she stormed out of the café, and Maya felt a rush of triumph.

Hesitating, Will looked after Lexie and then turned to Maya. But it was Jay who spoke. "Bud, you'd better go after Lexie. You'll have to talk to her sooner or later. Might as well get it over with."

Sighing deeply, Will hurried after Lexie.

Maya was left with Jay, who moved back to the seat where Will and Lexie had been.

The server, the same one as the day before, came over to take their order. "That was a big scene." He smiled, and there was a dimple in one of his cheeks. "Sweet potato fries?"

"Make that a double order," Jay said. "We'll need to revive ourselves after that battle."

"You got it. And chamomile tea?"

"Sure."

The server left, and Maya's feeling of triumph fizzed out to be replaced by shame. She had used her ability to see to say snide, hurtful things, and Maya knew without a doubt this was the wrong way to use that ability.

Jay stared thoughtfully at her. "You're something else, aren't you? I've never heard anyone talk to Lexie like that."

Maya rubbed her face. "I shouldn't have said those things. I went too far."

Jay grimaced. "You were a little harsh."

Maya took a deep breath. "No, I was mean, just like Lexie." After all that Maya had seen and done, she had thought she was beyond such pettiness, but apparently she was not.

Jay stared at Maya, and she realized he could see, too, not as much as Will, but it was strong enough, a lot like it was with Viola. "Of course he can," Maya thought sadly, wondering what was in store for Jay.

"Even though everything I said was true, I'm going to apologize tomorrow," Maya said.

"You might want to leave it alone."

"But we're going to be in a play together. It won't be good if we're mad at each other."

Jay leaned forward. "There's no way you're going to make it up with Lexie. Once you get on her bad side, you're there forever."

Maya sighed. "All right. How long have Will and Lexie been going out?"

"Not long, but she's been after him ever since we started high school. For nearly three years, Will slipped out of her clutches, but at a party this summer, she caught him." Jay grinned. "Lexie can be, ah, persuasive, and it would have taken someone made out of stone to resist her. Will can be aloof, but he's a guy."

Smiling ruefully, Maya could picture it. "It was never going to end well, was it?"

Jay shook his head. "She's not his type. And if Lexie hadn't been so obsessed, she would have realized he wasn't her type, either."

"Who is his type?" Maya asked, knowing the answer.

"You are. Will's been talking about you nonstop since yesterday. I've never seen him this way. Tell you the truth, I was getting sick of hearing your name."

Maya thought, "And it's not even my real one." Aloud, she said, "Jay, I'm not going to be here long, and I have a lot going on. It would be best..." Maya didn't finish the sentence.

Jay's bright face was serious. "Too late."

"I know," Maya said sadly.

From the kitchen pass-through, came the chiming of the bell. Glancing over, Maya saw someone peering through the window, but it wasn't the woman who had been there the day before. Instead, it was an older man who had high cheekbones and a long beautiful face, like the woman had. The man was looking at her, and nodding slightly, he disappeared back into the kitchen.

4: Maya Makes a Decision

That night at dinner Maya said, "I think I might have found the Accumulator."

Earlier in the day, Alexander had made bean burritos, but he was at work at the library, and it was only Alani and Maya at the table.

Alani stopped cutting her burrito. "Where?"

"He's a cook at a café called The Other Green Door. It's not far from the Little Bard Theater. I've been there a couple of times." Remembering that afternoon's scene, Maya grimaced, pushing around the salad Alani had made.

"Oh?" Alani asked.

"Yeah, twice with a guy named Will Henley, and once with Jay Valdez and a girl named Lexie Norton."

"And?"

"There's something different about that place, mostly because of the people who work there. They look like they stepped out of Rivendell, from *Lord of the Rings*, and I can't read them the way I can most people. They're a little like Chet, except I know he's not from Rivendell. Or if Chet is, then he's an evil elf."

"Do you think the people who work at The Other Green Door are from somewhere else?" Alani asked.

"I do."

"Want me to get my Book so we can get more information?"

"Sure."

Alani's Book said, "I can't see the cooks or the servers clearly. I only get a vague impression of them. But you'd better check them out."

"Okay," Maya said. "But tell me something. Did you send me to the Little Bard Theater because of Will and Jay?"

"Yes," the Book admitted. "You're going to need help, and there they were, all signed up for theater camp. Will's nearly as good as you are, except he hasn't had his eyes peeled, and Jay is pretty good, too. But don't dismiss Jay. His ability isn't as strong as yours and Will's, but he has a different way of looking at things, and that might come in handy. Besides, he can play the mandolin, and that also might come in handy. It seemed like a good idea to send you to the Little Bard Theater, even though your father and Inga are in charge. Are you upset that we didn't tell you about them?"

Maya shrugged. "At first I was, but not now. It's what you Books do. However, you could tell us a little more. Knowing what we're going to face might make it easier."

The Book hesitated, and Maya could tell it was deciding how much to say. "We've been talking about this. The Great Library's Book thinks we should share information on what you Americans call a need-to-know basis. To be fair, that technique has worked for a long, long time. Sometimes knowing too much makes it harder for Chance and gives a boost to Nemesis. We have to be careful."

"What about now?" Alani asked sharply. "After all that's happened, is it still a good thing to keep so much from us?"

"Everything's in flux," the Book answered slowly. "Cinnial's at the Great Library. Everyone's gone into hiding. Never before have we Books been so unsure about what to do."

The Book's voice sounded sad and a little afraid as well. Maya realized what a strain it was for Alani's Book—indeed for all the Books in exile—to be separated from the Great Library, the place where they had come into being, where they had been connected to the rest of the universe. But the Books and Time were no longer at the center. Instead, Chaos was.

"From now on, tell us what you can," Maya said.

The Book made a sound as though it were clearing its throat. "All right. There's Lexie. You've made her your enemy."

Maya sighed. "I know. I said things I shouldn't have said. I wanted to tell her I was sorry, but Jay said that it wouldn't make any difference."

"No, it probably wouldn't," Alani's Book said. "However, despite what's happened between you two, I have the feeling that soon you will have to make a decision about her. And when you do, choose carefully. Look closely."

Maya wondered nervously how Lexie was going to be involved in her plans. "I wish she'd just stay away from me."

"It would be better," the Book replied. "But she probably won't."

The next day at theater camp, parts were assigned, and Maya's hunches had been correct. She and Will got the parts of Hermia and Lysander, Jay was Puck, and Lexie was Titania, the fairy queen.

Lexie no longer sat next to Will. Instead, she sat across the table from him, and she was flanked on both sides by girls who had gotten the roles of her fairy attendants. Lexie only looked at Maya once, and Maya felt the full force of the blonde girl's anger.

"Man oh man," Maya thought, turning away. "Good thing she's not from Mortmain. She'd be right there with Cinnial." Maya immediately knew that she wasn't being fair. Will had broken up with Lexie to be with Maya. Lexie had every reason to be angry, and while there was something hard and selfish inside the blonde girl, there was a glimmer of something else, too—courage and intelligence.

Maya glanced at Will, who was sitting next to her, and all thoughts of Lexie went away. Again, it seemed as though there was nobody in the room except for the two of them, and all Maya wanted to do was to go somewhere else and talk with Will, to hear his stories, to be with him. Then Maya blushed as she thought about what else she would like to do. Maya's hands were in her lap, and Will put one of his hands over hers.

As Maya leaned a little toward Will, she heard her father say, "All right, time to get started. Today we're going to go through the play with everyone reading their parts."

When rehearsal was done, Jay asked, "To The Other Green Door for lunch?" As Maya and Will looked at each other and nodded together, Jay gave them a searching stare. "Do you two want me around?"

Although Maya wanted to be alone with Will, she had the feeling that Jay should come along, too. Maya sensed that what she would learn today would affect them all, and that Jay, along with Will, needed to be there from the beginning.

"Yes, you should come." Maya could feel Will's surprise—he wanted to be alone with her as much as she wanted to be alone with him. But Maya pressed on. "You must be hungry, the way we are, and ready for some sweet potato fries."

"Okay," Jay said slowly, looking from Maya to Will and then back to Maya, who smiled.

The Other Green Door was busy, as usual, but there always seemed to be one empty booth waiting for them in the middle of the café across from the pass-through in the kitchen. "Where the cooks can see what's going on," Maya thought, understanding that this booth was unofficially reserved for people like her, who might be of use.

The server with the dimple in his cheek came over to take their order. "You must be going to theater camp at the Little Bard Theater."

"We are," Will answered, who was beside Maya.

"Sweet potato fries?" he asked.

"Yeah," Jay answered. "Two orders. This time, I'm paying." He frowned at the menu. "Let's add a couple of plates of hummus and pita bread to go with those fries."

"You won't be sorry. Both the hummus and pita bread are homemade. And Chamomile tea?" the server asked hopefully.

"Of course."

The server paused. "Will anyone else be joining you?"

"No," Will answered firmly. "It's just the three of us."

When the server left, Jay regarded Maya and Will, who were sitting close together with their shoulders touching. "You sure it's okay if I'm here? I can leave right after we're done eating."

Before Will could say anything, Maya said, "It's best if you stay here." She could feel Will frowning at her as he tried to figure out why she would want Jay to stay, and Maya made what she hoped was the right decision—it was time to tell Will and Jay about the Great Library, the Books of Everything, and how she was connected with them. Then if they decided to get involved with whatever was going to happen next—and Maya still wasn't sure exactly what that would be—it would be their choice, made freely, the way it had been with Andy.

First Maya looked at Will, into those hazel eyes, and she nearly changed her mind as she thought wistfully about how fun it would be to have a summer romance and not worry about anything. Maya glanced at Jay, who was trying to decide whether he should smile or not, and she saw what a good friend he would be to both her and Will. But then the chiming bell rang, and Maya turned toward the kitchen. Both the man and the woman were there, staring at them all. Again, the man nodded slightly, and Maya knew she had to tell Will and Jay who she was and why she was there.

"Look, I need to talk to you guys," Maya said. "Could you come to my apartment afterwards?" Hesitating only slightly, both boys said they could. "Wait, let me call my friend Alani to see if either she or Alexander will be there. We'll need at least one of them."

Maya took the phone from her pack and called Alani. "Are you home and will you be there for a while?"

"I'll be here all afternoon," came the answer.

"Is it okay if I bring two friends over?"

"Will and Jay?" Alani asked.

"Yes," Maya answered.

"All right. When?"

"In about an hour."

"See you then."

Will and Jay frowned as they regarded Maya. Will shifted slightly. "Anne, what's going on?"

"First of all, my name's not Anne. It's Maya."

Jay shook his head. "Maya?"

"Yes," Maya answered. "Maya Hammond, not Anne Page."

"You have the same last name as Professor Hammond?" Will asked.

"I do," Maya answered, watching their astonished expressions.

"Are you two related?" Jay asked.

"We are." She would have said more, but the server had come over with their order.

"Two orders of sweet potato fries and chamomile tea," the server said, holding a tray with the steaming platters and three glasses of tea. "I'll be right back with the hummus and pita bread." After carefully setting the tray down on the table, he asked Maya, "Are you going to tell them?"

Startled, Maya looked at the server for a few minutes. Why would he know this much about her when she could only get the barest impression of him? But Maya decided to be truthful and direct with the server, the way she was going to be with Will and Jay. "If they're going to be involved with whatever is going to happen, they need to know the truth."

"I told Father that's what you would do," the server said. "By the way, my name is Thirret. Father is one of the cooks, and he would like to talk to you three after the café closes. Could you come back at around 4:30 or 5:00?"

"I can," Maya said, looking from Will to Jay. "What about you guys?"

"Nothing much going on at home tonight," Jay replied.

"Same for me," Will said, taking Maya's hand and squeezing it, letting her know that even though things had taken a weird turn, he was still with her.

Maya gratefully returned the squeeze. "We'll be back."

5: The Accumulator

Alani had bought an assortment of cookies from the Italian bakery and was fussing with tea while Maya, Will, and Jay sat in the living room of the apartment. A full platter and small plates were on the black coffee table, and Will and Jay sneaked longing glances at the cookies. Maya grinned. Even though the day had taken an unexpected turn, and they had had lunch at the café, Will and Jay were still hungry.

"Go ahead and have some cookies," Maya said. "You don't mind, do you, Alani?"

"Not at all," Alani called from the kitchen. "They're boys. I still remember how much my brothers used to eat."

"Dig in," Maya said, and Will and Jay each took a small plate and placed a few cookies on them. "Go on, take some more." Will and Jay didn't have to be told twice.

Not long after, Alani came in with a tray with a teapot, cups, sugar, milk, and spoons. The tray looked too heavy for the small woman, but she carried it with ease.

Will and Jay tried not to stare as Alani set the tray on the table and poured tea. "I know," she said, passing a cup of tea to each of the teenagers. "On your world it's unusual for an adult to be as short as I am. But on my world, my height is average."

Jay choked a little on his cookie and had to take a quick sip of tea.

Frowning, Will paused mid bite. "Your world?"

"My world," Alani repeated. "I'm from a planet called Copernia." She sat down on the small chair by the couch. "You're going to hear a lot of strange things today. None of it will make sense at first, but gradually it will." Her expression became sad. "I'm sorry you two are here, but things are desperate." Maya was sitting on the end of the couch next to Alani's chair, and the small woman reached over and squeezed Maya's hand. "This girl has done more than most can imagine, but there's a lot more to do. And Will and Jay, you have to decide how much you want to get involved."

Maya turned to Will, who was beside her on the couch, and to Jay, who was sitting in a chair beside Will. "I want you both to choose freely. I don't want you to be nudged by Chance." She shivered. "Or Nemesis."

Alani took a cookie. "Probably too late."

"Probably, but going forward, I want it to be their choice."

"Tell us," Will said as he considered Maya. "I knew right off there was something different about you."

Jay grinned uncertainly. "We just didn't know how different."

"But I don't care," Will added quickly.

"That's because you two can see," Alani said. "Just like me. Just like Maya. Go on, Maya, tell them about seeing, about what you've done. Then they can look at my Book." Alani's Apprentice Book was on a small table next to Alani's chair.

The telling took a long time, and the teapot had to be refilled twice. Maya began with meeting Chet on the train, ten years in the future, which was Maya's present; how Earth's Book of Everything came to her and took her back in time to Waterville's South End, where she met Andy; and how they had traveled through time and space to Caxton. She told them about the Great Library, where Books of Everything were made. Maya finished the first part of the story with coming back to Earth, discovering Andy was President Murphy, and that Humphrey, from Caxton, was in Andy's inner circle.

Jay held up his hand. "Wait a minute! That guy Andy from the poor part of Watertown..."

"Waterville," Maya interrupted.

"Whatever," Jay said. "This guy's going to be our president? Unbelievable!"

Maya rubbed her face. "I know. I was surprised, too. Earth's Book didn't tell me until after I saw Andy on TV and found out that he was president of the United States. Humphrey was right beside him."

Jay looked incredulous, and Will grinned a little. "Jay, after all that Maya's told us, you get hung up on Andy being president?"

Jay shook his head. "I know. But somehow that seems like the weirdest thing of all."

Maya smiled sadly. "Trust me, it gets weirder." She told them about Mortmain, Cinnial, and Bigly, about Chance and Nemesis, about how she had escaped without a Book's help from a cell in the Office and had followed the timeline to Earth to see her younger self and her mother walking into a corner store. Finally, how Professor Hammond was her father, but he didn't know this.

Jay sat in speechless astonishment.

Even the usually cool Will was shocked. "Shouldn't coming here and seeing your younger self have disrupted the space-time continuum?"

Alani laughed. "Not when Time is in charge."

"Why should we believe any of this?" Jay finally asked.

Alani passed him her Book. "Here, this is my Apprentice Book from the Great Library. Go to the letter *J,* look yourself up. When you've read enough, pass it to Will so that he can go to the letter *W.*"

Taking the red Book, Jay went to the letter *J,* looked down, blinked in surprise, and started reading. Nobody said anything while he read, and Maya felt on edge, wondering how both boys would respond to the Book. She fidgeted with her napkin, crumpling it into a ball and then smoothing it out again. As he had done often during the day, Will placed his hand over hers, and the fidgeting stopped.

As Maya looked at Will, different impressions came to her—his unflappability, his amiability, his steadiness all combined with a firm, almost fierce, resolve. When Will wanted something, he did not easily give up. "Like Elspeth," Maya thought, smiling at Will, who smiled back at her, and she knew right then that they would make a good team—his calmness would help steady her, and Maya's tendency toward action would energize him.

After a while, Jay stopped reading, made a puffing sound as he exhaled, and passed the Book to Will, who turned to the letter *W*. Will read even longer than Jay had. Cookies were crunched, tea was sipped, and finally looking up, Will said, "I believe you, Maya. I believe it all."

Jay sighed. "Me, too. Even though I wish I didn't. So what now?"

Maya answered, "I think the cook at The Other Green Door is someone called the Accumulator. Alani's Apprentice Book believes the Accumulator will have something that will help us defeat Cinnial or at least be able to tell me where I can get it."

Nodding, Will closed the red Book and passed it back to Alani. She considered it for a few minutes and then without opening the Book, set it on the table beside the chair.

Alani's small face was serious. "I'm going to tell you a little more than my Book is willing to tell you. My Book thinks you will have to go to a place we call Outside Time, which is where the Accumulator and his family come from. We don't know much about it. It's a dimension that has its own rules and laws, different from ours. Most cultures have stories about a place like this. Here, you would call it..."

"Fairyland?" Jay asked.

"Or Elfland?" Will suggested.

"That's right," Alani replied. "Sometimes the old legends have more truth than anyone can imagine."

"Elfland," Maya repeated, both enthralled and terrified, and she thought about how the Accumulator and the servers—long, slim, and elegant—did look like elves.

Alani leaned forward. "From what little we know, Outside Time is enchanting but extremely dangerous. I wanted to go there with you, but my Book advised against it. My ability to see isn't as strong as it is with the three of you, and neither is Alexander's. My

Book said that you, Will, and Jay would make a better team." She stared at her hands. "That Alexander and I would get in the way and might not even make it back. And also that we're needed here."

Jay swallowed. "What about us? Will we make it back?"

"My Book thinks you will but is not certain," Alani answered slowly. "I thought you two needed to know this before you decided whether you want to go with Maya."

"Maya, you'll go whether or not we come with you?" Will asked.

Maya answered, "Yes, I've come too far. Cinnial has to be stopped."

Alani looked up. "What happens at the Great Library will ripple across the universe, even to someplace as remote as Earth. Now that Cinnial is at the Great Library, Chaos is in control, and Time is on the sidelines. Lies will gain more and more power. Facts will hardly matter."

"It's kind of that way now," Jay said.

"I know," Alani answered. "But it could be much worse. There are places on Earth where dictators are in charge, and facts don't matter. It could be that way nearly everywhere."

Maya thought about Andy and his respect for the truth. "Andy made things better, didn't he?"

Alani said, "He will eventually. Remember, Andy's still a senator right now. And in this time, Maya, you're only six."

Will blinked. "I'm eleven years older than Maya?"

Jay snorted. "You just figured that out?"

"Yes. No. Oh, shut up! There's been a lot to take in," Will shot back, but he was smiling.

Alani grinned. "You were indeed born eleven years before Maya. But that's not too much older. Or at least eventually it won't be."

Will considered Maya. "No, I guess it isn't."

Maya flushed and changed the subject. "So now you know about Cinnial and the Great Library. What are you going to do?"

Will's voice was firm. "I'm going with you, Maya."

"Jay, what about you?" Alani asked.

Jay looked from Maya to Will. "I'm going, too."

Alani said, "All right. Thank you, Will and Jay. It will be a big relief to know Maya won't be alone. When do you have to go back to The Other Green Door?"

"Soon," Maya answered, standing up, and the other three stood up, too. "The café should be about ready to close by now."

Alani kissed Maya on the cheeks, and she squeezed the boys' hands. "Good luck, you three, and be careful. Alexander and I will be here, waiting for you when you come back."

Maya nodded. "Thanks, Alani."

"I wish I could do more," Alani replied soberly. "But I think we'd better listen to the Books. There's too much at stake for us to just go blindly off on our own."

Will and Jay also nodded solemnly, and the three left.

At The Other Green Door, the lights were off, and even though it wasn't dark yet, the windows were black. The door was locked, but Thirret was sitting in a booth by the door, waiting for them, and he immediately opened the door when Maya knocked. As soon as they came in, Thirret closed the door and said, "Everybody's waiting for you in the backroom, where we take our breaks when the café isn't busy. Follow me."

Maya, Will, and Jay followed Thirret through the kitchen that smelled both sweet and spicy, the scent reminding Maya of a faraway land. He led the teenagers to a room off the kitchen that looked as though it had come from the middle of a forest. There were skylights in the ceiling, and along with the side windows, there was plenty of light for the small trees in pots that ringed the room. The walls were painted green and the floor an even darker green, the color of moss. In the middle of the room was a round oak table and chairs. At the table sat Thirret's father, tall and straight. A woman—the other cook—and two servers sat by him. With them all grouped together, Maya could see that they were all part of the same family. They all had dark eyes and skin and long black hair. The men wore ponytails, and the two women had braids that went below the middle of their backs.

"Here they are, Father," Thirret said. "Right on time."

"I am not surprised," Thirret's father said. "In this place, Time means a lot to them. It is the force that gives them life and moves them along." He motioned to the empty chairs. "Please have a seat." Maya, Will, Jay, and Thirret sat down. The man continued, "My name is Pawel Greenwood, but I am also known as the Accumulator." He motioned to the woman. "This is my wife, Khirra." Then to the two servers. "My nephew Dagan. And my niece Jacinda, whom we call Jace. You've already met our son, Thirret."

Smiling, Maya nodded. "I'm Maya Hammond. And this is Will Henley and Jay Valdez."

"Welcome," Khirra said, and her voice was as musical as Maya had expected it to be. "We have been waiting for someone like you for a long time."

Dagan frowned. "Aren't they a little young, even by human standards?"

"They are," Pawel agreed. "But none of the others who went could see the way Maya can, and it's strong in Will and Jay, too."

Will rubbed his face. "There have been others?"

"Yes," Pawel's expression was impassive, but there was a look of sorrow in his eyes. "Elves."

"What happened to them?" Jay asked.

Khirra looked as sad as Pawel. "They never came back."

Jace spoke for the first time. "They are either imprisoned or dead."

"In Elfland?" Maya asked softly.

Pawel replied, "Something like that. Except we call it Elferterre."

"Better start at the beginning," Khirra said. "And tell them how we got here."

6: To Elferterre

Pawel began, "We might be from different dimensions, but greed, cruelty, and the grasping for power are present in our land, just as they are in yours. Our world is as big as yours is, and it shares many of the same features. Some parts are wooded, some parts are mountainous, some parts tropical, some parts are desert. My family is from the woodlands, from a kingdom called Norlander."

"With a beautiful capital city called Foretcour," Khirra put in. "Enough elves, but not too many. Plenty of room for trees and birds and things that grow. Or at least there was when we left. And nowhere near as polluted as it is here on Earth."

Pawel said, "My family is one of the ruling families. There are four in Norlander: The Greenwoods, the Fernleaves, the Willowdales, and the Ashglades. Khirra comes from the family Willowdale and so do Dagan and Jacinda. For years and years, there was strife between the four families, and at times there were wars. Many elves died, but at last the families decided to work together instead of fighting. This cooperation lasted for a long while. There was peace. And plenty for all."

Pawel paused, and Khirra took up the story. "But the Ashglades, from the southern corner of Norlander, had long felt that they had given up too much when the families banded together. Kidnapping children from your world was outlawed, as was human bondage, but the Ashglade economy had depended on their cheap labor. Also, women became as equal as men, which many of the Ashglades did not like. For years this resentment simmered underneath." Khirra stopped, unable to go on.

"And then came Tamick." Pawel grimaced as though even the name caused him pain. "A kinsman of mine on my mother's side. Sly, clever, and smooth, Tamick Ashglade wormed his way up into the ruling council, and one by one, he turned the other members against my family and me, convincing the council that we had stolen from the kingdom, lied, cheated, and worse. Khirra and I were tried and found guilty, even though we were innocent. We weren't executed, the way Tamick would have liked. The other council members wouldn't go that far. Instead, we were banished to Earth. Dagan and Jace came with us. Their parents died when they were young, and we are their guardians." Pawel smiled affectionately at the two elves, and they smiled back. "Dagan and Jace are like a son and daughter to us."

Jace said, "Even though we were old enough to live on our own, we decided to come with Uncle Pawel, Aunt Khirra, and Thirret when they were exiled. We didn't want them to be alone."

Khirra's face was grim. "It probably wouldn't have been safe if you two had stayed behind."

"Probably not," Jace agreed sadly.

Maya asked, "Why don't you all just go back to Elferterre and fight Tamick? If he's that bad, I bet others would join you. What's keeping you here?"

Pawel lifted the right leg of his pants, and pulled down the cuff of his sock. Maya could see a faint shimmer. When she looked closer, she saw a nearly translucent chain cinched tightly around Pawel's ankle. Pawel explained, "These chains bind us here, and we all wear one. Each has a lock, and I have searched your planet for a key that might work. But as far as I can tell, the only thing that will open the locks is a special key from Norlander."

"Why would you think you could find a key on Earth?" Jay asked.

"There are many of us elves here among you humans," Pawel answered. "Some, like us, are exiles. Others come out of curiosity and decide to stay. The elves who come on their own bring items with them when they leave Elferterre. We call the items relics. I thought that maybe among these elves there would be someone who would have a key to unlock our chains. Or would know how to make one. But there isn't, and as long as we wear these chains, we can't return to Elferterre."

Will's face was still and serious. "Why would elves want to come here?"

Khirra replied, "With our looks and abilities, we do extremely well on Earth. Many rich and famous people are either elves or direct descendants. It's a way for elves from the lower classes to get ahead." She regarded Maya, Will, and Jay. "Even though you don't resemble us physically, it wouldn't surprise me if all three of you are descendants of elves. This is often true for humans whose ability to see is strong."

Maya thought about her pépère and her mother, about how tall and lean they were, and about their long but beautiful faces. There was something otherworldly about both of them, especially her mother. Maya wondered, were they descended from elves?

"But some humans who can see don't have elves as ancestors," Thirret added.

"No, they don't," Khirra said. "This ability is not limited to elves. However, it's often stronger with us because we are not ruled by Time on Elferterre."

Maya frowned. "If Time isn't in charge, then what is?"

Pawel said, "I think you know."

Maya did know. "Magic," she whispered.

Khirra's expression was both wistful and fierce. "A wild force that sustains all of Elferterre, and it allows us to see deep into the heart of things. Magic is here, too, but much weaker. So faint that sometimes it appears as though magic doesn't exist at all on Earth. But it does."

Jay looked around the room at the potted trees. "Why did you stay in New York? It doesn't seem like a place for woodland elves."

"It is not," Pawel admitted. "But it is close to one of the entrances to Elferterre that leads to Darkwood Forest in Norlander, where we came through to Earth. We did not want to stray too far. Also, New York is a city of food. Even though Khirra is from a ruling family, one of her talents is cooking, and she taught me how to cook, too."

Khirra shrugged. "In general, elves are good cooks, no matter what class we're from. We have a feel for food. Thirret is an especially good baker, as is Jace. Dagan, on the other hand, makes excellent spreads, noodles, and rice dishes. We all have our specialties."

"So cooking is how we make our living on Earth. We have had to work hard. Luckily we had our son, niece, and nephew to help," Pawel said. "We eventually saved enough to buy this café, close to the entrance of Elferterre."

Jace shrugged. "And here we are. In Brooklyn."

"Some of it's been good," Thirret put in quickly. "New York's a great place. Magic, from the entrance to Elferterre, spills into this city, and you can feel it thrumming through the streets, almost like a beat."

Khirra fondly regarded her son. "Thirret is the youngest. It was easiest for him when we came here."

Flushing, Dagan clenched and unclenched his hands. "Some of us can't wait to go back to Elferterre. And defeat Tamick Ashglade."

Jace, on the other hand, looked at Thirret, who smiled back.

Pawel turned to Maya. "But we need your help."

"You want us to find the key," Maya said.

"That's right," Pawel replied. "On the edge of Foretcour lives Galli, the locksmith who made our chains. He has a master key that will unlock them. Galli's workshop is a couple of day's journey from the entrance to Elferterre. If you decide to go, we will give you a map as well as other things to aid you."

"All right. But I need something to help me defeat someone named Cinnial, and I was told you could help me," Maya said. "Do you know about Cinnial and the Great Library?"

"Oh, yes," Khirra answered. "We know how he murdered Sydda and took over the Great Library. What a terrible blow for this universe. Unfortunately, an elf from Norlander works for the Association for the Preservation of Order. She was in the café not long ago and told us what had happened at the Great Library."

Startled, Maya asked, "APO? The organization on Earth that has one of Cinnial's Books?"

Khirra winced. "The elf's name is Jammisin Fernleaf, and she is now the director of APO. Many times, Jammisin has tried to talk us into joining APO, promising that they will help us return to Elferterre. But we have never been tempted. In her own way, Jammisin is as bad as Tamick, and we didn't want anything to do with either her or APO."

Maya shook her head, but then her thoughts turned back to the locksmith. "So what will Galli have that will defeat Cinnial?"

Pawel answered, "Along with making binding chains, Galli makes binding locks that will suck in a creature's essence. Once that lock is shut, the creature can't get out. When Cinnial is trapped, bring the lock to me, and I will take it back with me when we return to Elferterre. Cinnial will bother this dimension no more."

Jay blinked anxiously. "This Galli doesn't sound like a good guy. He let Tamick use his chains to trap you here."

Pawel's lips curled. "Galli goes along with whoever is in power."

Khirra shook her head. "As I'm sure you realize, Galli will not be willing to give you either the key or the binding lock. You will have to steal them."

Maya asked, "How will we know which are the right key and lock?"

"You must choose carefully," Pawel admitted. Getting up, he went to a desk at the back of the room and found paper and pencil. Sitting back down, he drew two characters—Б and Я. "The key and the lock will each have one of these." He pointed to each symbol. "The lock will have the Б, and the key will have Я."

As Maya stared at the paper, the characters disappeared, and she felt them settle into her memory.

"Oh," Maya said in surprise.

Pawel smiled. "That way you will not forget what they look like."

"That's one way of doing it," Maya replied. "Okay. That's all set. When do we go?"

For the first time, the elves laughed, an enchanting, rippling sound, and some of the tension left the room. "You are a girl of action," Pawel said in an approving voice.

Khirra stared thoughtfully at Maya. "But don't be overconfident. You have never been in our realm. There are many dangers.

Elves who were here voluntarily on Earth have tried to help us, and they did not succeed. Tamick Ashglade keeps a tight grip on things, but unlike our elf allies, you young humans are so small and insignificant that you might be able to slide in without being noticed."

"I've faced Cinnial and his henchman, Bigly. I'll be careful." Despite the danger, Maya felt it was worth taking the risk to go to Norlander. Maya was certain that if she could remove Cinnial from this dimension and trap him on Elferterre, then Astrid, Elspeth, Alani, Alexander, and all the other librarians would be able to return to the Great Library to make Books of Everything.

"When do we go?" Maya asked again.

"You could leave in an hour or so, if you are ready," Pawel replied. "I have plenty of supplies to give you. We elves like to be prepared."

"Wait a minute," Jay said. "I need to tell my parents I'm going somewhere. I can't leave without telling them anything."

"Yeah," Will agreed. "My father isn't home, but I should message him."

Khirra hesitated. "Time does not pass the same way on Elferterre as it does here. If all goes well, then they won't know you've gone. But you must use the same portal to leave as you use to enter. That portal will have a memory of you and where you belong in Time. If you use another portal, there's no telling where you will end up."

Pawel leaned forward. "This is important. Do not forget."

Maya replied briskly, "Right. You said you'd give us a map. The portal will be on the map?"

"Yes," Pawel answered, "and other portals will be on the map, too. But don't use a different portal unless you have no other choice. The map is easy to use. Press a button on the top of the case, and the map will come out. You only need to ask for directions, and the map will show you the way."

Maya turned to Will and Jay. "Are you two ready? Are you sure you still want to come with me?" They both nodded. "Okay. Let's go."

Thirret grinned. "Now you get to see some of the things Father has accumulated over the years."

Everyone stood, and Khirra said, "Dagan, Jace, and I will leave you three with Pawel and Thirret. Too many of us would be a distraction. Good luck to you all. We will be waiting anxiously for your return." She inclined her head toward them as did Dagan and Jace, who both looked hopeful and skeptical at the same time.

When the three elves had left, Pawel said, "Come with me."

In the kitchen, Pawel opened a door, and there were stairs that led to a basement. As Maya followed Pawel and Thirret down the stairs, she felt a slight crackling in the air, which energized her, making her feel as though each step was lighter.

Will was right behind her. "Do you feel that?"

"Yes," Maya answered in an enthralled whisper.

Thirret was directly in front of her. "It's magic. All the things Father has accumulated have magic. The magic comes off them, like a smell."

"Almost like a drug," Jay muttered.

"Almost," Thirret agreed. "You can see why it is hard for us to be away from Elferterre, where the magic is much stronger." They were at the bottom of the stairs in a long room filled with bins and shelves. "We often come down here to rejuvenate."

"It's one of the reasons why I have accumulated so many things." There was a gleam in Pawel's eyes, and Maya knew this wasn't the only reason.

Thirret laughed. "Plus, you like to collect stuff. You always have."

"That, too." Pawel grinned, and for the first time, Maya got a sense of the elf Pawel had been before he had been exiled—still a leader, but lighter, more playful, less burdened.

Pawel stared thoughtfully at Maya. "Your ability to see really is very strong. Not many people on Earth can look into an elf the way you just did."

Maya blushed. "I've had my eyes peeled, too."

Pawel said, "I know. Right from the start, I could see that you had. But I didn't expect the seeing to be so strong with you. It's too bad the other two haven't had their eyes peeled, but we must work with what we have. Now, let's find some clothes for you."

From a bottom shelf, Pawel removed an old wooden trunk and set it on a long table that was in the middle of the room. Opening the top, Pawel murmured in a language that Maya didn't understand, and out came tunics, vests, trousers, boots, and capes. Pawel passed each of the teenagers a bundle, and all the clothes were exactly the right size.

"That is some trunk," Maya said in admiration, and Jay whistled in approval.

Pawel patted the trunk. "Cost me a lot, but it was worth it. This trunk always gives me exactly what I need."

There was a small bathroom next to the room with the relics, and Maya went there to change into the clothes Pawel had given her. Running her hands over the smooth vest, she looked down at herself and smiled. "I sure am dressed for the part," Maya murmured, feeling like a player straight out of a fantasy game.

When Maya went back to the room with the relics, Will and Jay had changed and were ready for action. They all grinned at each other.

"Quite the trio," Thirret said approvingly. "You all look pretty sharp."

Pawel nodded but said seriously, "You will have to keep your heads down. As long as you do this, nobody will pay much attention to you as most elves think humans are too weak to worry about. In Elferterre's social order, elves are at the top, and humans are at the bottom. So watch what you say to an elf. And never, ever strike one."

"We'll be careful," Maya said.

"Good," Pawel replied curtly. "Your lives might depend on it."

The cheerful mood faded as Pawel gave each of the teenagers a large backpack. The map was in Maya's pack, but all the packs were filled with supplies they might need, including food, small pans, matches, and boxes of chamomile tea.

"What is it with you elves and chamomile tea?" Jay asked.

Thirret answered, "We're crazy about it. We elves feel about chamomile tea the way some people on Earth feel about chocolate. But on Elferterre, chamomile tea is rare and costly even for the ruling families."

"But so common here," Pawel said with a faraway look. "Having chamomile tea whenever I want is the one thing I will miss about being on Earth." He shook his head as if to clear his mind of thoughts of chamomile tea. "The tea bags will be your currency. But be careful not to flash the boxes of tea bags around. Humans do not usually have very much chamomile tea. A bag or two at the most, and even that is unusual. Carry only a few bags in the pockets of your trousers. The best thing to do would be to find a money changer and trade the tea for gold coins, which are our most valuable currency. But even then be on guard. Don't let the money changer know you have a lot of tea, and exchange only one bag at a time."

Maya could see that Will and Jay were trying not to laugh, and she had to bite her lip before saying, "We won't flash the tea around."

Both Thirret and Pawel gave her sharp looks that indicated they did not find anything at all humorous about chamomile tea.

Then Pawel turned his attention to the shelves. "Now for something a little extra."

To Will, Pawel gave a small silver ball. Pawel explained, "If you are in a tight situation, twist the ball to turn it on and throw it at your opponents. The ball will hit them all in the head, knocking them out."

"How will it know not to hit Maya and Jay?" Will asked.

"It will know," Pawel answered. "The ball will connect with you and realize who your opponents are. It won't work against an army, but it will take out many."

"Wow," Will said softly as Pawel wrapped the ball in a soft cloth and passed it to him. Will carefully put the ball inside his knapsack.

To Jay, Pawel passed a case, and Jay unzipped it, taking out a gleaming mandolin. Jay ran his fingers over the strings, and even with that simple movement, the notes that came out were ethereal and haunting. Jay asked in surprise, "How did you know I played?"

Pawel smiled. "I just did. And on Elferterre, we love music. If someone plays, we can't help but listen at least for a little while. This is even true for Galli. But it is not really Galli I'm concerned about. Right now, he is gone from home as he searches Elferterre for new spells to bind and lock."

"How do you know this?" Will asked.

"I have ways of keeping track of things even though I am in exile," Pawel replied enigmatically.

Jay frowned. "Doesn't Galli worry about anyone breaking in while he is gone?"

"No, he doesn't," Pawel answered. "Because he has guards. Imps. Don't let their small size fool you. They are quick and fierce and can take down an elf in minutes. Imps have a great resistance to spells and magic, which makes them formidable guards. Fortunately for you three, the imps do have a weakness—human music. It is like catnip to them, and they love it even more than elves do. But most people don't want anything to do with Galli's guards, which means these particular imps don't get to hear human music very often."

"Like hardly ever," Thirret added.

Pawel said, "Jay, with your music, you should be able to distract the imps while Will and Maya steal the key and lock. And the imps won't think a bunch of human kids will be worth worrying about. With any luck, you'll escape their notice."

"I hope so," Jay muttered.

Pawel didn't say anything. After attaching the mandolin case to Jay's pack, Pawel turned to Maya and handed her a little velvet box. When Maya opened it, she saw a small golden bee buzzing and vibrating softly. Maya quickly closed the box, and it seemed to her that she could still hear the faint sound of humming.

Pawel said, "This is even more dangerous than the ball I gave to Will. The ball will usually only knock its victims out. The bee, on the other hand, kills. You can only use it once, so think carefully before you do."

Maya tried to give the box back to Pawel. "I don't want this. I don't want to kill anyone."

But Pawel's long fingers closed Maya's fingers over the box. "Child, it is possible that you might not have a choice. With all the hazards you'll be facing, I expect you could probably use many more bees, but this is the only one I have. When you get to Foretcour, you should be able to find other things to help you. Maybe more bees. Maybe something else. That's why I gave you that much chamomile tea."

Swallowing, Maya stared at Pawel, and his expression was so serious that Maya said, "All right. But only if I have no other choice."

As Maya slipped the velvet box in her pack, she glanced furtively around the room. All the shelves had bins and cases, and the room had a humming undertone as different sounds came from various objects. Maya wondered what else was in this room below the café. "I'll never know," Maya thought as she slipped into her backpack. "But I'd sure like to look."

"Yeah," Thirret whispered. "Me, too. But Father doesn't let me come down here by myself. Mother used to be the only one allowed on her own. But now Jace can come here, too. She's an Accumulator-in-training."

Pawel cleared his throat. "Thirret?"

Thirret smiled innocently. "Yes, Father?"

"Are you ready to take Maya, Will, and Jay to the portal?"

"I'm ready," came the quick answer, and Maya got the sense that Thirret didn't mind that he was not an Accumulator-in-training. Thirret liked what he was good at—baking, being a server, helping to run the café—and he didn't feel the need to be good at anything else.

They all went back upstairs, and as they stood by the café's door, Pawel inclined his head toward Maya, Will, and Jay. "Good luck to you three. May you succeed in your mission."

Will and Jay shifted uneasily, but Maya inclined her head toward Pawel. "We'll do our best."

Pawel's voice was soft, almost affectionate, and grave. "I know you will. And it just might be enough." He murmured and made a circular motion that encompassed the three teenages. Maya felt as though something soft and light had embraced her.

Pawel explained, "I've put a little spell on you so that nobody will notice that your clothes are different from what most humans wear. Even though this is New York, there is a limit. The spell will go away as soon as you enter Elferterre"

The teenagers laughed, and with Thirret leading the way, they left The Other Green Door. Dusk was starting to settle over the city, but it was still light enough to see, and there were plenty of people on the street. Thinking about Elferterre, Maya absently noted some of the passersby: the mother and her children eating ice cream; teenagers strolling hand in hand; and Chet Addington, looking all around him as he went down the sidewalk. He glanced at Maya, but there was no glimmer of recognition as he passed her and quickly walked away from them.

Startled, Maya almost stopped, and Will, who was right beside her, asked, "What's wrong?"

"I saw Chet."

"The man who didn't smile?" asked Will. "The one from APO who's been trying to get Earth's Book of Everything?"

"Yeah," Maya answered.

Thirret said, "APO's headquarters isn't too far from here. It's on Fulton Street. Underneath a hardware store."

Maya blinked in surprise. "Underneath a hardware store?"

Thirret scowled. "The hardware store is just a front. You should see what's underneath. It's pretty elaborate."

"In a hardware store on Fulton Street," Maya repeated softly. "Now I know where APO is."

Thirret brought them to the subway station not far from The Other Green Door. Will, Maya, and Jay followed him down, down, down the stairs.

"This feels very Harry Potterish," Will said.

"Will we be taking a subway to Elferterre?" Jay asked.

Thirret laughed. "No." He made a slight waving motion with his hand, and nobody except for two people noticed as he led Maya, Will, and Jay a little beyond the platform where there was only a narrow ledge between the wall and the tracks. They all had to walk single file.

Thirret stopped in front of a section that looked like a normal wall except for a slight wavering that would be unnoticeable unless someone was looking for it. He said, "Portal, please open." The shimmering outline of a door appeared. "This is the portal that will take you to Darkwood Forest. Father can't bear to come here. It makes him too sad to be this close to Elferterre and yet not be able to enter."

Maya said, "We'll get the key. And the lock."

Thirret replied, "I hope you will, for this dimension's sake as much as for ours. Remember, follow the map back to this portal. If you take another portal, you'll be in trouble."

Maya patted her pack, where the map was tucked. "We'll remember."

"Before we go, I have one question," Jay said. "Do elves have pointy ears?"

Thirret laughed. "We do." He lifted his thick dark hair to reveal delicate pointed ears. They all grinned at each other for a few moments, then Thirret cleared his throat. "Time to go." He waved his hands in front of the shimmering door. "Portal, please allow these humans to enter Darkwood Forest." His voice was firm but polite. The air inside the door's outline crackled into an entryway, and Maya felt the hair raise on her arms and the back of her neck.

Thirret turned to Maya, "Remember to say please when you ask the portal to open. Rudeness puts them off, and they won't open if you don't say please."

"I'll remember," Maya promised.

One by one, they filed past him, and Thirret clapped them all on the shoulder as they went through the portal. To Maya, it felt like both a blessing and a warning at the same time. Before the portal closed, Thirret called after them, "When you see Hanss, say hi for me. And trust him. He's a cool cat."

7: A Cool Cat

It seemed to Maya that they had stepped out of a tree and found themselves in a meadow ringed by a dark forest. In some ways, Maya was reminded of the Forest of Arden, but this one felt even wilder, more unpredictable. Magic crackled all around them, and Maya shivered, feeling both exhilarated and apprehensive. When Maya turned back to look at the tree they had stepped through, the portal was gone.

Jay whistled softly, and Will shook his head in wonder.

"Have you ever been to a place like this?" Jay asked Maya.

"No," she answered, "not like this." Maya took out the map from her pack. It looked like a scroll, but when she pushed a button at the top, it unrolled into what looked like a small tablet and even had the glow of a computer screen. "Show us the way to Foretcour," Maya said. A route appeared on the screen, and she studied the map. "The pathway to Foretcour is nearby. To the right of us, I think."

In a daze from the magic, they all looked to the right, but Maya felt dizzy, finding it hard to focus. Putting the map back in the pack, she said, "I have to sit down."

"Yeah," Jay agreed. "Me, too."

Will didn't say anything, closing his eyes as they all sat down.

"I hope it gets better," Jay murmured.

Will's voice was faint. "I don't feel as though I could walk ten steps. How far away is Foretcour?"

"Far," Maya answered miserably, thinking that even traveling with the Books had not been this bad. The queasy feeling had only lasted for a few minutes, but this dizziness showed no sign of going away anytime soon.

"It will pass eventually," a voice behind them said. The teenagers jumped and turned. Not far away sat a huge tawny cat with tufted ears and a thick white ruff. The cat seemed to be thoughtfully regarding them.

"Did that cat just talk?" Jay asked.

"I think so," Will replied.

"Yes, I did," the cat said. "And it would be more polite if you addressed me directly."

"Who are you?" Maya asked.

"I am Hanss," came the answer. "I used to live in Foretcour with Thirret Greenwood and his family before they were exiled."

Maya considered Hanss. "Why are you here in Darkwood Forest?"

The cat's voice was wistful. "I am waiting for my family to return. Especially for my boy, Thirret. And why are you here? Did Thirret show you how to use the portal? I thought I caught a glimpse of him."

As Maya regarded Hanss, she felt his sadness, his longing to be reunited with his family. "Yeah, Thirret showed us how to use the portal. I'm Maya, and this is Will and Jay. When we feel better, we're going to Foretcour to find Galli the locksmith, steal a key and a lock, and return to Earth so that the Greenwoods can unlock their chains and return to Elferterre. The lock is for us, to help trap someone in my universe."

Hanss stared steadily at Maya. "That won't be easy. A lot of others have come here with the same intention, but they did not succeed even though I helped them all. And they were elves, much stronger than you humans."

Jay said, "We're going to try anyway." He put a hand over his eyes. "If we can ever walk again."

"Pawel must have seen something in all of you, even though you are just young humans from the Other Side." Hanss stood, and his full tail plumed over his back. "You're not used to magic. Your system needs a while to adapt."

Will swallowed. "How long will it take?"

Hanss made his way toward where they were sitting, and he moved elegantly yet deliberately. "I am not sure how it will be for the three of you. I've never had anything to do with humans coming over from the Other Side. But lie down. Take a short nap. If you are lucky, when you wake up, you won't feel dizzy."

Maya, Will, and Jay did as they were told. Removing their knapsacks, they rested their heads against the soft grass in the meadow and closed their eyes. Hanss sat beside them and began to purr loudly. The purr enveloped them, and gradually Maya felt herself relax. The dizziness was still there, but it wasn't as bad, and breathing along with the purring, Maya slid gratefully into sleep.

When Maya woke up, she wasn't sure how much time had passed. The sun was shining, warm but not too hot, and Will and Jay were sleeping on either side of her. Gazing at Will's quiet face, Maya brushed a finger across his cheek. Waking up, Will smiled at her, and his hand reached out for her face. For a few minutes, they lay still, staring at each other, until Hanss said wryly, "You two seem to be feeling better."

Maya sat up, and to her relief she was no longer dizzy. "I do."

Will also sat up, and he actually laughed. "Me, too. I think I might even be able to walk."

Hanss was curled up beside Jay, who was beginning to stir. Hanss said, "Someone else came through the portal while you were sleeping." He motioned with his paw. "She's over there. Sleeping, too. Or maybe passed out. She had an even harder time than the three of you did."

Maya looked to where Hanss pointed, and on the ground not far away, she saw the form of a girl whose blonde hair covered her face.

But Maya didn't need to see the girl's face to know who she was. "Oh, no. Alani's Book was right."

"Lexie," Will whispered.

Jay was awake and sitting up. "Dear God, why is she here?"

Hanss growled softly, and his ears were flat against his head. "I knew there was something wrong with that girl the minute she came through."

Standing, Maya walked over to where Lexie lay. "Why did you follow us here?" Maya muttered, and leaning over, she saw that Lexie had been sick.

Lexie's eyes snapped open. "Go away, Anne."

"My name's not Anne, it's Maya."

"I don't care what your name is. I don't want to see your face."

"Then why did you come here?" Maya demanded impatiently. "Did you think we wanted to see your face?"

Moaning, Lexie sat up, wiping vomit from her cheeks and chin. "A blonde woman told me to follow you. She showed me where the door was, and she helped me get in."

"Nemesis," Maya said flatly. "I should have known."

Lexie's lovely face crinkled into a puzzled frown. "What?"

"Never mind. You need to go back. You shouldn't be here."

"You can't tell me what to do." Grimacing, Lexie tried to get up, but she fell back down.

Hanss came over to where Maya was standing. Sitting in grim silence, Jay and Will watched but didn't join them.

The cat's tail twitched. "That one's system really can't handle the magic. She's weak."

Lexie glared at Hanss. "Are you talking to me, cat?"

Hanss hissed. "Rude!"

Lexie's shoulders sagged. "Why can that cat talk?" Her expression was so forlorn and befuddled that Maya actually felt sorry for her.

"Is there some place we can go to make a fire, boil some water, and have a little tea?" Maya asked Hanss.

"Yes, my den is not far from here. You have tea?"

Maya stared down at Lexie, who had covered her face with her hands. "We do." Maya looked at Will and Jay. "Could you two come here? Lexie needs your help. She can't walk on her own."

Reluctantly, Will and Jay joined Maya, and she could tell that neither boy wanted to help Lexie. A flash came to Maya of Will's last exchange with Lexie, of the mean things she had said, of the threats even, to ostracize both him and Jay at school when it started in the fall. But Will had remained firm, telling Lexie that Maya was the one he wanted to be with and that threats wouldn't change his mind.

Maya felt such a surge of affection toward Will that she wanted to kiss him right then and there. Instead, she patted his back. "Will, Lexie needs our help. She's been mean, but we can't leave her here." Maya looked around, and in the distance she heard a shrill whistling sound. "There's no telling what will get Lexie if she's alone. She can't even walk."

"Maya is right," Hanss said. "Come night, it's especially dangerous here. This human girl would never make it until morning."

"All right," Will replied grimly, reaching down for Lexie, who hesitated only briefly before taking his hand. But Lexie couldn't stand on her own, and as her legs buckled, she nearly pulled Will down with her. Jay sprang to her other side, and between the two of them, they could keep Lexie upright as they moved her along.

"I hate this," Lexie muttered as they followed Hanss out of the clearing and into the woods. "I wish I had never come."

"Yeah, Lexie, we feel that way, too, but here you are," Jay replied.

Lexie's voice was tight with anger. "Shut up, Jay, you stupid little nerd. Nobody asked you. Nobody cares what you think."

Will's voice was firm. "Lexie, you're in no position to be telling people what to do. Not as long as you're here. And never with us again, no matter what. Do you understand?"

Will stopped. Jay stopped as well, and Lexie hung limply between them. Ahead of them, Hanss and Maya waited and watched.

Lexie glared at Will, but she didn't say anything. He frowned sternly at her as though Lexie were a wayward child. "I'm serious. Do you understand me?"

Lexie snapped, "Of course I do. But I'll never understand why you would choose that little freak Anne over me."

Maya called out, "My name's Maya."

"Whatever. You're still a little freak."

Clenching his jaw, Will let go of Lexie, who fell against Jay, nearly knocking them both to the ground. Will moved toward Maya and Hanss.

"Come on, bud," Jay called. "Don't leave me alone with her."

"No," came the firm reply. "I'm never touching her again."

"Will," Maya said. "Please."

Will's expression softened, but he shook his head, and Maya could see he was too angry to relent.

"Fine." Maya sighed as she went over to Lexie. "He's stubborn, isn't he?" Maya asked as she supported Lexie on the other side.

"Oh, yeah," Jay said. "Just wait."

"Never mind," Maya said. "I might be a little freak, but I'm strong."

"I hate you," Lexie whispered to Maya.

"I know," Maya whispered back. "But luckily I don't hate you. Or you would be in a pickle."

Lexie's face was hard with anger, but she didn't say anything else.

They slowly made their way into the forest. The cat's den wasn't far, but because of Lexie, it took them a while to get there. Occasionally, Will would turn back to see how they were doing, and Maya could tell that even though Will was stubborn, he had started to relent and would have taken Maya's place if she had asked.

But Maya didn't ask, thinking that it was better for Lexie to learn that her mean words had consequences. Maya had the sinking feeling that Lexie wouldn't be returning to Earth anytime soon, and it would be best if things were sorted out as quickly as possible. Lexie was used to running the show, but on Elferterre, things were different. It wasn't her show anymore.

"Or mine either," Maya thought with a slight shiver.

Hanss had made his den in the hollow of an enormous tree. There was plenty of room for one cat and even enough room for the four teenagers. But Jay, Will, and Maya didn't stay inside the den. As soon as Lexie was settled, they left her inside by herself and went to look for fallen wood for a fire. Before long they had each gathered an armful, and they returned to the small glade by the den, where Hanss told them how to build a fire.

Maya, who had often helped her pépère make fires, knew what to do, but she said nothing as Hanss instructed them. She sensed that helping them made Hanss feel useful, and that for too many years, Hanss had felt helpless as first his family had disappeared and then the rescuing elves had failed to get the key that would unlock the chains.

Before long, a small fire was going, and on it Maya placed a pot with water from a nearby stream that seemed to laugh as it rushed by. As soon as the water boiled, chamomile tea was made. Maya, Will, and Jay all had a tin cup and bowl in their packs, and Maya used her cup to make tea for Lexie.

Lexie was sitting up when Maya brought her tea, but Lexie's face was still pale, and she was slumped miserably against the wall of the tree. Without saying anything, Lexie took the cup and cautiously sipped the hot tea. When the tea was halfway gone, Lexie was sitting up straighter and didn't look as sick. Maya turned to leave.

"Wait," Lexie said. When Maya hesitated, a grudging "please" was added.

Maya sat down. She had no doubt that Lexie had many questions, and Maya decided to do what the Books of Everything did: Give as little information as possible while still telling the truth. "I'm becoming like them," Maya thought ruefully.

"Who are you really?" Lexie asked.

Maya could be truthful with this question. "My name is Maya Hammond. I live in Maine and New York."

Lexie shook her head. "What is this place? Why are you here?"

"This is Elferterre, and we are in the kingdom of Norlander. Elferterre is in a different dimension than Earth is, and that portal in the subway station brought us here. Will, Jay, and I are helping the Greenwood family. They own The Other Green Door." Maya stopped, not wanting to say too much about the elves.

"And?" Lexie asked.

"That's all I'm telling you. Lexie, you don't belong here. It's dangerous. As soon as you're well enough, you should go home. Go back to the tree where the portal is and say, 'Please open.' It will take you back to Earth"

Lexie stared thoughtfully at Maya. "Why did that woman send me here?"

"For no good reason," Maya answered firmly. "Her name is Nemesis, and she's not to be trusted."

"Nemesis? What kind of name is that?"

"Exactly what it sounds like. She's bad."

"She's so beautiful."

Maya could see how someone like Lexie, overly concerned with appearances, would be dazzled by Nemesis's looks. "I know. But Nemesis is as bad as it's possible to be. She's on Chaos's side."

"Chaos? What do you mean?"

"Two forces rule our dimension. One is Chaos, and the other is Time."

"I suppose Chaos is evil, and Time is good."

"Yeah," Maya answered. "You could put it that way."

"And what about Elferterre?"

Maya ran her hands over the soft pine needles that Hanss had used to line his den. "Magic rules Elferterre. It's strong here, and that's why you feel so funny. Will, Jay, and I felt that way, too, when we first came through the portal."

"But you're better now, and I'm not."

"We're all different, Lexie. You'll feel better eventually. And then it will be time for you to go home." Maya hoped that maybe if she said it enough, Lexie would actually go back to Earth.

"Yeah." Lexie fiddled with a silver bracelet she wore. Hanging loosely on her wrist, it was simple and lovely and had a single heart dangling from it. Maya realized that Will had given Lexie the bracelet.

"Why does he want to be with you when he could be with me?" Lexie asked, and if her expression hadn't been as sad, Maya would have laughed. But while Maya's fiery nature had often caused her to say things she would later regret, Maya had never laughed at anyone's pain. Then Maya saw something that surprised her—Lexie truly was in love with Will, which was why she was still wearing the bracelet.

"Somehow our personalities go together," Maya answered.

"How old are you?" Lexie asked sharply.

Maya gave Lexie the same answer she had given Will. "Sixteen going on forty."

But Lexie didn't laugh. Instead, she sighed. "Could you leave me alone for a while? I'm tired."

"Sure."

As Maya left, Lexie closed her eyes and settled into the bed of pine needles.

Will, Jay, and Hanss were sitting around the fire.

Jay poked at the fire with a stick. "How is her majesty doing?"

"Better," Maya answered.

"Is that girl royalty?" Hanss asked incredulously.

Will laughed shortly. "No, but Lexie thinks she is."

The cat's whiskers twitched. "That human is trouble. I can feel it."

"I know." Maya's voice was rueful. "But what could we do? We couldn't just leave her there."

Nobody said anything, and Maya could tell they all grudgingly agreed with her. Seeing her knapsack set with the others away from the fire, Maya decided to change the subject. "Is anybody hungry? Pawel packed us some food, and you know what good cooks the elves are."

Both Will and Jay grinned. "Of course we're hungry," Jay said.

In her pack, Maya found bundles of lentils and spices folded in brown paper bags. In another bag was flatbread to go along with the soup. Soon two pans of simmering lentils were on the fire. Maya knew that one pot wouldn't be enough for the four of them, especially with Will's and Jay's appetites, and fortunately each backpack had a small pan as well as a bowl and a cup.

"Would you like some soup?" Maya asked Hanss.

"No," the cat answered. "I'll get my own meal."

Hanss left, and Maya, Will, and Jay studied the map while the lentils cooked. When the stew was ready, Maya put the map away. Hanss hadn't returned, but they decided that since he wasn't joining them, it didn't matter when they ate.

Maya brought some stew and bread to Lexie, who reluctantly woke up to take them from Maya. One look at Lexie's stony expression told Maya that the blonde girl didn't want any company, and Maya left.

Maya and Will shared a bowl. Extra spoons had been packed, and as they gratefully ate their spicy stew, dusk settled over the forest. She could hear little chirps, rustlings, and high-pitched squeals, but somehow, Maya felt safe by the fire.

"Really good," Will said with a smile between mouthfuls.

"Sure is," Jay agreed.

Maya scraped the bowl with some of the tasty bread to get the last bits. "The Greenwoods know how to cook."

After the pots, cups, and bowls had been rinsed with water from one of the canteens Pawel had given them, wiped dry with a small towel, and put back in the packs, Jay asked, "Want to hear some music?"

"All right," Maya and Will said together.

Jay took the mandolin from its case and strummed it gently. "It's in tune," Jay said, surprised.

Hanss had returned and was sitting by Jay. "It's an elven instrument. It will never go out of tune."

"Sweet," Jay said, strumming a little louder. "I'm going to play some songs my abuela used to sing. She had a temper, but she was smart and brave. Maybe the songs will bring us some luck."

"My mémère is brave, too." Swallowing, Maya felt her eyes sting with tears. Where was her mémère now? And was she safe?

Shaking his head, Will didn't say anything, and as Maya brushed away the tears, she got the impression that Will's grandmothers were not a big part of his life. Smiling sadly, Will remained silent as he put his arm around Maya's shoulders, and she leaned against him.

Jay sang in a tenor, and when his voice, strong and true, blended with the golden notes coming from the mandolin, Maya felt transfixed, almost as though she were under a spell. As Jay sang songs in Spanish that were sad, happy, and rousing, Maya simply stared in wonder. Beside her, Will was doing the same thing.

When Jay finished, even he looked a little astonished, as though he couldn't believe the power of his own voice and the music.

Hanss said, "Jay, you might succeed where others have failed. I have never heard such a voice coming from a human. Look, the woodland sprites have come to hear you sing."

"My voice is better here than it is on Earth," Jay said as they all turned around to look at the bobbing lights that hovered among the trees beyond the small glade. Maya could barely hear the high-pitched voices of the sprites as they spoke to each other.

"Naturally," Hanss replied. "You're on Elferterre."

8: Captured by Ogres

When the fire had burned down, Maya, Will, and Jay followed Hanss into his den. Although it was dark, the forest was aglow with the light of the sprites, and Maya could make out Lexie's outline as she lay huddled against the tree's wall. Maya settled beside Lexie, but the blonde girl didn't say anything. Will lay on the other side of Maya, and as she moved toward him, taking in his warmth and his smell, Will kissed the top of her head and put his arm around her.

Hanss sat by the opening, and his front paws moved around in a weaving motion. It seemed to Maya that Hanss was using magic to make some kind of protective barrier.

When Hanss was done, he confirmed Maya's hunch. "There. That will keep most things from getting us yet still allow you to go outside, should you need to. However, don't go too far. The forest is especially dangerous at night and just before the sun comes up. I've woven a spell around the glade, but because the area is bigger, the spell isn't as strong as it is on my den's door. Be careful if you go out."

Jay, who was on the other side of Will, said sleepily, "We won't go anywhere. We'll stay right here."

"Good," Hanss replied with a purr, curling up beside Jay.

But the next morning, Lexie was gone, and Maya was the first to notice. "Oh, no."

Will sat up quickly. "What?"

"Lexie's not here."

Will's voice was hopeful. "Maybe she went back home."

"Maybe," Maya said, but she had a feeling that Lexie hadn't returned to Earth.

As Jay stirred beside him, Hanss opened one eye. "I'm glad she's gone. I hope I never see her again."

However, when Jay, Will, and Maya went to the stream to wash their faces and fill their canteens, they discovered that Lexie hadn't gone home. In the soft dirt by the stream, there were huge footprints that had four toes, and beside them were smaller prints. Inside one of the huge footprints was the silver bracelet with the heart.

Will picked it up. "I gave this to Lexie." Will's voice had a rueful tone, as though he couldn't understand why he had wanted to give anything to Lexie.

Maya shrugged. "You liked her once. I liked another boy, too."

Putting the bracelet in his pocket, Will frowned. "But not anymore?"

"No, he changed," Maya answered, thinking of Andy. "A lot."

"Never mind about that," Jay said. "Let's get back to the den and see if Hanss knows what might have happened."

Hanss did know. "Lexie was captured by an ogre. Probably Novok. He's always nosing around here." Hanss sniffed. "He'd like to eat me, but my magic is stronger than his, and he can't get me when I'm in my den."

"Lexie must have gone to the stream to wash up," Maya said slowly. "Before the sun was actually up, but light enough to see."

"And Novok got her." Jay's voice was glum. "What's he going to do with Lexie?"

"Oh, he'll eat her." Hanss looked from Jay to Maya and Will. "I suppose we'll have to rescue that dratted girl."

"Of course we do," Maya said. "Lexie is a pain, but she doesn't deserve to be eaten by an ogre."

"Probably more than one ogre would eat Lexie," Hanss said. "No doubt Novok will invite his brothers Bainah and Tronen to come over and have roasted human. It's a delicacy for ogres. There are not many humans in these woods. Too dangerous for them. In a way, that's good. It means Novok won't just gobble Lexie down. He'll wait to kill her at the last minute so the meat will be fresh for his special feast." Maya, Will, and Jay shuddered while Hanss shook his head. "It won't be easy to get Lexie away from Novok. Ogres are strong, and despite their bulk, they can move fast. I've had near misses with ogres more than once."

Will's voice was firm. "We have to try."

"Yeah, we do," Jay added quickly.

"I know." The cat's whiskers twitched, and nobody spoke for a while. Finally, Hanss said, "I think I have an idea. But Maya, you'll have to be translated with a potion so that we can trick Novok."

"Translated into what?" Maya asked, having a bad feeling about this.

"Into Erman, a female ogre that Novok is sweet on. I've seen them together in the woods. Novok's so besotted by Erman that she could talk him out of anything, even roasting a human. With any luck, you can go to his cave and get him to give you Lexie. Then you two can escape before the potion wears off."

Will frowned. "Why does it have to be Maya?"

"Because she is the smallest of the three of you," Hanss answered. "There is a better chance the potion will work longer on her."

"Why don't you take the potion?" Will asked, staring intently at Hanss. "You're the smallest here."

Hanss stared back at Will. "This is true. However, my cat nature will never let me be anything but what I am. Even if I looked like Erman, Novok would be able to tell right away that something was fishy."

Jay smiled. "Or catty."

Will laughed, Maya rolled her eyes, and Hanss yowled in a way that could have been either a laugh or a protest.

Jay continued, "But seriously, Maya's a good actor. If anyone can pull this off, she can."

Maya could tell that Will was still going to object, and she said quickly, "I'll do it. I've faced worse." Will continued to frown at her. "Really, I have. Do you have a better idea?"

"What about the ball Pawel gave me?" Will reached into his pack, pulled it out, and unwrapped the silver ball.

Hanss blinked. "Pawel must be desperate if he gave you that ball. They're rare, even on Elferterre, and I am amazed that he found one on Earth. Unfortunately, that ball doesn't work well against a creature with a skull as thick as an ogre's. It might stun Novok, but it wouldn't knock him out, and you'd never get away from him in time. As I said, those ogres can move fast. That's how Novok got Lexie without us hearing anything. He probably knocked her out before she even had time to scream."

"What about this?" Maya asked, reaching into her pack to take out the box with the bee. Maya opened the box, and the bee buzzed expectantly. "Not now," Maya whispered, and the buzzing stopped.

Hanss yowled in surprise. "Pawel gave you a bee, too? By my paws, he's pulling out all the stops. The bee should work against Novok, but I think it would be best to try to trick the ogre and only use the bee if you have to. Who knows? Something even worse might come up when you really need that bee."

"Okay," Maya replied quickly, putting the bee away.

"Right," Hanss said. "Now where were we?"

"We were talking about turning Maya into an ogre called Erman," Jay said. "Where will we get the potion?"

Hanss answered, "From a sprite named Kai, whose specialty is potions. He'll have something to help us."

"Will he want to?" Jay asked.

"Oh, yes," Hanss replied. "I've saved him from the gliders more than once. When Kai is out at dusk gathering ingredients for his potions, he's not as careful as he should be."

"The gliders?" Maya asked.

"I'll tell you about them later," Hanss said. "Let's go find Kai so we can get started."

Not far from where Hanss lived, there was a stand of tall silver trees with glittering white leaves. In the morning sun, the trees sparkled with such a bright beauty that Maya, Will, and Jay simply stood and stared, unable to speak. High up the trunk of each tree, there were several holes, and sprites of various colors flew in and out of the openings. Underneath the holes were little decks that wrapped around the entire tree, and small wooden chairs, brightly painted, were grouped on each deck. In some of the chairs sat sprites holding tiny mugs. The chairs faced the rising sun, and the sprites seemed to be greeting the day.

"Wow," Jay said.

"Unbelievable," Will added.

"Lovely." Entranced, Maya was beginning to understand how much magic changed a world, how it permeated everything, making the beautiful more beautiful.

"And the ugly even uglier," Hanss said, regarding her thoughtfully.

"Can you read my mind?" Maya asked, startled.

"I can," Hanss replied. "But mostly I choose not to."

Maya grinned. "Well, that's considerate."

The cat's mouth twitched into something resembling a smile. "I don't want to be too pushy."

Maya, Will, and Jay followed Hanss as he walked among the silver trees. Maya noticed that small spikes, going a quarter of the way up the trunks, were embedded in all the trees.

"What are the spikes for?" Maya asked Hanss.

"To keep out the gliders."

"Which you'll tell us about later," Jay said.

"Right," Hanss replied, stopping by a tree in the middle of the stand. "The gliders don't come out until dusk, which means we don't have to worry about them right now. We need to focus on the problem at hand."

"Hanss," a high voice called down.

"Kai, could you come here? Pawel sent three humans to Elferterre, and we need your help."

"I'll be there in a flash."

A blue blur flew from the deck and landed on the cat's back. But Hanss didn't seem to mind, and the sprite, who had a human body with wings as long and as lacy as a dragonfly's, gave the cat a pat before fluttering up to regard the teenagers. Kai wore a blue tunic edged with silver and matching blue pants. His dark hair was cut short enough to reveal tiny pointed ears.

"Pawel sent humans?" Kai asked. "That's a first."

"All the elves he sent failed," Hanss replied.

Kai's voice was sad. "That they did. So who do we have here?"

Hanss introduced Maya, Will, and Jay. "Unfortunately, there's a fourth one, a human girl named Lexie."

"And where is she?"

"Novok got her."

Kai made a tsk-tsking sound. "Not good for the human girl. Novok will eat her. And he'll probably invite his rotten brothers to join him. How do you want me to help?"

"Do you have enough of your translation potion to turn Maya into Erman?"

Kai stared critically at Maya. "Possibly, but I'm not sure how long it would last. I know she's small for a human, but compared to a sprite, she's enormous."

"Here's what we'll do," Hanss said. "We'll go to Novok's cave in the Gray Hills. Maya can take the potion and try to get Lexie away from Novok. If this works, we can carry on with that plan. If it doesn't, then we'll go with Will's plan."

Kai asked, "What plan is that?"

Hanss told Kai about the silver ball and Maya's bee.

"H-m-m-m," Kai replied. "We need another backup plan. I'll come along and bring a few more vials of potions, just in case."

"Thank you, Kai," Hanss said gratefully.

Kai waved a small hand. "Come on, you know I owe you a few. Plus, you aren't as good with translation spells as I am."

"Still." Hanss blinked affectionately, and Kai's responding smile was also affectionate.

Maya was moved by the bond that connected these two creatures who were unalike, and she wondered if it could ever be this way on Earth, where humans often didn't extend their affection to each other much less to different species. Maya knew that humans loved their pets, but she could tell that the attachment between Kai and Hanss was different, based on respect and equality rather than dominance.

After a breakfast of tea, flatbread, and sweet purple berries that grew by the stream, Maya, Will, and Jay, guided by Hanss and Kai, set out for Novok's cave, about an hour's trek from where Hanss lived. Golden-specked sunlight filtered through the trees, and wherever it fell, there was a sparkling glow, making the leaves that were yellow shimmer and gleam. They passed a gorge with a waterfall that beckoned to them: "Come here, come here."

Maya felt strangely drawn by the waterfall's lovely rushing voice, and she could tell that Will and Jay did, too.

"Don't listen to it," Hanss said. "That waterfall is not to be trusted."

Kai flitted beside Hanss. "Righto! The voice is friendly now, but if you get too close, it will roar, pulling you in." Zipping toward the edge of the water, Kai shouted, "We know your tricks. You can't fool us." Then he shot back to the cat's side.

Maya, Will, and Jay jumped as the waterfall roared at the retreating sprite, and Maya felt as though something was tugging at her. Maya was able to resist but knew that if she had been closer to the waterfall, she might have gone over the edge.

Hanss said, "Kai, you know you shouldn't do that. Someday you'll be caught."

"Never!" came the sprite's saucy answer. "I can outfly that poky waterfall."

Hanss sighed but didn't say anything to Kai.

"Are all waterfalls like that here?" Maya asked.

Hanss shook his head. "No, that one has a bad attitude. The water comes from the Gray Hills, which is ogre territory."

Kai flew in a little circle around Maya. "Think how you'd feel if you started out in ogre territory."

"Not good," Jay agreed.

"Lucky our stream doesn't come from the Gray Hills," Kai said.

"We wouldn't live near it if it did," Hanss replied.

"Where does that water come from?" Maya asked.

"From one of the sweetest springs in the forest," Hanss answered. "And the water blesses all who live near it."

Kai zipped in a figure eight between two trees. "Some creatures don't deserve that blessing."

"Maybe not," Hanss agreed with the flick of his tail. "But the water doesn't discriminate, which is the way it should be."

"Sure, sure, sure!" Kai called, disappearing into the forest.

"Wow, Kai has a lot of energy," Maya said.

"That he does. For years and years, I've been trying to convince him of the benefits of short naps in the afternoon, but he never listens."

Kai returned in a blue blur, skimming over the cat's fur and ruffling it, and Hanss swatted amiably at the sprite. Maya, Jay, and Will laughed, and for the rest of the morning, except for Kai's aerial stunts, the woods were quiet. By late morning they came to the edge of the forest where there was a small field edged by a large mass of stone hills.

"Here we are," said Kai. "There are caves all through those hills, a regular ogre village. They'll mostly be in their caves. As a rule, ogres don't come out until night. That's why they're so pasty pale. Do them good to get a bit of sun."

"Where does Novok live?" Will asked.

Kai pointed to the left to an opening. "Over there. The younger ogres all live in caves on the edge of the hills. The older ones live deeper in, where it's safer. I will say this, the ogres do take care of their elders. Novok probably would have saved some of Lexie's fingers for his grandparents, who don't get out much anymore. Ogres love the snap and crunch of human fingers."

Thinking about this, Maya shuddered, but she realized that in a way ogres were much like other creatures who hunted and killed to eat. Nevertheless, Maya didn't want Lexie to be their next meal.

"All right," Maya said. "I'm ready."

"I don't like this," Will replied.

Hanss growled a little. "Me, neither, even though I suggested it. But if all goes well, no one will die."

"Good luck," Jay said softly.

With a gleeful expression, Kai rubbed his hands together before digging into a tiny pack he had brought. "Let's see if we can trick Novok. But, Maya, do it as fast as you can. There's no telling how long the potion will last."

"I'll do my best."

"Open your mouth, tip your head back, and let me give you the potion. Your fingers are so big that I doubt you'd be able to handle the vial without crushing it or spilling the potion."

Maya did as she was told and felt a sprinkling of something bitter on her tongue. Kai chanted, "Translate Maya, the human girl, to Erman, the ogre. Translate, translate, translate!"

As soon as Kai was done chanting, Maya felt funny. Her hands tingled, and it seemed as though she was being stretched in all directions. She heard Will and Jay gasp, and looking down at herself, Maya saw pale massive arms and stubby fingers. She stared at Will and Jay, who were now much shorter than she was, and even with so much going on, Maya enjoyed being taller than they were. When she touched her head, Maya felt long thin hair instead of short bouncy curls.

Kai shrieked with delight. "Holy stream, it worked! Now go, Maya, go!"

Maya loped out of the forest toward Novok's cave and was amazed by how fast she could run. In no time, Maya was by the cave's opening, and stopping by the entrance, she looked down at herself. She was wearing a white shirt with ruffles around the neck and a long red skirt. She was also wearing gold hoop earrings, and when Maya shook her head, she could feel the earrings move against her thick neck. Her feet were bare, and there were four toes on each foot, just as there had been on the prints at the stream.

From the cave, a gruff voice called, "Who's out there?"

"It's me," Maya called back, startled by how deep her voice had become.

"Erman?" Novok asked hopefully.

"That's right. I heard you captured a tasty human. Can I take a look?"

"Course you can. Come in, come in."

Maya took a tentative step inside the cave, which was much cleaner than she had expected. In the middle, there was a long table with benches, on the wall were shelves with crockery, and a big wooden bed was at the far end. Underneath the shelves was a cage, and Lexie sat inside, weeping softly.

Feeling Lexie's fear and grief, Maya put a hand to her face. She had to get Lexie away from this place. Soon.

Large, pale, and heavy, with a protruding chin and a bulbous nose, Novok was sitting at the table. He wore a white shirt—free of stains—a brown vest, and brown trousers. But his feet were bare. There was a big pencil behind his fat ear, and several books were spread out in front of him. With a start, Maya realized that Novok was going through cookbooks. Looking up, he beamed at Maya, and she could feel how much he loved Erman.

Novok pointed to the cage. "Look at that human," he said proudly, like a small child who had caught a frog.

Maya forced herself to smile. "Oh, lovely! When was the last time we had a human?"

Novok's broad face was scrunched in thought. "Not for a long, long time. Me and my brothers caught a bunch who were trying to get to one of the portals in the forest. Must have been four or five years ago."

"Too long!" Maya said with a deep trill as she bent down to look at Lexie, who screamed and scrambled to the back of the cage.

"Damn right," Novok replied with a proud rumble. "What do you think of her?"

Maya pretended to consider Lexie. "Luscious looking, but..."

Novok stood quickly. "But what?"

Maya could hear the worry in his voice, and she pressed her case. "The human's a little thin, don't you think?"

The ogre hurried over to the cage and peered at Lexie, who covered her face with her hands. "Is she?" Novok asked anxiously.

"Nothing to her," Maya said. "Look at those arms and legs. They're long but skinny. Hardly any meat on them."

Novok sighed, and his shoulders drooped. "The human won't go far, will she? I was hoping to have a nice little party. You, me, my brothers, and the new couple that moved in a few caves down. Thought it would be a good way to get to know them." He glanced at her. "I was even planning to save a finger for you. My grandparents don't need all of them."

Novok's expression was so adoring that for a moment Maya felt sorry for him. If her plan worked, there would be no human fingers for Novok to share that night.

"Tell you what," Maya said, forcing herself to move a little closer toward Novok, who smelled sour and greasy. "How about if I take the human home and fatten her up? Then when she's ready, I can give her back to you for the feast."

Novok beamed at her. "You'd do that for me?"

"Of course I would," Maya answered, unsure of how much give and take there was in their relationship. Maybe Novok was the giver, and Erman was the taker. But Maya knew there was no time to worry about the nuances of ogre courtship. She had to get Lexie away before the potion wore off and there would be one more human for Novok to roast. Maya pointed to the cage. "Give her to me, and I will return her fat and saucy."

Giggling with delight, Novok went to the shelves, dug into one of the pots, and produced a key. He brought it over and unlocked the cage. Lexie started to shriek.

Novok said severely, "I'll conk you on the head again if you keep making that racket. And don't even think of biting Erman, or there will be big trouble. Do you understand me?" Lexie continued to scream, and Novok cuffed her across the head. It was a light slap, but Novok's big hand left a red mark on Lexie's face. Choking in fear and pain, Lexie stopped screaming. "There you go." He shook a large finger at her. "Now, I don't want to hear that you've been any trouble." Grabbing Lexie by the leg, Novok pulled her with ease and lifted her out of the cage. When Lexie started to struggle, Novok held up a warning finger, and she stopped, biting her lip to keep from crying out.

Novok handed Lexie to Maya, who took the light bundle in her arms. "What a nice little freak you are," Maya crooned. Blinking, Lexie stared at Maya, who winked.

"What's a freak?" Novok asked.

"Oh," Maya replied airily. "It's just a word I made up to describe someone who's little and funny looking."

"Freak," a bemused Novok repeated.

"Off we go," Maya said, jostling Lexie as though she were a baby. As Lexie stared at her, Maya could tell the blonde girl was hoping against hope.

Novok's fleshy lower lip protruded into a pout. "No kiss?"

A kiss? Maya took a step back, but then she saw how much Novok expected one, and she didn't want to arouse his suspicions. Holding her breath, Maya gave him a quick kiss on his bristly cheek. "Lexie, you really owe me," Maya thought.

"All right, then," Maya said aloud, keeping a firm grip on Lexie. "I'll start fattening this girl up."

"Okay," Novok rumbled in his deep voice. He followed her to the cave's entrance and watched her scramble down the hill onto the field. Maya had no idea where Erman's cave was, but breaking into a jog, she went back the way she had come, planning to head to the woods as soon as Novok couldn't see her anymore.

When she was nearly out of the ogre's sight, Maya began to relax a little, thinking that maybe the plan was actually going to work and that she, Lexie, and the others would be miles away before Novok was any wiser.

But then Maya's hands tingled, and she felt a contraction. A minute or two later, her arms and legs began to shrink. "Oh, no!" Maya cried, falling to the ground with Lexie, who landed on top of her.

Novok could still see them. "What's going on?"

"Nothing!" Maya yelled back gamely as she watched her arms return to normal.

Novok roared, "You're not Erman!"

With a mighty thud, Novok leaped from his cave and rushed down the hill toward Maya and Lexie.

9: Exit, Pursued by Ogres

Maya was in a daze, but she scrambled to her feet. "Run!" Maya yelled to Lexie.

Lexie didn't hesitate, and the two girls sprinted toward the forest. Behind them, Maya could hear Novok's pounding feet as he gained ground.

"I'll get you!" Novok yelled, and his voice sounded all too close.

Beside her, Lexie choked back a sob, and Maya felt her own throat close with fear. "We'll never get away," she thought, and her shoulder twitched in anticipation of being grabbed by Novok's large hand.

But that hand never came down on her shoulder. A blue blur whizzed around Maya's head. "Open your mouth," came Kai's high voice. Maya did as she was told, and she felt something bitter on her tongue. Kai chanted, "Big human turn small, translate into a sprite. Translate, translate, translate."

Before she shrank, Maya yelled to Lexie, "The sprite's a friend. Do what he tells you to do."

Maya's hands tingled, and with a pop, she became a sprite. Like Kai, Maya was blue, and she stared in amazement at her gossamer wings.

"Maya!" Kai screamed, and his voice no longer seemed high. "Watch out! Flap your wings. Fly away!"

Novok's fat fingers nearly had her. Maya's wings beat desperately, and she shot up like a small blue rocket. Maya zoomed past

Novok's grasping hand, and soon she was looking down at the bald spot on his head.

"Ha, Novok!" Maya yelled, exhilarated by being able to fly as swiftly as a sprite. "You can't catch me."

"I'll get you!" Novok boomed. Cracking like thunder, his voice sounded even deeper and louder than it had when Maya had been ogre-sized.

"Oh, no you won't." Maya knew that she should leave the ogre alone, that she should fly away while she had the chance. But Maya couldn't resist one parting shot, and she dived toward Novok.

"No, Maya!" Kai called out.

Maya ignored the sprite. Instead, she buzzed the ogre's head, and her wings were moving fast enough to rustle Novok's sparse hair. With a rapid snap, Novok's hand reached for Maya, and he might have caught her if Kai hadn't flown to her side, grabbed her arm, and pulled her out of reach.

Kai's face was bright with anger. However, Maya felt nothing but glee as they flew away from the howling ogre. Lexie was waiting for them on a tree branch by the edge of the forest.

Unlike Maya, Lexie was red, and she shook her tiny head as they settled on the branch beside her. "I've got to hand it to you, Maya. You're brave. But sometimes you're not too smart."

Still angry, Kai folded his arms across his chest. "That was a stupid thing to do. Ogres are quick. Novok nearly had you."

Maya knew that Lexie and Kai were right, and although she nodded contritely, Maya still felt exhilarated. "I wish I could just fly and fly," Maya thought.

Noting Maya's elated expression, Kai grinned reluctantly. "Oh, never mind. Thanks to me that big oaf didn't get you. Come on, let's go join the others. It won't be long before Novok organizes a hunting party to track you and Lexie. He knows the potions will wear off soon. We shouldn't hang around here."

"Okay," Maya agreed meekly.

Before they flew from the branch, Lexie said in an offhanded way, "Thanks, Maya."

Maya nodded in response, sensing how hard it was for Lexie to thank anyone, much less someone who had taken Will. But Maya could tell that Lexie had been changed by her time in the cage. Maya wasn't sure how deep this change went, but facing death had chastened Lexie. It had made the blonde girl realize that in this land there were many things beyond her control.

Kai, Maya, and Lexie flew back to where Jay, Will, and Hanss were waiting. As the three sprites settled on the ground, the boys stared in amazement at Lexie and Maya, but before they could ask any questions, Kai said, "You can hear the story later. Right now, we've got to get out of here. Novok, his brothers, and friends are going to come looking for us." The sprite dug in his pack and produced three more vials. "This is all I have." Kai looked from Will to Jay to Hanss. "If I turn the three of you into sprites, then we can put some distance between us and the ogres. We might even be able to make it most of the way home."

"If you must," Hanss said with a sigh.

"Oh, come on!" Kai replied. "It will be fun to fly together. I've been wanting to fly with you for a long time."

The cat's whiskers twitched. "I like having something solid under my paws."

Kai laughed. "It will do you good to go through the air."

Hanss shook his head in protest, but he opened his mouth and let Kai transform him. Soon six sprites zoomed through the woods. Will was blue, like Maya; Jay was green; and Hanss was a luminous gray.

Kai and Hanss led the way, with Lexie and Maya close behind. Jay and Will whooped with glee as they followed them. Grabbing Maya's hand, Will pulled her close, and they wove their way through branches and underneath leaves that had become big green canopies. Up and down they flew together, always keeping the others in sight. With all the swooping, Maya felt breathless, a little dizzy even, but flying next to Will filled her with such joy that she didn't want the trip to end.

However, as they passed the roaring falls, Maya felt her hands tingle, and she said to Will, "We need to fly close to the ground. The potion is wearing off."

Will sped toward the ground, banking up just in time to avoid crashing, and Maya tumbled into herself, skidding among the ferns.

Ahead of her Lexie was doing the same thing, and not long after, Hanss, Jay, and Will returned to their true forms. In a blue flutter, Kai flew alone around the humans and the cat.

Jumping to their feet, Will and Jay whooped and gave each other a high five.

"That was crazy!" Jay said, brushing his dark hair away from his face.

"A real rush," Will agreed, looking at Maya, who blushed and laughed but didn't say anything.

Even Lexie's normally haughty face was bright from the excitement of flying.

"I need to groom myself," Hanss said, twitching his tail.

"You need to get out of here," Kai replied sharply. "The ogres can't move as quickly as we did, but they're fast. Soon enough, they'll be back at the stream, where Novok caught Lexie. From there they'll fan out, tracking you."

"You're right," Hanss agreed quickly.

"You're taking them to Foretcour, to Galli's?" Kai asked. "And you'll stay in Arbor City tonight?"

"Yes," Hanss answered. "But we need to go to my den first so that Maya, Will, and Jay can collect their packs."

"What about me?" Lexie's voice was low.

Maya surprised herself by asking, "What do you want to do?"

"I should go back home," Lexie said slowly. "I was almost killed."

"You should," Maya agreed. "We have a mission here. And we need to focus on that, not on you."

With glittering eyes, Lexie looked at Maya. "I know. But I don't want to leave. I want to go with all of you and see what else is here. I've never been anywhere like Elferterre. I've never felt like this before. And to fly!"

For a moment, Maya didn't know what to do, but she remembered Alani's Book's advice. "Look at me," Maya commanded. Lexie did as she was told and didn't flinch when Maya's hand cupped her face.

Maya stared into Lexie's blue eyes and saw a rich child who had been given everything she had ever wanted; Maya saw a vain, arrogant mother who had loved Lexie the only way she knew how—by making Lexie the center and never encouraging her to think about anyone else; but Maya also saw that while Lexie was self-centered, she was also brave and smart and had the potential to learn. Finally, Maya saw that if Lexie went back to Earth now, then the blonde girl would grow up to be exactly like her mother, hard and selfish. But if Lexie stayed on Elferterre, there was a chance that the experience would improve her. Maya couldn't deny Lexie this chance to grow into something better than she was now.

Maya patted Lexie's cheek. "All right."

Lexie's eyes were wide. "I can go with you?"

"Yes," Maya answered, taking her hand away.

"What?" Will asked incredulously.

"No way!" Jay exclaimed.

Hanss licked a paw and ran it across his face. "You might want to rethink that decision."

"No," Maya said firmly. "Lexie belongs with us."

Hanss considered Lexie. "You will have to do exactly what you are told."

"I will."

The cat's whiskers twitched. "It's dangerous here. And you are not in charge."

"I know that," Lexie answered. "I was almost eaten by an ogre."

"You might not make it back." Hanss stared steadily at Lexie. "Many who are stronger have not."

Lexie hesitated, looking from Maya to Will to Jay and then back to Hanss. "I understand. But I don't want to leave. Not yet."

Kai flew around Lexie. "Good! That's settled. Now you all have to get out of here. With any luck, you can get to Arbor City before the ogres get you. I'll come with you to the edge of the forest. Then you're on your own."

"What about lunch?" Jay asked hopefully.

"It has been a while since breakfast," Will added.

"No time," came Kai's twitter of an answer.

"Kai is right," Hanss said. "The sooner we're out of the forest, the better it will be. You humans are no match for the creatures that live here."

Nobody grumbled out loud about not having lunch, but when they reached the den, Hanss said, "If you can eat while you walk, grab some bread, and then let's get going."

As Maya reached for her pack, she got a flash of Novok and his hunting party. There were about twenty of them, entering the woods, and they were moving fast.

Rather than looking for bread, Maya slipped into her pack. "Kai and Hanss are right. We have to hurry. There are at least twenty ogres coming our way. We can eat later."

Kai flew around Maya. "Oh, ho! That girl can really see."

"Yeah," Maya replied. "Now let's get going."

"Will your magic protect us if the ogres get to us?" Jay asked Hanss.

"I don't know," Hanss answered. "I've never had to use it against twenty ogres. Only against Novok and his brothers. They usually don't hunt in such big parties unless they're going after something really good."

"Like us," Will said.

"Then let's not waste time." Lexie spoke with some of her old authority. "I was almost eaten by those ogres. I might not be so lucky the next time."

"Right," Maya agreed.

"Go on," Kai said. "I'll catch up with you later." And off he flew.

Hanss led the four teenagers away from his den to a faint path that wound through the trees. "This will take us to Arbor City," Hanss said.

For a while, nobody spoke. Hanss was in the lead, and they walked along at a brisk clip. Second came Jay, followed by Lexie, and then Will. Maya brought up the rear, listening and reaching out with her mind as she moved along the path. Maya felt the presence of small creatures that hummed, fluttered, and flapped. She heard bigger creatures rustle among the trees and bushes, but they kept a safe distance between themselves and the path. In the background, coming closer and closer, the ogres pounded through the woods. Their speed amazed her, and Maya knew that she, Will, Jay, and Lexie would never be able to outrun Novok and his hunting party.

"Hey!" Maya called loudly, stopping. "We're not going to make it to Arbor City. Even though we got a head start on the ogres, we won't be able to outrun them. We need another plan."

Skidding to a stop, the others turned.

"We could find a place to hide, and I could try to weave a strong enough spell," Hanss said.

Will patted his pack. "I have my ball. Maybe it's time to use it."

Lexie impatiently brushed the hair away from her face. "I'm not going back into a cage, waiting to be slaughtered by an ogre." Her voice was fierce. "I'll kill myself first."

"Luckily, you won't have to," came a chipper response as Kai flew toward them. "I brought some more potions. It's not good to be translated too many times, so this time I brought potions to help you run really fast. But after the running potion wears off, you will be tired. You will need to rest. And you will be hungry. Very hungry."

"In Arbor City, there's The Trotting Horse Inn that caters to humans," Hanss said. "We can stay there for the night."

"All right!" Kai called. "Tip your heads back, swallow the potion, and run as you've never run before. Because if I'm not mistaken, the ogres are by the roaring waterfall."

Heads were tipped back, and as soon as Kai had sprinkled potion on all the tongues, he yelled as loud as his tiny voice allowed, "Run, run, run! And don't stop until you've reached Arbor City."

Maya felt a surge spring from her feet and course throughout her body until it was vibrating, and off she ran, following the others. Through the woods they sprinted. The cat's furry body was a straight line as he skimmed over leaves and needles. Because the teenagers were bigger, they made more of an impact as they ran. Leaves and needles skittered to each side, and by the time Maya passed, the path was down to bare dirt.

"The ogres won't have a hard time tracking us now," Maya thought, but somehow she didn't care. All Maya wanted to do was run, and every muscle in her body joined together in a joyful blaze of movement. The speed that Kai had given her was nearly as exhilarating as flying.

"I feel like the Flash!" Maya heard Jay yell, and in front of her, Will made a loud whooping sound.

Maya tried to pause, to cast her senses into the forest to find the ogres. Shaking with the effort of staying still, Maya found the ogres, who were by the stream not far from the den.

"They are gaining on us!" Maya shouted.

"Run faster! Run, run, run!" Kai urged, his bright voice whipping them forward.

The cat and the four teenagers ran faster. Maya's blonde curls flew around her face, and the trees on either side of her were a blur. Ahead of them, the path had widened, and the trees had thinned out. But behind them, the ogres were getting closer, and Maya could hear them roar as they pursued their prey.

"We're not going to make it," Maya thought in a panic.

"Don't look back," Kai said. He was flying by her head. "Just keep running. You're almost out of the woods. The ogres can't leave this forest. Elven magic binds them here."

Hanss burst into the fields surrounding Arbor City. Next came Lexie, Jay, and Will.

"No!" Novok's angry roar engulfed Maya, who was on the forest's edge. Novok sounded close enough to grab her, and once again, Maya's shoulders twitched as she waited for the ogre's big hand to clap down on her.

"Go, go, go!" Kai's high voice blasted in her ear.

The sprite's urgent voice gave Maya the strength and the energy to run even faster. Shooting out of the woods, Maya crashed into Will, who was heading back to the forest to look for her, and she knocked them both to the ground.

Angry ogres howled in rage as they stood inside the tree line not far from where Maya and Will lay. Gasping, Maya sat up and stared at the ogres as they strained against the magic that kept them in the forest.

Glaring at her, Novok raised his fist. "I'll be waiting for you. Don't think I won't. We'll be patrolling this forest. And if you come back, we'll get you."

Too spent to come back with a stinging retort, Maya shook her head as she stood on shaky legs. She thought about how Novok was right—the ogres would have another chance to get them. Maya,

Will, Jay, and Lexie would have to go through the woods to get back to the portal that would take them back to New York City. And the ogres would be on the prowl, looking for them.

But as she stared at Novok's angry face, Maya couldn't resist sticking out her tongue at the ogre, and she felt absurdly gratified by the answering roar.

"What the hell, Maya!" Will exclaimed. "They nearly got us." But when he looked at Maya's upturned face, Will grinned, putting an arm around her.

Maya grinned back, and on legs stiff from so much running, they hobbled to join the others.

Behind her, carried by a breeze, Kai's faint voice called, "Good luck to you all."

10: At The Trotting Horse

The Trotting Horse Inn was on the far edge of the small walled city, away from the elegant houses that lined a park, away from the main street with the shops, away from the gleaming white public hall that stood taller than any other building. The inn was among modest but tidy houses and, as Maya soon realized, in the human part of the city. While many humans did wear simple trousers and tunics—the way Maya, Will, and Jay did—others wore clothes that were not as plain, and some of the women wore calf-length dresses with lace collars and cuffs.

Lexie, in her jeans, sandals, and flowered shirt, was the one who stuck out, and the guards had frowned at her as she passed through the city's gate. But when they saw Hanss, the guards waved everyone through the gate.

"I need new clothes," Lexie had muttered. "Those guards are staring at me."

"Yeah and not in a good way," Jay added.

Will stopped, digging into his pack, and the others stopped, too. "Here," he said, passing his cloak to Lexie. "This might look a little weird on such a warm day, but not as weird as what you're wearing."

Lexie took the cloak. "Thanks." Her voice no longer had an angry edge, and she even smiled a little at Will, who nodded noncommittally.

With his tail held high, Hanss led the teenagers away from the busy center to side streets that were mostly empty. "We probably should have waited until night," the cat said, looking back at the kids, who followed wearily behind. "But with those ogres screaming at us, it seemed best just to come into the city. Voices carry, and it wouldn't have been long before the guards came out to investigate. Lucky for us, Arbor City is sympathetic to Pawel and his family. His kinswoman, Hedwight Greenwood, is the mayor, and while she doesn't help me directly, she looks the other way when I come through with various elves. That's why the guards at the gate let us in."

"But you don't usually come here with humans, do you?" Will asked, tiredly running a hand over his face. "Those guards looked surprised to see us."

"No," Hanss replied. "I have never come here with humans. I'll have to visit the mayor tonight to explain what's going on. I know where she lives, and it's best that no one sees me talking to her. Mayor Greenwood has to be careful. Tamick Ashglade's spies are everywhere, even in this small city. Fortunately, the mayor only chooses those who are loyal to her to guard the gates. Those guards aren't likely to tell any-one that I came through with four humans, one of whom was oddly dressed."

Maya, Will, Jay, and Lexie drooped with fatigue as they followed Hanss into the tidy inn with its public room on one side of a staircase and a dining area on the other side. A thin man stood behind the bar, and he stared in surprise as Hanss came in with the weary teenagers.

Hanss nodded at the man. "Good day, Orvul."

Orvul continued to stare. "Good day, Hanss," he finally replied.

"You're surprised that I'm here with this group of young peo-ple," the cat said.

Orvul nodded. "Don't usually see you with our kind."

Maya could tell that Hanss was choosing his words carefully. "They are friends. They've traveled a long way and are exhausted. Do you have any rooms available?"

"I have two rooms, numbers five and six, upstairs on the right at the end of the hall." Orvul reached for two keys that hung on hooks on the wall by the bar. "Good thing you came when you did. The evening crowd isn't here yet." Stepping forward, Maya held out her hand, and Orvul gave her the keys.

Hanss pointed a paw at Lexie. "This human needs different clothes. She came unprepared. Any chance you can get her some?"

Orvul regarded Lexie. "I should be able to find something. Standard workwear all right?"

"That would be just fine," Hanss replied. "That's what the others are wearing. And we can pay for everything. We have chamomile tea."

Orvul's eyes were wide with surprise. "Do you now? Well, don't flash the tea around down here. Pay me when I come up with the clothes or the food. You don't want anyone knowing that you're carrying chamomile tea. Most of my customers wouldn't think of robbing you, but when it comes to chamomile tea, all bets are off. Plus, there are more than a few I'm not sure about."

"We'll be careful," Hanss said. "And many, many thanks."

Orvul lowered his voice even though there wasn't anybody else in the room. "We humans are grateful to the Greenwood family. They gave shelter to those of us who escaped from southern Norlander when times were bad. Here in Arbor City, we could live freely, and we still can. Now upstairs you go. I'll be around soon with some clothes for the girl."

Clutching the keys, Maya trudged up the stairs behind Hanss, who no longer held his tail high and walked slowly as if going up each step was almost too much for the cat. Maya felt the same way, and she sighed with relief when they reached the top.

"I never thought going up the stairs would be so much work," Maya heard Will mutter behind her.

"Yeah, me too," she replied.

Maya gave the key to room five to Will, and she unlocked the door to room six. Hanss went with Will and Jay, and Lexie followed Maya. There was only one bed, but neither girl cared. Without taking off their shoes, Maya and Lexie collapsed onto the bed. Dizzy with weariness, Maya fell into a deep sleep, not even moving when the edge of Lexie's cape flapped across her face.

A knocking on the door woke Maya up. "You two awake yet?" Will's voice called. "Jay and I are really hungry. We're ready to eat."

Lexie muttered, "For God's sake, go away."

Maya rubbed her eyes. "Give us a minute."

"Do you want Hanss to order some food for you two?" Will asked. "And out here on a chair by the door, there are some clothes for Lexie."

Maya's stomach rumbled. "Yes, order food for us. I'm hungry, too."

Lexie put a hand over her own rumbling stomach. "So am I."

The girls sat up, and they both leaned against the headboard.

Lexie yawned. "I've never been so tired in my life. Even when I've stayed out all night."

Maya was about to agree, but then she thought about her time in the Office, about how Bigly had tortured her, about how afterwards she hadn't even been able to walk.

"I've been more tired," Maya said simply. "Once."

With curiosity, Lexie regarded Maya. "You've had quite a life, haven't you?"

"Yeah," Maya answered slowly. "I guess I have."

"Maybe you can tell me a little about it tonight. Before we go to sleep." Lexie's voice was soft, almost sympathetic, and Maya heard something new in Lexie's tone—respect.

Maya smiled at Lexie. "All right."

"Hey!" Will called from the other side of the door. "The food's here. Is it all right to come in?"

"The door's unlocked," Maya said. Before their nap, she had been too tired to think of locking it.

The door burst open, and Will, followed by Jay, came into the room. Hanss walked beside them and leaped onto the bed. Behind Will and Jay came Orvul, carrying a large tray heaped with food. He set it on a table by the windows.

"I'll be back up with drinks," Orvul said.

Will and Jay settled on the bed, and it wasn't long before Orvul came back with four pints on a tray.

"Beer?" Will and Jay asked joyfully.

"It seems to me that you are all too old for milk," Orvul observed wryly. "Not adults, but close enough."

Jay grinned. "Yeah, we are."

As Orvul began putting the four pints beside the steaming bowls, Maya slid off the bed, went to her pack, and pulled out a box of chamomile tea. "How much do we owe you?"

Orvul nearly dropped a pint. "That's a lot of tea!"

"It's common where I come from," Maya replied. "Do you want the whole box? We have more."

Orvul was silent for a minute, and Maya could tell the innkeeper was struggling with himself as he tried to decide how much tea he should take.

"How about half the box?" Lexie called from the bed.

"That's enough," Orvul answered quickly. "More than enough. Maybe too much."

"No," Maya said, handing him the tea. "You deserve it. We're safe here, and that's worth a lot more than chamomile tea."

Slipping the tea bags into the deep pocket of his apron, Orvul regarded her for a few minutes, and Maya could tell he had caught a glimpse of her mission. Orvul inclined his head. "You might be small, but you are wise."

Lexie snorted. "You should have seen her buzz the ogre's head when she was a sprite."

"Or stick her tongue out at an ogre when we barely escaped from the forest," Will added, his eyes gleaming.

Orvul smiled. "Scrappy." He shook his finger at the others. "Nevertheless, you should listen to her."

"Come on," Hanss said as Maya blushed. "You're going to give her a swelled head."

Saying nothing but still smiling, Orvul left.

Jay rubbed his hands together. "Let's eat!"

Will and Jay carefully pulled the table over to the bed. There were also two chairs, and Will and Jay brought them over as well. Maya and Lexie sat on the edge of the bed, Will and Jay sat on the chairs, and they all tucked into the food—chickpea stew and a loaf of whole grain bread, cut in slices. Even Hanss had some stew. A small plate had been provided for him, and they all shared some of their stew with the cat, who ate with as much gusto as the teenagers did.

For a while, the only sounds were spoons scraping against bowls interrupted by sips of beer, which was too bitter for Maya's taste, and she only drank half a pint. When she saw Will staring pointedly at her glass, she said, "Go ahead. You can have it. I'm done."

Taking the glass, Will grinned at her, and as Maya looked into those hazel eyes that crinkled at the edges, she wondered how she could bear to be parted from him when their mission was done. Maya had known Will for less than a week, but it seemed as though they had always been together. As Will's grin faded, and he quizzically regarded her, Maya shook her head. There was no point in worrying about this now. Their mission wasn't even close to being finished.

After sighing and wiping his mouth with a napkin, Jay was the first to speak. "Hanss, are elves vegetarians?"

Hanss had been washing his face, and he stopped to answer. "They are. Elves are so attuned to the magic that binds everything in this world that they can't bear to eat other creatures."

"So the humans are vegetarians, too?" Will asked.

"Yes," Hanss said. "Their ancestors are stolen babies and young children from your dimension. The humans here have never known any other way of eating."

Maya thought about the ogres and their zeal for hunting. "Tell us about Darkwood Forest."

"Long ago," Hanss said, "ogres, gliders, and other big creatures who hunted lived among the elves, whose magic was strong enough to keep the predators at bay. But then the humans who were brought here grew up and started having babies. And more babies. Humans mature faster and reproduce more quickly than the elves. When the humans were freed, they were allowed to go where they wanted, but because they are not as strongly connected to magic as the elves are, the humans became sitting ducks, if you will. It wasn't safe for them to leave the walled cities and towns and go into the countryside. But the humans went anyway. They wanted their own land and farms. When the humans left the cities, the slaughter was terrible. So the elves made a decision that is debated to this day. All the big predators—including the ogres—were rounded up and brought to Darkwood Forest. Then the elves wove a spell to keep them there."

Maya frowned. "Darkwood Forest is like a prison, then."

Hanss said, "Unfortunately, it is. A vast one with thousands and thousands of acres, but a prison all the same. The binding spells must be maintained, and the forest is surrounded by small cities with elves whose job is to maintain those spells. Arbor City is one of those cities."

"Could the ogres promise not to eat humans and then be released?" Lexie asked.

"Possibly," Hanss replied. "But cooperating with the elves comes hard to ogres. Too many years of animosity between them. Too much hatred. Too much distrust, especially after having been prisoners for many, many years."

Even though Maya feared the ogres, she could understand their anger and resentment toward the elves. No matter how big or beautiful, a prison was still a prison, and no creature liked having its freedom curtailed.

"I need to go tell Mayor Greenwood about you," Hanss said. "I'll be back as soon as I can." He gave them each a stern look. "Keep to your rooms. We don't want anyone finding out who you are, where you came from, and what your plans are."

"We'll stay up here," Maya promised.

"Don't worry about us," Jay said. "We'll be fine. Especially if you ask Orvul to bring us each another pint of beer."

Not saying anything, Hanss twitched his tail as he went over to the door and waited for someone to open it. With a flourish, Jay obliged, bowing a little as the cat left.

"Humph," Hanss said as the door closed behind him.

But a little while later, Orvul brought up four more pints.

11: Too Much Fun

As Maya listened to Jay, Lexie, and Will sing in the tavern downstairs, she thought about how at least their intentions had been good. They had meant to stay upstairs in their rooms and have a quiet chat. But then Jay had decided it was time for music. Fetching his mandolin from the room next door, Jay sat down on a chair and began to play. This time he sang songs that Will and Lexie knew and Maya had vaguely heard of: "Hanging by a Moment," "Save Tonight," and "Otherside." Lexie, whose voice was also strong, sang with Jay, and Will sang harmony.

Jay had left the door open, and it wasn't long before several other people stood in the hall and listened, clapping after each song. A red-haired man went downstairs to get the singers more beer, and he was joined by some of the patrons. Soon the hall was crowded with people listening to Jay, Lexie, and Will, and someone suggested, "Why don't you all come down to the tavern? That way, everyone can hear you, and you can have a pint whenever you want."

"Sounds like a plan," Jay agreed, and before Maya could say anything, he got up, following everyone downstairs.

Will turned to Maya. "I'll go get him."

"Come right back up," she called as he left the room.

Lexie smirked. "What's the chance that they're going to come right back?"

"Almost zero," Maya replied.

"We'd better go get them."

"Right."

Shutting the door, Lexie quickly put on the clothes Orvul had brought her, and they went downstairs. Will and Jay were already singing, and Maya could feel the music pulling her, drawing her into the tavern. Maya couldn't even see Will and Jay. Too many people were clustered around them. Lexie elbowed her way through the crowd, and it wasn't long before her strong voice joined with Jay's and Will's. Maya wriggled her way toward Will, Jay, and Lexie, and she tried to get the singers' attention. But they hardly noticed her. Short of grabbing the mandolin away from Jay, Maya knew that she wouldn't be able to reach them. The music and singing had them in a tight grip and wouldn't let go. And Maya figured that if she tried to take the mandolin away from Jay, a ruckus would ensue, causing an even bigger scene than simply letting them play and sing. Defeated, Maya made her way to the bar and sat down on a stool at the end, where if she peered through the swaying, clapping people, she could see Will, Jay, and Lexie.

"Want a beer?" Orvul asked as he listened to the singers.

"No, thank you," Maya said.

"Good idea," Orvul replied. "Someone's got to keep a level head."

"Yeah. Do you have anything else to drink?"

"I have Elf Spirits."

"Elf Spirits?" Maya asked suspiciously. She had had enough potions for one day.

Orvul laughed. "It's nothing much. Just some bubbly water with flavors."

"Oh," Maya said. "Sparkling water."

"Yes, something like that."

Orvul brought her a glass filled with a clear liquid that fizzed. Maya took a cautious sip. The drink was light and tasted like a combination of berries, both familiar and unfamiliar. And although there was no magic in it—or at least not much as there was magic in everything on Elferterre—the drink was refreshing, making Maya feel less tired.

"Good, isn't it?" Orvul asked.

"Sure is," Maya answered. "Just what I needed."

"Think your friends have had enough beer?"

"I do."

But the tavern was crowded, and Maya and Orvul couldn't keep track of where the beer was going. It was when the music got louder, more boisterous, and the songs more vulgar that Maya realized Will, Jay, and Lexie had had too much beer.

Orvul, busy behind the bar, raised his eyebrows when he looked at Maya, who shook her head and shrugged.

A woman came into the tavern and sat down on an empty stool beside Maya. She had dark curly hair that came to her shoulders and was simply dressed in a purple tunic and a skirt. But when Maya looked at the tunic, she noticed it was trimmed with embroidered stars and moons in an opalescent white that seemed to shimmer. Maya reluctantly looked away from the stars and the moons to regard the woman, whose green eyes glimmered with humor and whose broad lips quirked into a smile. Maya couldn't tell exactly how old the woman was, but she seemed to be about the same age as Lily.

Orvul came over and asked the woman, "Do you want the usual, Myranda?"

"Why, of course," Myranda answered.

Orvul looked from Maya to Myranda, and Maya could tell that he wanted to say something. Instead, he shook his head, left, and returned with a drink that was nearly as luminous as the moons and stars on Myranda's tunic.

"Here you go." Orvul set the drink in front of Myranda, but he didn't leave.

"You have something to say to me?" Myranda asked. "Well, go ahead. You know I don't bite."

"No," Orvul replied in a low voice, "you don't bite."

"Oh, come on," Myranda said. "Have I ever done anything bad to you or your family or to anyone else in this city?"

"You have not," Orvul replied. "And I'd like to keep it that way."

"No reason why it should change." Myranda's voice was neutral, but in a flash, Maya got a sense of the woman's power. "Orvul's right to be careful," Maya thought.

Myranda took a sip of her drink, regarded Maya, and took another sip. "Orvul, you don't have to worry. I know this one is special. I could tell the minute I came in, even though she is sitting quietly to one side while her friends whoop it up and make fools of themselves."

"They're just having a little fun," Maya said, stung by the note of rebuke in Myranda's voice. "What's wrong with that?"

Myranda's laugh was as melodious as her voice. "Nothing at all. As long as your friends don't have too much fun. Despite what it might look like, with all the music and good cheer, not everyone in here is a friend. Are they, Orvul?"

"They are not," Orvul agreed, still hesitating.

"Go on, Orvul. Tend to your business. Surely you know I can't pull anything over on this girl."

Orvul's forehead was wrinkled with worry, but he smiled a little. "All right. Hanss brought her and the others to the inn, and they were supposed to stay in their rooms."

"Did he?" Myranda asked, and for the first time she looked surprised. "Well, well. But you know how kids are. They never do what they're told."

"Isn't that the truth," Orvul muttered, moving away to serve other customers.

Myranda winked at Maya. "Orvul's son is supposed to be here helping out tonight. But the son, ah, had other plans. He'll be here much later."

Maya smiled, and Myranda smiled back, asking, "What's your name?"

There seemed to be no point in lying to this woman. "Maya," she replied.

"And when did you have your eyes peeled, Maya?"

Maya stopped smiling. "How did you know?"

"I can see, too," Myranda answered softly.

Maya was not surprised, thinking of Orvul and how he had caught a glimpse of their plans. Maya guessed it was the magic, which affected everything, even the humans, helping them see more than what most people on Earth normally saw.

Myranda nodded as though reading Maya's thoughts. "You had your eyes peeled recently, didn't you?"

Maya rubbed her face. "A few weeks ago, I think. I've traveled so much that I really don't know how much time has passed."

There was a metal straw in Myranda's glass, and she used it to swirl her drink. "You're young to have traveled this far."

"I know, but that's the way it is."

"Right. What about your companions? I took a peek at them before I sat down. I'm assuming they're more useful than they look right now. But then again, they haven't had their eyes peeled the way you have."

Maya sighed. "No, they haven't."

"And you're in love with the boy with the hazel eyes, aren't you?"

"His name is Will. And, yeah, I am."

"Will is in love with you, too. And even though you're both young, it's the real thing." Myranda shook her head as Will clambered onto a table and started to sing "Happy Together." As Will sang, he looked around for Maya and spotted her sitting by the bar. The rest of the song was directed at Maya, who squirmed in embarrassment on the stool. When Will was finished, he bowed with a great flourish toward Maya. Blowing her a kiss, Will jumped down, amid much clapping.

Looking puzzled, Myranda asked, "What does this mean: 'If I should call you up, invest a dime'?"

Maya answered, "I think it means calling someone on a pay phone and using money, a dime. That's an old song. It was written long before I was born."

"What's a pay phone?"

Maya thought for a moment and carefully chose her words. "I'm from away, and where I live, we have devices that let us talk to people who aren't close by. We call them phones. Back in the day, there were lots of booths with phones where you could pay to make a call. But now most people pretty much carry their own phones with them." Maya added quickly, "Small ones."

"I see," Myranda said. "Like a two-way." She pulled a metal case out of her pocket. When Myranda flipped open the cover, Maya saw a round screen with some knobs below it.

Myranda said, "That's how we call people here."

"It's kind of like what we have where I come from," Maya replied, thinking of the phone she had left behind at The Other Green Door. Pawel had told the teenagers that their phones wouldn't work on Elferterre and that it would be best to leave them behind.

Myranda studied Maya. "And you come far from here, don't you?"

"Yeah," Maya agreed. "Very far."

"All four of you do, even Will?" But it was more a statement than a question.

"All four of us, even Will," Maya agreed.

Myranda frowned a little. "I can help you get Will up to speed."

Maya blushed, and her voice was sharp. "What do you mean?"

Looking at Maya, Myranda laughed. "Not like that. No, that's between you two, and I don't think he needs any help in that department. I mean I can help him see even more. And his dark-haired friend, too. The blonde girl doesn't have much talent in that way. Although she can see a little, I'm not sure she's worth bothering with."

Maya was shocked. "You want to peel their eyes?"

"Why, yes. I'm a witch. I can do such things. And I think it would be a big help to you if those boys could see as much as you can."

A witch. Somehow, Maya was not surprised. After all, this was Elferterre.

"I don't know," Maya said slowly. A part of her yearned to have Will be even more observant and sharper than he already was, but another part didn't want Will to have the responsibility that came with seeing. As the Toad Queen had said, "Once it is done, it is done, and you will be different from most of your kind."

Leaning on the bar, Myranda considered Maya. "I know. To really see is a burden as well as a gift."

"Yeah." Maya felt her eyes sting with tears.

"But it should be their choice, not yours." Myranda's voice was matter of fact, but there was a slight edge to it. "You've got to admit that they have a long way to go before they catch up with you. If indeed they ever do."

Maya turned to Myranda. "I know. So go ask them. You're the witch, and I'm just a kid."

At first Myranda didn't say anything. She sipped her drink, and when she was done, Myranda stared directly at Maya. There was a tugging, but Maya had faced Cinnial, who, in his own way, was just as powerful as Myranda. Shaking her head, Maya closed off her most private self away from the witch.

Myranda's lips quirked into a reluctant grin. "You're a great deal more than that, my dear. And you know it."

Maya grinned back. "Maybe."

Myranda's voice was low. "Stay with me. Be my apprentice. I haven't met anyone like you for a long time. I could teach you a lot. I could teach you how to use magic."

For a moment, Maya was tempted to stay with Myranda and to learn how to use the magic that crackled throughout Elferterre. Maya could envision herself becoming more powerful than she had ever imagined, stronger than she would be in her own universe, even mightier than Cinnial. But then Maya thought about the Great Library and Earth and the chaos that would spread if Maya stayed on Elferterre and didn't return to confront Cinnial.

"Thank you," Maya said. "I'd like to. I really would. You could teach me a lot. But I have things to do."

Myranda bent toward Maya. "You could come back after you've dealt with those things."

Maya hesitated. Yes, she could, and Myranda's offer became even more tempting, shimmering like a big prize. But another image came to Maya—the Great Library, serene yet powerful, and it tugged at her even more insistently than Myranda's offer of magic.

Maya's voice was sad. "I can't. But thank you very much."

Myranda's voice was sad, too. "Ah, well. It was worth a try even though I was pretty sure what your answer would be." She patted

Maya's cheek, and Maya closed her eyes, feeling the warmth from the witch's hand. "So what do you think? Do you want me to ask the two boys if they want to have their eyes peeled? Not tonight. They are in no shape to make such a big decision. But tomorrow, after they've recovered from their hangovers."

Maya opened her eyes. "Yeah. Ask them. You're right. It should be their choice, not mine. But why do you want to do this for them?"

Myranda's eyes glittered, and she looked around. "Let's just say that I think peeling those boys' eyes would benefit a great many, near and far."

A voice by Myranda's feet startled both Maya and the witch. "What are those kids doing down here? They were supposed to stay in their rooms." The voice belonged to Hanss, and he twined around the legs of Myranda's stool.

"Hanss!" Myranda called in delight. Sliding from her stool, she gathered Hanss and settled back on it with the cat on her lap.

Maya was surprised by the way Myranda had scooped up the dignified cat as though he were a playful kitten. But Hanss didn't protest and actually looked pleased as he curled up in Myranda's lap, hitting her in the face a few times with his fluffy tail. Myranda laughed as she brushed the tail away, and Maya could see the strong bond that connected the two.

Noting Maya's amazed expression, Myranda laughed. "After all, I am a witch."

"And I'm a cat," Hanss added. "But I repeat my question. What are those kids doing down here, and why are they attracting so much attention?"

"I couldn't stop them," Maya replied glumly. "Jay started playing and singing, and it wasn't long before he came down here where more people could hear him. And where Jay went, Will and Lexie followed. I tried to get them to come back upstairs with me, but they wouldn't come. So I stayed down here to keep an eye on them, and I met Myranda."

Hanss shook his head. "I should have known something like this would happen. But what could I do? I had an errand to attend to."

Myranda ran her hand over the cat's back. "Of course you did. And if they hadn't come down here, then I never would have seen them. I've offered to peel the boys' eyes."

Hanss looked up at Myranda. "Have you?"

"It would help, wouldn't it?"

"Yes," Hanss replied. "It would. Will and Jay are good, but they're green, and really being able to see would help with that."

"Yeah," Maya said. "Seeing certainly makes you focus."

"Although seeing didn't stop you from buzzing that ogre when Kai's potion turned you into a sprite," Hanss pointed out.

Myranda laughed in delight. "Did you do that, Maya?"

Maya felt her face flush. "I did."

Hanss growled in disapproval.

"Come on, Hanss," Myranda said. "Maya's just a kid. We were young once, too. Remember?"

"Barely," Hanss replied, but he began to purr as Myranda scratched his head.

Myranda's hand became still. "Hanss, look at whom those foolish kids are talking to."

The singing and playing had stopped. Most of the people had gone back to their tables and were sitting down, but Jay, Will, and Lexie were standing and talking to a man with a round, cheerful face and a wave of brown hair that flipped to one side.

Hanss purring came to an abrupt end. "I knew something like this would happen."

Maya regarded the man. "He looks ordinary."

"Look closer," Myranda suggested. "Barint Dover is anything but ordinary."

Maya focused on Barint and saw the man for what he really was, devious, malicious, and not to be trusted. But Barint had a hard, false shell of good humor that was wrapped tight around him like a thick blanket. Maya understood that few people were able to see the real Barint. Until it was too late.

"Oh, no!" Maya said.

Myranda sighed. "Right? If I weren't a good witch, I would have changed Barint into a toad long ago. I still might, if he gets in the way."

"Steady, Myranda," Hanss said coolly. "Barint has friends in high places. Let's just hope those kids are discreet."

Maya watched as Jay, Will, and Lexie laughed and talked with Barint as though they were old friends who hadn't seen each other in a long time. And without a doubt, Maya knew they weren't being discreet.

Not far from Jay, Will, and Lexie, a bald man with no eyebrows or eyelashes watched the teenagers as they spoke with Barint.

Maya stared at the man, and Myranda followed her look. "Now he seems like someone to worry about, doesn't he?"

"Yes," Maya agreed, but as she considered the bald man, Maya saw something gentle, almost radiant.

"Looks can be deceiving," Myranda observed. "An old cliché, but true. His name is Ehren Robinwood, and he travels from town to city with wonderful carvings that he and his mother create. Hanss, this is our lucky day. Ehren wasn't supposed to be here until after the Summer Gathering."

"Indeed." But the cat's tail was swishing as he watched Will, Jay, and Lexie continue to talk with Barint.

"Time to break up the party, don't you think?" Myranda asked. "With all the beer those three have had, it shouldn't be too hard."

"Past time," Hanss replied, jumping from her lap onto the floor. "Make them good and sick. Teach them a lesson."

Myranda laughed. "I won't be too hard on them. I'll just give a nudge to whatever was going to happen on its own." She winked at Maya. "That's mostly what we witches do anyway."

Murmuring softly, Myranda gazed at Will, Jay, and Lexie. With her left hand, Myranda made a small circular motion, counterclockwise, around her stomach.

Soon the teenagers' goofy expressions went away to be replaced by queasy looks that grew increasingly desperate. In a bunch, with their hands over their mouths, they ran from the tavern and left Barint to stare after them. Then he spotted Myranda. For a moment his mask slipped away, and Maya caught a glimpse of a snarling man. But it didn't take long for Barint to compose himself, and in a moment the affable expression was back.

Myranda raised her nearly empty glass. "Cheers, Barint."

Smiling, Barint shook his head, but he couldn't quite keep the hard glitter from his eyes, and without saying anything, he quickly left the tavern.

"Take that, you old canker," Myranda said.

"Barint's not that old," Hanss replied. "But he's certainly a canker. I'd better go after those kids and make sure nothing happens to them."

"Go ahead, Hanss. But they'll be all right. Barint won't want to be around them as they puke up their guts. When they're done, they'll stagger up to their rooms and pass out on their beds."

Thinking about sleeping in the same bed with Lexie, Maya grimaced. "I don't know if I want to be around them either."

"Why not come spend the night in my cottage?" Myranda asked. "I have a sweet guest room that's just waiting for someone like you. Then, Hanss, you can bring the kids around tomorrow whenever they've recovered. It probably won't be until afternoon."

Hanss looked up at Myranda. "You won't steal Maya away from us, will you?" he asked anxiously, his tail twitching.

"Stealing is a harsh way of putting it."

"Myranda," Hanss scolded, batting at the hem of her dress.

Myranda laughed ruefully. "What? I had to try to get her to stay with me. You must have known that I would. But don't get your whiskers in a twist. Maya refused."

With narrow eyes, Hanss regarded Maya, but when she smiled and nodded reassuringly, Hanss said, "Humph!" and left, holding his tail high and straight.

"Can't say as I blame him for being a little snippy," Myranda said with a sigh. "It's been a hard time for Hanss. In truth, it's been a hard time for many of us." The witch's voice was so low that Maya had to bend to hear what she said. "But never mind. Come back to Lavender Cottage with me. I'll show you how to use a little magic. It won't be much in such a short time, but you'll know more than you do now. And with the way your friends are going to feel tomorrow, we won't have to worry about getting up early. We can stay up as late as we want."

"All right," Maya agreed.

They both slid from their stools, and Maya followed Myranda out of the bright tavern into a dark night with sparkling stars. As if in response, the stars on Myranda's tunic twinkled even more brightly.

12: At Lavender Cottage

Myranda's cottage was even farther from the center of things than The Trotting Horse was. Not near any other house, the cottage was by a small woodland on the edge of the walled city. Maya followed the witch through a field with tall plants that seemed to nod at them as they walked among the leafy stalks.

"My babies," Myranda crooned, and a pleased murmur mingled with the nodding.

Low and made of stone with a thatched roof, Lavender Cottage was exactly the way Maya had envisioned a good witch's home to be.

Stopping by the purple front door, Myranda passed her hand over the knob. "Open, please."

Without a sound, the door opened, and Maya followed Myranda into the cottage. Myranda flipped a switch by the door, and the small room was filled with glowing light from orbs on the wall. Maya had seen the same kind of orbs at The Trotting Horse, but with all that had happened, she hadn't had time to think about where humans and elves got their power on Elferterre.

"Do you have electricity here?" Maya asked.

"Electricity?" Myranda frowned. "I don't know that word."

"Where do you get the power for your lights?"

"Oh, I understand. It comes from the same place as everything else does on Elferterre."

"From magic?"

"That's right."

"I wish we could get our power from magic," Maya said wistfully, still looking at the orbs. "I bet magic doesn't pollute Elferterre the way our power pollutes Earth."

"Earth? From the Other Side?"

"Yeah."

"I thought that's where you and your friends might be from." Myranda went over to a stove that looked much like an electric stove on Earth did. "No, our power doesn't pollute. Tea?"

"Yes, please."

Myranda filled a purple kettle with water and set it to boil. While Myranda made tea, Maya looked around and was delighted with what she saw—a jumble of books and knickknacks and stones and pictures. There was hardly a bare place on any wall, shelf, or table. But instead of feeling cluttered and closed, the room felt cozy yet vibrant, and Maya was certain that out of the corner of her eye, she caught a glimpse of a knickknack moving every now and then. There was a galley kitchen with a round table at the end, and it reminded Maya of the one in Alani and Alexander's apartment. A sitting area abutted the kitchen, and two overstuffed chairs faced a fireplace. Beside each chair were two small tables.

"Let's go sit by the fireplace," Myranda said. "It's more comfortable there. I made butter and seed cookies today. Would you like some to go with the tea?"

"I would," Maya replied. "Thank you."

Soon they were sitting by the fireplace. With a wave of her hand, Myranda had started a fire, and even though the night was cool rather than cold, the fire's warmth felt good. As Maya munched a cookie and drank tea, she tried to remember the last time she had felt this relaxed. Then it came to her—it was when she had traveled with Jeam and Captain Creb.

Myranda smiled. "Don't get too comfortable. I want to show you a little bit of magic before you go to sleep."

"It's so nice here," Maya murmured.

"It's home," Myranda said, looking affectionately around the cottage. "And home is best."

Maya thought about her home in New York City, just down the street from the corner store where she had lost and found the little red pocketbook with the gold handles. Before Maya's father had left to be with Inga, home—with its art and books and color—had been the best place to be. Even as a young teenager, Maya hadn't minded being with her parents, especially with her father, who always filled a place with his energy, his curiosity, and his lively mind. When Maya was around her father, she was never bored, and she knew that he liked being with her as much as she liked being with him. Although their arguments had sometimes escalated into fights, her father had always encouraged her to speak her mind. Not one to hold a grudge, Maya's father would never stay angry with her for long, and Maya had felt exactly the same way about him. Until he left.

Then it was only Lily and Maya, and while Maya loved her mother, the house no longer brimmed with conversation about books and movies and politics. Instead there was silence, and it wore on Maya until she thought she would go crazy with her own sad thoughts. In desperation, Maya had found reasons to go over to her friends' houses. On weekend after weekend, Maya had left Lily alone with her paints and her canvases.

"Do you think your mother was lonely?" Myranda asked, closely watching Maya.

"Yeah," Maya answered, brushing away tears. "I shouldn't have left her so much. But I couldn't stand to be home. It was too quiet." She stared at Myranda. "Can you read minds?"

"I can," Myranda answered, setting her mug on the small table by the chair. "But mostly I don't. You can, too, in a way, I think."

Maya sighed. "Kind of. Sometimes I get thoughts, but not usually. At least not on Earth. Mostly what I get is like clips from a movie. I can see and hear what has happened. I can feel people's emotions. Sometimes I can even see what will happen, but that always comes to me in a flash, and I can't control it."

"I understand," Myranda said. "Your power is different from mine, probably because it comes from Time rather than Magic. Stronger, in some ways, even though it's not fully developed yet. However, it leads to the same place."

"What place is that?"

"Illumination."

"But nobody can see everything," Maya said, thinking again of what the Toad Queen had said.

Myranda smiled. "That's right. Often we are surprised. Sometimes in a good way, like when I saw you tonight. I could tell immediately that you weren't just an average teenager watching her foolish friends sing and carry on. Then when Orvul said Hanss had brought you, I knew something was up. Even though you are all young and human. Did Pawel send you here? Did you come from the city where he lives in exile?"

"Yeah, New York City. Pawel sent us here to steal a key from Galli. It's a key to unlock the chains the Greenwoods are wearing. I'm also going to steal a lock so that I can trap Cinnial, a really, really bad guy in my own dimension." As briefly as she could, Maya told Myranda about Earth, Books of Everything, the Great Library, and Sydda.

Myranda stared into the fire. "I've heard of the Great Library. I bet it's a wonderful place."

"It is," Maya replied simply. "One of the best places in our universe. But now Cinnial has taken over, and he'll ruin it."

"Cinnial sounds like a tough customer."

"He's a rotter."

"In Norlander, we have our own rotters, and that's why Pawel is in exile." Myranda shook her head. "Pawel has never sent humans before. But then again, all the elves he sent have never returned, and I suppose Pawel must have thought it was time to try something new. Given that your friends learn to control their wagging tongues, you might be able to succeed where the others have failed. Nobody will expect a group of human teenagers to try to steal anything from Galli. And Hanss left you alone to go to the mayor to let her know why you are here?"

"Right," Maya replied. "The guards at the gate were pretty surprised to see us with Hanss. Especially Lexie, who was wearing clothes from our world. So Hanss wanted to tell the mayor what was going on."

Myranda frowned. "I hope your friends haven't spoiled things by telling Barint too much."

"Me, too. I should have tried harder to bring them back upstairs."

Myranda waved her hand. "Oh, they wouldn't have come anyway. The music and the applause had them all in a tight grip. At least Barint won't try anything too obvious, like hitting your friends over their heads and dragging them from their rooms. Too risky for Barint. He might get caught. Instead, Barint will be more subtle. That's how he is anyway. Barint will probably try to lure your friends so that they will go with him without attracting any attention. When they are all away from the city, he will have others waiting to take your friends prisoner and bring them to Foretcour, to Tamick Ashglade. At least that's what I'm guessing. Even though I'm a witch, Barint's pretty good at keeping his thoughts away from me. However, we won't let him get your friends, will we?"

"I hope not. But will Barint just follow us when we do leave and capture us then?" Maya asked anxiously.

"Yes," Myranda answered. "So you'll have to sneak out when he's not looking and be miles away before he realizes you're gone. Don't worry. I can help with that."

Maya said, "Good thing you're on Pawel's side."

Myranda sighed. "If only it were enough. But I'm just one witch here in the hinterlands. I'm good, but I don't have the power that Pawel and Khirra have, which is why we need them to come back."

For a while, absorbed with their own thoughts, Myranda and Maya gazed at the fire. Finally, Myranda said, "Let's get started. We need to sleep at least a little tonight. If Will and Jay decide to have their eyes peeled, we won't get much rest tomorrow. We'll have to watch them to be sure everything is all right."

"Like Feste did with me," Maya said, thinking sadly of the slight man and of how much she still missed him.

"I know. People come, and people go. So do cats, dogs, and other creatures we love. And we're never ready, no matter how old we are or how much loss we've seen."

Again, Maya and Myranda stared moodily at the fire.

Leaning forward, Myranda clapped her hands, and Maya jumped. "Enough of this. Time for lessons."

Myranda told Maya about magic, about how it was everywhere on Elferterre. To use this magic, Maya had to focus on it, gather it, and direct the magic where she wanted it to go.

"Spells help concentrate the magic," Myranda said. "But if you're good enough, you can do it on your own."

"Are you good enough?"

"Not quite, but I'm nearly there. It takes a long time for a human to learn. It's much quicker for elves."

Myranda taught Maya a simple spell: How to levitate small objects. "But magic has a price. Using it takes a lot of energy. You get stronger as you go along, but at first you won't be able to do much without resting."

"Like with the potions the sprite Kai gave us," Maya said.

"Potions are the worst," Myranda said. "They amplify the magic in a burst. But sometimes potions are just what you need."

"Without it, we never would have escaped the ogres."

"Ogres," Myranda said with a sigh. "They have long memories and hold grudges. Plus they like to eat humans."

"They almost got us." Maya told Myranda about what had happened with the ogres. "Good thing we had Hanss and Kai to help us. We never would have made it without them."

"That's why Hanss stayed behind. He wanted to go into exile with his family, but Pawel thought it would be best for Hanss to stay here, keep an eye on things, and make friends with creatures who would be willing to help. Like Kai."

Maya thought of how lonely Hanss was, of how much he missed Thirret. "I hope I can help the Greenwoods come back."

"Me, too. Now time to practice."

Focusing on the magic came easy to Maya. She could feel it swirling around her. However, gathering it and making it work with the spell was far more difficult. But finally, from the table beside her, Maya was able to lift a carved wooden man with a hat, and the man squealed as he rose from the table. Maya jumped as the little man swore and came down with a clunk.

Myranda laughed. "Oh, Gus. You're all right."

"No thanks to her." The wooden man gave Maya a dirty look as he got up. "Why didn't you have her try with a rock? They're just lumps of stone."

"They're heavier than you are. You're just the right size and weight. But now, I think, Maya is ready to try with some rocks, even though they're not quite the lumps that you think they are."

Gus didn't say anything. Folding his arms, Gus stood by the lamp, and he returned to his inanimate self. Beside Gus was a woman with curly hair, and she seemed to be laughing at the wooden man. A cat lay by the woman's feet, and for a moment, it twined around Gus's legs before settling beside him. Gus's grumpy expression went away to be replaced by a reluctant grin.

Blinking at Gus, the woman, and the cat, Maya had many questions she wanted to ask, but Myranda kept Maya to the task at hand—lifting objects. On one of the shelves of a nearby bookshelf, there was a row of five rocks.

"Lift those rocks. First one, then the others. Focus on the spell, focus on the rocks. Lift, lift, lift."

"Lift, lift, lift," Maya chanted to herself. By the end of the evening, Maya could lift all five rocks. Up they went. Down they clattered on the shelf. Exhausted yet exhilarated, Maya fell back into her chair.

Myranda had made more tea and had refilled the plate of cookies. Thirsty and hungry, Maya gulped her tea and munched some cookies.

When Maya was finished drinking and eating, Myranda said, "Good job. Now I am going to give you one more spell to memorize but not to practice until later. You're too tired right now. Here's a throwing spell to use once you've lifted a rock or a branch or whatever you choose to lift."

Even though Maya was tired, she was still attuned to the magic, and the spell danced as glittering words in front of her. Myranda's voice whispered in her ears until Maya said, "Yes, yes. I'll remember." The voice faded slowly, but the words were planted in Maya's memory.

Myranda said, "There. Now you have two spells. To lift and to throw. And the magic is in the throwing, not in what you throw. Say, rocks for example. Might be just the thing if you have to face Galli's imps, who are used to dealing with the direct magic that the elves throw at them. Those imps can pretty much deflect most spells that come their way. But throwing rocks is a kid's gambit, and the imps won't expect it, even though you are young. The only humans who can do something like that are witches and wizards, and we are far and few between." Myranda smiled a little. "I expect you will catch those imps completely off guard."

"A kid's gambit," Maya thought as she turned down the blankets in the pretty guest room that had flowered wallpaper and a matching quilt. The purple sheets smelled faintly of lavender, and Maya gratefully folded the top sheet under her chin as she settled into bed. Tired, Maya wondered how Will, Jay, and Lexie were doing. "Probably not too well," Maya said to herself as she fell asleep. "Idiots." She would have a few things to say to them tomorrow.

Maya slept until late morning. When she woke up, the sun was shining into the room, and the flowers on the wallpaper were aglow. Maya could smell something delicious cooking, and she could hear Myranda talking to someone, a man. Myranda had let Maya borrow a nightgown and a bathrobe, and slipping into the bathrobe, Maya left the bedroom.

The bald man with no eyebrows and eyelashes was sitting at the round table, which was set for three.

"Good morning, sleepyhead," Myranda said. The witch was wearing a flowered kimono, and she stood by the stove.

"Good morning," Maya said, nodding shyly at Ehren. "I'm Maya Hammond."

Ehren smiled gently. "So I've been told. I'm Ehren Robinwood. You're from the Other Side?"

"I am. From a planet called Earth," Maya said, looking at Myranda. "Do you need any help?"

"No, no. Almost done with the eggs and the sprite cakes. Tea is on the table. Help yourself."

There was a large teapot with a ring of running cats, and when Maya reached for it, the cats actually spun around. Maya laughed as she poured the tea.

"Different on the Other Side?" Ehren asked.

Maya grinned as she set down the teapot, and a ginger cat batted at the tail of the black cat in front. "Very different. We don't have magic there the way you do here. Where I come from, painted cats don't come to life and race around a teapot."

Ehren shook his head. "Must be a strange kind of place."

"To us, it's normal," Maya replied. "And this is strange."

"Ehren, it all depends on what you're used to." Myranda came to the table carrying two plates—one had scrambled eggs and the other had the sprite cakes, which looked like small pancakes. Myranda sat down. "All right. There is jam and butter. And tea. Do we need anything else?"

Ehren smiled in delight at the food. "Not a thing. You're a good cook, Myranda. Always a pleasure to have one of your breakfasts, especially after being on the road."

"You're welcome here anytime. You know that."

With a sly, affectionate grin, Ehren regarded Myranda. "I do know that."

"Ehren, I have a favor to ask."

Ehren helped himself to some sprite cakes. "You want me to give the kids a ride to Foretcour, don't you?"

"Yes," Myranda replied.

"Then of course I will," Ehren said, carefully spreading butter on one of the sprite cakes. "Mother sent me here even though we should be getting ready to go to the Summer Gathering. She had a feeling you might need my help."

Myranda sighed. "Oh, Ehren. Why aren't more people like you and your mother?"

Ehren took some eggs. "Because they haven't had our experiences. And truthfully, I wouldn't wish some of my experiences on anyone."

"No," Myranda said, patting his arm. "It's more than that. There's something good inside the two of you that can't be corrupted."

Ehren shook his head. "I wouldn't put it exactly like that. Both my mother and I have to work at being good, same as anyone."

"Let's agree to disagree," Myranda said.

Ehren helped himself to another sprite cake. "Right. No point in arguing."

Maya knew it was rude to pry into Ehren's past, but she peeked anyway and saw how a witch with a face that was beautiful but cold had cursed him, causing all his hair to fall out.

Ehren grimaced. "I got on Gyllis's bad side."

Myranda shuddered. "Maya, I hope you never meet her. Gyllis gives witches a bad name."

"Am I likely to meet her?" Maya asked in a low voice, not liking the image of the witch even though she was beautiful.

"No," Myranda answered. "With the exception of Ehren, Gyllis rarely bothers with humans who aren't witches and wizards. She thinks it's beneath her. But Gyllis lives in Foretcour, in the royal chateau with Tamick and his family. So try to steal that key and lock as discreetly as you can. Keep a low profile. You don't want her on your trail."

Ehren stared seriously at Maya. "Myranda told me Pawel sent you."

"He did," Maya replied.

"Better have a talk with those friends of yours," Ehren advised. "Hope they didn't give too much away last night."

"I'll talk to them, all right," Maya said fiercely, stabbing a sprite cake. "They're coming over later."

Ehren stared admiringly at Maya. "I just bet you will."

"Size is no way to judge a person, is it?" Myranda asked.

"Sure isn't," Ehren agreed. "Looks don't always tell the true story."

Despite her irritation with Will, Jay, and Lexie, Maya grinned. "But sometimes it's good to be small. You get away with more before anyone notices."

Myranda raised her teacup. "To not being noticed."

Ehren raised his cup. "Hear, hear."

Maya clinked her teacup with the others, and on the teapot, the cats raced around and around.

13: Lexie Makes Her Case

When later that day Hanss finally brought Will, Jay, and Lexie to the witch's cottage, Maya was resting in the garden—a buzzing, fluttering, twittering place that was bursting with flowers, vegetables, birds, and insects. To the side of the cottage, under a pergola, there was a patio with a table and chairs. Maya had spent some of the afternoon lifting rocks, and after a while, she had even managed to throw them a short distance. Ehren had left, and Myranda was inside the cottage, getting ready should Will and Jay decide to have their eyes peeled.

"It's not a sure thing," Myranda had said. "They might decide not to. But I want to be prepared, just in case."

"Right," Maya had replied, thinking about how Chance was everywhere, even on Elferterre.

As Hanss led Will, Lexie, and Jay into the yard, Maya called, "I'm over here."

Will, Jay, and Lexie jumped and then stared sheepishly at Maya. Their faces were pale, and there were dark circles under their eyes. Will and Jay looked downcast, and for a moment Maya actually felt sorry for them. Both Will and Jay could see enough to know how careless they had been the night before and how that carelessness might have put their mission in jeopardy. Lexie couldn't see as much, but she saw enough to know she had done something wrong.

"Good afternoon, Maya," Hanss said as they all headed toward the patio. "I'm assuming you have something to say to these three fools. I couldn't bring myself to do it. I was too angry. Besides, they're your friends. It's up to you to tell them how stupid they've been."

Will and Jay flinched, looking at a point past Maya.

Lexie flinched, too, but held her ground. "All right, cat. You've made your point with your silent treatment. We don't need a lecture, too."

Hanss hissed fiercely at Lexie. "Oh, but you do. I'll leave you with Maya and go see Myranda."

With his fluffy tail high, Hanss walked away, slipping into the cottage through a cat door that Maya hadn't noticed before.

Will, Jay, and Lexie came over to the table, and Maya motioned for them to sit down on the three empty chairs. Most of Maya's anger was gone. After an hour of lifting rocks and trying to throw them, she was too tired to be angry. Also, Maya saw how ashamed they were, even Lexie, who held her head high and refused to look away. Part of Maya admired Lexie for not backing down, and she realized that this was something they had in common.

But Maya knew she had to talk to them about what they had done last night, and she rubbed her tired face. Yet again Maya felt as though she were sixteen going on forty, an adult rather than a teenager.

Will was the first to speak. Leaning over, he put his hand on her arm. "Maya, I am so sorry. We should have listened to you and stayed upstairs. We never should have gone down to the tavern."

For the first time, Lexie looked contrite. "And we never should have drunk so much beer."

Jay sighed. "But we're performers. We love to hear people clap and tell us how good we are."

As she considered the three, Maya understood what she should do. Rather than scold them, the way she would have done if she hadn't been tired, Maya would instead play on their emotions and make them feel even more guilty than they already did. Maya pushed away the uncomfortable feeling that she was being as manipulative as the Books of Everything were.

Maya pursed her lips. "I know you're sorry. I can see that. And nobody's perfect. After all, I did buzz that ogre, and if Novok had caught me, it wouldn't have been good." As Will, Jay, and Lexie relaxed and looked a little brighter, Maya knew it was time to deliver the thrust of guilt. "But that guy you were talking to last night? His name is Barint, and because of what you probably said when you were too drunk to know any better, you've put us all in danger."

Will and Jay flushed, and Lexie protested, "The guy with the funny hair that flipped to one side? He was just some little nerd who was sucking up to us. He's lucky we bothered with him at all."

Will and Jay didn't say anything. Instead, they looked abashed. Lexie, on the other hand, needed more convincing.

Maya said crisply, "That little nerd is a spy. Barint works for Tamick Ashglade, and he's been sent here to keep an eye on things, to make sure nobody comes from our dimension to help free Pawel and his family so that they can return to Elferterre. And what did you all say? Did you give Barint any reason to think we weren't from Elferterre?"

Lexie finally lowered her gaze and stared at her hands. "Maybe."

"Yeah, we did," Will said, looking miserable.

Jay looked just as miserable. "Even though we didn't tell Barint we came from Earth, we told him we came from a place that didn't have much magic, and we went on and on about how awesome it was here. We told him how we had been turned into sprites and what a blast it was to fly through the woods. We're supposed to meet Barint this afternoon. He offered to show us around today."

Maya sighed. "I bet he did. As prisoners, all the way to Foretcour, where you would be interrogated." Maya grimaced. "And tortured. You know how torture looks bad in the movies? Well, I can tell you that it's even worse in real life."

Lexie looked up with a start. "You've been tortured?"

"Yes, I have," Maya answered. "In our dimension. On a planet called Tufrak by a troll named Bigly who works for a guy named Cinnial, who's trying to take over our universe. Bigly used a device on me that dug deep into my brain. The device drilled so hard that blood came out of my ears and nose. It nearly killed me. I couldn't even walk when the torture was over, and other trolls had to drag me back to my cell, which was pitch black. No light, no bed, no chair. Just a hard floor. And death, if I hadn't managed to escape." Maya's voice caught at the end as she remembered the intense pain and the fear, and she no longer cared about making Jay, Will, and Lexie feel guilty. Instead, Maya wanted them to know how terrible it would be for them if they were caught and brought to Tamick Ashglade, whose methods might be different from Bigly's but who would be just as harsh.

Lexie stared in shock at Maya, and so did Will and Jay, who had not been told the details of how Maya had been tortured, only that it had happened.

Lexie spoke first, and there were tears in her eyes. "Maya, I'm sorry. I had no idea."

Maya saw that Lexie was sincere and that this was a breakthrough for the arrogant girl. Usually, Lexie was not the one who apologized. Instead, others apologized to her.

Will cleared his throat, and his voice was strained. "Maya, I don't even know what to say. I can't stand thinking about how you were tortured."

Jay clenched and unclenched his left hand. "We've been real jerks."

As Maya stared at their remorseful faces, she felt a surge of affection for all three of them, even Lexie. Maya could no longer be angry with them because of their careless behavior. None of them had seen the things that she had seen. Hanss was right: Will, Jay, and Lexie were green. But they were learning.

Maya's voice was gentle. "No, not jerks. You just didn't know. But now you do. And you need to be more careful."

"Well, well," Myranda said, coming onto the patio. A tray with tea and cookies floated beside her, and Hanss walked on the other side. "I guess Maya has convinced you about the error of your ways."

Jay frowned. "She sure did."

Will ran a hand through his hair. "If we've ruined things..."

Lexie's voice was glum. "We might as well go home."

The tray glided over to the table and settled with a gentle clink. From the garden shed to the side of the patio, a door opened, and two chairs scooted out to join the others at the table.

Myranda sat down on one of the chairs, and Hanss jumped up on the other. The witch's voice was soothing. "Nobody has to go home just yet. Fortunately, Maya met me last night, and I can help you with some of your problems. By the way, I'm Myranda, and I know you are Will, Jay, and Lexie." She inclined her head to each teenager in turn.

Maya said admiringly, "Myranda's a witch and knows how to use magic."

Myranda smiled. "But you three probably have already figured that out because of the floating tray and the scooting chairs."

The teenagers all laughed, and the mood lightened a little.

"You'll be able to help with Barint?" Will asked hopefully.

Myranda poured cups of tea. "I will. And I've found you a ride to Foretcour with an artisan named Ehren Robinwood."

Maya looked pointedly at Lexie. "Gyllis, a witch, cursed Ehren and took away all his hair. Don't stare or say anything mean when you meet him."

Lexie's back was stiff. "Come on, I wasn't raised to be totally rude." Maya looked up at the pergola but didn't say anything. "I wasn't," Lexie protested. "I've met important people. I've been to more galas and parties than any of you could possibly imagine." Will shook his head. "All right, maybe not more than Will. But I know how to be polite."

Maya thought, "When she wants to."

"That's good to hear," Myranda said softly but sternly as she considered Lexie. "Because despite his humble ways, Ehren is going to be one of the most important people you will have ever met on Elferterre. When you travel with Ehren, you will be relatively safe. His goodness helps keep bad things away. Not everything, of course. In the end, Gyllis was too powerful for him. But his goodness keeps out a lot."

Lexie asked, "Why did Gyllis curse Ehren?"

Myranda passed Lexie a cup of tea. "For revenge. Gyllis loved Ehren, but he didn't love her back. Right from the start, Ehren could see her cruel, hard nature, and he knew they wouldn't be a good match. Gyllis took away his beautiful curly hair so that nobody else would love him. But guess what? Gyllis failed. Despite having no hair, eyebrows, and eyelashes, Ehren is loved by many."

Lexie's hand trembled, and tea sloshed out of her cup as she and Will exchanged quick glances then looked away from each other. Maya wondered what Will had said to Lexie when he broke up with her.

"There, Lexie," Myranda said in a crisp but soothing voice. "You're not as bad as Gyllis. At least not yet. And you have some choice in the matter. Just as Gyllis did. So choose carefully in the upcoming days."

Lexie didn't say anything. Instead, she looked away, taking a sip of tea, and Maya felt sorry for the blonde girl who was hearing more harsh words in a few days than she had ever heard in her whole pampered life.

Maya thought hopefully, "And yet she wants to stay with us."

After cups of tea had been passed out and cookies offered—for once, Will and Jay refused—Myranda said, "All right, Will and Jay. You have a decision to make."

Will looked coolly from Myranda to Maya. "You've been talking about us. And not just because of what we did last night."

"We have," Myranda replied.

"What about me?" Lexie asked in a small voice.

Myranda said, "Lexie, this time it isn't about you." She turned to Will and Jay. "Maya told you about seeing, didn't she?" Both Will and Jay nodded.

"She didn't tell me," Lexie said. "But I think I know what you mean."

Myranda's voice was firm. "Lexie, please don't interrupt. Let me finish, and then you can ask questions."

"All right," came the sulky reply.

"Now, then," Myranda continued. "You two know about seeing and specifically how you both can see things that others cannot. Just like Maya. And you also know that Maya had her eyes peeled so that she can see even more."

Maya could tell that Lexie was about to say something, but Myranda held up a finger, and the blonde girl was silent.

Will stared intently at Myranda. "You want to peel our eyes."

"That's right," Myranda replied, smiling slightly.

Jay ran his hands through his hair. "Wow!"

Will looked at Maya, who had clenched her fists without knowing it. She thought, "Please say no, please say no."

"Yes," Will answered simply. "I'll have my eyes peeled."

Jay said, "If Will does it, then I'll do it. And it's forever, isn't it?"

"It is forever," Myranda replied. "I had my eyes peeled when I was a little older than you are, and my eyes are still peeled. But, Jay, just because Will has agreed to have his eyes peeled doesn't mean you have to."

Jay turned to Maya. "Are you glad you had your eyes peeled?"

"Sometimes yes, sometimes no," Maya answered honestly. "Without having my eyes peeled, I couldn't have done the things I've done. But now I'm different from most people. And I feel..." Maya stopped.

"Alone," Myranda finished gently. "Maya feels alone. I'm not going to lie to you. Being able to really see sets you apart from everybody else. But it will also give you an edge that most people don't have."

"And we'll need that edge, won't we?" Jay asked. "If we're going to get that lock and key from Galli."

"I'm afraid so," Myranda answered. "Galli is an elf, and he naturally draws his power from Elferterre and its magic. You humans are no match for him or the imps who guard his house. Elves have tried to steal that key from Galli, and they have failed."

"Yet here we are," Jay said with a bemused smile.

"Here you are," Myranda agreed. "At the beginning of your journey. Will, are you sure you want to have your eyes peeled?"

"Yes," he answered without hesitation, and Maya could tell that Will would not go back on his decision. "Last night, Maya was the only one who knew we shouldn't be drinking so much beer, singing, and attracting attention. If we had been able to see more, then we might have known, too."

"Possibly," Myranda said. "But don't expect instant enlightenment. You'll continue to make mistakes. Just not as many."

Will's jaw was set. "That's bound to be better than what we did last night." Maya was sitting beside Will, and he reached for her hand, giving it a squeeze. "And when I have my eyes peeled, you won't be alone."

Unsure of what to say, Maya stared at Will, and then she looked at Myranda, who shrugged and smiled sadly. "Will," Maya finally said, "we're not from the same time. When we're done here, I have to go back to my own time."

"I don't care," Will replied. "I'll wait until you're old enough. I'll find you."

Maya couldn't look away from Will's hazel eyes. She felt his affection come over her in waves, and Maya saw that while Will didn't love easily, he was as firm about his affections as he was about everything else. And the reason that Will had been able to suddenly break up with Lexie was that he had never truly been in love with her to begin with.

In wonder, Maya shook her head. No flash of insight came to her. "I don't know," Maya whispered.

"Yes," Will replied, staring at her intently.

Myranda cleared her throat. "We'll let these two have their moment. Jay, what's your decision?"

Jay threw up his hands. "Of course I will."

Myranda spoke sternly, "Jay, the choice has to be something you make for yourself, not because Will is doing it. And Will, the same goes for you. I know you love Maya, but this will affect your whole life."

Will's back was straight. "I'm an only child. My mother died when I was ten, and my father's a workaholic. Before I met Maya, I pretty much thought about myself all the time, about what I wanted to do, and it's been that way for a long time. But after meeting Maya and coming to Elferterre, I can see how small my life has been. Now I have a chance to do something big. And after we're done here, I'm supposed to go to school and worry about grades? And about who likes me? And about which parties I'm invited to? No, I can't go back to the way I was before. Even without having my eyes peeled, I've seen too much. I want to have my eyes peeled and go where it takes me."

Thinking about what Will had just said, Maya sat in shocked silence. It was true for her, too, only more so. After having her eyes peeled, after all she had done, how could she go back to school, to her old life? Maya shook her head, pushing that thought away. She had to focus on what they were doing now, not worry about what she would do when all this was over.

"Dude, you're right," Jay said. "We've seen too much. We can never go back to the way we were before."

"What about me?" Lexie asked in a rush, no longer able to remain silent. "Am I supposed to just hang around while these guys have their eyes peeled, whatever the hell that means? I know you think I'm shallow and selfish. And maybe I am. But I feel the same way that Will and Jay do. I've come too far to go back to the way I was before."

Myranda's voice was gentle. "Lexie, you do not have the same abilities as Will and Jay do. I'm sorry, but that's the way it is. You got looks, status, and personality. But your ability to see to the heart of things is limited, and peeling your eyes wouldn't give you that much more. Be content with what you have."

"No," Lexie said fiercely. "I will not. All right, maybe I'm not as good at seeing as those guys are, but I can see a little bit, can't I?"

Myranda considered Lexie. "I suppose you can. Being the alpha girl requires some measure of seeing. You have to have a feeling about whom you can intimidate and whom you have to fight."

Lexie turned to Maya. "And I knew I would have to fight you from the very first when you marched down the aisle at the theater in that stupid outfit."

"Was your outfit really that stupid?" Myranda asked Maya.

Maya grimaced. "It was. My friend Alani bought it for me. I had just escaped from Tufrak, and I didn't have anything else to wear."

Lexie snorted. "Maya looked like a clown."

"And yet," Myranda murmured.

"No kidding," Lexie replied. "I could tell Maya was trouble, right from the start."

Myranda considered Lexie. "I guess you have a point. Maya, what do you think?"

"I don't know," Maya answered slowly. "Lexie, this is a big thing. You shouldn't want to do it because you feel left out."

"I know," Lexie said. "But even though I might never be as good at seeing as the three of you, I want to be as good as I can be. Besides, you never know how I might be able to help you if I have my eyes peeled."

Maya got a flash of Lexie talking with an elf—tall, tattooed, dangerous—and because she had had her eyes peeled, Lexie knew exactly how to handle the elf's aggression.

"Let her do it," Maya said, blinking a little from the vision. "She might be able to help."

"Very well," Myranda said. "Let's get started."

14: Team Earth

Off the kitchen an enclosed porch ran along the side of Myranda's cottage. On the wall against the cottage, there were shelves with jar after jar of herbs, dried flowers, and ointments. There was a long table between two sets of cupboards, and on the table there were six wide rings next to gloves, gauze, and a small jar of gleaming needles. Screened windows were along the other wall, and under the windows were three cots and two chairs. A warm breeze, smelling of lavender, blew in from the sunny gardens not far from the cottage. But the porch, with its overhang, was cool and dim, despite the warm breeze.

As Myranda led them onto the porch, Jay asked, "How long will it take us to recover?"

"About a day," the witch answered.

"Will it hurt?" Lexie asked.

"No," Myranda replied. "I'll give you something so that you won't feel what I'm doing."

"Would it hurt if we didn't have that?" Will asked.

"Yeah," Maya said quickly. "A lot."

Surprised, Myranda stopped. "You weren't given anything?"

Maya shook her head. "No, the Toad Queen just did it."

Myranda whistled. "Wow. But luckily I'm the one who will be peeling eyes today, not the Toad Queen. Now take your shoes off and lie down on the cots."

Will, Jay, and Lexie did as they were told. Nobody, not even Lexie, said anything, and Maya could see that they were nervous. "They should be," she thought.

Myranda went to the table and picked up a purple bottle with a dropper. "All right," the witch said, "I'm going to put a couple of drops of this on your tongue. It will put you into a sort of sleep. Open your mouths."

Three mouths were open then closed. Maya sat between Will and Jay. Both were lying with their heads toward her, and Maya put one hand on Will's arm and the other on Jay's arm. Myranda, sitting by Lexie, did the same thing to the blonde girl.

Maya said softly, "I'll be right here the whole time, and so will Myranda. You won't be alone. We'll take care of you."

Will tried to smile. "Promise you won't leave?"

"I promise," Maya answered.

"You won't take off with Ehren while we're out?" Jay asked, grinning impishly even though he was afraid.

"No, I'm not going anywhere. I won't leave you."

Will's voice was drowsy. "This has been one hell of a ride, but I wouldn't have missed it for anything."

"Me, neither," Jay murmured.

"Yeah," Maya agreed, thinking about how their journey was just beginning. She patted Will's cheek. "Go to sleep," Maya whispered. Then she patted Jay's cheek. "You, too."

Within five minutes, Will, Jay, and Lexie were still. Their breathing was slow and deep, and although their eyes were open, it didn't seem as though they could see anything. When Myranda passed her hand over their eyes, there was no blinking.

Myranda said, "They're ready." Pursing her lips, she looked at Maya. "I still can't believe you weren't given anything to help with the pain."

Maya thought of the impassive Toad Queen. "I don't think she had anything to give."

"Probably not," Myranda said, going over to the table. She passed gloves, gauze, and two of the rings to Maya and then took a needle from the jar. "Shall we start with Will?"

Putting on the gloves, Maya swallowed. "Yes. Do him first."

"I thought so. Here's what we're going to do. Put the rings over Will's eyes. They will hold his eyes open. When I'm done, there will be blood. Quickly take off the rings, and put the gauze over his eyes. After that, we'll put the rings back on. Just in case Will stirs and tries to rub his eyes. Then we'll move on to Jay and finally to Lexie."

Maya swallowed again.

"Are you all right to do this?" Myranda asked. Her gloves were on, and she gripped a needle between her thumb and her forefinger.

"I'm okay," Maya said.

"Are you sure? I don't want to have to tend to you, too."

"You won't have to. I'm fine."

"Put the rings on Will's eyes."

Giving him a quick kiss on the forehead, Maya put the rings over Will's eyes. Although his eyes were still unseeing, they were opened wide by the rings, which adhered to his face.

"Good, good," Myranda said softly. Then, as quick as the Toad Queen had been with her slashing nails, Myranda used the needle to flay one eye and then the other. All the while the witch murmured, and Maya felt the spell settle on Will's face. Maya choked back a sob as she looked at Will, whose eyes appeared to be totally gone, but then the blood began to pool, and Myranda ordered curtly, "Time for the gauze."

Taking a deep breath, Maya removed the rings, which easily came off, and placed the gauze over Will's eyes.

"Now put the rings back on," Myranda said.

Maya put the rings back on, and they adhered to the gauze, which wasn't soaked with as much blood as Maya had expected.

"It's amazing how fast it stops," Myranda said. "And how soon the eyes heal."

Maya felt a little limp, but she remembered how quickly her own eyes had healed. "Yeah, the next day I was off with Feste to the Golden Toad. We were trying to stop Sir John from doing something foolish."

"But you didn't succeed," Myranda said sympathetically.

"No," Maya answered sadly, remembering how Sir John had punched Feste in the face. "Not at all."

Myranda sighed. "Let's move on to Jay."

Within an hour, all six eyes had been peeled. And although there was an occasional soft moan, Will, Jay, and Lexie lay still.

"Now we wait," Myranda said. Her gloves were off, and she sat between Lexie and Jay. "That seems to be a lot of what we witches do. It helps to be patient."

"I'm not patient." Maya's gloves were off, too, and she settled on the chair between Will and Jay.

Myranda smiled. "I wasn't, either, when I was young. But over the years, I've learned."

Hanss called from the kitchen. "Is it over?"

"It's over," Myranda assured him.

"I think I'll just stay in here," Hanss said.

"Probably just as well," Myranda replied. "Best to keep the cat hair out of this room. At least until tomorrow."

"Like you don't shed," Hanss said.

Myranda laughed. "Come on. Be honest. I don't shed as much as a cat does."

"That's because you're practically hairless, naked like a newborn rat."

"Hanss!" But the witch's lips quirked into a grin. "Why don't you go take a nap?"

"Good idea," came the short reply, and Maya could picture the cat's tail twitching.

"Cats can be a little touchy," Myranda whispered.

"They sure can," Maya whispered back.

"I heard that," Hanss retorted.

"Go take your nap."

Maya heard a snippy yowl, but Hanss didn't say anything else.

Night came, and the sky turned a deep blue before it went black. Fireflies blinked on and off just beyond the screens. They reminded Maya of sprites, and she wondered what Kai was doing. All around, Maya could hear the call of small creatures as they hunted in the dark. She heard the scurrying of smaller animals as they tried to escape, sometimes successfully, sometimes not. There was an especially loud squeak just outside the porch, and Maya shuddered as a little life force flickered out.

"I know," Myranda said softly. "Sometimes nature can break your heart. But hunting is the way many creatures earn their living. Most don't have a choice, the way we do. I've put a protection spell around the bird boxes, but that's the only way I interfere. I just can't stand the thought of something eating those baby birds."

"Yeah," Maya agreed. Closing her eyes, she felt the pulse of life and magic. Time wound its way like a silver thread through the magic, and another darker thread followed, sometimes intersecting the silver thread.

"Time and Chaos," Maya whispered, opening her eyes.

"Even here," Myranda said.

"Even here," Maya repeated.

Vibrating alongside Time and Chaos were Chance and Nemesis, and Maya wondered if they looked the same on Elferterre as they did on Earth.

Throughout the long night, Maya and Myranda kept vigil. When Will, Jay, and Lexie reached to rub their eyes, Myranda and Maya guided their hands away. When the three became increasingly restless, Myranda gave them each another drop of the tincture, and they lay still.

Myranda had made a pot of bean soup and some biscuits. Sometime during the night, spoons, bowls of soup, and plates of biscuits whisked onto the porch, and Maya and Myranda ate gratefully. These were followed by glasses of water and bowls of berries sprinkled with something sweet.

When Maya and Myranda were done eating, the bowls and plates whisked themselves from the porch, and Maya heard a gentle clink as they settled into the kitchen sink.

As the night wore on, Maya's head began to bob, and she fought to keep her eyes open.

"Go ahead and take a little nap," Myranda said. "I'll be right here, and I'll wake you up if I need you."

Maya slid into sleep, not waking up until dawn. Coming to with a start, she looked down at Will and Jay, who were sleeping peacefully. She glanced at Myranda, who looked tired but was still alert, and then at Lexie, who was also sleeping.

"All is well," Myranda said. "When they wake up, we can take off the gauze and the rings."

Not long after the sun rose, Will woke up.

Myranda removed the rings and then the gauze. "Looking good," she said, peering into his eyes.

"Do they?" Will asked Maya anxiously.

"Yeah," Maya answered. Will's eyes were still red, but most of the blood was gone.

"Didn't believe me?" Myranda teased.

Will considered Myranda. "You don't lie, but you don't always tell the whole truth, do you?"

"The peeling worked." Myranda laughed, patting his arm. "Now you have to learn when to see and when not to see."

"What do you mean?" Will asked.

"Only look when it's important," Myranda said. "Don't pry if you don't have to. Even though you can see, you should still respect people's privacy."

"It's hard at first," Maya said. "But it gets easier as time goes by." She thought of Feste and Duke Owen and how they had been with her after her eyes had been peeled. Then Maya thought of Andy, who had betrayed her by stealing Earth's Book of Everything.

"I'd punch his face if he was here," Will said grimly. "How could he do that to you?"

Maya sighed. "Sometimes people do bad things. I know I have. Haven't you?"

"Yeah," Will answered, his voice fierce. "But nothing like that."

"Maybe not. But as soon as you met me, you dumped Lexie."

Will sat up and looked over at Lexie. "That was different."

"Was it?" Maya asked. "Don't you think Lexie felt betrayed?"

Sitting down next to Lexie, Myranda patted the girl's cheek. "I'm sure she felt terribly betrayed."

"But dumping Lexie didn't involve a whole planet and a Book of Everything," Will insisted, meeting Maya's gaze. "Just one vain girl."

"I know," Maya replied. "But the point is, when you can really see, you understand how people feel. And it's harder to be angry with them. At least most of the time. I knew Andy was sorry and ashamed of himself. He didn't have to tell me. Sir John, too, when he killed Feste, his very best friend. And they tried to make up for what they had done."

"Did they succeed?" Will asked.

"Maybe," Maya answered, not really sure if either Andy or Sir John could ever make up for what they had done. "They tried, anyway. That has to count for something."

"It does," Myranda said in a low voice. "But what they have done will be with them for the rest of their lives. And it might come back to them when they least expect it."

Will shifted on the cot. "Maybe I should apologize to Lexie for the things I said."

Maya finally got a flash of what Will had told Lexie, of how even though she was pretty on the outside, Lexie was ugly on the inside, and he could hardly stand to look at her. Maya said, "Yeah, maybe you should. And now that Lexie has had her eyes peeled, she might even accept your apology."

Myranda smiled gently at Lexie. "Don't feel too sorry for her. This girl's got spunk, and nothing will keep her down for long. But for all her arrogant ways, Lexie did love you, Will. So maybe you two should have a talk when she's recovered."

"All right," Will said. "That's what I'll do."

Not long after, Jay and Lexie woke up, and Maya and Myranda instructed them as they had instructed Will. When the three had recovered, Myranda left to make sprite cakes and scrambled eggs. As Maya and Jay helped in the kitchen, Will said to Lexie, "Let's go to the patio. I need to talk to you."

Lexie looked from Maya to Myranda, and when they both nodded at her, she said, "Okay."

For the first time, Lexie's voice sounded open to what somebody else was feeling. Although Lexie's talent for seeing was small, Maya sensed that in some ways the blonde girl would gain the most from having her eyes peeled. Even a slight improvement would nudge Lexie forward, stopping her from becoming the hard, selfish woman her mother had become.

Myranda watched Will and Lexie leave the cottage. "We made the right decision."

"Yeah," Maya said.

"Lexie's different already," Jay added, sitting down at the table. "I never would have thought it was possible. That girl's been a pain in my ass for a long time."

Myranda flipped a sprite cake. "She is different. After all, it's not every day that you have your eyes peeled. But don't expect too much. Lexie will always be somewhat arrogant and more than a little bossy. She was raised that way, and now it's part of her nature. But at least it will be softened as she gets a glimpse of how other people feel."

Later, when Will and Lexie came in, the tension between them was mostly gone. Lexie even smiled at Maya, who smiled back. To her surprise, Maya saw that while there would still be an occasional squabble—she and Lexie were too strong-minded not to get on each other's nerves—Maya also saw that they would become friends. And even more important, they would be able to work well together.

As they all sat down to eat breakfast, Myranda raised her teacup. "To Team Earth. May your mission be successful."

Teacups were clinked, and yet again, on the teapot, the cats raced around and around.

On his own chair, Hanss yowled in approval.

Blinking rapidly, Maya tried not to cry as she thought about how good it felt to be part of this team, to be with people her own age, from her own planet, who could see nearly as much as she could.

15: Farewells

Myranda decided that Will, Jay, and Lexie needed more rest and that they should all spend one more night at Lavender Cottage before they traveled with Ehren. Nobody argued.

As they all sat on the patio, having a midmorning snack, Maya didn't say anything, reflecting on how the day after she had had her eyes peeled, she had traveled to the Great Library. Chaos had tried to tear her apart, but Time had saved her.

"What?" Will asked, staring intently at Maya.

Maya grinned. "I didn't say a word."

"You didn't have to," Will replied.

Jay shook his head. "You think we're soft."

"Not exactly soft," Maya protested.

"Pampered." Lexie frowned. "Because we are not having it as hard as you did after your eyes were peeled."

Myranda laughed. "Maya, with these three, you'll no longer be able to get away with thinking one thing and saying another. And I expect that here, with Magic in charge, thoughts will be easier to read than they are on Earth."

Staring hard at Will, Jay, and Lexie, Maya said, "I can block my thoughts. Don't think that I can't."

Lexie smirked. "Not all the time, I bet."

Maya glared at Lexie. "Don't push me."

Lexie leaned in closer to Maya, and neither girl backed away.

Myranda clapped her hands and said sternly, "Now, now. Let's just settle down. Maya, you will have to get used to Lexie, Jay, and Will seeing more than they did before they had their eyes peeled. And Will, Jay, and Lexie? You will have to learn to back off. Besides, Maya is right. She had it much harder than you did. The Toad Queen peeled Maya's eyes without giving her anything to take care of the pain. Then Maya watched her mentor die. After that, on to the Great Library with just an acorn to help her get there. So count your blessings. And Maya, try not to lord it over them."

Suitably chastened, they grinned in embarrassment at each other.

Maya was the first to speak. "I've never had friends who could see as much as I can. It will take some getting used to."

Jay frowned. "And we need to give you some space."

"But it's hard," Lexie said, looking around. "So much is clearer now."

Will didn't say anything. He simply pulled away from Maya's thoughts, and she sighed with relief, realizing that there was such a thing as too much togetherness.

"Sorry," Will said softly.

"It's all right," Maya replied.

Myranda stood. "There, that's a start. But now I'm going to leave you. I'm going downtown to suss out how much Barint knows. It won't be easy. He does his best to avoid me. But I might be able to get bits and bobs from other people. I'll be gone for a while."

"We'll be fine here," Hanss said. "It's a perfect afternoon for a nap."

"A nap?" Will asked. "We just woke up."

But even as Will protested, Maya could tell how tired they all were, and she remembered that not long after she had had her eyes peeled she had slept for days at the Great Library. "Get some sleep," Maya said gently. "When we get to Foretcour, there probably won't be time for naps."

"Maya is right," Myranda added. "Rest while you can."

The witch left, and Will, Jay, and Lexie went back to the cots on the porch.

Hanss curled up on one of the chairs. "This sun feels good. Not much sun in the woods." The cat purred as he fell asleep.

While everyone slept, Maya practiced picking up rocks and then throwing them. She knocked over a garden ornament, a gnome, who swore at Maya before getting up and resuming her gnomish pose among the flowers.

"Sorry!" Maya called, thankful that she hadn't broken anything.

"Be careful," came the gruff reply.

After more practice, her aim improved, and Maya could actually direct the rocks at their intended target, a large tree nearby that seemed impervious to the pelting rocks. At least it didn't complain.

With a smile, Maya surveyed the rocks scattered by the tree's base. She was about to practice some more when she heard a voice call, "Maya, over here!"

Standing by the gate was an elven child with ragged clothes and a shining face.

"Who are you?" Maya asked, feeling as though she should know the child.

"Never mind. Just come with me."

Maya only hesitated for a moment. There was something compelling about the child, and Maya knew she should follow her.

"Quickly," the child urged, leading Maya into the field with the tall plants, which were all bending in one direction, away from the cottage.

"Follow them," the child said. "I have to go now."

Maya looked where the plants were pointing, but when she turned back, the child was gone.

The plants tapped Maya's back, pressing her on, and Maya hurried toward where they pointed.

"Faster, faster," the plants whispered.

Maya ran faster until she came to the edge of the field and saw a pale-haired man trying to extract himself from the twining plants that had wrapped themselves around him. Taking out a knife, he began to slash viciously at the stalks.

A keen wail arose from the plants he attacked, but other plants asked, "Do you see?"

Snarling, the man slashed his way out of the stalks. Before sprinting away, the man gave Maya a fierce look.

"Did you see?" the plants asked again.

"I did," Maya murmured, knowing she would meet this man again, and it would not be a good encounter.

As for the child?

"That was Chance," Maya said aloud, and the plants nodded in agreement.

As Maya made her way back to the cottage, she was grateful for having met Chance, but at the same time Maya was aware that if Chance was around, then so was Nemesis. The two never seemed to be far apart, always checking on each other. And hadn't Maya felt them both during the night?

Hanss was awake and alert in his chair when Maya got back to the patio.

"I almost followed you, but I knew you were in good hands," the cat said. "And what did Chance show you?"

"A man with pale hair. He was spying on us, I think."

The cat's whiskers twitched. "There are spies everywhere, now that Tamick is in charge. Mayor Greenwood has to let them be. If anything happens to the spies, then she'll have to answer to Tamick."

"Then it probably won't be long before Barint knows where we are."

"I'm afraid so."

"I hope Myranda comes back soon."

"Me, too," Hanss said.

Maya ran her hand across the table. "I wonder why Chance plays such a big role both here and in my dimension. Why don't Time and Magic just take charge? Wouldn't it be easier?"

Hanss didn't say anything for a while. Instead, he licked his paw and washed his face. When Hanss was done, he said, "Time and Magic can't control everything. Don't forget that there is always Chaos to deal with. I think that Magic and Time give Chance so much latitude because if they didn't, things would be too rigid. There wouldn't be room for the unexpected, for that spark of creativity that always throws Chaos and Nemesis off. And where would we be without creativity? My world and your world would be pretty flat, don't you think?"

"It would," Maya agreed, unable to conceive of a world without creativity.

While Will, Jay, and Lexie were still napping, Myranda came back and told Maya that Barint's spies were everywhere, watching for Maya and her friends. From the inn, Myranda had brought the teenagers' backpacks, which had trailed behind the witch like invisible puppies and had plopped down around the patio table, winking back into visibility as soon as Myranda took away the cloaking spell.

"Leaving won't be easy," Myranda said. "The spies will be watching the road out of the city. You four will have to be hidden in Ehren's caravan. I will give you something to help shield you from prying eyes. It won't work indefinitely with elves, but it should work pretty well with humans. They'll still see you, but they won't notice anything special about you. You'll just be a group of teenagers traveling with Ehren. Not the ones that Tamick's spies are looking for."

Then Maya told Myranda about the man with the pale hair.

Myranda ran a hand through her own dark curly hair. "One of Barint's spies! Time for a change of plans. You need to leave right now. Go wake up the others, and I'll call Ehren. Hurry!"

Maya rushed into the cottage, woke up the others, and told them what had happened. Myranda gave everyone extra clothes—tunics and pants that were much nicer than the ones they were wearing—as well as small shining brooches of a moon and a star. Jay, Will, Lexie, and Maya stood in a row in the parlor as Myranda fastened the brooches on their tunics. "The brooches will help protect you from Barint and his spies. Right now, your ability to see blazes forth, and these brooches will dim that energy. However, don't get too cocky. They won't work against strong magic, but every little bit helps, and you four will need all the help you can get."

Jay laughed. "Thanks for the encouragement."

Myranda hugged him. "Don't lose that puckishness."

"We'll be careful," Will said firmly.

Myranda hugged Will. "I know the others will be able to count on you. Especially now that you've had your eyes peeled."

When Myranda came to Lexie, the blonde girl's voice was almost shy. "Thank you very much for all that you have done."

"And you are very welcome," Myranda replied, hugging Lexie. "You've come a long way. With any luck, you'll go even further."

Myranda stopped in front of Maya, and the witch's face was sad. "Even though we just met, I'm going to miss you."

Maya hugged Myranda, taking in the witch's lavender scent. "I'm going to miss you, too."

After they were done hugging, Myranda stared searchingly at Maya, who knew the witch was trying to decide how much she should say. Finally, Myranda said solemnly, "Be careful. Think before you leap into action."

"Not my style." Maya grinned, and beside her, Will frowned.

"I know," Myranda murmured. "I know."

Before anyone could say anything else, the front door opened, and a voice called, "I see everyone is ready."

Myranda wiped tears from her cheeks. "Ehren, come in."

Ehren stepped into the cottage. "Goodbyes are always hard."

"That they are," Myranda said with a sigh. "But you've got to leave now. Barint knows you are here. And he and his spies will be watching my house as well as the road from the city. The sooner you're gone, the better it will be."

"You give those kids something so that they won't be noticed as much?"

"Of course I did, and Hanss, too, if he'll wear this." Myranda held up a purple collar with a small brooch attached.

"I suppose," Hanss said. "Even though I hate having a collar around my neck."

Myranda nodded sympathetically as she snapped the collar into place.

"You got the substitutes ready?" Ehren asked.

"I do." Myranda waved her hand, and four figures appeared. Shadow versions of Maya, Will, Jay, and Lexie stood silently in the kitchen.

"That is weird," said Jay, peering at the image of himself.

"No kidding," Will agreed.

Lexie frowned at herself. "They look like ghosts."

"In a way, they are," Myranda said. "But as long as nobody gets too close a look, which they won't, these four will do the trick. You'll be well out of the city before Barint realizes you're gone. All right, kids and cat. Ehren and I will create a little diversion while all of you slip into the trailer. Sit low on the floor, and stay there until Ehren tells you the coast is clear."

Hand in hand, Myranda and Ehren left the cottage together. Looking wistfully around the cottage, Maya hated to leave, but Will's voice was firm. "Let's go."

Ehren's truck, huge with wooden sides, was parked by the cottage, and attached to the truck was an enclosed wooden trailer with its door open. Clutching their backpacks—Myranda had given Lexie one of her own—the kids bent low and scooted into the trailer. Hanss passed them in a blur. As soon as they were all inside, the door shut with a click. In the dim light, the kids settled on the floor by shelves with secured bins, and Hanss pressed against Jay.

Outside, Maya could hear Myranda and Ehren say sorrowful farewells.

"Goodbye, my darling," Myranda crooned.

"I always hate to leave," came Ehren's regretful reply.

There was a silence, and Lexie asked softly, "Are they kissing?"

Maya wished she could peek out one of the windows in the trailer, but she didn't dare stand up. "I think they are."

"Not totally an act, is it?" Will asked, shifting closer to Maya.

"No, not at all," Maya replied, thinking back to the conversation the first morning when Ehren had joined them for breakfast. Maya had seen that there was a connection between Myranda and Ehren, but absorbed with her own troubles, Maya hadn't realized how deep it was.

Outside, Ehren said tenderly, "I'll be back as soon as I can."

Myranda's voice filtered into the trailer and drifted into the small stand of trees and bushes across the road. "I know you will. Be safe. Stay away from Gyllis."

"I never go to the royal chateau. Everything I need is on the edge of the city. Besides, Gyllis doesn't like me anymore without my curly hair. She thinks I look ugly."

"I like you just the way you are."

"I know you do."

There was another silence, and finally, they heard Myranda call, "Goodbye, my love."

"Goodbye, sweetheart," Ehren said. A door opened and slammed shut as Ehren got into the truck. Silently and smoothly, the truck moved forward down the small road that went by Myranda's house.

Maya could feel that the truck and the trailer were being watched by someone—a woman—hiding among the trees across the road from Myranda's house. Maya sat still, as did the others. She sensed the woman's attention turn from the truck to the house, where Maya knew their shadow selves were moving around. Maya understood that the witch's plan had worked, and for now, at least, the spy thought the four of them were still with Myranda at the cottage.

The others realized it, too, and they all sighed at the same time.

Will settled into a more comfortable position. "I think we tricked that spy," he said in a low voice.

"Yeah," Maya replied. "But even so we have to be careful. We can't see everything. And there are plenty out there who are stronger than we are."

"Don't be such a buzzkill," Lexie said. "Let us enjoy what we have at least for a little while."

"Sorry," Maya muttered, stung by Lexie's rebuke.

Jay frowned. "No, Lexie. Maya's right. We shouldn't get too cocky. There's a lot out there that can get us. We almost didn't make it out of the woods when the ogres were after us."

Instead of putting Jay in his place, the way she usually did, Lexie agreed with him. "I know. But still. We're on the road with Ehren, who by the way doesn't look anywhere near as bad as I thought he would. And we could all tell that we tricked Barint's spy. Can't we be happy for just a little while?"

Lexie stared earnestly at Maya, who knew the blonde girl had made a valid point. "Jay, you're right, but so is Lexie. While none of you should get too cocky, you should feel good about how much you can see. As far as I know, people on Earth don't get their eyes peeled. So you're way ahead." Maya's voice became low. "I just don't want anything to happen to any of you. I want you to be careful."

Lexie leaned over and put her hand on Maya's arm. "I know. I can see that." She shrugged. "But I can never let anything pass. That's how I am. The words just come out."

Maya smiled a little. "And sometimes we need to listen to you."

"Hoo boy!" Jay said, rolling his eyes.

"We are so together," Will added with a smile. "Maybe we should all sing a happy song."

"Wise guys," Lexie said, settling back down.

But they all grinned at each other as the truck wound through the city, away from Myranda's cottage with the four shadowy figures who had fooled the woman hiding among the trees.

Ehren drove to the city gate, where the guards waved him through without checking the trailer.

"That was lucky," Jay said.

"Not lucky at all," Hanss replied. "Mayor Greenwood lets Ehren come and go as he pleases. She knows whose side he's on."

Maya frowned. "I bet Barint does, too."

"Oh, yes," Hanss agreed. "But thanks to your shadow selves, Barint thinks you're still in Myranda's cottage."

Maya wondered if this was true. Would Barint send someone to trail Ehren, just in case? But Maya didn't say anything. Will, Jay, and Lexie were still tired from having their eyes peeled. Lulled by the motion of the truck, their heads began to droop. One by one, they settled against their packs, and it wasn't long before they were asleep.

Hanss curled up against Jay's legs. "A short nap would be nice." Soon the cat was asleep, too, and the trailer was quiet.

Will was pressed close to Maya, and every so often she smiled down at him. Even at rest, his face was resolute, and Maya got a glimpse of how this firmness had helped Will make it through his mother's death and his father's long absences. Maya reflected on her own childhood and realized how lucky she had been to have had both parents for so long. And even though her father now lived far away, Maya knew that he thought of her often and missed her as much as she missed him. His leaving had felt like a betrayal, and that sting would be with Maya for a long time, but it wasn't as sharp as it had been. After finding Earth's Book of Everything, after going across the universe, after facing all that she had faced, Maya's hurt and anger were slipping away. She was simply too busy to worry much about her father and Inga. Besides, in her short time at the Little Bard Theater, Maya could see how well they went together.

Shaking her head, Maya yet again felt sorry for her mother, whose concerns were mostly centered on shapes and colors and patterns. Quiet Lily was no match for the sharp, lively Inga, who could argue about Shakespeare and about who was right for which role in *A Midsummer Night's Dream*. The wonder was that Maya's father hadn't left sooner.

"Oh, Mom," Maya sighed. But then an image came of her mother in a house in the Maine countryside, and with her mother was a tall, thin man with a gentle smile, who didn't need someone to argue with, who was comfortable with silence.

Maya blinked. "Mom, I hope it's true. I don't want you to be alone."

Because if everything went the way she thought it would, Maya knew the time would soon come when her mother would be alone.

16: Tagen Robinwood

The truck and the trailer motored on until late afternoon, sometimes going over bumpy roads, sometimes going over smooth roads. Maya heard other vehicles whiz by, and she was tempted to peer out the small high windows in the trailer. But Ehren had not stopped to tell them that it was safe to be seen, and Maya sat scrunched on the floor, next to Will, who slept peacefully. As did the others. Occasionally, Hanss would wake up and look at Maya, who would shrug, and the cat would nod, settling back into sleep.

Once there was a strange clunking sound alongside the trailer, and by one of the windows, Maya saw the head of a large mechanical rooster with a bright red metallic comb. Squealing softly, Maya covered her mouth with her hand as she stared at the rooster. Beside her, Will stirred but didn't wake up, and Jay and Lexie lay still, sleeping soundly. Coming to with a start, Hanss looked around, and Maya pointed toward the window, where the rooster's head bobbed along.

"Nothing to worry about," Hanss said softly, settling back beside Jay. "Just some show-off who likes a different mode of transportation. The driver sits low, which means he or she can't see into the trailer. On the other hand, the rooster can see into the trailer. The pellets that fuel the rooster animate him. But there is nothing unusual in this trailer for the rooster to notice. Just four kids and a cat and a lot of bins."

As Maya stared at the dark gleaming eye of the rooster, she knew that Hanss was right. The rooster briefly considered Maya and then turned his attention to the road ahead. Maya longed more than ever to get a better look at this strange machine. But Maya stayed where she was, not wanting to attract attention. Eventually, the rooster's head jerked past all the windows, and its clunking sound faded into the distance.

"Must be kind of a rough ride," Maya said.

Hanss shook his head. "Some fools will do anything to stand out."

"Yup," Maya agreed, grinning as she thought of how the driver must look.

When the sun slanted low on the horizon, the truck and the trailer turned onto a side road, went along for a while, and then stopped. Opening his eyes, Will sat up as did Jay and Lexie.

"Are we there yet?" Lexie asked.

"I'm hungry," Jay said.

"Me, too," Will added.

Maya looked at the ceiling but didn't say anything.

The door opened, and Ehren's luminous face peered into the trailer. "All right, kids. It's safe to come out. You must be hungry and ready to stretch your legs."

Jay scrambled to his feet. "That's for sure."

They all stepped down from the trailer to find themselves beside a large field dotted with purple, red, and yellow flowers. In the field there were stands of trees, and the countryside was clear, clean, and lovely. Maya simply stood and stared for a few moments, taking it all in. On the edge of the field, by the road, was a small cottage made of white stones, and lush gardens surrounded the cottage. Not far from the cottage was a barn also made of white stones.

"My mother's house," Ehren explained.

"Will she mind if we're here?" Maya asked.

"Not at all," Ehren answered. "I've already called and asked. And remember, she's the one who sent me to Arbor City. She had a hunch I'd be needed, and I always listen to her hunches. You four can sleep out here by the trailer." He pointed to a ring of stones. "And we'll make a fire. Mother always likes a good fire."

The door to the cottage opened, and a small woman with curly white hair stepped outside. Smiling, she walked briskly toward them. "Ehren!"

"Mother!"

The two embraced, and Ehren's mother fondly patted his back. "So here they are," she said, looking at the teenagers.

"Here they are. Maya, Will, Jay, and Lexie," Ehren replied, pointing to each one. "This is my mother, Tagen Robinwood."

Will stepped forward. "Very pleased to meet you, Mrs. Robinwood."

Grinning, the old woman waved her hand. "We don't stand on ceremony here. Just call me Tagen. The four of you must be hungry after traveling all afternoon with Ehren."

"Really hungry," Jay agreed.

"Come on, then. I've made stuffed mushrooms with cheese, and there are baked potatoes and carrots to go with them."

As they followed Tagen to the cottage, the old woman asked, "How is the lovely Myranda?"

Ehren smiled. "As lovely as ever."

"And useful as well," Tagen said. "I like that about her. After all, handsome is as handsome does. Looks only go so far."

Lexie frowned, and Maya blushed, remembering what she had told the blonde girl at The Other Green Door.

Tagen had reached the cottage, and turning, she considered the teenagers. "Still, it doesn't hurt to be young and good looking." She winked at them. "Enjoy it while you have it."

"Now, Mother," Ehren said with affection. "They're just kids."

Tagen laughed. "So they are. Plenty of time for them to find out about wrinkles, bunions, and creaky knees. That's all in the future. Many years away." Peering at them, she stopped smiling. "Ah, maybe many, many years away."

Maya stared at the old woman. "You can see, too. That's why Ehren always pays attention to your hunches."

"Yes," Tagen admitted. "But I've never had my eyes peeled, the way you four have. Didn't want to. I can see enough for what I do."

Maya sighed. "I know what you mean."

Tagen shrugged sympathetically. "Some of us have more of a choice than others. I'm just an old lady who carves little figures and lives in a field full of flowers."

"Maybe so, Mother," Ehren said. "But you sure can cook as well as carve."

Tagen smiled. "You know how to make your old mother feel good." She opened the door. "Come in, come in."

Tagen's cottage was bigger than Myranda's—there were separate rooms rather than one open space—but it was as cozy and welcoming as the witch's home. There was a parlor by the kitchen and next to that a dining room, where a table was set with red and blue crockery.

"There's a bathroom off the parlor where you can wash your hands if you like," Tagen said.

"Oh, yes," Lexie said with a sigh, heading into the parlor.

Tagen laughed. "Some always like to go first."

Jay grinned. "That's Lexie." But he sounded amused rather than critical.

"I heard that," Lexie called from the bathroom before shutting the door.

After hands were washed—and faces, too—everyone settled at the table. Food was passed around, glasses were filled with water, and they ate. For a while, nobody said anything, but after plates had been scraped clean and strawberries and cream had been served for dessert, Maya asked, "Is it obvious that we can see?"

Tagen sat back in her chair. "No. When Ehren called to let me know you were coming, he told me that Myranda had peeled your eyes. I'm guessing those brooches are from Myranda and will help cover that fact."

"Yes, they are," Ehren answered. "When they wear those silver brooches, there should be nothing special about those kids to attract anyone's attention."

"Nothing at all," Tagen agreed, looking around at each one. "You're from the Other Side?" she asked in a hesitant voice. "Ehren told me that Pawel Greenwood sent you here to help him and his family."

"We are," Jay replied. "You know about the Other Side?"

"All we humans do," Tagen said. "It's where our ancestors came from." She was silent for a few moments. "There are stories about the Other Side. Some consider it to be our homeland."

Ehren patted Tagen's shoulder. "Now, Mother. Don't be getting sad. We were both born here. Elferterre is home to us."

Tagen shook her head. "But my mother wasn't born here, and neither was my father. Both were brought to Elferterre when they were children."

Will's voice was gentle. "We call our planet Earth, even though it's mostly a water planet."

"Earth," Tagen repeated. "Yes, that's what my father called it. When he came here, he was old enough to remember a few things from the Other Side, unlike my mother. He lived in a small village, and there were horses and carts but no motorized vehicles. There was some kind of fight, and both his parents were killed. His neighbor was an elf, who had gone to the Other Side to study the way humans lived. She brought my father to Norlander. Told my father he'd have a better life with her family on Elferterre, and he agreed to come."

"Did he have a better life?" Lexie asked.

"I think so," Tagen answered. "On Earth, Father's family was poor, and there was never really enough to eat. In Norlander there is always plenty to eat. Still, Father thought of the Other Side as home, and even though he lived here most of his life, I think a part of him always wanted to go back."

Swallowing, Maya said in a rush, "On Earth, there are motor vehicles now and too many people, and there's plastic everywhere, even deep in the ocean, and our energy is so dirty that it's changing the climate. Some places get too much rain. Others don't get enough, and there are terrible fires." She covered her eyes with her hand.

Ehren and Tagen stared at Maya. "Is this true?" Ehren finally asked, looking from Will to Lexie to Jay.

"I'm afraid so," Jay replied, and Will nodded sadly.

"Yeah," Lexie answered. "Even though my parents won't admit it."

Will turned to Maya. "And it doesn't get better, does it?"

Maya took her hand away from her eyes. "No, it's getting worse." Seeing Ehren's and Tagen's puzzled looks, she added, "We come from different times. I'm slightly ahead of them. In their time, I'm six. It's kind of complicated."

"I should say so," Ehren remarked in his gentle voice. "How do you keep it all straight?"

Maya shrugged. "Somehow, I do." Then she asked Tagen, "What about your mother?"

Running her spoon around the bowl, Tagen collected the last bits of strawberries and their juice. "Mother was taken as a baby. Stolen, if we're going to be honest. With her brown curls and blue eyes, she must have been irresistible when she was little. Her generation was the last one that was taken. Soon after she came here, the Greenwoods took charge. No more stealing babies. And humans were set free. They no longer had to serve elves."

Will leaned forward. "It must have been hard living alongside the ogres."

Tagen shuddered. "Those ogres! They killed a lot of humans. My father remembers that there were roving bands of ogres that hunted during the night and broke into people's homes. It wasn't safe for humans to live outside the cities, but of course they did. They wanted to have their own land and their own homes. They wanted to get out from under the elves. A lot of people figured it was worth it to move into the countryside, even though there were ogres and other creatures who ate meat." Tagen shuddered again. "Imagine, eating flesh."

Maya didn't have to imagine it, and she knew that it was the same for Will, Jay, and Lexie. Until Maya had come to Elferterre, she had eaten meat on a regular basis. "But not anymore," Maya thought, and Will nodded in agreement.

Tagen's voice was sad. "The ogres got Father's first wife, and before I was born, a sister was taken. In the countryside, every family was affected. The slaughter was terrible, and the Greenwoods felt it had to stop."

Hanss, also on a chair, spoke for the first time. "The elves tried negotiating with the ogres, but it didn't work. Ogres like the taste of human flesh too much. And although they look dim, ogres are, in fact, smart and cunning hunters."

Tagen said, "So all the ogres were rounded up and put in Darkwood Forest, where they are bound by magic. Both my mother and father said what a big relief it was when ogres no longer roamed the countryside."

Maya shivered. Even though Hanss had told them about how the ogres had been imprisoned in the forest, it was different hearing the story from Tagen and Ehren, whose family had been torn apart by the violence.

Lexie's voice was low. "I was nearly eaten by an ogre. If Maya hadn't saved me, I wouldn't be here."

Tagen looked from Maya to Lexie. "That's a story for the campfire. Will and Jay, why don't you help me clean up while Lexie and Maya help Ehren with the fire? I do love a good campfire, and it's always best when there are lots of friendly faces around it."

While Jay and Will stayed behind to help Tagen, Maya and Lexie followed Ehren outside to gather wood from the woodshed. Camp stools and a small table tucked in the shed were also gathered.

"Do either of you know how to start a fire?" Ehren asked.

Lexie shook her head, but Maya answered, "I do."

"Well, go ahead, then," Ehren said. "Mother always likes to mix things up with boys and girls. She thinks it's good for them to learn to do different things."

"Your mother is right." Lexie's voice was brisk. "Maya, teach me how to make a fire. I always let others start them when we're on the beach."

"Okay," Maya said, and she showed Lexie what to do.

By the time Tagen, Will, and Jay came out carrying trays of iced tea and cookies, a small fire crackled in the stone fire pit.

Tagen said with a smile, "What a nice little fire." She settled on a stool. "All right, tell me about how Lexie was almost eaten by an ogre."

The others sat down, too, and the story was told in parts by Lexie, Jay, Will, and Maya. Because they had all had their eyes peeled, the teenagers instinctively knew when to talk and when to let the story pass to someone else. Maya wanted to leave out the part about buzzing Novok's head, but she knew that she'd never get away with it, that this story would follow her as long as she was with Will, Jay, and Lexie. When there was a pause in the right place, as Lexie took a breath to describe what it was like to be turned into a sprite, Maya blurted out what she had done to Novok.

Throughout the storytelling, Ehren's and Tagen's faces had been serious, but when Maya told in a rush how she had buzzed Novok's head, they both laughed.

"Shouldn't have done it," Ehren said. "But it does make a good story."

"And a good story is quite a gift," Tagen added.

Ducking her head, Maya glanced at Will, who was looking at her with a combination of affection and exasperation, and Maya got the sense that this was how it would be for them as long as they were together. Maya also knew that sometimes she would be the one who felt this combination of emotions, and she understood that feeling this way was part of being a couple.

Tagen cleared her throat. "Lately, there have been rumors about the ogres and the forest."

Ehren's voice was quiet. "I've heard them, too. But do we really want to talk about the rumors right now? It will spoil the evening."

"Yes, I do because we both know what we've heard is more than just a rumor," Tagen replied. "Pawel Greenwood sent these four to help, and they have to know what's at stake here, what will happen if they fail."

All the laughter was gone, and Hanss and the four teenagers sat still as they waited for Tagen to tell them what she had heard. "There's been talk that Tamick Ashglade wants to release the ogres from the forest. To let them roam free the way they once did."

"Why would Tamick want to do this?" Will asked.

"Because he's a dirtbag," Jay said fiercely.

"Dirtbag," Tagen repeated. "We don't say that here, but I get the meaning. And it's a good description of Tamick Ashglade. I'll have to remember that word. Yes, Tamick is a dirtbag, as Jay put it. He wants to release the ogres for a number of reasons, but mostly it's because Tamick thinks there are too many humans in Norlander. We reproduce faster than elves do, and Tamick is afraid that if the elves are outnumbered, then they will be at a disadvantage even though elves are stronger in magic than we are and live longer than we humans do. And if the ogres cull us and terrorize us, then we humans would have no choice but to return to the cities and work for the elves again."

"For cheap," Ehren added. "Very cheap. Because once again, we would have to live under their protection. We wouldn't be able to strike out on our own, and our options would be limited." He gazed lovingly around his mother's farm as dusk settled over the fields and trees. "This land is fertile, and it gives us everything we need. We have to work hard, but the land never lets us down. The sun, the wind, the rain, and even the cold always come together to make things grow and then rest."

"It's the magic," Tagen said softly. "Under it, everything thrives. My father told stories of how crops often failed on the Other Side, how people went hungry when that happened."

Maya had heard stories like that, too. Her great-great grandparents had been potato farmers in northern Maine, in the County, as it was called. Mémère Celine had told Maya about the farm, of how during good times there had been enough money for Christmas presents, sometimes even for big presents like skis. But the good times hadn't lasted.

"My great-great grandparents lost their farm during hard times," Maya put in. "They had lots and lots of land. Then they had to come to Waterville, a small city, and work in a factory and live in an apartment."

Ehren shook his head in sympathy. "Never heard of anyone losing a farm here. Have you, Mother?"

"Never," Tagen replied. "But if the ogres are released, one way or another, plenty of humans would lose their farms, and this would mean less competition for the elven farmers."

"Win-win for the elves." Lexie's voice was sad. "This kind of thing happens on Earth all the time."

Jay brushed his dark hair away from his face. "Rich people in power always grab everything. They don't share because they're greedy and don't want to lose their power."

Will and Lexie frowned, and Maya could tell that they wanted to argue about this. Lexie opened her mouth and then shut it. Will shrugged and sighed.

"It can be different for you," Ehren said softly, looking at Will and Lexie. "You're not your parents. You can take a different path."

Tagen considered Will and Lexie. "You already have. You've seen Elferterre. You've had your eyes peeled. So this is your chance to be different."

"Yes," Will said.

Lexie's voice was doubtful. "Maybe."

Maya thought, "Lexie likes her life the way it is." And who could blame her? Until now, life had bent in Lexie's direction, and it was no surprise she wanted it to stay that way.

Tagen regarded Lexie. "Don't sell yourself short, my dear. When your time to act comes, you might surprise yourself. Now, enough of this. Ehren told me that you are good singers and that Jay plays the mandolin. Let's have some music."

Maya raised her hand. "I'm not a good singer."

Tagen grinned. "I'm not, either, and Ehren is even worse. We can listen while those three sing."

Jay fetched his mandolin, and he, Will, and Lexie sang many of the same songs they had sung at The Trotting Horse. But they left out the bawdy songs. As they sang, the fire burned down, and the stars glittered brightly in the dark night.

"No mosquitoes," Maya thought with a smile as she listened to the three sing. Of course not. This was Elferterre.

17: Getting to Know Each Other

The four teenagers were given sleeping bags to set up around the fire pit.

"I'm too old for that," Tagen said with a laugh. "I need to be in my own bed."

Ehren laughed, too. "I'm getting that way myself. Used to be able to sleep on the ground, but now I want to be in a bed."

The sleeping bags came from the attic in the cottage, and there were more than enough to go around.

"You have a lot of sleeping bags," Lexie said, surveying the supply of rolled bags lined up on shelves under the eaves.

"I never know who Ehren is going to bring home," Tagen said, passing a sleeping bag to Lexie. "Or how many. He just seems to attract people."

"He's so kind and gentle," Lexie said, and her expression was affectionate, soft even.

Maya blinked in surprise as she took a sleeping bag from Tagen. Lexie really was changing all the time.

Tagen stood still. "No witch could take that away from Ehren. She would have had to kill him first, and lucky for us all, Gyllis wouldn't go that far."

"She loved him too much," Maya said.

Tagen sighed. "That's right. Even hard souls can love."

Neither Tagen nor Maya looked at Lexie, who blurted out, "I'm not as hard as I used to be."

Tagen patted her arm. "We know."

Smiling, Maya looked out the attic window and saw gardens, fresh-cut fields, and rolling hills.

"So pretty here," Maya said. "It reminds me a little of where my grandparents live."

Standing next to Maya, Tagen gazed at her farm. "It is pretty. I love this farm. When it comes time to leave, it won't be easy. My husband and I bought this piece of land. I've lived here for a long time."

"Why would you have to leave?" Lexie asked.

"I'm getting older," Tagen replied. "Right now, we make just enough to keep this place going, with me and Ehren pretty much working full time. But I'm slowing down. The time will come when I won't be able to pull my own weight. And among other things, we have to pay to have the gardens plowed and the hay mowed. What we need is a good horse, but a horse is expensive."

"Wouldn't taking care of a horse be a lot of work?" Lexie asked.

Tagen shook her head. "Not a mechanical one. The pellets to keep it going cost quite a bit, but with the work those horses can do, it would be worth the expense. Those horses can even plow snow, which would be very helpful when Ehren is gone for several days in the winter with the truck. We wouldn't have to pay anyone to plow the driveway when it snows."

Maya didn't say anything but thought, "No, they won't have to leave. They'll find a way. And maybe I'll be able to help." How, she did not know, but the notion settled inside her, and Maya felt certain that she would be able to do something to assist Ehren and Tagen.

When Lexie and Maya came down from the attic, Jay and Will had already set their sleeping bags around the fire, now down to glowing embers. Maya put her sleeping bag next to Will's, which was a little apart from Jay's and Lexie's. They stared at each other as Jay and Lexie fell asleep. Reaching out, Will touched Maya's face, and she knew he wanted her to join him in his sleeping bag.

Maya shook her head. No, not yet. Nodding, Will removed his hand from her face and settled into his sleeping bag. Smiling, Maya fell asleep.

The ground was surprisingly soft, and nobody complained the next morning when Ehren came out to fetch them. "Time to get up. Mother and I have a nice breakfast ready for you."

The teenagers were still in their sleeping bags, and Will and Jay scrambled out of theirs as though a bee had stung them.

Jay rubbed his hands together. "Breakfast!"

"Let's go!" Will said.

"Oh, my God," Lexie moaned. Her blonde hair was messed around her face, but she was still lovely, and Jay stared at her intently before looking away. Lexie continued, "Don't you guys ever get enough to eat? Go on ahead of us. There's only one bathroom anyway."

Jay grinned. "All right." And he, Will, and Ehren headed toward the cottage.

Maya and Lexie sat up, both trying to smooth their hair into place. It was easier for Maya because her hair was short and curly.

Lexie squinted critically at Maya. "Those curls are cute, but really you have dark hair, don't you? Your roots are starting to show a little."

"Yeah, I dyed it so someone wouldn't notice me."

"Most girls want to be noticed."

Thinking of Humphrey, Maya shivered. "Not by this guy. He's really bad, and I had to warn Andy, I mean President Murphy, about him."

"President Murphy?"

"If things ever settle down, I'll tell you about it. Will and Jay already know."

"I always thought my life was exciting until I met you."

Maya grinned. "Don't worry. You're catching up."

Lexie grinned back. "Yeah, almost being eaten by an ogre must have given me some points. And then having my eyes peeled."

Maya crawled out of her sleeping bag. "Like I said, you're catching up."

Lexie didn't get out of her sleeping bag. "Maya, I have a question to ask you. With all that's going on, I know it's a stupid one. But do you think Jay likes me?"

Maya was in the process of rolling up her sleeping bag, and she stopped. "Jay?"

"I know. He's such a nerd. I've always called him names, and he thinks I'm a spoiled mean girl. Which I am." Lexie shook her head. "Or was. I don't know. It's confusing. Anyway, since I've had my eyes peeled, it seems different between us."

"You're friends now," Maya said cautiously.

Lexie shrugged. "I'm wondering if it's more than that."

Maya thought about Jay and how he had looked at Lexie that morning. "Maybe it is. How do you feel about it?"

"I don't know," Lexie replied, getting out of her sleeping bag. "This is new. Ever since I started high school, I've had a thing for Will, but now that I can really see, that's different, too."

Maya looked away from Lexie. "Yeah." She turned back to the blonde girl, who was rolling up her sleeping bag. "Lexie, I'm sorry. I didn't want to get Will involved. But somehow I couldn't stop it."

Lexie stared ruefully at Maya, who blinked anxiously. "I know. I understand. You two..." She shrugged. "Will thought I was pretty, but he didn't really love me. It's all right now. Or at least mostly it is."

Putting her hand on Lexie's shoulder, Maya didn't say anything, and Lexie didn't pull away.

Lexie said, "One of the reasons I was so mean to Jay was because of how close he was to Will. I always thought he stood between us. But he didn't, did he?"

Taking her hand off Lexie's shoulder, Maya thought about Jay and Will and the way their tight friendship bound them together. "I don't think so. At least not too much."

"No, it wasn't about Jay at all. It was about me." Lexie's expression was sad, and once again Maya felt sorry for her.

Maya said, "Lexie, there's more to you than what most people see. When I first met you, I knew you were smart and brave. That's why I didn't tell you to go home when you wanted to stay on Elferterre with us."

Lexie took a deep breath. "I get that from my father, but I feel as though I'm being pulled between him and my mother. Mom is always obsessing about the way I look and what I'm wearing and how much I weigh. It's exhausting." She stared down at her tunic and pants. "If Mom could see me now, she would have more than a few words to say. My father wants me to look nice, but he wants me to think about other things, too. Like taking over the family business. But Mom has different ideas. She wants me to be a TV journalist or the wife of a politician. She wants me to be seen."

Maya understood what it was like to be pulled between two parents. Even though her gentle mother had never insisted that Maya be anything other than what she was, Maya knew that the bond she had with her father had often excluded her mother. It hadn't been deliberate. For Maya and her father, words and stories were the center, and Maya and her father simply didn't see things the way Lily did. All the same, it was two against one even though it wasn't on purpose. As a young child, Maya had sensed this and had felt bad about it, but there was nothing that could be done to change things. Maya and her father were the way they were just as Lily was the way she was.

"Maybe on Elferterre, away from your parents, you'll have a chance to think about what you really want to do," Maya said.

"Maybe," Lexie agreed. "But right now I feel more confused than I ever have. As though I'm being pulled in a third direction, one I hadn't even considered."

"I think you probably are."

The two girls looked at each other, and Lexie said, "I'm not going to figure things out this morning, am I?"

"Nope."

"Then I guess we'd better have breakfast."

"Good idea," Maya replied.

"I do have one more question."

"What?"

"Do you think Jay is cute?"

"Well, yeah. But I like nerds."

"I never thought I did. But then again, Will is a nerd, isn't he?"

Maya gave Lexie an exasperated look. "Of course Will is a nerd. He likes Shakespeare."

"I like Shakespeare, too," Lexie said slowly.

Maya smiled. "Let's go have breakfast."

Tagen and Ehren had made muffins and an egg casserole, and there were more strawberries, fresh from the garden, to go with the meal.

"Delicious," Lexie said, helping herself to seconds. "I've never eaten so much in my life, but I don't feel as though I'm gaining any weight." She looked down critically at herself. "I might have even lost a few pounds."

Ehren said, "That's what happens when you're always on the move."

"Speaking of being on the move...you're going to something called Summer Gathering in Foretcour?" Maya asked. "What exactly is Summer Gathering? We left so quickly that you never had a chance to tell us."

Ehren answered, "Summer Gathering is a big fair on the edge of Foretcour. It lasts for two weeks, and it's where Mother and I make most of our money for the year. From the things we carve. Artists come from all over, and the city is packed."

"With so many people coming to the Summer Gathering, it will be perfect for you to move around without being noticed," Tagen said.

"Will you be coming, too?" Jay asked.

Tagen looked around the table. "If there's enough room for me. At the Summer Gathering, it's better to have two at the table."

Ehren smiled. "Sure, there's enough room. You sleep on a cot in the trailer, the way you always do, and I'll sleep in the backseat of the truck, the way I always do. We'll bring sleeping bags, and the kids can sleep outside the same as they did here."

"And we can ride in the trailer the way we did when we came from Arbor City," Will said.

"Not too uncomfortable for you?" Tagen asked. "There's room for a couple of you in the truck. You could take turns."

Looking around at each other, the teenagers shook their heads. "We're good in the trailer," Maya said.

"Mother," Ehren said in his gentle way, "when they sit in the trailer, it gives them a chance to talk among themselves."

"Of course it does," Tagen replied. "All right, then."

After breakfast was done, and the kitchen was cleaned, everyone helped Ehren and Tagen pack the truck. In the trailer covered wooden boxes were secured as were tables and chairs. Sleeping bags and pillows were tucked in among the boxes and tables, and by the time they were ready to leave, the trailer was more crowded than it had been when they had left Myranda's cottage. Still, there was room for a cat and four teenagers. All the small windows were open, and a breeze blew in, bringing in fresh air. The ride to Foretcour would be cozy but comfortable.

Before they left, Maya handed Ehren a box of chamomile tea.

"Oh, my!" Tagen gasped.

Ehren tried to pass the box back to Maya. "It's too much."

But Maya wouldn't take it. "No, it's not too much. Without your help, we wouldn't have made it this far so fast. Besides, we have more." Ehren didn't say anything, but his expression was stubborn. "Please, Ehren. We can afford to give it to you. Really."

Tagen put her hand on Ehren's arm. "Son, let them be generous. It does the soul good."

"Doesn't seem right for the kids to give us so much chamomile tea," Ehren said slowly, but he gave the box to his mother. "Here. You keep it safe. Do we want to bring this much to Foretcour?"

"We do," Tagen answered, putting the box into a large flowered handbag she carried. "The truck and the trailer all need new wheels. At Summer Gathering, I was hoping to make at least enough to buy some tires for the truck, but now we can get some for the trailer as well. And Foretcour has the best prices for tires. We'll get them after the fair is over."

"All right, Mother. All right." But Ehren was smiling. "Many thanks, Maya."

Maya smiled at Ehren. "You're welcome. And Ehren, just so you know, chamomile tea is common on the Other Side. It doesn't cost much at all."

Ehren shook his head. "Sure is different over there."

"It certainly is," Maya agreed.

Soon the truck and trailer were on the road. In the trailer, the four teenagers and the cat sat close to each other, but after all they had been through together, it didn't seem too close. They used the sleeping bags to lean against, and Will put his arm around Maya. Jay did not put his arm around Lexie, who sat regally even though she was on the floor and settled against a sleeping bag. But their shoulders almost touched, and neither made any effort to pull away. Hanss, as usual, was curled up against Jay.

Jay grinned. "What are we going to talk about among ourselves?"

Lexie's voice was firm. "Maya is going to tell me everything that's happened to her, and how it brought us here. Will and Jay, I know you've heard her story already, but I haven't."

"That will take us all the way to lunch," Will said comfortably, smiling at Maya and giving her shoulder a squeeze. Maya smiled back at him.

"But I don't mind hearing it again," Jay said. "It's a long, complicated story. I could use a refresher course."

"Yeah," Will agreed.

"And I haven't heard it at all," Hanss put in. "All I know is that Pawel sent you here. I, too, would like to know more."

"Okay." Maya rubbed her face and began. "For me, it really started on a train from New York to Boston with the man who didn't smile, the woman who was afraid, and the Book of Everything."

Even though Maya finished well before lunch, it took a long time to tell the story. Lexie interrupted now and then as did Will and Jay. Hanss asked a few questions as well.

When Maya was done, Lexie shook her head. "And to think I let Nemesis tell me what to do. But it wasn't just that. I had to see where you were going."

"Chance might have been involved, too," Maya said. "Did you notice a slight woman with brown hair and blue eyes?"

"No," Lexie answered. "But I wasn't looking for anyone else. All I wanted was to follow you and find out what you were up to."

"I bet Chance was involved somehow, too," Hanss said. "At least on Elferterre, Chance and Nemesis work nip and tuck against each other. That pale-haired man who spied on you at Myranda's cottage? Strong possibility that Nemesis sent him."

Maya shivered. "We better watch out in Foretcour. I don't think we've seen the last of him."

"There are five of us," Will said in his firm voice. "He won't get us."

Maya wasn't as sure about this as Will was, but she didn't say anything more about the pale-haired man. Instead Maya said, "Now tell me a little about yourselves. Even though it feels like we've been together forever, I hardly know anything about any of you."

Hanss told how Thirret, Pawel's son, had rescued him when he was a kitten. Hanss had fallen into a stream, which had swept him miles away from his mother and his litter mates, all the way to the summer home in the woods where Thirret and his family were staying. Hanss was nearly dead by the time Thirret plucked him from the stream, pressed the water out of his lungs, and blew a healing breath into the kitten's tiny mouth.

"From then on, Thirret was my boy," Hanss said simply.

Maya smiled at the cat. "Not hard to understand why."

"Did you ever see your mother again?" Will asked, and there was a catch in his voice.

"I did," Hanss answered. "But by then I had been with the Greenwoods for a while, and I wanted to stay with them. My mother didn't mind. She thought it was excellent for me to be with one of the ruling families. Of course, she couldn't foresee what would happen to the Greenwoods, how they would be exiled. Even the Greenwoods, who can see so much, didn't anticipate what Tamick Ashglade would do."

"Nobody can see everything," Maya said, yet again thinking of the Toad Queen. "Not even the elves. Will, you go next."

Looking down at his hands, Will spoke about his mother, about how she had played board games with him and had read stories to him. And had taken him for walks where they had looked at leaves, flowers, and lichen. Or shells on the beach and crabs and barnacles in tidal pools.

Will said, "When my mother died, my father hired a nanny. Kay was all right, but she wasn't my mother. My father worked all the time, and I hardly saw him. Then he married my stepmother, and she's not at all like my mother. She's into business, just like he is, and they're never home. They go to galas and openings and parties. For business, they go to Asia and Europe. Sometimes I go with them, but mostly I stay at home because I'm in school."

"What did you do all by yourself?" Maya asked Will.

"I wasn't always by myself. I had friends. When I wasn't with them, I read and watched movies."

Jay said, "And then he met me. We went to plays together and we hung out all the time and played video games. Not to brag, but I usually kicked his butt."

Smiling a little, Will shook his head. "Not even close."

Then the smile went away. "Even before my mother died, my father was gone a lot. When my mother was dying, I asked her about it. I was so mad at my father for being gone all the time. But my mother said that mostly it had been all right, that she had had me, drawing, and writing. She told me not to be angry with my father. That work for him was the same as nature was for her."

"What did she die of?" Maya asked gently, blinking back the tears.

"Cancer," Will answered, looking up and swallowing. "Even if you have money, it can get you."

Feeling Will's loss and loneliness, Maya held his hand, and for a while, nobody said anything.

"Lexie, what about you?" Maya finally asked.

Lexie said, "I have a little brother named Charlie, and what a brat that kid is. He's six years younger than I am, and he's always trying to horn in when my friends come over. If I lock my door, he kicks on it until I scream at him and threaten to slap him. But usually I have to bribe Charlie with something before he goes away. Like a trip to a diner to get hamburgers and fries. Mom feels that it's beneath her to go to a diner. My father wouldn't mind, but he's like Will's father. Always working. So the only time Charlie gets to go is when I take him."

"That's nice, Lexie," Jay said, and his voice was soft, almost affectionate.

Lexie shrugged. "Charlie's just a kid. He hates going to the fancy places my mother likes to go." Then she grinned. "But don't feel too bad for him. Charlie's a pain in my mother's ass. One time, at a big party at our house, Mom drank a little too much, and she fell asleep in a chair by the pool while the party went on. She had been swimming. Her hair was a mess, and the sundress she wore over her bathing suit was all scrunched and sideways. Charlie took a picture of her and shared it with his friends online. The caption was "Guess Who Had Too Much to Drink at the Party?" But then his friends shared the picture. Lots of people saw it, and my mom was really embarrassed. After that, Mom never drank too much at a party again, but her friends still tease her about the time she fell asleep in a chair by the pool while there was a party at her house."

Not knowing what to say, Maya, Will, and Jay stared at Lexie, who grimaced and shook her head.

"Your brother shouldn't have done that," Hanss said.

"No, he shouldn't have," Lexie agreed. "It was a mean thing to do. But Mom is always after us about the way we look. Always. She never, ever lets up. And there she was in that chair, looking like a mess. It kind of served her right."

Again, there was silence.

"Did Charlie get in trouble because of that picture?" Jay finally asked.

"He sure did," Lexie replied. "After the picture incident, my father had a talk with Charlie. Usually Dad lets Mom handle everything, but this time he stepped in. I don't know what Dad said, but Charlie's never done anything like that again. To tell you the truth, I think Charlie really was sorry that he had embarrassed Mom so much. He's not usually that mean. He just got carried away."

Hanss made a tsk-tsk sound. "Like most young creatures, Charlie acts first and thinks later. No impulse control."

"That's Charlie," Lexie agreed. "And it doesn't help that he's not afraid of anything. Or anyone. Not even my mother, who's not someone you mess with."

"Brave," Maya said. "Like his sister."

Lexie actually blushed. "Oh, I don't know."

"Yes," Maya insisted.

"Maybe," Lexie said slowly, then grinned. "And Charlie has done plenty of other stuff, too. Fortunately, nothing as bad as what he did to Mom when he took her picture. I could write a whole book about Charlie's exploits."

"It would probably be a bestseller," Jay put in. "Kids would love to read a book like that."

They all laughed in agreement, and when they had stopped, Maya asked, "Jay, what about you?"

"I only have one sister, Maria, who is in college in Rhode Island, and she's not nearly as interesting as Charlie is. But I have a big extended family, lots of aunts, uncles, and cousins. And we all sing and play instruments. When we get together, it's a sound and a fury." Jay grinned. "Sometimes the neighbors complain, and sometimes they come and join us. There's always a lot of food. Plenty for everyone. That usually helps."

"It's a lot of fun when Jay's family gets together," Will said wistfully, and Maya knew he was thinking about his own lonely house with too many rooms and not enough people.

"We always like to have you sing with us," Jay replied, smiling at his friend. "My parents are professors at NYU, just like Maya's father, but they've never met him. The first we heard of Maya's father was when I signed up for theater camp. My mom and dad both teach in—surprise, surprise—the music department. So I guess I was doomed to play and sing."

But Jay's expression indicated that he didn't feel doomed at all, that he took great delight in being able to sing and play. Maya saw how Jay's love of music wove through him like a bright band of color, sustaining him the way words and stories sustained Maya and her father. With a shiver, Maya understood how painting, stories, and music all came from the same place, deep within and without, illuminating those who created, read, looked, and listened.

Lexie glanced at Jay. "Are you going to tell Maya how you've won music awards, three years in a row, at our high school, for playing the saxophone and for singing? And how you'll most likely win again this year?"

Jay said, "No, I wasn't going to mention it."

Lexie gave Jay a stern look. "Well, why not? You're good. Probably the best in our school. You should be proud of this. Even Mom comments on how good you are, and she never likes to praise anyone except for me and Charlie."

Astonished, Jay stared at Lexie. He opened his mouth to say something, then closed it.

Will grinned. "Jay, I've never seen you at a loss for words before."

Jay blushed, and Lexie looked triumphant.

Jay seemed to be gathering himself for some kind of response, but the truck stopped, and all Jay could manage was "Do you think it's time for lunch?"

Lexie laughed. "Except when you're hungover, food is pretty much on your mind all the time, isn't it?"

With a serious expression, Jay faced Lexie. "No, that's not all I think of."

Now it was Lexie's turn to be quiet, but the door opened, and Ehren called, "Time for lunch. Mother packed a nice picnic for us. But don't worry. When we get to the Gathering, there will be plenty of special treats to eat. Then you'll have to pace yourselves. The food can be kind of rich. You don't want to overdo, or you'll be sorry."

Without saying anything, the cat and the teenagers got up, and they all blinked as they left the dim interior to go out into the bright sunshine.

# 18: To the Summer Gathering

Ehren had pulled the truck and the trailer into a parking area by a large field overlooking a shimmering lake surrounded by mountains. In the field, there were plenty of tables and benches, and many of them were filled with elves and humans who had stopped for lunch. Maya saw that there were other trucks and trailers in the parking area, and she guessed that they were all headed to the Summer Gathering. As they made their way to an empty table, people waved and said hi to Ehren and Tagen. Maya was relieved that nobody gave her or the other teenagers a second glance, and she thought, "The brooches are doing their job."

Tagen carried a large basket, Ehren brought a cooler, and when they reached the table, Tagen set out a loaf of crusty bread, butter, pickles, grapes, carrots, and cookies. She also removed small wooden plates, cloth napkins, and knives. Ehren opened the cooler and took out brown bottles and a selection of cheeses.

As Will, Jay, and Lexie glanced at each other, Ehren said, "Don't worry. It's not beer. It's a root fizzy drink that we get at the store."

Taking a bottle and twisting off the cap, Maya took a sip. "It tastes a lot like root beer but with an extra sparkle. Delicious!"

"Next time, don't drink so much beer," Tagen said, winking as she passed bottles to Will, Jay, and Lexie, who flushed as they took the root fizzy.

Ehren laughed. "I think they learned their lesson."

"Yeah," Jay said ruefully. "We sure did."

Ehren stopped laughing, and his expression was serious. "At the Summer Gathering, there's beer, and there is a lot of other stuff as well. Have fun, but be careful."

"We're not going to the Summer Gathering to have fun," Maya reminded Ehren.

"So don't worry," Lexie said, and there was a slight edge to her voice. "Maya will keep us in line."

Maya faced Lexie. "Come on!"

Lexie took a crisp pickle and bit into it with a crunch. "Admit it. You never back off for one minute. You're relentless."

Maya was about to argue, but she knew it was true, and instead she shrugged. Will gave her hand a gentle squeeze. He, too, knew it was true, but he didn't mind.

Tagen regarded Maya. "I know you can't let your guard down, but maybe tonight, after we're settled, you can have a little fun. There's so much to see at Summer Gathering. And you probably won't come back to see it again."

Jay grinned at Maya. "How about it, Captain Hammond? Can we have one night off. Please? Pretty please?"

Maya smiled. "All right, all right. Tonight we can have fun, but tomorrow it's back to work."

Jay saluted. "Aye, aye!" His impishness broke the tension, and everyone laughed.

"When will we get to Foretcour?" Will asked.

"By midafternoon," Ehren answered. "The fair opens at dusk, and we want to be ready. While Mother and I set up and then tend our table, you four can take a look at the sights."

Maya thought, "And maybe scope things out while we're having fun." Will, Jay, and Lexie gave her sharp looks. "What?" Maya asked, more than a little annoyed that they could all pick up on her thoughts so easily.

"You know what," Will said quietly.

"Point proven," Lexie added with a note of triumph. "You never back off even when you're supposed to be having fun."

Maya sighed. "I know, I know. And here's something to make you grumble some more. For the rest of the way, I was thinking of riding in the truck with Ehren and Tagen so that I can see some of the city and what's around it."

"Excellent idea," Tagen said. "Chances are you won't be coming back with us."

"Is there enough room for me, too?" Will asked quickly.

"Sure thing," Ehren answered. "Two in the front, two in the back."

"And Lexie, Hanss, and I in the trailer," Jay said, and for once Lexie didn't say anything. Instead, she smiled.

Soon after lunch, they were back on the road. Holding hands, Maya and Will sat in the backseat, and they each looked out the window by their side. The countryside had given way to more houses and towns, all gleaming with the same white stone that was used in the buildings in Arbor City. But no matter how big the community, there were trees and gardens and water and terraces. Every town had a park, sometimes more than one. The main streets were lined with small shops and larger stores. There were vehicles on the roads—including odd mechanical ones like the rooster Maya had seen earlier—but the roads didn't seem congested. Instead, many people walked and rode their bicycles, and there were special walkways and lanes for them.

The truck's side window was open. Maya dreamily stared out, feeling the wind ruffle her curls, and she was charmed and soothed by the lovely landscape. Even better, Will was beside her, exactly where she wanted him to be.

"It's so crowded on Earth," Maya said after a while.

"I wish it could be more like this," Will replied, and Maya could tell that he was as taken with the landscape as she was.

Turning her head, Tagen said, "It is pretty, isn't it? I have to admit that the elves know how to make things look nice."

Will and Maya looked at each other. Maya knew that Will had caught the tension in Tagen's voice and the underlying mixed feelings the older woman had about elves.

As if sensing this, Tagen added sharply, "No matter how it might look, it's not perfect here. The elves are always lording it over us. Even the good ones. And now with rumors about releasing the ogres from Darkwood Forest, there's more tension than ever."

Looking straight ahead, Ehren gripped the steering wheel. "If the kids succeed in their mission and Pawel and his family come back, things will be better."

Tagen regarded her son but didn't smile the way she usually did when she looked at him. "Maybe. But those elves will always think they're better than we are."

"Aren't they?" Ehren asked softly. "They're stronger and can use magic better than we can."

"Maybe so," Tagen agreed stiffly. "But we work hard. We're clever. We can imagine better than they do. Admit it. We tell better stories. And we're always tinkering and improving things. The elves are so planted in the flow of magic and depend on it so much that they have a hard time seeing outside it. While Magic gives them extra strength, it also blinkers them in a weird kind of way. Chance willing, Maya and her friends will succeed where the elves have failed."

"True." Ehren grinned. "And that will throw those elves in a tizzy. Four human teenagers doing what elves could not."

Tagen laughed, and the strained feeling between them went away.

But Maya stared thoughtfully at Will as she reflected on how there was always a struggle for power, and it didn't matter if the beings were humans, trolls, or elves. She remembered the stories Mémère had told her about how hard it had been for the French Canadians when they had come to Maine to work in the factories.

Mémère had said, "Those maudit politicians in Augusta even made it against the law to speak French at school. But I did sometimes on the playground, and when I got caught, the teachers made me write on the chalkboard, *I will not speak French at school.*"

Thinking about this, Maya frowned, and Will nodded. His responding thought was to note how the top groups always wanted to control and exploit those at the bottom.

"Is there another way?" Maya asked silently.

"I don't know," came the equally silent reply. "But we should talk to Pawel about it when we get back."

"If we have time."

Even Will's thoughts were firm. "We'll make time."

Smiling, Maya squeezed his hand. "All right, we'll make time."

"A little silent communication going on there?" Tagen asked shrewdly.

"Sorry," Maya replied, not knowing if it was rude or not to communicate this way with Will. Even after she had had her eyes peeled, she had never been able to communicate with anyone so directly. "Except for Ariel," Maya thought. And now Will, Jay, and Lexie. Maya supposed that Myranda was right—being on Elferterre amplified their ability to communicate with thoughts.

"No need to apologize," Ehren said. "Myranda and I communicate like that all the time. Handy."

"Especially when you're young," Tagen said dryly.

Maya smiled shyly at Will, and he smiled back. What she wanted more than anything was to kiss him, but not here in the truck with Ehren and Tagen in the front seat.

Will's thought was loud and clear. "Later, if Captain Hammond thinks we have time."

Grimacing, Maya nudged him with her elbow, and Will grinned.

By midafternoon, they had reached the outskirts of Foretcour. There were more homes and businesses, but again nothing felt crowded or rushed. Maya had taken out her map, which was now only a map of Foretcour rather than of the surrounding area spreading out from Darkwood Forest.

Maya said, "Show me where the Summer Gathering is."

On the eastern edge, an area glowed, and the words *Summer Gathering* appeared.

"Where are Galli's house and workshop?" Maya asked.

Some distance away, another spot shimmered, and the words *Galli's House* and *Workshop* lit up.

"How far apart are they, do you think?" Maya asked, passing the map to Tagen.

"About ten miles. It would be a long walk," Tagen answered, passing the map back to Maya. "Maybe Ehren can take you first thing in the morning before the fair starts."

Ehren nodded, but Maya said doubtfully, "Maybe." She didn't want Ehren to be even remotely connected with the robbery.

Maya thought, "We need to find another way."

Will squeezed Maya's hand. "I agree," came his silent reply.

"Good," Maya answered just as silently as she put the map in her bag. Aloud she said, "Pawel said I would be able to find something in Foretcour to help us when we break into Galli's house."

"There will be plenty to choose from at Summer Gathering," Ehren replied. "You'll have your pick of things."

Maya said, "Maybe something to go along with the bee." Something that could fly and zip through the magic.

Will frowned. "Don't forget my ball."

"I won't," Maya replied. "But a ball's not a creature, and I want another creature. I don't know why. I just do."

"You'll find something at the Gathering," Ehren repeated. "You have enough tea to pretty much buy anything you want."

"Right," Maya answered. Her hand went to her pocket, where she had tucked some bags of tea.

"But be careful. Don't flash it around."

"I'll be careful."

Three large tree-lined boulevards led to Foretcour, and Maya was struck by the beauty and the elegant order of the city. Even the smallest houses with tiny yards had flowers spilling out of boxes and pots. Red, yellow, purple, and orange blossoms stood in jaunty contrast to the white buildings, bringing life to the cool stones. Ehren took the right boulevard and drove to a huge field with many acres on the edge of the city. In the distance large white buildings glowed in the afternoon sun, and one had a glittering gold dome.

"That's the city center," Tagen said, pointing in that direction. "It's where Tamick Ashglade and his cronies get together to decide how to torment us next."

Ehren didn't argue. Maya understood that even someone as kind and as positive as Ehren couldn't dispute what Tagen had said.

Large tents covered most of the field, but the edges were left for the vendors to camp out during the night. An air of shimmering expectation hung over everything, and some of the tents seemed to twinkle.

"Wow," Maya said, feeling the pull.

"Yeah," Will agreed.

Ehren laughed. "Told you that you'd want to take some time off to look at the sights."

"In Norlander, this is the fair of fairs," Tagen said simply.

Ehren parked next to a blue and white striped tent not far from the center of the fairgrounds.

"Here's where we'll set up," Ehren said. "Then we'll go to the edge where we'll camp."

"You're not worried about someone stealing your stuff while you're gone?" Will asked.

Ehren laughed. "Not at all. The Gathering is well guarded. You'll see."

From the trailer, Maya, Will, Jay, and Lexie helped bring out the boxes with the things Ehren and Tagen had carved. They also brought out tables, chairs, and shelves.

"Sure is nice to have these kids here," Tagen said wistfully. "Makes unloading the trailer faster and easier."

"You bet," Ehren replied, smiling at the teenagers. "But Mother and I will unpack the boxes and set up. We have a system. Would you like to take a peek first?"

"Yes!" Maya answered, and the others nodded.

They knelt by the boxes, and Maya opened one of them.

"Fantastic!" Lexie exclaimed.

"No way," Will murmured.

"Unbelievable," said Jay.

"This is Elferterre," Maya reminded them, and they all nodded.

Various little figures that had been carefully packed blinked and stared up at them. Some were human, others were animals, still others were birds, and the details of their faces, clothes, feathers, and fur were exquisitely carved. One, a young child, waved at them. A bird chirped. A fox barked. A girl stuck out her tongue.

"Are they alive?" Lexie asked breathlessly.

"In a way," Ehren answered. "Magic animates everything here, even wood, stone, and paper."

"And water," Maya said, remembering the waterfall in Darkwood Forest that had wanted to pull them in.

"Especially water," Ehren agreed. "You have to be real careful around water. Even when it's placid."

"Water's moody," Tagen added. "You have to be extra polite to it. Something as small as a puddle might give you a nasty surprise."

Ehren reached into the box and tenderly removed a white fox, who settled contentedly in his palm. "But the wood doesn't allow them to move as freely as if they were flesh, like you and me. So even though they can move a little, they are more or less rooted to where they are put. Placement is very important, and they shouldn't be alone. They need company, the same as we do."

"This means we have a following," Tagen said. "People come back year after year to buy companion pieces."

Ehren gently placed the fox back in the box. "The right combination of figurines makes a house a home."

"How?" Lexie asked.

"It's hard to explain, but when they are happy, the figurines give off a good feeling to a home."

"You carved Gus, didn't you?" Maya asked suddenly, thinking about the little figurine she had lifted and dropped at Myranda's cozy cottage.

"I did," came Ehren's answer. "As well as the woman, Mauve, and her cat, Cleone. They keep Myranda company while I'm away traveling to sell our little pieces."

"Of course," Maya said, remembering the close feeling that the three figures seemed to have for each other.

Will blinked. "Oh, brave new world."

"How are we ever going to go back to our own?" Jay asked.

"It will be flat," Lexie put in.

Hanss didn't say anything, but Maya caught his thoughts: four more to miss.

"There, now," Tagen said. "We have to set up before the fair opens. Off you go for a look around."

Ehren reached into his pocket and pulled out his wallet, not leather, made out of some kind of smooth black material. He took out four crisp bills and handed one to each of the teenagers. He briefly explained their worth, and Lexie was the one who understood best. Out of her flowered bag, Tagen removed a small purse and gave them each some silver coins.

"Use these to buy something to eat and drink," she said. "Save the bills for something big."

Ehren looked around at the other vendors setting up their wares. Nobody seemed to be paying attention to them, but he said in a low voice, "Why don't you leave your bags in the truck? After we're done, it will be locked."

The teenagers nodded. They didn't have to be told that Ehren didn't want them to carry boxes of chamomile tea around with them as they explored the fairgrounds.

Digging through a crate with cloth pouches for customers to carry their figurines, Tagen found four dark green ones to give to Maya, Will, Jay, and Lexie. "To hold your money," she said.

Thanking her, the teenagers took the bags, tucked their money inside, and slid them into the roomy pockets of their trousers.

"How long will you be here?" Will asked.

"Late into the night," Ehren replied. "The gates open at dusk, and the fair doesn't close until midnight. If you get turned around, just ask the way to the Carvers Tents. They put us all here in one place."

Jay grinned. "Great!" He looked at the others. "Let's go. Hanss, are you coming with us?"

"No," the cat answered. "I have friends to catch up with. I'll see you later." And he slid out beneath the wall of the tent.

Will took Maya's hand, and hesitating only a little, Jay reached for Lexie's hand. For a moment, Maya could imagine that the four of them were ordinary teenagers, on a date even, about to explore one of the most exciting fairs they had ever been to. Maya smiled, feeling a burst of happiness as she thought about a night off with her friends.

"She relaxes," Jay joked.

"Finally," Lexie said.

Will didn't say anything aloud, but his hazel eyes crinkled at the edges as he smiled at Maya.

As they started to leave, Tagen said, "Have fun, but be careful. And, remember, don't talk back to the elves."

19: Across Two Universes

As the sun set, the lights twinkled on, inside and outside the tents, and it seemed as though the field was aglow with the light of hundreds of tiny stars. All kinds of beings were at the fair: short, tall, fat, thin, wrinkled, smooth, scaled, bald, hairy, brown, green, blue, and white. Maya was dazzled by the wondrous diversity of the denizens of Elferterre. The teenagers wandered through a crafts area, and peering into the various tents, Maya and Lexie got a brief glimpse of scarves, tunics, jewelry, hats, and cloaks. They wanted to stop for a better look, but Will and Jay hustled them on.

"Can you smell that?" Will asked.

"Oh, yeah," Jay replied.

Maya sniffed and caught the mouthwatering scent of food being fried.

Lexie could smell it, too. "That figures. Okay, we'll get something to eat, but then we're going to look at other things. Don't think we're not."

"Deal," Will and Jay said together.

They followed their noses as the scent of various foods—some sweet, some salty—curled around them, enticing them, drawing them in. When they came to the edge of the food section, the field dipped, and hundreds of food stalls spread out before them.

"Be still my trembling heart," Jay said as if in a dream.

"It reminds me of Smorgasburg," Will murmured.

Even Lexie was impressed. "Look at that."

Maya smiled. "Let's go."

As they wandered by the stalls, even Will and Jay were daunted by all that was offered—little cakes, noodles, rice dishes, spicy beans, cookies, something that looked like popcorn, drinks, breads, spicy nuts, sweet nuts, honey balls, ice cream. On and on it went. Maya was the first to stop for a paper cone filled with spiced nuts. It reminded her of something she could get in New York City, and Maya was comforted by the familiarity. The warm nuts tingled her tongue, and with all four digging in, it wasn't long before nuts were gone. After that it was on to honey balls, spicy beans, noodles, and cake. Naturally, after all that food, they had to have something to drink.

They had stopped beside a beer tent, and Will, Jay, and Lexie looked at Maya.

"One beer," Maya said firmly. "And no more."

"Aye, aye," Jay said.

"Lead the way, Captain Hammond," Lexie commanded, but her tone was not sharp, and grinning, Maya led them into the tent to an empty table.

However, Will's expression was serious. "Remember what happened last time."

"Yeah," Jay and Lexie said together, and one beer each was all they had. Except for Maya. The bitter taste of beer did not appeal to her, and instead she had a fizzy ginger drink.

When they had finished, the teenagers wandered through another craft section, and a high buzzing sound drew Maya into a tent where there were tables and tables of metallic insects, many of them vibrating. Most of the artisans were elves, whose long hair was twined in multiple braids, and their bare arms were covered with swirling tattoos.

As Maya approached one of the tables, she could see that the tattoos changed shape, much like a neon sign. Two elves, a male and a female, stood behind a table swathed in a rich green fabric, and not smiling, they regarded Maya, Will, Jay, and Lexie. Maya recognized the male from the flash she had had on Myranda's patio about how Lexie could be useful, and he had a hard, coiled energy. "We need to be careful," Maya thought.

Insects of various kinds hummed on the table, but in the far corner, almost hidden in a fold of cloth, there was one that looked like a cross between a dragon and a butterfly. As Maya bent over to regard the small creature, the dragonfly opened its eyes.

"I will be able to help you," the tiny creature said silently, its wings fanning slowly.

Maya looked around, to see if the others had heard, but they were peering at different insects, and the two elves didn't seem to notice, either.

"You're talking to me?" Maya asked just as silently.

"Of course I am. Who else?"

"How do you know I need help?"

"I can see past the brooch that the witch gave you. Even though it can't move the way I can, we are both made of the same element, and it can't trick me."

"What about the elves?"

"They are made of flesh. They can be fooled for a while but not for long. Be quick about your purchases."

"All right." Maya put her hand down, and the dragonfly crawled onto her palm.

The dragon said, "You will also need something else to help cover your tracks and to pick locks. You will need a spider. Look closely. There is one that is beside me, hidden even more beneath the fold."

With her free hand, Maya gingerly pushed open the fold, and there sat a gleaming black spider, who with eight tiny eyes, regarded Maya. "Yes, you will need me, too."

The spider skittered beside the dragon, and holding both of them in her palm, Maya turned to the female elf. "I want these two."

The elf frowned. "You have expensive taste. I'm not sure you can afford them."

Setting the dragon and the spider on the table, Maya reached into her pocket and pulled out the pouch Tagen had given her. Maya took out all the money she had, but the elf shook her head. "Not nearly enough."

Will, Jay, and Lexie dug into their pockets and added their money to Maya's.

"Still not enough," the elf said.

"Come on!" Lexie exclaimed.

"Really." The elf glanced quickly at her partner, who was helping other customers and wasn't paying attention to the exchange. "Those two are precious," the elf said in a low voice, and Maya knew she didn't want to sell the dragon and the spider, which was why the small creatures had been put to one side, nearly hidden.

In one pocket of Maya's trousers were the four bags of chamomile tea. Maya took out the tea bags, and the elf gasped. "Where did you get those? Did you steal them?"

Maya shook her head. "No, I got them honestly."

Now the elf's partner noticed what was going on, and frowning, he came over, staring intently at Maya, and his eyes narrowed as he looked at the tea she held.

Tossing her blonde hair, Lexie said, "Her father's always spoiling her, but this time he outdid himself. Four bags of chamomile tea? Really?"

Maya made herself laugh sheepishly. "Yeah, I know."

Lowering her voice, Lexie leaned toward the elves. "Her father's never home. That's how he makes it up to her. By the way, my name's Lexie."

Maya could see that both elves were struck by Lexie's beauty, and they relaxed a little.

"I'm Duca," said the female elf. "And this is Balric."

Lexie nodded regally at them, and they nodded back.

Duca stared longingly at the tea. "Well, some human parents do spoil their children. It's the same for elves, too."

"But not for us," Balric said darkly.

"No, not for us. We were not spoiled." Duca continued to gaze at the tea bags. "All right, four bags for the dragon and the spider. His name is Aiken, and hers is Orlaith. They have more life than most of our creations. The metal I used to make them is rare. So be careful with them."

Maya was about to give Duca four tea bags, when Lexie put her hand on Maya's arm. "Four bags? Are you kidding? For one little dragon and spider?"

Aiken stared coldly at her, and two puffs of steam escaped from his small nostrils. Beside him, Orlaith impatiently tapped her tiny front legs.

Lexie gazed sweetly at Aiken but did not back down. She regarded Duca and Balric. "One bag is plenty."

Balric's voice was soft, and there was a thrum of danger in it. "You have a lot of confidence for a human. Where are you from?"

But Lexie smiled. "I'm from away. And my parents raised me to be confident."

Balric considered her. "Where?"

Duca intervened. "What does it matter where she's from?" Glancing briefly at Maya, she turned to Lexie. "Two tea bags."

Lexie pretended to consider. "All right. Two bags. Even though that still seems like a pretty high price."

Gazing at Aiken's small gleaming scales and Orlaith's delicate legs, Maya didn't think the original price was high at all. Four bags of chamomile tea for these exquisite creatures? But Maya didn't say anything, knowing it would look weak, not to mention stupid, to back down from the deal Lexie had made. After putting two tea bags back in her pocket, Maya handed the other two to Duca, who tried not to grab them but was not entirely successful.

Duca passed Maya two small black boxes that when opened looked like little nests. "This is for Aiken and Orlaith when you are carrying them."

With something that sounded like a chirp, Aiken curled up in his box, and Orlaith settled gracefully into hers. Before Maya closed the boxes, the dragon said silently, "When you need me, I'll be ready."

"And so will I," the spider added just as silently.

"Okay," Maya thought.

Maya put the boxes in the empty pocket of her trousers, and when she looked up, Maya noticed Duca was staring wistfully at the pocket. Maya looked sympathetically at Duca, but the elf sadly shook her head.

Balric moved closer to Duca's side. "We need that tea."

"I know," she replied softly.

His voice was hard. "Then let it go. They're not pets."

Duca swallowed. "I know that, too."

Leaning over, Maya put her hand on Duca's arm. "I'll take good care of Aiken and Orlaith."

With something that sounded like a snarl, Balric pulled Duca away. "Don't you touch her! Are you humans done here?"

Scowling, Will stepped forward. "Don't talk to us like that."

Elf and human stiffly regarded each other, and for once, Maya wasn't sure what she should do, wondering if there was going to be a fight and knowing who would lose.

But again, with a toss of the head, Lexie intervened, pulling on Will's arm. "Oh, let's go! I'm tired of looking at bugs. I want to see the jewelry."

Following Lexie's lead, Maya took Will's other arm. "Yeah, me, too."

Jay said, "Come on, bud. Time to go."

Balric didn't say anything, but Maya caught the elf's ugly thought: "I'd like to smash that human's face."

As Maya, Lexie, and Jay hustled Will out of the tent, Maya caught one more thought, this time from Duca. "Thank you," came the grateful farewell. "I know you'll take good care of Aiken and Orlaith."

Once outside the tent, Jay said sharply, "What the hell were you thinking, Will?"

Will was rigid with anger. "I was thinking that elf had no right to look down on us like that."

Jay faced Will. "Doesn't feel too good, does it?"

Lexie and Maya let go of Will's arms, and he regarded Jay. "No, it doesn't."

Jay's shoulders twitched. "Well, now you know what it's like."

"Yeah," Will answered thoughtfully as his anger went away. "It's different here."

"What's different," Jay said, "is that all humans, no matter what color they are, are on the bottom here. So watch what you say, and keep your head down."

After her experiences with Cinnial and Bigly, Maya knew what it was like to be on the bottom, and she sighed in agreement. Even Lexie looked chastened. Nobody said anything as they walked away from the tent with the buzzing insects. The teenagers kept walking until they came to a large dark tent that seemed to glimmer even more than the others did. Outside, leaning against a podium, was a tall, thin elf who sparkled along with the tent. He wore a shimmering deep blue jacket with a matching top hat, and after considering the teenagers, the elf grinned crookedly.

"Step right up," the elf beckoned, his coaxing voice pulling the teenagers closer to the tent.

Maya felt as though she could resist, that maybe she should, but somehow she didn't want to. The elf and the tent beckoned.

The elf leaned a little toward the teenagers, as though they were all privileged to be part of a great secret that most of the other fairgoers would never be aware of. In a voice soft but clear, he said, "This might look like a normal tent, but inside you will be taken across the universe to places you've never imagined in your wildest dreams."

Maya smiled a little, knowing that she had seen things that perhaps even this elf couldn't imagine.

Noting Maya's expression, the elf's voice became lower. "So you think you've seen it all, little human?"

"Don't call her that," Will said sternly.

"Will," Jay warned.

"Oh, I meant no disrespect," the elf said smoothly, looking briefly at Will before turning back to Maya. "Being small has its advantages, doesn't it?"

Maya regarded the elf and understood that even though he was working at this fair, he could see as much as she could, and her brooch couldn't block his sharp gaze. "It does," Maya replied coolly but honestly.

The elf pursed his lips. "But nobody can see everything."

"That's right," Maya agreed.

The elf's voice was softer still, but Maya heard him. "Even you can learn a few things. What do you say? Do you dare come in?"

Maya thought of traveling across her own universe with Time. "Yes, I do."

"Brave one," the elf murmured, and he tipped his hat to Maya. Speaking louder, the elf addressed the others. "What about the three of you? Do you dare take this trip? It's not cheap."

Will stepped forward. "Where Maya goes, we go."

"Right," Lexie said, and Jay nodded.

The elf rubbed his hands together. "Very good. Now how will you pay?"

Deciding to go straight for the chamomile, Maya took the two remaining tea bags from her pocket. "How about with this?"

The elf laughed. "Of course you have chamomile tea. Yes, that will do. Come inside. You may call me Lucius." He peered at them one by one. "And your names?"

The teenagers introduced themselves. With a nod, Lucius stepped down from the podium and led them inside the tent, securing the door, not only with rope and hooks but also with waving hands. In the dim light, Maya could barely see the elf and Will, Jay, and Lexie.

When Lucius was done, Maya asked, "We're the only ones?"

"You're the only ones," Lucius replied, holding out his hand. Maya placed the tea bags on his palm, and with a motion so quick it was almost a blur, the elf's hand went to his pocket, and the tea bags were gone. Lucius smiled pleasantly, but Maya caught a dark undertone. "I want to be able to monitor travelers, and I only take a few at a time."

"Monitor what?" Jay asked, and Maya could tell he was having second thoughts.

"Why, your trip," came the answer. "I do it with all customers, no matter what kind of creatures they are."

"Where will we go?" Lexie asked, and although her voice was steady, Maya caught her nervousness.

"That depends on the individual. You might all go to different places. Or you might go to the same place. I can never tell. But rest assured that you will all go where you need to."

Lucius waved his hands again. With a burst the light increased, and Maya could see there was a tent inside the tent. The smaller tent glowed and pulsed, as though it really was the center of something strange and mysterious.

Lucius took them inside the smaller tent, where there were four comfortable chairs with high backs. Next to the chairs was a low free-standing shelf with a carafe and four small glasses. In three of the glasses Lucius poured a thick liquid to the top, but the fourth glass was only filled halfway. He passed the three full glasses to Will, Jay, and Lexie, and Maya received the one that was half full.

"Why does she get less than we do?" Lexie asked. "Is it because she's the smallest?"

"No," Lucius replied with amusement. "It's because she won't need as much as you three. Being bigger does not always mean being the best."

Lexie gave Maya a sharp look. "So I've discovered."

Lucius laughed. "Some lessons are bitter. But don't worry, pretty one. You will have your day. Now sit down, all of you, before you drink. I want you to relax. Don't worry too much about the drink. It's only a potion that will heighten your senses. When it wears off, you will be yourselves. But," and he winked at them, "you will very much remember where you've been. And that will be a good thing." Then Lucius added in such a low voice that Maya wasn't sure if she had heard him correctly, "Pawel will thank me." In a louder voice he said, "Sit down, sit down. And drink."

What could Maya, Will, Jay, and Lexie do now but follow his instructions? The four sat down into chairs that folded around them with a hug. Feeling secure rather than trapped, Maya drank the liquid, which was sweet and bitter at the same time. She was glad she was sitting down because the potion, like the other two she had taken, worked quickly. Maya felt the liquid travel through her whole body, and her lips, hands, and feet tingled.

"Now it begins," Lucius said in a deep voice as he took the small glasses from the teenagers. The lights dimmed, and above them, projected on the roof, was a mass of swirling stars and galaxies, shimmering and beckoning. Chiming music, at first low and then becoming louder, tugged at Maya, pulling her out of her seat and drawing her upward. Except when she looked back, Maya saw that she was still sitting in the chair, and she understood that this time only her spirit, not her body, was traveling. Beside her, the spirits of

Will, Jay, and Lexie soared upward, and for a brief moment they traveled together, but Magic sizzled beside Maya and eventually enveloped her, pushing her faster and faster, leaving the others behind.

"Wait!" called Will.

With Magic propelling her, Maya couldn't wait. She zoomed beyond one set of stars, planets, and galaxies, through what looked like a dark passageway, and then burst into another universe. Here Time, gentler but still firm, took over from Magic. Maya sped past a beautiful blue planet, and she knew it was Earth. Maya desperately wanted to go to Earth, to her own planet, but Time propelled her onward, and Maya didn't struggle, trusting that Time would bring her to where she should be. Her senses blazed as she traveled, and Maya was so filled with marvel that she wondered how she could ever return to her body.

"I wish I could just stay among the stars," Maya thought, knowing this wasn't exactly true. She would miss the people she loved—her mother, her father, Mémère, Pépère, Will, Jay, and even Lexie. "But that would soon pass," a voice said. With a start, Maya realized the voice belonged to Time. "And then you would forget them. Your spirit can't stay apart from your body for too long. It's a risk traveling this far, but it will be worth it. And I will help you when you need it."

Thinking about the danger of her spirit leaving her body, Maya shivered as she went faster and faster, bursting toward another blue planet and traveling at such speed that Maya couldn't even think anymore. Then Maya stopped. It wasn't jarring, the way it would have been if she had been traveling with her body. Instead, Maya simply wasn't moving anymore, hovering in front of a familiar place, a white castle with towers and turrets.

Maya's thoughts returned, and her spirit was filled with joy. "I'm at the Great Library!"

20: The Great Library

Maya's spirit slid through the big doors of the front entrance and zipped through the main stacks that were completely empty of people from the mainland. She stopped, hovering by Sydda's old office, and saw Cinnial, who was now in charge of the Great Library. He sat at the desk, and on the shelf behind him, in the big stand where the Great Library's Book of Everything once rested, was Cinnial's own Book, and Maya felt its malicious consciousness. Maya was sure they would notice her spirit, but Cinnial didn't look up. He was frowning at papers on his desk, and his Book, in a sharp voice, was telling Cinnial that he had better get up to speed, that being in charge of the Great Library was much different than being in charge of one little planet on the outskirts of a small galaxy.

"I realize this," Cinnial replied tersely.

"You'd better ramp up production of our Books and start getting them to other planets."

There was a pause before Cinnial said, "The Great Library's equipment is not as well suited to our Books as our own equipment in Mortmain is."

"Then bring some of our own equipment here," came the edgy response. "And make it work."

Now it was Cinnial's turn to be edgy. "As you know, we've tried. We brought some of the old equipment to the Great Library, but it, too, doesn't work well here. Which means Book production is down until we figure out how to make everything run. Now back off. I'm doing my best."

The Book's tone was softer but no less menacing. "The Great Library's Book is out there, plotting against us. We need to get up to speed."

Maya expected Cinnial to bellow at his Book, but instead he ran a hand over his tired face. "I know."

She sensed that Cinnial's Book was absolutely correct—managing the Great Library and, by extension, the universe, was not as easy as controlling one planet that had been in crisis, ripe for someone like Cinnial, a tyrant, to step in and take over. With a burst of glee, Maya thought, "Uneasy lies the head that wears a crown." Maya also sensed that something else was bothering Cinnial, but she couldn't tell what it was, and she didn't dare look too closely and attract his attention.

Before Cinnial could pull himself away from his own dark thoughts and notice her, Maya flitted to the next office, which had once belonged to Astrid. Julian sat at the desk, and he looked no less frazzled than Cinnial, but his Book was closed on the shelf behind him, and Julian was staring moodily out the open door. As Maya's spirit hovered in the doorway, Julian jumped.

"What are you doing here?" Julian asked. "You're supposed to be in the basement of the Office." Then he peered more closely at her. "I see. Your spirit has left your body."

"Yes," Maya answered neutrally, coming in and hovering in front of Julian's desk. She realized that Bigly had not informed either Cinnial or Julian that she had escaped from the Office. Good. Let Julian think she was still there. She certainly wasn't going to tell him otherwise.

Julian sighed. "Can't blame you for skipping out. Must be hell, what you're going through."

"Yeah," Maya agreed, remembering the pain, and her spirit shuddered involuntarily.

"Why are you here?"

"Oh, I don't know," Maya answered lightly but truthfully. Why had Magic and then Time brought her spirit here? Maya still wasn't sure, but she knew there was a reason. "Just looking around."

Julian frowned sympathetically. "I suppose it's nearly the end for you, and you wanted to come to the Great Library one last time."

"Maybe so," Maya said. It would be even better if Julian thought she was dying and therefore no threat either to him or to Cinnial.

"You don't have any tricks up your sleeves, do you, my girl?" Julian peered at her sharply, as though getting a sense of her thoughts, and Maya knew she had to proceed carefully.

Maya lifted her transparent arms. "These sleeves don't hold much."

Julian smiled. "I guess they don't."

"So how are things going now that Cinnial's in charge?"

Again, Julian peered sharply at her, but Maya kept her thoughts neutral, which was easier to do without her body. Maya understood that her spirit's flickering translucency extended to what she was thinking, making her thoughts as difficult to see as her shadow body.

After a moment's hesitation, Julian shrugged, and Maya knew her ploy had worked. "What difference does it make what I tell you? You'll be dead soon anyway." Maya's thoughts chimed in false agreement, and Julian continued, "Ever since Cinnial killed Sydda and burned the Ancient One, things have not gone according to plan. Book production has nearly halted, and the soldiers and staff don't feel at home here. They're not used to things that are green and growing. They don't like how the Great Library looks like a castle on the outside but is modern and bigger on the inside. And they hate that the center of the library has an atrium with trees, running water, and ferns."

"Must be strange for them," Maya agreed, remembering how cold and barren the city of Mortmain was.

"It is. Then there are the folks across the channel in Watertown."

"What about them?"

"They're just plain odd. They never once protested when Cinnial took over the Great Library. They hardly said anything. And

Cinnial, who can move most anyone with his looks and his talk, doesn't seem to be able to move them. Whenever he holds rallies, they come, and they clap politely when he's done. But nobody cheers and screams the way they did on Tufrak when Cinnial held a rally. And none of us, not even Cinnial, can read the citizens of Watertown. It's as though they are blocked off from us."

"I wonder why," Maya said.

Julian lowered his voice. "I think it's that damned tree, the Ancient One. Cinnial had it chopped down and then burned. It's affected the people somehow. I know it has."

"Have you mentioned this to Cinnial?"

Julian shook his head. "No. He's not in the mood to hear such things. Sometimes it's best just to keep quiet. When Cinnial is angry, someone has to pay. It wouldn't be me. He'd probably take it out on someone lower down the chain of command. And with all the troubles we're having, we don't need that right now. Morale is bad enough as it is."

Maya could feel something—not Time—tugging at her spirit, as though someone was trying to bring her back to Elferterre, and she knew she should leave soon. But there was one more thing Maya needed to see before she returned.

"I've got to go," Maya said as her spirit wavered.

"Yes." Julian's expression was sad. "I don't suppose you have much time left. Maya, I'm sorry it had to end this way for you. If only you had gone along with Cinnial. With your talents, you probably would have been one of his favorites. Maybe even fill in for the daughter he never had. But you just wouldn't give in."

"Nope, that's not me. Sometimes my mémère calls me a *tête de pioche*."

"A what?"

"That's French for stubborn."

Julian smiled a little. "I admire that about you. And Cinnial would, too, if he had paid more attention. But he had his mind on other things."

"Yeah, like taking over the Great Library and killing Sydda."

Julian rubbed his eyes. "Ever since his Book was rejected, Cinnial has been obsessed with taking over the Great Library.

Tufrak wasn't enough for him. No mere planet would have been. It had to be the Great Library. I tried to talk Cinnial out of killing Sydda, but he wouldn't listen. And with Cinnial's Book egging him on, there was nothing I could do."

Maya's spirit was still with sadness, and she saw how sorry Julian was.

"Sydda was our teacher," Julian said. "But I am bound to Cinnial."

"I know," Maya replied, and now she flickered with grief over all that had been lost. She thought about how Julian's life would have been much different if he hadn't decided to follow Cinnial.

Julian's voice was soft, resigned. "I pledged my loyalty many years ago."

"I know that, too. Goodbye, Julian."

"Goodbye, Maya."

She left one parting thought. "Remember, you can still change your mind. You can follow Chance rather than Nemesis. It's your choice."

Maya didn't stay to hear the response. Her spirit zoomed from the Great Library, and the tugging became more insistent, urging her to return to Elferterre. Maya heard a voice say, "Come back! You've been gone too long." It sounded like Will's.

"Not now," she said firmly. "I have one more thing to do. I have to find out what's happening with the people in Watertown."

Instead of returning to Elferterre, Maya zipped across the channel to Watertown. Time seemed to agree; she could feel it guiding her along. The tide was out, and Maya skimmed across the rippled sandbar that was hard enough to walk on during low tide. But nobody was walking across the sandbar, and remembering how empty the Great Library was, Maya understood that the people of Watertown were no longer allowed to check out books. For the first time ever, the Great Library was closed to them.

Maya's spirit was downcast as she thought about what a blow this must be for the people of Watertown. But she knew why Cinnial would do this. For someone who always wanted to be in control, it was dangerous to let people have access to the world of stories and ideas, to have them question and think. Maya knew that as long as Cinnial was in charge, the Great Library would be closed to the citizens of Watertown and beyond.

"Another reason to get him out," Maya thought as she flew past the docks and onto the tidy streets of Watertown, where there were flowers everywhere, and there was a general feeling of comfort. Most of the homes were stone or brick, and while they were not big, they were well taken care of. The people went about their business much the way people did in any small city, and on the roads there were cars powered either by electricity or by some other fuel that did not require an exhaust pipe. Lots of people walked, others rode bikes, and Maya immediately liked Watertown. She could even picture herself living there.

"Of course I like Watertown," Maya thought. "It's near the Great Library."

But then Maya noticed that on the sides of the stores and office buildings, large screens had been set up, and various messages flickered across them. "That's what Cinnial did on Tufrak," Maya reflected, and she stopped by one of them to look more closely.

An image of Cinnial's handsome face came on the screen, and he spoke with passionate intensity about how he and his forces had come to liberate the Great Library, Watertown, all of the planet Bellefour, and indeed the whole universe from the tyranny of Sydda and the Books of Everything. Cinnial paused in his message, and he seemed to be staring directly at Maya and whoever else was listening.

Maya shivered a little, but then she noticed that except for her, nobody else was listening. Or watching. Men, women, and children walked by without even glancing at the screens, and they appeared to be unmoved, unperturbed by what Cinnial was saying.

Cinnial continued, "All these years you have been fed lies by the Great Library. Fake news about how good the Books of Everything are and how they have been sent to help people progress. But what really happens is that planets struggle everywhere across the universe, and the Great Library doesn't lift a finger to help them. Instead, Books are instructed to let people figure things out for themselves, and all the Books do is drop hints now and then. In the meantime, people die because they don't know about germs and antibiotics. On one planet, it took people thousands of years for them to figure out that they had to wash their hands before delivering babies. How many mothers and babies died because of this? Why the hell didn't the Books just tell the people to wash their hands? Would that have been so hard?" Cinnial's jaw was clenched, and he shook his forefinger at whoever might be listening—in this case, Maya. "That kind of tragedy will never happen now that I'm in charge. I can fix things, and I am the only one who can do this. The Books I send will direct people right from the start, and there will be no more senseless deaths."

Cinnial's image went away to be replaced by clean, happy people clustered around a woman with a Book. Gentle but stirring music played as the woman instructed the people, who nodded in agreement. Their blissful expressions indicated that they were the most fortunate folks in the world to be taught by someone who had one of Cinnial's Books.

"Looks good, doesn't it?" said a voice next to Maya.

Maya's spirit jumped. A young man with sandy hair and an upturned nose was standing next to her. He looked to be around eighteen or nineteen, and he was wearing tan overalls and work boots caked with dirt.

"You can see me?" Maya asked in surprise. Maya had supposed that she would be invisible to average people who didn't have the ability to see the way she and Julian could.

"We can all see you," the young man said. Except he wasn't talking. Instead, the young man was communicating with her directly with his thoughts.

Maya studied the man closely and could see a faint glow around him. Glancing around, she saw that other people were watching them closely, and they, too, had a faint glow.

The young man laughed. "I was sent over to discover whether you're a good witch or a bad witch."

Maya laughed, too. "I am not a witch at all."

"We know that. We can tell that we're looking at a spirit, but we're wondering why you're here. By the way, I'm Kip."

"I'm Maya."

"Maya? Oho! We've heard of you. You were the one who was allowed to leave with an Apprentice Book, weren't you?"

With a pang, Maya thought about Ariel. "Yeah, to go to a little planet called Ilyria that's far, far away from here."

The screen had changed again, and one happy scene after another flashed before Maya and Kip as cities were restored, poverty was eradicated, and diseases were cured.

Kip snorted. "What a crock of a story."

"You don't believe Cinnial?"

Kip studied Maya's spirit. "You're here to help, aren't you?"

"I hope so," Maya answered cautiously.

With a frown, Kip regarded the screen. "Cinnial makes it sound as though all he has to do is send a Book to a planet, and everything will be great. But it doesn't work like that, does it? People aren't always ready to hear what the Books have to say. The Books can nudge them in the right direction, but they can't do much more. It can take a long, long time to convince people to go in the right direction. And sometimes it doesn't work at all. Even on Bellefour, our planet."

Maya thought about Sir John, how he had stolen Earth's Book of Everything and left the Forest of Arden, even though the Book had tried to talk him out of it. But Sir John wouldn't budge from his plans. His mind had been made up. "Yeah," Maya said slowly, "you got that right."

"There's only one way you can make people change fast, and that's through force. But Cinnial won't show that picture on his screens."

"It wouldn't exactly help Cinnial's cause," Maya said, "to show soldiers enforcing his orders by killing people and throwing them in jail if they don't listen."

Kip shook his head. "Cinnial says that fake news came from Sydda and the Great Library's Book of Everything, but he is the one spreading lies. His news is fake." He turned to Maya. "Why are you in Watertown?"

"Time and Magic helped me get here. To see what's going on. To see how you've all changed."

Kip confirmed Julian's suspicions. "It's the Ancient One. When the tree was burnt, its ash fell everywhere, on what we ate and what we drank. The tree is a part of all of us now, which means that Cinnial doesn't have any power over us. In fact, we can see him better than he can see us."

Maya was about to respond, but she heard a firm voice call, "Maya Hammond! Come back to Elferterre now. You've already been gone too long." Maya knew that voice, but somehow she had forgotten whom it belonged to.

"I have to go," Maya said uneasily to Kip.

"Your spirit needs to return to your body," Kip agreed.

"But I'll be back," Maya said. "Next time with my body. And when I do, I'll need your help."

"I'll be ready, and so will a lot of the others. We'll come up with a plan. My house is on 15 Oak Street. Come find me. If you don't remember, I bet Time will help you."

"All right."

The voice called again. "Maya, come back. Please!" Maya heard a note of desperation in the voice.

Maya said, "See you later, Kip."

Kip smiled. "See you, Maya."

Maya's spirit flew upward, and she took one last loving look at the Great Library, at the bright white walls and the towers that soared high.

"Maya!" the voice called.

"Coming!" Maya replied. But who was calling her? Was it Andy? No, not Andy. He was now President Murphy, and his voice was deeper than the one that was calling her. Unsure of where to go or what to do, Maya's spirit hovered above the Great Library. Maybe she should just stay here, where she knew she belonged.

"I can stay in Watertown with Kip," Maya thought. "I remember him. And 15 Oak Street."

But something gathered her hesitant spirit, something Maya had felt before. "Time," came a deep whisper, both inside her head and everywhere.

"That's right," Maya said. "Time." She had felt it guide her before, and she knew she would feel it again.

"Will you take me back?" Maya whispered. "I don't remember where I'm supposed to go."

"Yes," came the answer.

Wrapped tightly by Time, Maya's spirit soared back the way it had come, past stars, through galaxies, past Earth. She came to the dark passage, and Time passed her to another force, Magic, which crackled and tingled around her as it led her back to Elferterre.

"Time and Magic are helping each other," Maya thought in a daze.

"Maya!" There was that voice again. It was stronger now. Maya could hear it clearly, but she still couldn't remember whose voice it was.

Magic released Maya, and she fell into her waiting body.

"For God's sake, Maya. Come back!"

Maya opened her eyes. And there, staring at her, was a teenage boy, his expression tense and fearful.

Then Maya remembered. "Will," she whispered.

"Thank God," he said, choking a little as he held her close. "You're back."

"Give her some air," a voice commanded. Maya saw it was Lucius, the elf with the top hat, and he, too, looked concerned. Will reluctantly pulled away, and Lucius said, "You must have taken quite a journey."

"I did," Maya replied. She was still whispering. It seemed that was all she could manage.

Leaning over, Jay squeezed her shoulder. "Welcome back, Captain Hammond."

"Thanks," came the raspy reply.

Jay stepped aside, and Lexie stood by Maya. Her face was wet with tears, and her eyes glittered with anxiety, anger, and affection. "What a little pain you are! You had us worried sick."

Maya tried to grin, but she could feel that the edges of her mouth had only lifted slightly. "Sorry."

"You'd better be." With a quick motion, Lexie kissed her, except it wasn't on the cheek. It was square on the lips.

Maya blinked at the blonde girl as Will exclaimed, "Lexie, what the hell!"

Lexie jumped back. "I'm just glad to see her, that's all," she said in a rush. "I didn't mean anything by it."

Will glared at Lexie. "You'd better not."

Lucius intervened. "You two can sort this out later. Right now, Maya needs to recover."

"How long have I been out?" Maya asked.

"Too long," Lucius replied crisply. "We really did think we had lost you. But here you are."

"I nearly was lost," Maya murmured. "I traveled from this universe to my own universe and then back again. Both Time and Magic helped me."

For a moment, Lucius looked surprised. "Working together, were they? That hardly ever happens. I'm assuming it was worth the trip."

Looking at the anxious faces of her friends, Maya whispered, "Yes. Yes, it was."

21: Watched

Once Maya had recovered enough to stand—with the help of a sweet-tasting liquid that Lucius had assured her wasn't a potion—Will helped her to a little cart waiting outside the tent. Lucius, Jay, and Lexie followed them.

"Bring the cart back when you're done," Lucius said after Maya was settled, and Will was in the driver's seat.

"All right," Will replied, pushing a button that started the engine.

Lucius patted Maya's shoulder. "You may be small, but you can certainly travel."

"I sure can," Maya agreed wearily. This trip had been even worse than the last, when she had escaped from Bigly and the Office. At least then she hadn't nearly forgotten who she was.

"You'll be all right," Lucius said briskly. "Going across two universes is bound to take it out of you."

Despite her fatigue, Maya grinned at Lucius. "Yup."

Lucius grinned back. "There's a good little human." Will glowered at the elf, and Lucius waved him off. "Don't give me that look. You know I admire her. And that's saying a lot. I don't admire many elves, never mind humans. Now take Maya back to Ehren and Tagen's campsite."

Shaking his head, Will drove away, leaving Jay and Lexie to follow behind on foot. It was early morning, and except for a few elves and humans checking their tents, the fairgrounds were empty.

"I was out all night?" Maya asked, her voice a little stronger.

"Oh, no," Will said grimly. "You were out longer than that. You were gone two nights and a day in between. We had to tell Ehren and Tagen, and they were as worried as we were. They stayed with us a while but had to get some sleep and then go to their tent. Lexie, Jay, and I took turns being with you."

Maya leaned wearily against the seat. "I'm sorry to have worried everyone."

Will glanced at her. "Yeah. That's how it is with you, isn't it?"

Maya sighed. "I'm afraid so."

"And I just have to get used to it?"

"I don't know, Will," Maya said slowly. "I can't see everything. I only get flashes. But this is how it is right now."

Will took a deep breath. "It isn't easy being with you."

Maya touched his cheek. "I know."

Will leaned against her hand. "I've never been so scared in my life. Even Lucius thought you might not come back."

"Time and Magic helped me," Maya said. "And so did you. I heard your voice calling me."

"Across that distance?" Will asked in amazement.

"Across that distance. Except I couldn't remember who you were. I was beginning to forget everything. My spirit was gone from my body too long."

Will was silent, and Maya could tell that he was thinking about all that had happened. "And we haven't even completed our mission," Maya thought.

"No kidding," came Will's grim thought in reply.

The motion of the cart lulled Maya to sleep, and she woke up when they stopped beside Ehren's truck and trailer, which were parked beside a large stand of trees. Many other trucks and trailers were parked on either side, stretching in a long line beside the trees. Ehren and Tagen were sitting on stools by a small fire pit, and when they saw Maya and Will, they leaped up, rushing toward the cart. Not speaking, they both hugged Maya, and when they were done, Ehren lifted her from the cart and brought her inside the trailer, where a cot was set up.

"Isn't this where Tagen sleeps?" Maya asked wearily, barely able to keep her eyes open.

Ehren kissed her forehead. "Don't you worry about that. Just rest. Mother can sleep in the backseat of the truck."

"Where will you sleep?"

"Out with Will, Jay, and Lexie. I'll be just fine. Really I will." He kissed her again on the forehead and patted her cheek.

Feeling safe and cared for, Maya smiled as she fell asleep. When she woke up, the light was bright, and she judged it was early afternoon. Will was sitting on a stool beside the cot.

Maya smiled at him. "I haven't slept a whole day, have I?" she asked, glad that her voice was no longer a whisper.

Will smiled back. "No. It's still the same day as when you came back. It's early afternoon."

Maya sighed. "Good."

Will kissed her on the forehead, on the cheeks, then on the lips. "Where did you go when your spirit left your body?" he asked gently.

"To the Great Library."

Pulling away, Will sat up straight. "What the hell! No wonder you were gone so long."

Sitting up, Maya laughed. "Right?"

"It really wasn't funny." But Will's expression was soft as he considered her, and Maya could tell that now that she was safe, his anxiety for her was slowly fading.

"I know. But, Will, it was so worthwhile to go to the Great Library."

"What did you find out?" a voice asked. It was Jay, and he and Lexie were standing in the doorway.

"Come in," Maya said. "And I'll tell you."

Jay and Lexie settled on the floor by the cot, and Maya told them what she had discovered at the Great Library—that things weren't going well for Cinnial, both at the Great Library and in Watertown, the small city across the sandbar.

Maya said, "Cinnial burned a tree called the Ancient One, and when he did, all the people in Watertown got some of it in their bodies."

"How?" Jay asked.

"Ashes fell on the water and on their food in their gardens." Maya pictured the glittering ash coating everything. "They ate it and drank it."

Lexie shuddered. "That sounds creepy."

"In a way, I suppose it is," Maya replied slowly. "But it's changed them, and that's a good thing. This means that Cinnial can't influence them the way he usually does with people. When he lies, it doesn't matter. The people of Watertown are able to see right through them." Will, Jay, and Lexie didn't say anything as they considered this. Maya ran her hand through her curls, and her face was bright. "I met a guy named Kip. He could see my spirit, and he communicated to me with his thoughts. He and other people in the city are going to help me when the time comes."

"That is good," Jay agreed.

"How is Kip going to help you?" Lexie asked.

"I'm not sure. But now that Kip knows about me, he'll be thinking about ways to help. He told me where he lived so that I could go there when I go back to the Great Library."

"Go back?" Will asked.

"Yes, Will," Maya answered softly. "Who did you think was going to trap Cinnial?"

Will shook his head. "I don't know, but I didn't think it would be you. I figured you'd give the lock to someone older, someone more experienced from the Great Library."

Maya was silent for a moment as she thought about how much she should reveal about the Books' strategies. Maya decided to be honest, and she regarded Will, Jay, and Lexie, who had all become dear to her despite the short time they had been together. "In the long run, the Books of Everything are good, but they use children. Mostly teenagers. It throws off the adults, who dismiss us, especially when they're as small as I am."

Jay smirked. "Nobody should dismiss Captain Hammond."

"That's for sure," Lexie agreed. "No matter what she's wearing."

They all laughed.

Maya continued, "Cinnial and his Book will be on the lookout for a force to take back the Great Library. They won't expect me. As far as they're concerned, I'm in the basement in the Office, and my time is nearly up. Cinnial and his Book won't bother keeping track of what I'm doing. They have bigger things to think of."

"How do you know this?" Will asked.

"I talked to Julian at the Great Library. He thought I was still at the Office. Bigly hasn't told them yet about my disappearance."

"Probably doesn't dare to," Jay said.

"Probably not," Maya agreed. "And I hope that little worm never does."

Will frowned. "I wonder if Julian will tell Cinnial that your spirit visited the Great Library."

"I don't think he will," Maya answered. "He's changed in ways nobody expected, not even Julian himself."

After explaining so much, Maya felt weary, and she slumped against her pillow. "I need to sleep again, and I probably will on and off for a couple of days. Sorry, but that's the way it is when I travel so far without a Book to help me."

"That's all right," Will said, touching her cheek. "The fair goes on for two weeks. We still have plenty of time."

"Good," Maya replied. "But before I sleep, I'd like to talk to Lexie. Alone."

Shrugging, Will stood, and Jay did, too. Following Jay to the door, Will paused as though he wanted to say something. But Will remained silent as he went outside.

Lexie sat down on the stool where Will had been sitting. "Well," she said.

"Well," Maya agreed, and the two girls stared at each other.

Lexie grimaced. "I feel as though I've been called to the principal's office."

"I'm not that bad, am I?" Maya asked.

"No, not that bad," Lexie agreed, smiling nervously. "But almost."

Maya decided to come straight to the point. "You like girls as well as boys?"

"I guess I do," Lexie answered slowly. "I really hadn't thought about it that much until it looked as though you were gone and were never coming back. It scared me so much. It scared us all. It was such a relief when your spirit returned to your body that I just had to kiss you. I meant it to be a kiss on the cheek."

"But it wasn't," Maya said gently.

"No, and it surprised me as much as it surprised everyone else. Then I knew. Actually, I think I've known for quite a while, but I didn't want to admit it. I've always liked being around girls. A lot. This sure doesn't fit in with my mother's plans for me, which have always involved having a good-looking husband." Lexie frowned. "Someone like Will. Maybe even Will. Mom was always after me to go out with him. Both of our families have a lot of money and influence, and if Will and I got married, then we'd have even more."

Maya put her hand on Lexie's arm. "When you go back to New York, your mother is going to be in for a big surprise. Not just about that but about other things as well."

Lexie sighed. "No kidding. I'm not looking forward to it."

"I don't blame you. But you'll do all right."

"I hope so," Lexie said, biting her bottom lip.

Maya patted Lexie's arm. "You will."

Lexie put her hand over Maya's hand. "And about the kiss? It won't happen again. While I like to be in charge and probably always will, I'm not going to push myself on anyone ever again the way I did with Will." Her expression was firm. "Ever." Then her expression became rueful. "But I did love him, even though he really does seem to be the one for you."

"I know," Maya replied, squeezing Lexie's arm. "As for Will..." Maya paused. "At the Great Library, I could hear him calling to me. Across two universes."

"That has to mean something."

"Yeah, but I don't know what. Don't forget that we come from different times." Maya's eyelids fluttered, and she settled against her pillow. "I have to sleep now. Sorry."

"Don't be sorry. Sleep, and we'll all watch out for you while you do. When you're rested, we'll tell you what we saw. It will help with our mission here."

"Good," Maya mumbled as she fell asleep. "And thanks so much."

Maya was aware that Lexie patted her cheek before leaving. In her pocket, Maya felt the warmth of the little dragon through the box, and somehow it soothed her as she fell asleep. In her own box, Orlaith moved back and forth, but instead of being afraid of the spider, Maya felt comforted to know she was there, too.

First, Maya dreamed about the dragon. She saw Aiken soar through the air. Soon Maya was soaring, too, as though she were a dragon. Flames shot from her mouth, and she burned twigs and leaves that had fallen on the ground, leaving a little trail of fire as she went.

"I don't want to start a fire," Maya thought with alarm.

"Relax," Aiken's crisp voice instructed. "This is just a dream. I'm showing you what the fire can do."

Aiken's fire was small, but it burned white hot with precision, going in a straight line wherever he wanted it to go, even through a spell of woven magic used to protect a warehouse on the edge of the city.

Then Orlaith showed Maya what she could do. What Aiken burned, Orlaith wove and repaired, and when she was done, the spell looked the way it had before turning to cinders.

"No wonder you two cost so much," Maya said with wonder. Aiken proudly blew tiny round smoke puffs, and Orlaith's eyes glittered with pleasure.

On the edge of her dream, someone was watching her movements, but Maya only caught a shadowy glimpse.

"A spy," Orlaith said. "We have to be careful."

"I always have to be careful," Maya thought regretfully, remembering how easy everything had been before she had gotten involved with the Books of Everything. She had never worried that anyone was spying on her.

"We'll be with you," Aiken said. "And so will the others. You won't be alone."

Somewhat comforted, Maya settled into a deep sleep that had no dreams.

When Maya woke up, Tagen was sitting by her side, and she asked, "Thirsty?"

"I am." Dreaming about all that fire had parched her lips.

Tagen picked up a mug on the floor by the stool and passed it to Maya. "Drink this."

Maya hesitated. "What is it?"

Tagen smiled. "Don't worry. It's not a potion. It's just a tonic, a little pick-me-up that I made from flowers, weeds, and herbs in and around my garden. I brought some for me and Ehren. There are long days here at the Gathering, and by the end we sometimes need a pick-me-up."

Taking a sip, Maya made a face. "Bitter."

"I know. Just drink it. You'll be glad you did."

Maya drank it all, shuddering when she was done. "Tagen, that tastes awful."

Tagen patted Maya's shoulder. "Never mind. You'll feel better soon."

Tagen was right. Within moments, Maya did feel better, and she sat up in surprise. "Will it last?" Maya asked.

"It should," Tagen answered. "But if it doesn't, I have more."

"Where are the others?"

"Lexie is helping Ehren. That girl sure knows how to sell things. Lexie has a knack. I swear we sell twice as much when she's at the table. And she never lets anyone talk her down. With elves as well as humans. And that is no small thing here on Elferterre." Tagen sniffed. "Those elves think they are so much better than we are."

Grinning, Maya removed Aiken's and Orlaith's boxes from the pocket of her trousers. She opened the boxes, and the dragon and the spider blinked at them before crawling out and settling beside Maya. "The elves who sold these two wanted four bags of chamomile tea," Maya said.

"Four bags," Tagen marveled, considering Aiken and Orlaith. "Still, they are wonders and look as though they are worth it."

As Aiken chirped with pleasure, and Orlaith waved a dainty leg at Tagen, Maya replied, "Yeah, that's what I thought. But Lexie talked the elves down to two bags."

"She has her talents, doesn't she?" Tagen asked. "Even though she can't see as well as you, Will, and Jay."

"She does," Maya agreed. "And to think Myranda and I thought that Lexie shouldn't have her eyes peeled because it wouldn't be worth it. And where are Will and Jay?"

Tagen laughed. "Where do you think? Getting something to eat. I'll bet they'll bring something back for you, too."

"Good." Maya pressed her hand to her grumbling stomach. "I'm hungry."

A little while later, Will and Jay came back with bags and bags of food, more than enough to feed six people.

As they unpacked boxes and packets, Will said sheepishly, "We bought way more than we should have."

Jay sighed. "But it all looked so good."

Will passed a container and a wooden spoon to Maya. "I bought this for you."

Inside was a fragrant noodle soup, flavorful but not too spicy. "Perfect," Maya said after sipping from the spoon. "Thank you."

Tagen left, taking two boxes of spicy beans and rice, and Lexie soon returned. Will and Jay brought in two more stools from the campfire and set them up next to the other stool. For a while, nobody said anything. They just sat and ate—black, blonde, and brown heads bent toward the food. As Maya watched them, she blinked to keep herself from crying. Maya felt safe and secure, surrounded by people who not only cared about her but understood her as well.

"What?" Will asked, looking up from his food.

"I'm so glad you're all here," Maya answered softly. "I couldn't do this without you."

"Aw, shucks!" Jay said, grinning affectionately at her.

"Someone has to keep you in line," Lexie said.

"I wouldn't want to be anywhere else," Will added firmly, and Jay and Lexie nodded.

Maya swallowed. "All right. Now tell me what you saw when your spirits left your bodies."

"We didn't leave Elferterre," Lexie said. "We didn't even leave Foretcour."

Will set his empty container on the floor. "But we scoped out Galli's house and the surrounding area. And we have a plan."

"Tell me," Maya said, leaning forward. Beside her, on the blanket, the little dragonfly and spider eagerly leaned forward, too, listening to what Will, Jay, and Lexie had to say.

And at the edge of the field, far enough away not to be easily noticed, a man with pale hair watched Ehren's trailer.

22: The Man with the Pale Hair

The next morning, Maya felt much better and didn't need another dose of Tagen's pick-me-up. "Thank God," Maya thought with a shudder, remembering the bitter taste. She felt well enough to join the others outside. On a table by the trailer, underneath a canopy, was a camping stove with three burners and a griddle where Ehren was cooking sprite cakes. At the other end of the table, Tagen was lining up mugs for tea, and on one of the burners, a kettle was steaming. Clustered on stools around the fire pit, Jay, Will, and Lexie sat and waited eagerly.

As Maya came out of the trailer, Jay clapped. "She emerges!"

Maya blushed.

Lexie gave her a critical look. "There are showers here. After we eat, I'll show you where they are."

Maya blushed even more, realizing how ragged she must look.

Will smiled at her but didn't say anything.

Tagen waved her hand at Lexie. "I'd like to see what you'd look like after your spirit traveled across two universes."

Laughing, Lexie pointed at Tagen. "Touché! I wouldn't look any better. Maybe even worse. My hair is so fine it would be tangled like a rat's nest if I stayed in a chair for two nights waiting for my spirit to come back."

Sitting down on an empty stool, Maya looked around for Hanss, but she didn't see him. With a start, Maya realized she hadn't seen him since the night they had left Tagen and Ehren's tent to explore the fair. "Where's Hanss?"

Jay shrugged. "Don't know. We haven't seen him since we got here."

"I hope he's all right," Maya said, and she could tell Jay was worried about Hanss, too.

"I bet he is," Tagen replied as she poured hot water into the mugs.

Ehren flipped a batch of sprite cakes. "Probably running around with his own kind. I wouldn't worry about him. With that lot, he'll be safe."

"His own kind?" Jay asked. "And what do you mean by that lot?"

Tagen laughed. "Remember when we told you the grounds were well guarded? Have you seen big cats roaming around?"

"Yeah," Jay answered cautiously.

Ehren grinned. "That's the cat patrol, and they guard the fairgrounds."

"Cats?" Lexie asked incredulously. "What can a bunch of cats do?"

"These cats can do quite a bit," Ehren replied. "And some of them can fly, so there are eyes in the air as well as on the ground. Not to mention claws and teeth. Most of them are larger than Hanss, who's a pretty big cat."

For a while none of the teenagers knew what to say as they pictured a pack of guard cats, larger than Hanss, in the air and on the ground. Finally, Maya laughed. "After all, this is Elferterre."

The others grinned, and Lexie said, "Our new favorite saying."

With a spatula in hand, Ehren regarded them. "I'm guessing there are no guard cats where you come from."

Will smiled. "Nope. And no flying cats either."

"How long should we wait for Hanss?" Jay asked. "We'd like to leave today."

"I bet he'll turn up soon," Tagen answered. "And if he comes here after you've left, we'll tell him where you're going first. He'll know how to find you. Hanss knows this city very well."

Jay sighed. "I hate to leave without him. But we don't have any way of letting him know."

"And we need to get going," Maya added. She had the uneasy feeling that they had been spied on, but there didn't seem to be anyone around now, making it a good time to leave.

Ehren smiled sadly, but he only said, "The first batch of sprite cakes are ready."

In a flash, the teenagers jumped up from their stools to gather plates, napkins, and forks that were set up on another smaller table. To go on the sprite cakes were butter, berries, and a special syrup that tasted a lot like maple syrup but was also different. The teenagers ate as Ehren cooked another full batch. After he and his mother had helped themselves, he said, "There are some left if anyone wants them. And I can make more afterwards if you're still hungry."

Will and Jay had finished their sprite cakes and looked questioningly at Maya and Lexie, who were still eating theirs. Her mouth full, Maya shook her head, and Lexie said, "Go on. Take them. You know it's what you want to do."

Will and Jay didn't ask twice. It wasn't long before they were sitting down again and digging into their second helpings. When they were done, Ehren made yet another batch, and there were no leftovers.

For a while nobody said anything. Tagen and Ehren glanced at each other and then looked around. On both sides of them, the vendors had left to go to their tents. It wouldn't be long before the fair opened for the day, and Maya knew that Tagen and Ehren would soon be leaving to go to their tent. It was also time for Maya, Will, Jay, and Lexie to leave, and everyone looked sad.

Ehren cleared his throat. "You kids have a plan?"

"Yeah," said Will. "We talked about it last night."

"Good," Tagen said. "And we have our story. You're a bunch of kids we picked up hitchhiking on the way to the Gathering. You stayed with us a couple nights and helped out a bit. Then you left. That's all we know."

"I hope it's enough," Maya murmured, thinking about what would happen if Ehren and Tagen were taken in for questioning.

Ehren shrugged. "If it isn't, it isn't. We need to do our part. After all, this is our land, too, no matter what some of the elves might think."

"Do you need food?" Tagen asked, ever practical.

"No," Maya answered. "We still have most of the supplies we were given before we came here." Although nobody seemed to be around to overhear them, Maya was reluctant to mention Pawel's name. Just in case.

"You still have enough…" Ehren paused. "Resources?"

"We do," Lexie said. "We've only spent about half of what we brought."

Ehren regarded them all. "I have enough money to give you in exchange for some of what you have. With Lexie helping, we sold far more than we expected. It will look less suspicious if you pay for what you need with our currency."

"Thanks," Maya said. "We were told to find a money changer, but this will be better."

"Safer," Tagen agreed, tenderly surveying the teenagers. "I'm going to miss all of you. What a good bunch of kids you are. And so brave. You know where to find us if you ever come back."

Maya swallowed. "We do."

Lexie looked tearful, and Will and Jay nodded sadly. Maya knew that like her, they all appreciated Ehren's and Tagen's help and how it would have been much harder to get to Foretcour without their aid. But along with helping, Tagen and Ehren had opened up their home and their hearts, and the teenagers would never forget this generosity.

Tagen sniffed. "Well, guess we'd better clean up before we go to the tent."

"Don't worry about that," Jay said. "We'll clean up."

"I won't say no," Tagen said with a sad smile. "We're running a little late."

Before Tagen and Ehren left, there were tears, hugs, and kisses. In the trailer, chamomile tea was exchanged for coins and bills, and each of the teenagers had a sizable stash that they tucked in pouches in their backpacks. Tagen pressed a key into Maya's hand. "Just in case you need somewhere to stay on the way back," she whispered. By that time it was midmorning, and Tagen and Ehren had to hurry to their tent. They looked back once before disappearing among the other tents. They waved at the teenagers, who waved back, and then the two were gone.

Surveying the jumble of dirty plates and mugs, Lexie cleared her throat. "All right. Time to clean up this mess."

But Jay said, "Why don't you two go to the showers? Will and I got up early, and we already took ours. We'll do the dishes while you're taking your showers."

Lexie grinned. "That's an offer I'm not going to refuse. Come on, Maya, before they change their minds."

Lexie took Maya to a tent not far away that had been set up as temporary showers. For two silver coins given to a small creature who looked like a goblin, Maya and Lexie received towels, washcloths, and small packets of soap for both body and hair. Inside the tent were stalls with benches and hooks, and as the warm water ran over Maya's head and body, she thought that it had never felt so good to take a shower.

When Lexie and Maya returned, the dishes were done, the campsite was tidy, and they all packed their bags. Will took the ball Pawel had given him and put it in his pocket. Jay plucked a couple of the mandolin's strings to see if the instrument was still in tune. It was. Aiken and Orlaith were waiting on Maya's cot.

"Where would you like to be?" Maya asked them.

"In one of your pockets but not in our boxes," Orlaith answered. "It's best that nobody sees us, but you want to be able to easily get to us. You can put us in the same pocket. We're small. There will be plenty of room for both of us, and we don't mind being close together."

Aiken blew a snort of steam in approval, and into one of Maya's side pockets they went. As she put their boxes in her pack, Maya could feel the small creatures settle into place and nestle against her leg next to the velvet pouch with the money. There was another box in her pack, and Maya could hear a slight hum as the bee reminded Maya about her presence. Frowning, Maya took out the box but was reluctant to remove the bee. She slid the box into the other side pocket. With a shiver, Maya thought about what it would be like to use the bee to kill someone.

"Only if I don't have another choice," Maya murmured aloud. She patted her pocket. "You're a last resort." The box buzzed loudly in response.

After packing, the teenagers consulted the map and headed toward the main gate that faced the center of Foretcour. The gates had opened, and crowds streamed into the fairgrounds. Once again, Maya was struck by the diversity of the fairgoers. There were humans and elves and all sorts of other creatures—some big, some small, some shaggy with hair, and some completely bald. On four square posts, two on either side of the entrance, sat four winged cats on small platforms. The cats were bigger than Hanss—Maya guessed they were the size of lynxes and weighed at least forty pounds. With narrow eyes, they surveyed the crowd coming in, and the big cats occasionally flexed their sharp curved claws, reminding fairgoers of what they would face if they got out of line.

Will whistled as he looked at the guard cats. "I wouldn't want to mess with those guys."

"Me, neither," Maya agreed quickly.

Lexie's eyes were wide. "Same here."

With a wrinkled brow, Jay regarded a large black cat that was nearest to them. "I wonder if they know where Hanss is."

"You could always ask," Maya suggested doubtfully.

Jay's laugh was shaky. "Yeah."

But the black guard cat had heard them, and with a paw filled with those gleaming nails, he motioned for them to go over to a section of the fence away from the entrance where there weren't many people. The teenagers hurried to that section, and with a strong but graceful flap of the wings, the guard cat joined them.

"You're with Hanss?" the guard cat asked, his voice deep and low.

"Yeah," Jay answered. "It's time for us to go, and we thought he might want to know. We hate to leave without Hanss, but we haven't seen him for several days."

The guard cat rumbled, and it almost sounded like a laugh. "Hanss has been having a good time. Maybe too good. And he's needed a lot of sleep to recover. But he'll want to know that you're leaving. Don't worry. He'll get the message."

"How will Hanss know where we are?" Jay asked.

The guard cat looked at Jay. "The guard will keep track."

"Of course you will," Jay replied quickly, taking a step back.

The guard cat rumbled again, and his voice was softer. "Don't worry. You have nothing to fear from me. I know you are a friend of cats."

Jay's voice was nearly a squeak. "How did you know this?"

"I could just tell." He glanced at Maya, Will, and Lexie. "You three, not so much."

"I like cats," Will protested.

"So do I," Maya said.

"H-m-m-m," came the guard cat's noncommittal response.

Lexie shrugged. "I prefer dogs."

With narrow eyes, the guard cat regarded Lexie. "I know that, too. Anyway, Hanss will get the message. You may go on your way. Hanss will be able to find you without any trouble." Without saying anything more, the guard cat flapped his strong wings and flew back to his perch, where he resumed surveying the crowd.

"Wow," said Will.

"That is some cat," Maya added.

Even Lexie was impressed. "No kidding."

Jay didn't say anything as he stared in bemused admiration at the four guard cats sitting on the posts.

Will clapped him on the shoulder. "Come on, Bud. Let's go."

"I'm glad those cats are on our side," Jay finally said as they walked through the gates.

Did one of the guard cats—a smaller tabby with blue eyes—wink at him? Jay was sure she had, and although none of the others saw it, they nodded in agreement when he mentioned it as they left the fairgrounds and headed into the city.

Lexie gave Jay an affectionate nudge. "After all, you're the one who's a friend of cats."

Grinning, Jay returned the nudge.

After briefly consulting the map, the four teenagers saw that their first stop was nearby and within easy walking distance.

"I'm a little nervous about this," Maya said as they went past warehouses.

Will shook his head. "You've gone across two universes. Why should this faze you?"

"I don't know," Maya replied. "It just does."

"Me, too," Lexie admitted.

Jay rubbed his hands together. "I'm looking forward to it."

"So am I," Will said.

"This isn't a video game," Lexie tartly reminded them. "It'll take a lot more than just pushing a button and swearing when things go wrong."

"I think there might be a lot of swearing," Maya added and was about to say more when the hairs on the back of her neck prickled. Someone was following them. She could feel it. Stopping, Maya turned around. The street was empty except for them, but there were plenty of alleyways leading off from the streets.

Lexie shivered. "I feel it, too."

"Yeah," Will said, and Jay frowned. Stopping, they all scanned the street, but there was nobody in sight. Will motioned with his head to the alleyway to their immediate right, and the other three nodded, following Will's lead as he slipped into it.

Straining to listen, hardly daring to breathe, they all waited. Maya was certain she heard footsteps, soft but steady, coming their way. Moments later a child walked by the alleyway. She was meticulously dressed in a silver tunic and skirt. Her long blonde hair was brushed smooth, and at first it looked as though she might go by without noticing them. But then the child stopped, looking directly at them, and Maya knew who it was.

"Nemesis," Maya said to herself.

The child smiled disdainfully at such an obvious remark. Turning back toward the street, Nemesis nodded, and then she was gone.

They heard more footsteps creeping, creeping toward them, and finally a man stood by the entrance to the alleyway. It was the man with the pale hair that Maya had seen in the field by Myranda's cottage. He was holding a small silver gun, and he pointed the gun right at them.

"Come out," the man commanded. "Now."

Reluctantly, the four teenagers left their hiding place. As she regarded the man, Maya sensed his resolve to capture rather than kill them.

Maya stepped forward. "You're not going to shoot us, are you?"

"Not unless I have to," the man answered, staring at Maya. "For someone so small, you've certainly caused a lot of trouble."

Maya shook her head. "What exactly have I done? I stayed in Arbor City. I've come to the Summer Gathering. Are those two things a crime?"

"Don't pretend to be innocent," the man said. Although he was younger and had brown eyes rather than light blue, there was something about him that reminded her of Chet, and Maya knew she had to proceed carefully. The man frowned at her and then at the others. "You've been with Myranda. You've traveled with Ehren and his mother. Worst of all, Hanss was with you even though he isn't here now, and that alone is enough to incriminate all four of you."

"How do you know this?" Maya asked.

"Because I've tracked you all the way from Arbor City. I waited, and I watched, even though you didn't see me."

Yes. There it was. The man with the pale hair was a tracker just like Chet and had the same ability to elude being noticed.

Will stepped forward, flanked by Jay and Lexie. "There are four of us and only one of you."

The man smiled. "True. But I wonder how many of you I could shoot if you tried to take me down. One? Two? Three? Even four? I'm pretty fast, and so is this gun. Do you want to risk it?" Knowing they didn't, he motioned with the gun. "Let's get going. I have a vehicle parked nearby, and we're going to go for a little ride."

Maya's thoughts raced as she considered the possibilities. Aiken was in her pocket. Could his fire help them? Perhaps he could blind this man with the pale hair.

Will's thoughts chimed in, "I have the ball in one of my pockets."

But before either Maya or Will could respond, she heard a flapping sound. Looking up, Maya saw four guard cats speeding toward them. The man with the pale hair heard it, too, and spinning around, he aimed his gun at the ginger cat who was in the lead.

"No!" Maya yelled, slamming into him with all the force she could muster, and while she didn't knock him over, she did make the man drop his gun. As the gun fell, it went off, and a small beam tore a big hole into the road. Maya shuddered as she thought about what that beam would have done to a person. Or a guard cat.

Then the cats flew onto the man with the pale hair, and they tore into him with such ruthless efficiency that he only had time to cry out twice before he fell to the ground and lay still as his blood pooled around him. Aghast, Will, Jay, and Lexie stared at his body.

Maya, too, was shaken, even though she had seen other violent deaths. "Did you have to kill him?" Maya asked the ginger cat, who seemed to be the leader.

"We did," the ginger cat responded, regarding her coolly. "Captain Isling's orders. He told us to kill anyone who might be following you as we brought Hanss to you."

"Captain Isling?" Maya asked.

"The big black cat at the gate," a smaller gray cat answered. "You spoke to him as you were leaving."

"Of course!" Jay exclaimed.

The gray cat continued, "This man would have taken you straight to Tamick Ashglade. And that would have been that."

"It certainly would have," a familiar voice said. Hanss had joined them, and he was slightly out of breath from running.

"Hanss!" Jay called joyfully. "You're back."

"Good to see you," Will said, as though he were at a social gathering.

"Sure is," Maya put in, relieved to see Hanss.

"What took you so long?" Lexie asked, but along with the others, she was smiling.

23: Two Wheels and Four Hooves

After thanking the guard cats and leaving them to take care of the body—none of the teenagers wanted to think too much about that—Maya, Will, Jay, Lexie, and Hanss continued down the street. Hanss looked perky, and he walked with his bushy tail straight up.

"You were gone for a long time," Jay said, a note of rebuke in his voice.

"I was," Hanss agreed. "But the guard was on the lookout for you, and I knew you wouldn't be able to leave without them noticing."

"We were worried about you," Maya said, her tone milder than Jay's.

Hanss was silent for a few moments. "I'm sorry. I haven't been to the Summer Gathering in quite a while, and it was wonderful to catch up with old friends. I knew you were in good hands, but I shouldn't have been gone for so long." Hanss gave a delicate cough. "I didn't plan to be, but somehow it just happened."

Lexie laughed. "Did you have a good time?"

Hanss purred. "I did."

"We had quite a time, too," Will said. "We went to a tent and met an elf named Lucius. He gave us a potion that made our spirits leave our bodies. We learned a lot, and now we have plans."

Jay rubbed his hands together. "And our first plan involves wheels. Big ones"

The cat's tail drooped at the end. "Dear Magic, no. Have any of you ever driven?"

The teenagers were silent. "I drove Lucius's cart," Will finally said.

Hanss shook his head. "But you're not talking about a cart, are you?"

"No," Jay admitted. "Something much cooler. And bigger. And faster."

Will couldn't keep the glee out of his voice. "Gyrocycles. We have enough money to buy two."

Hanss stopped. "Are you out of your minds? You could get us all killed on those things."

Despite her own reservations about riding on a gyrocycle, Maya came to Will's defense. "Hanss, how are we supposed to get back to Darkwood Forest? It took us nearly two days of steady driving from Arbor City. We can't fly. And we need to move fast as soon as we complete our mission." Maya looked around, and even though the streets were still empty, Maya decided to be cautious about what she said. "We can't just hang around and wait to hitch a ride back with our friends. Or even worse, walk."

Hanss sighed. "You're right. But oh my whiskers, I don't like this idea. Not one bit."

Maya couldn't blame the cat. She didn't like it either. But the day before, Will and Jay had argued fervently in favor of buying gyrocycles for their journey back to Darkwood Forest. That night in Lucius's tent, when their spirits had left their bodies, Will, Jay, and Lexie had found a shop that sold gyrocycles not far from the fairgrounds. They had slipped in, looked around, and noted the prices. While Maya had rested from her own adventures, Will and Jay had discussed with Ehren the pros and cons of buying gyrocycles. When Maya heard that Ehren supported—albeit reluctantly—the plan, she also agreed, even though she had misgivings and could tell that Lexie did as well.

"And guess who gets to drive?" Lexie asked, looking from Will to Jay to Hanss.

Will and Jay had the decency to look sheepish.

"It was our idea," Jay said defensively.

"And you two were lukewarm about it right from the start," Will added.

"So it seems only fair," Jay finished.

"It seems sexist," Lexie replied firmly, "that the boys should drive and the girls should ride as passengers."

Will and Jay were about to continue the argument, but Maya held up her hand. "Lexie, you're right. And so are you, Will and Jay. But we don't have time to argue about it. Now, come on. Let's get going. We have a mission to complete."

There was a strained silence as they walked to the shop—Wheels, as it was called—that took up the whole bottom floor of a warehouse. An elf with short dark hair sat at a desk by the entrance. Dressed in black, he looked young, about the same age as Thirret, Pawel's son. Paperwork was strewn on the desk, and frowning, he looked down at it. But when the door opened, the elf glanced up, and his frown went away to be replaced by a neutral, polite expression even though his customers were humans.

Maya thought, "Money is money, no matter who spends it."

The elf said, "My name is Terren. May I help you?"

Maya nudged Will and Jay, who stepped forward.

"We're here to buy two gyrocycles," Will answered.

"Fast ones," Jay added enthusiastically.

Terren studied them. "Have you ever driven one before?"

"No," Lexie answered for them, "they have not."

Will and Jay glared at Lexie, but Terren laughed. "Lucky for you the gyrocycles aren't that hard to drive. The problem is turning. You lean in whichever direction you want the cycle to go, but the cycles will always try to right themselves. You will need to come to an understanding with them. What you want is something that has spirit but is not too headstrong. I have just the cycles for you. But the question is, can you afford them?"

Lexie glanced at Will and Jay, and their angry expressions softened.

"Go ahead, Lexie," Jay said, and he even grinned a little. "Do your thing."

With Will and Jay looking on as Lexie haggled with Terren, Maya wandered to the back of the store, where long windows overlooked a large fenced-in lot that was littered with broken-down gyrocycles lying on the ground at various angles. Maya thought they were a sad sight, machines that had once been useful were no longer needed except for parts. Then, at the far end of the lot, Maya saw something that made her even sadder. A large mechanical horse, with its head down, leaned against the fence. Even though the creature was covered with rust, Maya caught a glimpse of how it had shined in its younger days when it was new and taken care of. Then the horse had been neglected, left in a field to rust when the family that had once owned the horse stopped farming, eventually sold their land, and moved to the city. The new owners had bought the farm for a second home in the country, and having no need of the horse, they had sold it to a junkyard. The owner hadn't been able to bring himself to strip down the once magnificent creature for parts and had kept it going with the pellets that animated it. When that owner had died, the horse went to his brother and then to a cousin and finally to the shop that sold gyrocycles. Why Terren kept the horse he could not say, but he put it in the back with the broken-down gyrocycles, and like the junkyard owner, Terren kept the horse going with fuel pellets. But the horse needed a farm. Without it, the lonely creature had no purpose.

Maya saw all this in a flash. And she knew exactly where the horse belonged—with Ehren and Tagen, where it would help them during every season. A door led to the lot, and leaving Lexie and Terren to argue about prices, Maya slipped out the door and wound her way around various gyrocycles, brushing against dirty wheels, stepping over scattered parts, until she came to the horse. Maya stopped a short distance away and then slowly, slowly walked toward the horse, which did not move. But one gleaming eye noted Maya's progress. Stopping directly in front of the horse, Maya held her hand out, and the horse nickered softly into her palm. Maya touched the horse's nose, and the large head lifted slightly. Two shining eyes regarded Maya, who stood still. She saw unhappiness in those eyes, then a sort of pleading followed by the faintest flicker of hope.

Maya whispered, "I know where you can live. Two people need you on their farm. If Terren will let you go, would you come with me?"

In response, the horse lifted its massive head and whinnied in a loud trumpet that ricocheted around the lot, leaped over the fence, and even made its way into the showroom. Squeaking in surprise, Maya jumped back, and the door to the showroom opened with a bang.

"What's going on out there?" Terren asked sternly, standing in the doorway.

The horse no longer slumped. Instead, the horse stood tall with a proud, arching neck.

Terren walked toward Maya and the horse. "I see."

Maya turned toward Terren, and her words came out in a rush. "I know a farm where he can live. The people there need him. They don't have much extra money, but they would take good care of this horse. I know they would."

Terren considered Maya, and his gray eyes glanced from the brooch to her face and back to the brooch. "Not quite the harmless little human that you appear to be, are you?"

Maya smiled. "Well, I am small."

Terren's voice was thoughtful. "So you are." He stood by the horse and put his hand on its rusty side. "This creature doesn't belong here. I meant to find a farm for him." The elf shrugged. "But somehow I never had the time. Always too busy with work. But I kept him going. I had a feeling that one day he would go to a farm. His name is Sheverre."

"Sheverre," Maya said softly, and the horse whinnied a ringing response.

"Maya, what are you doing?" Lexie had made her way across the lot and stood beside Terren. Looking from the horse to Maya, Lexie shook her head violently. "No way. The horse can't come with us. Don't give me that look. I'm not going to haggle with Terren for this rusty thing."

With ears pressed against his head, Sheverre glared at Lexie, and the blonde girl shook her finger at him.

"You're right," Terren said. "You will not be haggling with me over this horse because I'm giving him to you. One round a day with you is more than enough."

"What?" Lexie asked in surprise. "Maya, are you crazy? What are we going to do with this horse? Look how big it is. And it will never be able to keep up with us when we're on the gyrocycles."

"You're wrong there," Terren replied firmly. "Sheverre can run like the wind. He might look old and rusty, but I've kept his joints oiled and his hooves polished."

Maya and Lexie stared down at the shining hooves, and Sheverre lifted one leg after another. The motion was smooth and easy without as much as a creak.

Maya said softly, "Sheverre will be going to a farm where he is really needed."

Lexie sighed. "Oh, for God's sake."

Hearing defeat in Lexie's voice, Maya smiled and patted Sheverre's neck. The horse whinnied softly and rested his chin on Maya's shoulder.

Neither Will nor Jay said much when Maya told them about the horse. They only nodded briefly, unable to look away from the two gyrocycles with their massive black wheels and gleaming silver bodies. On each gyrocycle, there were seats for two people, and there was even a small case at the back, which when opened, made a place for Hanss to ride.

"What about our bags?" Maya asked, not liking the look of the machines. "Those cases won't hold all our stuff."

"The passengers can wear theirs," Will said slowly, and then shrugged. "Maybe we'll have to get rid of some things." Maya could tell he had not thought about the bags, and neither had Jay.

Terren provided the solution. "Sheverre can carry them. He has plenty of compartments where the bags can be stowed. He could carry them all, and you wouldn't have to ride with any of them."

Jay frowned. "Sheverre?"

"The horse Terren gave us," Maya explained patiently. "I just told you about him."

"Yeah," Jay replied, "but I didn't think he'd be big enough to carry our bags."

Lexie rolled her eyes. "Oh, just wait until you see him."

On the street, standing next to the gyrocycles, which had been wheeled outside and were on their stands, Will and Jay didn't say anything at first as Sheverre rounded the corner and made his way toward the teenagers. With their mouths slightly open, Will and Jay stared at the massive horse, who stopped next to Maya.

Will finally said, "Maya, what the hell?"

Maya sighed. "I seem to hear that a lot from you."

Jay looked up at the sky. "I wonder why."

With her head, Lexie motioned toward Will and Jay. "Sorry, Maya, but this time I agree with the boys. But Terren has assured us that the horse will be able to keep up with us." With narrow eyes, she regarded the elf. "Haven't you?"

Grinning, Terren raised his hand. "By Magic's honor."

Lexie snorted. "Right. So there you have it. By Magic's honor."

With a cool expression, Terren regarded Lexie. "For a human, you are very confident." He glanced at the others. "You all are."

Maya shifted uneasily, and Lexie replied, "We come from far away, and in our land, humans are raised to be confident."

"And where might that land be?" Terren asked softly.

"Never mind," Lexie snapped.

Terren blinked. "You're right," he replied with a note of regret. "Humans are probably better off without us."

Maya thought, "Not that we're so great on our own." But she didn't say anything.

Will and Jay spent a while learning how to ride and steer the gyrocycles. They zoomed around the still nearly empty streets near the shop. There were a few close calls as the gyrocycles almost spun out of control, and once, grazing the side of a building, Will came to a skidding stop not far from where Maya and the others were waiting.

Terren winced. "Good thing most of the warehouses are closed for Summer Gathering."

"Yeah," Lexie replied with a toss of her head. "There's no telling how many elves they might have taken out."

"And that would not have been good," Terren murmured as he considered her, Maya, and Hanss.

In a flash, Maya saw what would happen if any human harmed an elf—the beatings and the imprisonments that sometimes stretched over a lifetime.

Maya's voice was soft. "We have to be careful."

Terren's voice was even softer. "Very. You're on dangerous ground here."

"I know," Maya answered, sensing that Terren had caught a glimpse of their mission. But when she looked keenly at him, the elf simply shrugged.

Within an hour, Will and Jay had learned how to drive the gyrocycles safely enough to meet Terren's approval.

"All right, you're ready to go." Terren looked as though he didn't quite believe his own words. "In one of Sheverre's compartments, there are bags of pellets to keep him going for a while. Feed them to him the way you would a normal horse."

"How often and how long?" Maya asked.

"Once a week should do it, but more often depending on how hard he works. There's a scoop in one of the bags. Give Sheverre a scoopful when he seems to be slowing down."

"All right," Maya replied.

Terren frowned at the teenagers. "Watch yourselves. The closer you get to the center of the city, the more folks there will be, even though it's Summer Gathering."

"We'll be careful," Maya said seriously as she scrambled on the gyrocycle behind Will.

Lexie climbed on behind Jay. "If you go too fast, I will pinch your arm. Don't think I won't."

Jay muttered, "Oh, I believe you."

"Good. Because I'm not kidding."

Hanss jumped into the open case, and his ears were flat against his head. "I can hardly wait."

As Sheverre trumpeted that he, too, was ready, Terren grinned reluctantly. "Off you go."

In front of Will, there was a stand for the map, and Maya slid the map into the stand. She watched in wonder as the map perfectly adjusted itself to fit in the stand. Will did not ask the map for directions, and Maya knew he would do it later when Terren was out of earshot. The elf seemed sympathetic, but like Maya, Will understood that there was no point in taking chances. Or implicating Terren when the robbery would most certainly be discovered.

"All set?" Will called to Jay.

"All set," Jay replied.

With Sheverre trotting beside them, they drove away from the shop, slowly at first, and then a little faster as Jay and Will gained confidence. Terren had been right; Sheverre had no trouble keeping up. Will gave the map instructions, and he and Maya were in the lead as they left the commercial section and headed to the outskirts of the city, where Galli lived.

Maya thought, "This is not too bad."

"Come on," came Will's answering thought. "This is great."

Maya shook her head. "No, not great. Just not too bad."

Will laughed but did not respond.

The roads became more crowded, but most of the traffic was on the other side of the road as all manner of beings headed to the Summer Gathering. Many of the elves and humans drove small cars filled with children. Occasionally a gyrocycle whizzed by, and regardless of who was driving, Will and Jay received a salute. It wasn't long before Jay and Will were saluting back. A variety of vehicles were also on the road—tiny egg-shaped carts driven by froglike creatures with bulging eyes; larger ones in the shape of pigs with imps at the wheel; and all kinds of other mechanical animals, even horses. Maya had worried, a little, that Sheverre would look out of place as he trotted behind the gyrocycles. But she needn't have worried. Sheverre fit right in with all the other strange and wondrous vehicles on the road.

24: Song and Dance

The plan was simple. When their spirits had left their bodies, Will, Jay, and Lexie had discovered that there was a large park across from Galli's house and workshop. While Maya, Will, and Hanss stole the key and lock, Jay and Lexie, by singing and entertaining, would draw attention away from what the thieves were doing. The gyrocycles and Sheverre could be hidden in the thick bushes that grew in the park.

"With my looks and our music, everybody will be focused on us, just the way they were at The Trotting Horse," Lexie had said the night before at Ehren and Tagen's campsite.

Maya's reply was half stern, half joking. "Not exactly the same way, I hope."

Lexie had answered sharply, "Don't worry, Captain Hammond. We'll behave. We've learned our lesson. You don't have to keep reminding us."

"Uh-huh," Maya had said, not backing down. Then shaking her head, Maya reluctantly grinned, and Lexie grinned back.

As Maya sat behind Will on the gyrocycle, she thought about all the lessons that her three friends had learned in a short time. Despite the mishap at the tavern, Will, Jay, and Lexie had quickly discovered how dangerous it was to make even one wrong move.

"We're not complete idiots," came Will's thought in response.

"I was thinking on my own," Maya replied. "You need to let me do that. I don't always barge in on you, do I?"

Will apologized, and Maya was left alone with her thoughts.

There was only one near mishap as they drove to Galli's house, and it involved trying to turn the gyrocycles. Both gyrocycles jerked and skidded as Will and Jay made a right turn. Hanss yowled, Lexie shrieked, and catching her breath, Maya dug her hands into Will's waist so hard it made him wince.

"Sorry!" came Will's firm thought. "It won't happen again." Then, "Behave!" he called sharply to the gyrocycle.

Glancing back at Jay, Maya saw his flinty expression, and she could tell that he was as resolved as Will. At the next turn, the gyrocycles only pushed back slightly, to show that they had some spunk, and after that, the turns were smooth. Maya remembered her experience with the ladders at the Great Library and how one of the ladders had actually bucked her to the floor. Reprimanding the ladders, Maya had told them exactly what she thought of their childish behavior, and only then had the ladders settled down. This memory tugged at Maya, and she had the feeling that somehow the ladders would be important later on.

"Ladders?" Will asked silently.

"What did I say about barging in?" Maya asked reproachfully.

"I really didn't barge in this time," Will replied. "The image of flying ladders just came to me from you."

Maya thought about how this often happened to her with other people, and her tone softened. "Strange, isn't it, how those ladders popped up?"

"Sure is."

But there wasn't anymore time to think about the wayward ladders at the Great Library. The map indicated that they had come to the street with Galli's house and workshop, and a dot of light flashed as they drove by the large timbered-framed home that dominated the other smaller timbered-framed houses on the street. Maya got the sense that although Galli had done well for himself, he preferred to live away from the center of things even though he was, in his own way, one of the most important elves in Foretcour. Maya understood that his locks and keys made him a valuable asset, no matter who was in charge. An image came to Maya of the tall, gaunt elf, of how his furrowed brow and calm demeanor masked an intense ambition to always be on the side of the elves who were in power. How those elves ruled didn't matter to Galli as long as he was paid well and was left alone to study the crafts of binding and releasing. These crafts were his obsessions that fueled him with a white-hot energy.

Will's back twitched. "Galli is terrible," he said aloud.

"Yeah," Maya replied, also aloud. "There's no mercy in him."

"Pawel told us Galli won't be home. That's lucky for us. But we have those imps to worry about. Good thing I have my ball."

"I hope we don't have to use it."

"Oh, I don't know," Will said. "I wouldn't mind throwing that ball at somebody who deserved to be hit on the head."

"Will!"

"Not to kill. Just to knock out," Will added quickly.

Maya made no reply and instead gave his arm a light pinch, not enough to hurt but firm enough to let him know what she thought about his eagerness to use the ball. Grinning, Will didn't say anything either.

Guided by the map, Will and Jay drove the gyrocycles to the far end of the park, where they slipped in the back entrance, which was as deserted as the area by the warehouse. Driving side by side, Will and Jay scanned the edges of the narrow road for a clump of bushes dense and high enough to hide two gyrocycles and one large horse. Behind them, Sheverre followed faithfully, and Maya could hear the clop, clop, clop of his metal hooves on the road. Turning, she looked at the metal horse, who nickered back at her. Maya smiled, glad that they had rescued this intelligent creature from his solitude at the gyrocycle shop. With a shiver, Maya had the feeling that soon the time might come when they all would be grateful that Sheverre was with them.

Not far from Galli's house, they found the stand of tall bushes that they had been searching for. The teenagers got off the gyrocycles, and Will and Jay wheeled them into the bushes. Sheverre looked at Maya.

"You have to go there, too," Maya said. "And wait for us until we come back. It's very important that you stay here and don't come looking for us. Do you understand this?"

The great horse nodded in assent and quietly joined the gyrocycles. The bushes closed around him, and there was no sign of either horse or cycles.

Jay whistled in appreciation. "That really is some horse, isn't it?"

"Yeah," Maya said. "Sheverre's special. And he'll have a good home with Ehren and Tagen."

Will kissed Maya on the head. "You were right to want Sheverre to come with us."

"Maybe," came Lexie's grudging response, but she was smiling slightly, and Maya could tell that Lexie had come around, too.

In the park, almost across from Galli's house, Hanss, Maya, and Will stood to one side as Jay and Lexie went to the center of the green. The street was quiet and empty, and Maya was not surprised. There had been a lot of traffic heading in the direction of the Summer Gathering. But Maya knew of one group that had stayed home, and she waited anxiously, hoping that the imps would be drawn by the music.

"You're not the only one," Will said silently. "Is it all right to communicate this way?"

"Yeah," Maya thought. "From now until we have finished. You don't even have to ask."

Will smiled. "Just checking."

"Me, too?" Hanss asked.

"You, too," Maya answered.

Jay took the mandolin out of its case, and Lexie cleared her throat a few times. Shrugging, they looked at the empty street, but with the first song—"Save Tonight"—Lexie and Jay gave it everything they had, even though the only ones to hear and watch were Hanss, Maya, and Will. Rippling outward in a wave, the song and the music cascaded in both directions up and down the main road and onto side streets. It slid under doorways and through glass, entering every house, including Galli's. For a while, the streets remained empty, but slowly, slowly, doors opened as various servants crept out of the houses not only on Galli's street but also from all around the block. There were many humans as well as some of the froglike creatures with the bulging eyes. They all made their way to the green and stood transfixed as Jay and Lexie sang.

"Come on, imps," Maya thought, and beside her, Will waited tensely.

When the song was over, Jay nodded at the small audience, and Lexie bowed gracefully, her blonde hair a shimmering wave. There were more than a few admiring gasps. As Lexie and Jay got ready to start another song, the door to Galli's house burst open as six imps raced out and joined the other spectators.

"There they are!" came Will's relieved thought.

"Finally," Hanss added silently.

The largest imp had a tuft of brown hair that stood up straight and pointed ears so large they looked like small sails. Clearly, he was the leader.

Turning to the other imps, he said in a voice both piping and brisk, "Alrighty, now. You knows we're not supposed to be out here gaping at the singing humans. But I don't think Master Galli would mind very much if we listened to a song or two."

Maya thought in relief, "Pawel was right. Galli is gone. Otherwise, the imp wouldn't be talking about him that way."

Will sighed, and Hanss meowed softly.

The imps continued their discussion.

"Brosk, we can keeps an eye on the house while we listens," a smaller one squeaked.

"Yes, we can," came a high-pitched chorus. "No problems, Brosk."

Folding his skinny but wiry arms across his chest, Brosk, the large imp, nodded.

"Both elves and humans knows what we can do." This came in a boastful peep from the second largest one who had a fringe of black hair.

Brosk snorted. "They sure do."

The imps were smaller than Maya had pictured. But an image came to her of the quick guards wielding sharp, sharp knives that had cut through elven magic almost as soon as the spells were uttered.

Blood gushed, and Maya saw what had happened to the elves who had come before them to steal the key that would unlock the chains binding Pawel and his family. Pawel had been right. With such a fierce force, Galli could go wherever he wanted and not worry about intruders. Even a stealthy elf could not get past the vigilant imps, who were normally immune from most distractions. Except, as Pawel had told them, human music.

The humans and the froglike creatures eyed the imps cautiously, and they would have gone back to the homes they were cleaning if Jay hadn't started playing "Semi-Charmed Life." Brosk caught sight of Hanss, and the imp frowned fiercely at the cat, who remained cool and calm. Brosk might have come over to investigate, but the music tugged and pulled at him until he turned away from Hanss to watch Jay and Lexie play and sing.

Watching the imps' rapt expressions, Maya could see exactly how bewitching Jay and Lexie's music was to the fierce little creatures. Surrounded by music, the imps stood transfixed, and on each pointed face there was a smile that looked almost dreamy.

Glancing at the imps from time to time, Jay and Lexie played and sang even better than they had at the tavern and at Tagen's house. They sang as though their lives depended on it, but with assurance rather than desperation. Flowing through Jay and Lexie, the music wrapped itself around all who were watching, and it wasn't long before everyone was humming and swaying. Many of the froglike creatures did a little jig, which Maya found endearing. Like the imps, the gentle froglike creatures could not resist human music.

"Time for us to go," came the thought from Will.

"Yeah," Maya replied, even though she, too, was reluctant to leave the swirling song.

Hanss twitched his tail in agreement.

Slowly, they moved unnoticed away from the crowd and the music. The cat and the two teenagers walked to the main road, and finding side streets, they circled to the back of Galli's house, which was surrounded by a high wall. There were houses behind Galli's yard, but Maya felt certain that nobody was around to see them. Jay and Lexie had drawn everyone to the park.

Looking at the wall, Hanss gave a low growl as they walked the perimeter without finding a door, and they returned to where they had started.

"Now what?" Will asked. "It looks too high to climb."

"I don't know." Maya felt Aiken and Orlaith stir in her side pockets, and she took them out.

They clambered up her arms to her shoulders and regarded the wall. For a moment they didn't say anything.

"Bet there is an opening here somewhere, don't you think, Orlaith?" Aiken asked. "He would want a way out, just in case. We can't see the opening because Galli has put a spell on it."

Orlaith waived her front legs in agreement.

"Stay here," Aiken said to Hanss, Maya, and Will. "Orlaith and I will see what we can find."

The spider climbed onto the dragon's back, and off they whizzed, skimming along the side of the wall. When they came to a corner, they zipped around the edge, disappearing from sight.

Will and Maya were silent as they waited. The music was faint but audible, and every once in a while there came cheering and clapping.

"We wouldn't be able to do this without Jay and Lexie," Will said aloud.

"No, we wouldn't," Maya replied, thinking that she wouldn't have been able to do any of this without the help of her three friends and Hanss. Knowing she didn't need to say anything, Maya put her hand on Will's arm, and Will covered her small hand with his own larger one.

He would have kissed her, but there was a buzz and a whir as Aiken and Orlaith rejoined them.

"We found the opening, and I have illuminated it," Aiken said. "Galli's magic is strong, but I'll be able to take care of it."

"And I'll be able to weave it back so that it won't look as though anyone broke in," Orlaith added.

Following Aiken and Orlaith, Will, Maya, and Hanss made their way around the wall, to an alley that separated Galli's wall from the wall of another house. In the dim light was a shimmering outline on Galli's wall, similar to the portal at the subway station in New York that had taken the teenagers to Elferterre. Aiken flew around the door, and his eyes glowed brightly. By the light of his eyes, Maya and Will could see the bright strands of woven magic that would keep them out, and Maya realized that this door had no wood, metal, or stone. It was completely made of strands of magic.

"Tight and strong," Aiken said, with a note of approval. "But not too much for my fire."

Orlaith rubbed her two front legs together. "And I can reweave as soon as you are done stealing the lock and key."

"Were you two made for something like this?" Maya asked in wonder. "To help thieves?"

"Not really," Aiken said. "Mostly we're just for show, to use at parties and on holidays. But luckily, you humans came by at the right time and rescued us from the humdrum yet humiliating life of being an ornament. For that we will be ever grateful."

Hanss twitched his tail. "Enough talk. Time to get going. Who knows how long Jay and Lexie will be able to hold those imps?"

Aiken blew a puff of steam at the cat who, with a twitching tail, stood his ground, but Orlaith clacked four legs together. "The fur creature is right. Time to burn through the web of magic. We need to be as quick as we can."

Aiken snorted again but turned toward the door. A line of white-hot fire came from his mouth and with a sizzle disintegrated the various strands of magic, one by one. When there was a hole big enough for Will and Maya to climb through, Aiken stopped.

"No point in burning more than I have to," the tiny dragon said. "We don't need to make unnecessary work for Orlaith."

Orlaith regally inclined her head toward Aiken. "Much appreciated."

Gazing through the hole, Hanss said, "I've never gotten this far with any of the elves that Pawel sent."

Will and Maya stared at the cat. "Never?" Will finally asked. "Why not?"

Hanss shook his head. "They didn't let me come with them to Galli's house. In case..." The cat stopped, and his whiskers trembled.

"Turns out, they were right. None of them got through the imps, and I always had to go back to the forest by myself when the elves didn't return from their mission."

"How?" Maya asked.

"I could always hitch a ride back with someone," Hanss replied. "Either directly or indirectly. I can squeeze into small places and hide."

Aiken cleared his throat. "Do we have to discuss this right now? Remember, the two humans can't play and sing indefinitely."

"Right," Hanss agreed briskly. "But before we go in, I am going to put a shielding spell over us, just in case. You never know who will be watching."

Meowing to himself, Hanss sat up on his hind legs. With both paws, he gestured in a circle around them all. Then Hanss waved up and down, and Maya saw thin strands of magic fall on her arms and legs. She felt it settle on her head and her back, and Maya really did feel as though she was hidden.

"From now on, no talking," Hanss said softly. "We must communicate solely through our thoughts."

Right, right, right came the silent responses.

"Let's go, then." Hanss slid through the hole Orlaith had made, and the others followed him into a small yard dominated by a long, low building—Galli's workshop.

25: A Kid's Gambit

Galli's workshop proved to be harder to break into. Not only was there a web of magic, but there was also an actual door with a gleaming lock.

However, Orlaith was undeterred. "If Aiken can burn through the magic, then I can get us in."

"Of course I can," came Aiken's quick reply, but Maya caught an undertone of fatigue in the little dragon's response and understood that his energy was not infinite. She hoped that this was the last web of magic that Aiken would have to burn.

As Aiken worked on the strands of magic, the others watched. Behind them, Galli's house was a large, hulking presence, and Maya wondered if it, like so many things on Elferterre, was animated and watching.

When Maya silently asked Hanss, the cat replied uneasily, "Perhaps. I feel it, too. We need to get in and out as soon as possible. I don't know how long my magic will last."

Will's thoughts were apprehensive. "Maybe the imps aren't the only ones guarding the workshop."

Maya didn't say anything. She had the feeling that Will was right and that the house could sense what they were doing, even if it couldn't see or hear them.

It wasn't long before Maya's suspicions were confirmed. As soon as there was a hole in the web of magic, Orlaith skittered up the door and thrust an elegant leg into the lock. Quivering with concentration, Orlaith probed and prodded until there was a loud click, and the door swung open. Immediately, a large booming sound came from the house—rhythmic, insistent—and to Maya it sounded like the crack of doom. "Why didn't Pawel warn us?" Maya wondered but then immediately knew the answer. Like everyone else, Pawel couldn't see everything.

Will looked back once at the house before turning toward the workshop. "Let's go!"

They all hurried into the dim workshop, which tingled with magic, much like the cellar at The Other Green Door did. There was a long table in the middle of the workshop, and on either side, running along the walls, were dark wooden cabinets with rows and rows of little drawers—all locked, Maya was sure.

"Where could that lock and key be?" Will asked in a murmur, shaking his head against the noise the house was making. "There must be hundreds and hundreds of drawers."

Trying to ignore the house's thumping, Maya studied the cabinets. "Not in those cabinets. Galli would hide them away somewhere," she answered aloud. There seemed no point in being quiet any longer.

Orlaith, who was on the floor, clicked her legs together. "In a safe. I can feel it nearby just waiting to be picked."

The thumping grew louder, and Will and Maya looked at each other. It wouldn't be long before the imps discovered what had happened. Jay and Lexie were good, but there was no way their music could compete with the booming house.

Then Maya felt the shielding spell slip away. Now they would be visible to everyone, imps included.

As the thumping became a throb that was almost painful, Maya said to Orlaith, "Show us."

But Will took the ball from his pocket. "You go, and I'll stay here."

Maya wanted to argue with Will, but his stern look silenced her, and she knew he was right. The time had come to use the silver ball Pawel had given them.

Aiken settled on Will's shoulder. "I'll stay with the boy and help teach those imps a lesson." A puff of smoke came from each nostril. "They'll be sorry they tangled with us."

Hanss hesitated, looking from Will to Maya.

"Go with her," Will commanded. "Do what you can to keep her safe in case we fail."

Thinking of the fierce imps and how they could easily tear Will apart, Maya choked back a sob and followed Hanss and Orlaith to another door. The spider picked the lock, and the door swung open. In this room—Galli's office with a desk and chair—the magic was so strong that Maya could almost taste it as it seemed to coat her mouth and tongue. There was a switch by the door, and when Maya flipped it, a light came on. At the back of the room, on the wall, was the safe.

"Let's see what I can do," Orlaith murmured.

"Go, go, go!" Maya urged.

Orlaith hurried to the safe and then skittered up the wall to the lock, which unlike most safes, required an actual key to open it rather than a combination of numbers. Maya thought this made perfect sense for an elf whose specialty was locks and keys.

Orlaith inserted a leg into the opening and felt around. This time there were no clicks. "Not going to be easy," she muttered.

The house was no longer booming, and from the other room, Maya heard the imps confront Will and Aiken.

"A human boy?" came Brosk's incredulous voice. "A lone human boy broke into Galli's workshop?"

"A lone human boy?" another imp echoed.

"What the hell!" yet another imp shouted.

Maya felt the imps hesitate in disbelief as they regarded Will. She knew that in this brief pause lay their only hope of surviving this encounter with the imps, who would not expect Will to have a ball that could knock them out. The imps probably hadn't noticed Aiken, either. They were too flabbergasted to discover a human boy had succeeded where elves had failed.

"Now!" Maya's thoughts urged Will and Aiken. "Throw that ball and use your fire."

The silence vanished, replaced by screams and high-pitched yelps of pain.

Maya turned to Orlaith. "Hurry!" she cried, wondering how many locks and keys would be in the safe.

After what seemed like an age but wasn't actually that long, Orlaith proclaimed in triumph, "Got it!"

The door swung open, and peering inside, Maya could see a green velvet pouch. Grabbing it, she spilled the contents onto Galli's desk and regarded the assortment of keys and locks. With a trembling hand, Maya searched through them, and her fingers picked over ones that glimmered and sparkled. But Maya couldn't find the ones with the symbols that Pawel had imprinted in her memory. Over and over, Maya went through the locks and keys, and in despair she cried, "I can't find them. They're not here."

Hanss stared intently at the jumble on the desk. "Where, where, where?"

"What about these?" Orlaith said, and with one leg she lifted up a stack of papers. Underneath were a lock and a tiny key, both dull and tarnished.

"Those old things?" Maya asked impatiently.

"Look closer."

Maya grabbed the lock and key and saw the symbols, Б and Я, on them.

"Yes!" Hanss cried in triumph.

"Were they hiding?" Maya asked Orlaith.

"I think they were. When you emptied the pouch, I saw them shoot to one side and tuck themselves under that pile of papers. I'll wrap them tight so they won't be able to escape."

In motions so quick that Orlaith was a blur, the spider covered the key and lock in thick webbing. The key and lock tried to jerk away, but they were no match for the firm weave that bound them. When Orlaith was done, she said, "You have a pouch in your pocket. Put them in there and tie the strings in tight knots. You don't want to take any chances."

Maya did as she was told, folding the pouch and pushing it way down into her pocket, where it would be safe.

Then Maya noticed how quiet it had become. "Will!" she cried, looking up.

But he was standing by the doorway, and Aiken perched wearily on his shoulder. There wasn't even a scratch on Will, but his face was flushed with excitement.

"Did you find them?" he asked.

"Yes, they're in my pocket." Maya put a hand to her cheek. "The imps?"

"Knocked them all out," Will said with quiet pride. "That ball is something else. It moves so fast! And Aiken distracted the imps with his fire as the ball went around and conked them all on the head."

For a moment, Maya wished she could have seen the ball do its job. "Are the imps dead?"

"No, just knocked out. And we should get going. There's no telling how long they'll be out. They're little but tough. Especially that leader, Brosk. At first I didn't think he'd go down. But finally he did. The ball had to hit him three times. Little dirtbag."

"Will is right," Hanss said. "We need to leave now. No point in putting things back the way they were or repairing the webs of magic. It'll be clear to Galli what has happened." He hesitated. "We should finish off the imps while they're unconscious."

Will stared at Hanss. "Just murder them in cold blood?"

"Yes," the cat replied. "Those imps are vicious. They've killed many a good elf."

"No," Maya said firmly. "We don't do that. We're the good guys. Now let's go." She held out her hand for Orlaith and Aiken, who skittered and flew onto her palm. Into her pocket they went, and Maya, Will, and Hanss hurried to the door leading outside.

The cat's whiskers twitched, but he said, "All right. Let's go, then!"

The knocked-out imps lay in a cluster in the doorway, and Maya, Will, and Hanss had to pick their way around the unconscious bodies. As Maya stepped over Brosk, it seemed that he twitched a little, but he didn't wake up. There was a snarl on his face, and Maya wanted to be far, far away when he woke up. A part of her wondered if Hanss was right. Maybe they should kill the imps.

"I can't," Maya thought as she finally made her way over the small bodies. "I just can't."

Maya, Will, and Hanss hurried back through the opening Aiken had burned in the wall's door. As soon as they were through, Maya saw Jay and Lexie at the far end of the wall, looking for some way to get in.

Maya waved. "Jay and Lexie! Over here."

They all raced toward each other.

"Did you get the lock and key?" Lexie asked.

"Yes," Maya answered.

"Good!"

"Did you use the ball on the imps?" Jay asked.

Will's face was still flushed with excitement. "I did. And it was epic."

Will would have gone into further detail, but Hanss cut him short. "We have got to get out of here now. We don't know how long the imps will be unconscious, especially that head imp. We can have a discussion when we're safe."

Nobody argued. They ran back to the empty park, found the road that curved along the back, and raced toward the clump of bushes where Sheverre and the gyrocycles were hidden.

But someone was not far behind, and Maya could feel a hot presence bearing down on them. She knew who it was, and she glanced back to see Brosk running furiously, his little legs pumping like pistons. And he was gaining ground.

Will, Jay, and Lexie looked over their shoulders and saw the imp speeding toward them. Brosk was close enough for them to see his livid, murderous expression. In one hand, the imp gripped his knife. Maya knew he was carrying more than one and would be able to retrieve them in a flash.

Will stopped suddenly, facing Brosk. "Go to the gyrocycles!" he yelled to the others. But instead of running away, Maya, Hanss, Lexie, and Jay stopped, too.

Will fumbled in his pocket for the ball.

"Oh, no you don'ts. Can't fool me twice," Brosk cried, throwing the knife at Will.

Then, to Maya, it seemed that Magic slowed down Time and showed her what would happen if Brosk wasn't stopped—the knife would reach Will before he could throw the ball. It would hit him in the chest, slicing into his heart and killing him.

"No!" Maya screamed. "Help us!"

She felt Magic surround her and propel her toward Will. Maya hit Will with such force that she knocked him out of the way, and the sharp, sharp knife hit her instead, stabbing her in the arm. They both fell to the ground, and with a startled grunt, Will dropped the ball. Crying in pain, Maya saw that Brosk was almost on them. The imp had another knife in his hand. Maya could feel Brosk's hot, angry intent as he focused only on the two of them. He wanted to slit their throats.

But Brosk was fooled a second time. On either side of the road, rocks trembled in anticipation of Maya's command. In a flurry, she hurled them at Brosk, who was caught by surprise. As rocks hit him one after another, the imp fell with an anguished cry and dropped his knife. More rocks rained down on the imp until he lay still, and his breathing came out in shallow gasps. For a while, nobody said anything as they stared at Brosk. Maya's arm burned with pain, and she had no more energy to lift and throw rocks. Clutching her arm, she sat huddled on the road.

In a daze, Will looked for the ball, which had rolled over to the side of the road. Will rose on shaky legs, but Jay hurried to retrieve the ball as Lexie ran to Maya. Then they were all distracted by a mighty clatter. Hurtling down the road, Sheverre raced to the fallen imp. The metal horse reared on its massive hind legs and brought its front legs down on Brosk.

The imp didn't even have time to cry out as Sheverre crushed his head and his body. Blood spurted in every direction, some of it spraying Maya and Lexie, who were crouched nearby.

Lexie and Maya screamed, and Jay and Will winced as they looked at the mash of flesh, bones, and blood that had once been Brosk.

But Hanss remained calm. "Should have killed that imp to begin with. Now let's go before the rest of them come." Sheverre nickered in agreement.

Lexie helped Maya to her feet and gave her a questioning look.

Maya nodded. Yes, pull it out.

Lexie yanked the knife out of Maya's arm. Maya screamed and then stood trembling as she clutched her oozing arm.

After handing the ball to Will, Jay said in admiration, "Maya sure took down that imp."

Stuffing the ball into his pocket, Will didn't say anything. His mouth was an angry line as he searched Sheverre's compartments for one of the packs. He grabbed the first one he came to—Maya's as it turned out—removed it with a jerk, rummaged inside, and pulled out a cloak. Taking Brosk's knife from Lexie, he sliced off a length and wrapped it around Maya's arm.

Glaring at her, Will tied the strip in a knot so tight that it made her wince.

"Will," Maya thought, but his thoughts were closed to her, and tired from hurling rocks and being stabbed, all Maya could do was sigh. She knew there would be a fight, and Maya's shoulders drooped. Right now, a fight with Will was the last thing she wanted.

With quick, furious motions, Will stuffed the cloak and the knife into the bag and the bag into Sheverre's compartment.

"Maybe Maya should ride with me," Jay suggested tentatively.

"No," Will said curtly. "She rides with me."

Despite her exhaustion, Maya felt a surge of anger when she heard Will's peremptory tone. Holding her head high, Maya said, "I'll ride with Jay."

Will's eyes were narrow as he looked from Maya to Jay, and Lexie put an arm on his shoulder. "It will be better that way," she said. "Let me ride with you."

"Fine," Will said tightly. "We'll hash it out later." He stared at Maya. "Don't think we won't."

Swallowing to stop herself from crying, Maya followed Jay to the gyrocycle and let him help her onto the seat. He climbed in front of her and waited for Will and Lexie to get on their gyrocycle to lead the way. Hanss jumped into the box behind Maya.

Soon they were heading down the road, and Sheverre cantered behind them. Where they were going, Maya didn't know, and a part of her didn't care. Her eyes stung with tears, and her arm throbbed.

"I saved his life," Maya finally said in a trembling voice. "Time sort of stopped, and I could see that the knife would have gone right to Will's heart."

"Yeah," Jay said. "But what if it had gone to your heart instead? Didn't think of that, did you?"

Maya sniffed. "No. Magic was helping me, and I knew the knife wouldn't go to my heart."

Jay's voice was affectionate. "Of course you did. But Will didn't, did he?"

Maya had to admit he didn't, and she sniffed again.

"Try not to worry about it too much. He'll get over it. Eventually. Just lean against me and rest," Jay said.

With a grateful sigh, Maya wrapped her good arm around Jay's waist and slumped against his back. She heard Jay chuckle.

"What?" she asked faintly, thinking there wasn't much to laugh about right now.

"I can see that up ahead, Lexie and Will are having, ah, a discussion. You know Lexie. She doesn't hold back. But this might be a good thing. By the time we get to Ehren and Tagen's house, he'll be all worn out from fighting with her and won't have the energy to fight with you."

Despite her low spirits, Maya smiled a little, knowing Jay was right about Lexie, and she even felt a little sorry for Will. And of course they were going to Ehren and Tagen's house. That's why they had been given a key at the campsite.

Hanss had been silent, but Maya heard him say, "You did the right thing, no matter what Will thinks. I saw it, too. If you hadn't acted, we'd all be dead. That imp was fast, but you were faster."

And she felt his soft paw pat her back.

26: Little Lion

Maya rode in a swoon to Ehren and Tagen's cottage. Not even stopping once for a break, they reached the cottage by late afternoon. Maya's arm throbbed more painfully than ever, and as she slid off the gyrocycle, she fell to her knees. Jay helped Maya to her feet. She started hobbling to the cottage's front door, but rushing over, Will bent to scoop her up.

"No," Maya said through gritted teeth. "I can walk."

"Come on, Maya." Will's voice was weary. Jay had been right. After squabbling with Lexie, most of the fight was gone from Will.

Maya sighed. "All right." And she let Will gather her into his arms.

The key was retrieved from Maya's pocket, and soon she was lying on the sofa in the parlor. Lexie first removed the strips of cloak tied around Maya's arm and then her tunic top. The wound, throbbing and red, was examined, and Maya heard Hanss say in relief, "The knife was not poisoned, but that wound needs to be tended. Let's see what Tagen has here to help."

Hanss gave orders, and Will, Jay, and Lexie followed his instructions. They bustled around the cottage, finding salve, tablets to ease the pain, bandages, and a cloth to clean the wound. Aiken and Orlaith climbed out of Maya's pockets and perched on the edge of the sofa. Salve was put on the wound, and Maya bit her lip as she felt it burn into her. The knife had gone deep, and the salve oozed all the way down. Gauze and a clean bandage came next. In Maya's pack, Lexie found another tunic and helped Maya put it on. Exhausted, Maya fell back onto the sofa, and Lexie covered her with a blanket.

"You really are a little freak," Lexie said affectionately, patting Maya's cheek.

"I know," Maya replied wearily.

Jay leaned over and kissed her forehead. "Maya's not a freak. She's a little lion." He stared pointedly at Will, who looked at his hands.

Even though her arm was throbbing, Maya grinned. "Well, my birthday's in August, and I'm either six or sixteen."

Laughing, Jay and Lexie left to fix supper, and Will settled beside her on the floor.

Maya wanted to sleep but knew that she and Will needed to talk. Her eyes fluttered shut, but Maya reluctantly opened them. "Will..."

"Shush," Will said gently. "We don't have to talk now."

"Yeah, we do. Are you still mad?"

Will shook his head. "No. By the time we got here, Lexie had taken it right out of me."

Maya looked into his eyes and saw the doubt there. "But?" she asked.

"You just act without thinking," Will said slowly. "And you hope things will turn out all right."

Although Maya knew there was some truth to what Will said, she was still stung by his words. "Will, I see things that you can't see. At least not yet. You've just had your eyes peeled. Magic showed me what would happen if I didn't do anything. The knife would have gone straight into your heart and killed you."

"It could have killed you."

"No, Will. Magic was working with me. I knew I wouldn't be killed."

Will shook his head. "How can you be so sure? The knife got your arm."

"An arm is not a heart. My arm will heal."

Will rubbed his face. "Does it ever occur to you that you might be wrong?"

Maya lay still as she thought about this. Sometimes, even now, Maya wasn't sure what she should do. However, when it came to Time and Magic, Maya understood that she should trust what they showed her.

Maya answered slowly, "I don't always think I'm right. But when I know, I know."

"What the hell is that supposed to mean?" Will asked curtly.

Shifting to get a better look at Will, Maya winced as she bumped her bandaged arm.

"Be still," he said sternly.

Maya settled back into her original position, flat on her back. She stared at the ceiling. "Sometimes, but not all the time, I feel connected with things, and I can see different possibilities. In our universe, Time shows me. Here, it's Magic. Hasn't that happened to you, Will?"

"Once in a while," Will admitted slowly. "But apparently not as often as it does with you."

"As I said, I've had my eyes peeled longer than you have."

Will's voice was low. "Plus, you're better than all of us put together."

"Don't say that. I'm not."

"Yeah, you are. Which is why if anyone takes a knife, it should be one of us rather than you. What if Magic had been wrong? What if that imp had killed you? Where would we be? Do you think one of us could go to the Great Library and do what you're going to do? What would we do without you?"

Knowing Will meant two things by that last sentence, Maya twisted around to stare at him, and she didn't care that her arm seared with pain. "Will, do you think I would let you, Jay, or Lexie die if I could do something to stop it? Do you really?" Reaching out with her good arm, she grabbed Will's hand. "Never! So don't even think about it."

Squeezing Maya's hand, Will stubbornly shook his head.

"Never," Maya repeated fiercely.

Jay and Lexie had come back into the room and were leaning against the sofa.

"Will," Lexie said, "when there's a fire, most people run the other way. It's what any sensible person would do. But a few people run right toward the fire even though they might get burnt. Maya's that kind of person, and there's nothing you can do about it. That's how she is."

Will's eyes glittered as he looked at Maya. "I know."

Maya looked at her three friends. "You're all the same way. Will and Jay, you came with me to Elferterre without even hesitating."

"I did hesitate a little," Jay put in.

"All right," Maya admitted. "Maybe a little. But not for very long."

"No," Jay agreed. "Not for very long. I couldn't let Will go without me."

"And I go where you go, Maya," Will said, stroking Maya's cheek.

Pressing Will's warm hand against her cheek, Maya turned to Lexie. "And you. I think you're the bravest of us all. After coming to Elferterre, getting really sick from Magic, and then nearly being eaten by an ogre, you decide to come with us rather than go back to Earth. Now how sensible was that?"

Lexie looked pleased but waved her hand. "Well, I couldn't let you guys have all the fun."

They all laughed, and the mood shifted. Jay kissed Lexie, who smiled, and Will kissed Maya, who smiled as well.

Then a shiver of premonition came to Maya, and it chilled even her throbbing wound. The premonition was so dire that it made her doubt everything she had just said about trusting Time and Magic. Quickly, Maya blocked her thoughts so the others wouldn't see what she had just seen, and Maya knew what she needed to tell Will, Jay, and Lexie. "There's something else you should know."

Lexie looked at the ceiling. "Dear God, what now?"

"I'm not the only one," Maya said slowly. "There are others. Out across our universe, there are other librarians and Books of Everything coaching other teenagers. If something happens to me, take the lock and find one of them. Earth's Book of Everything will help you. In your time, it is still on Earth."

The mood changed again, and there was a shocked silence. Maya continued, "I'm not kidding, guys. What? Did you think the Great Library would put all its eggs in one basket? With me? Come on!"

Will finally spoke, "I'm going to be honest. I hadn't thought about it at all. Everything's happened so fast. I met you and bam! Here I am on Elferterre, running from ogres, having my eyes peeled, traveling without my body, stealing a lock and key, and then fighting imps."

Jay drummed his fingers on the back of the couch. "Yeah, not much time to think about the master plan, was there?"

"I suppose not," Maya said. "But now you know. So promise me you'll take the lock if I don't make it. If Chaos is stronger than Magic. Or Time."

Will stared intently at Maya. "Nothing is going to happen to you. Do you hear me? Nothing. I won't let it."

Maya sighed. "Will..."

"I'm serious."

"I know. But..."

"No buts," came Will's quick retort.

Maya shook her head. "Promise me you'll take the lock and key," she insisted.

"I promise." This came from Jay, and his normally impish face was serious.

"So do I," muttered Will, looking the saddest Maya had seen since he had spoken about his mother's death.

"And so do I!" Lexie snapped. "I wouldn't let those two geeks go off on their own. Someone has to remind them that they can't stop to eat whenever they want."

Maya laughed in relief as did the others. But then overcome by all that had happened on Earth and on Elferterre and by what would happen if her vision was correct, Maya covered her face with her hands and began to weep. Blinking rapidly, Will stroked Maya's head.

"Oh, Maya!" Lexie said, and she began to cry, too.

Jay put his arm around Lexie, and she wept on his shoulder.

On the back of the couch, Aiken blew little puffs of smoke in sympathy, and Orlaith clacked her front legs together.

"Sorry," Maya gulped between tears. "Sorry!"

"Don't be sorry," a voice said. It was Hanss, who had been quiet the whole time. He jumped on the couch and nestled on her lap. "You are carrying a heavy load."

Maya took her hands away from her face to look at Hanss, and putting both paws on her wet cheeks, the cat began to purr. Maya felt the purring travel from his paws through her face to her whole body. She breathed in time with the purring and slowly stopped crying.

"There," Hanss said tenderly. "There, there. Remember, Magic won't let you down."

Warm and comforted, Maya closed her eyes, settled into the sofa, and fell asleep.

When Maya woke up, it was morning, and the sun was shining in through the windows of the cottage. In a comfortable chair by the sofa, Will was asleep, slumped against the back and with both legs draped over an arm. Nobody else was in the room, and the house was quiet with sleep. Maya sat up carefully. Her arm was stiff and sore, but it didn't feel too bad. Maya decided that Tagen's salve must have done its work. She went to the bathroom, shook her head as she regarded her tired face in the mirror, and washed up. When Maya came out, the house was still quiet. Looking out the window, Maya saw that the sun was not high. It was early morning, and there was no reason to wake the others.

But Maya was hungry. She opened the refrigerator, but except for some butter and a few jars of jam, there was nothing much in there. Of course there wasn't. Ehren and Tagen wouldn't leave food to spoil in the refrigerator while they were gone. Knowing there were chickens and a garden, Maya grabbed a couple of bowls and headed outside.

Birds were singing, the air was fresh and clean, and all around was green, green, green. Before going to the coop, Maya stood on the porch and breathed deeply, smelling the sweet air and listening to the morning song. The coop was behind the cottage, and the hens looked at her expectantly when she came in. The door to their large yard was closed, and Maya supposed that someone came over a couple of times a day to tend the chickens while Ehren and Tagen were gone. In a room off the coop, there were big covered metal containers filled with grain, and Maya fed the chickens. She found an outdoor spigot and gave them fresh water, too. Then she let the chickens out, and there was a clucking and a rush as most of them hurried outside. Some of the hens stayed on their nest-boxes and watched her with gimlet eyes as she went over to them. But they didn't try to peck Maya's hand as she gathered eggs.

Putting the bowl of eggs in the shade, Maya went to the garden, not far away. There were still strawberries to be picked, and Maya quickly filled the bowl. A long black snake hurried by, not far from where Maya was picking, but she watched it without jumping or squealing. Maya had never been afraid of snakes.

Just as Maya was done picking, Sheverre came out of the fields and joined her on the edge of the garden. Setting the bowl of strawberries next to the eggs, Maya went over to the great metal horse and put her hand on his neck. She sensed that Sheverre had been patrolling the property while they slept, on the lookout for anything that might harm them.

"A guard horse as well," Maya murmured. "No wonder Tagen was so keen to have a horse like you."

Sheverre nickered, and his eyes glittered proudly.

"Do you need some pellets?" Maya asked, and Sheverre shook his head.

"I gave him some last night." Will had come outside, and he walked toward them.

"Good."

After the emotional day they had had yesterday, Maya felt a little shy around Will, and she could tell he felt the same way. What had been said needed to have been said, but it was still sobering, and it put a distance between them that hadn't been there before.

Will cleared his throat. "How are you feeling?"

"I'm okay, Will. Really, I am. My arm hardly hurts at all. It must be Tagen's salve. I'll be ready to go when you all are."

"I'm sorry about yesterday." He looked at her hand but didn't take it. "Hanss is right. You're carrying a heavy load, and I just made it worse. But when I saw what you did, I was really scared. You knocked me out of the way without thinking twice. And then the knife hit you when it should have hit me."

Shaking her head, Maya reached for one of Will's hands and squeezed it. "Will, I understand. We're all carrying a heavy load. Maybe the Books of Everything shouldn't use us this way. But they do. And I can see their point. Nobody is expecting a bunch of teenagers to steal from Galli and beat Cinnial. And Hanss is right. We should trust Magic."

"Yeah." Holding hands, they were silent for a few minutes. Then Will said, "I have something for you."

"You do?"

"Don't sound so surprised. Why wouldn't I buy something for you?"

"Oh, I don't know. Between having our spirits leave our bodies, riding gyrocycles, stealing a lock and key, and fighting imps, there's been so much free time."

Will laughed. "While you were resting at the campsite and we took turns staying with you, there actually was a little free time." He reached in his pocket and pulled out a velvet pouch. Opening it, he removed an exquisitely carved female lion. "Jay is right. You are a little lion."

In wonder, Maya took the lioness, who nodded regally. "She's beautiful, Will. Thank you so much."

Will hugged her, and Maya winced. "Sorry!" he said.

"It's all right." She could hardly stop looking at the lioness.

"Did Ehren or Tagen carve her?"

"No, she came from another table." Will kissed the top of Maya's head. "The minute I saw her, I knew she should be with you, even though you already had quite a collection."

"But she will be with me always," Maya said simply, reluctantly putting the lioness back in the pouch and then into her empty side pocket. "And I don't think the others will."

Will smiled, and his eyes crinkled around the edges the way they had when they first met. He looked at the two bowls not far from where they stood. "Are those strawberries and eggs?"

"Sure are. Are you hungry?"

"Did you even have to ask?"

As they grinned at each other, Maya was relieved that the easiness between them was back. They each picked up a bowl and headed for the house, where Jay and Lexie were waiting for them.

They made tea, fried the eggs, and ate the strawberries. After having their breakfast, they tidied the cottage.

"I still have a little chamomile tea," Jay said when they were done.

"So do I," Will added.

"Leave the rest with Ehren and Tagen?" Lexie suggested.

"Good idea," Maya replied. "Along with most everything else. It will be easier to travel without so many packs."

Maya's pack was already in the house, and the other packs were retrieved from Sheverre. In the empty box on Will and Maya's gyrocycle, they put in a pot, matches, bags of soup, spoons, and bowls. The imp's knife went in, too, even though nobody really wanted it. But they all agreed it would be best to bring the knife. Just in case. The half empty bags were left on the dining room floor, and the rest of the tea went on the dining room table, along with a little picture of Sheverre that Lexie had drawn.

"That's pretty good," Jay said, looking at the drawing.

Lexie winked at Jay. "I have many talents."

Jay laughed. "I bet you do."

Will and Maya laughed, too, but then the teenagers were silent as they looked wistfully around the cozy cottage, cheerful and safe. Nobody wanted to leave. The last leg of their journey was through Darkwood Forest, and the teenagers—especially Maya—thought about the dangers that waited for them there.

"Ogres," Lexie said with a shudder.

"And gliders," Hanss added.

"You never did tell us what those were," Jay replied.

The cat's whiskers twitched. "Big, big snakes that come out at night to hunt. The gliders can see in the dark, and when they move, they skim a few inches above the ground. Which makes them really, really fast. But with any luck, we should be out of the forest before nightfall."

"Right," Jay muttered.

Lexie snorted. "What could possibly go wrong?"

As she tucked the key under the doormat, Maya thought with a shiver, "What, indeed?"

But after saying goodbye to Sheverre, Maya resolutely put all thoughts of ogres and gliders out of her mind. She had decided to trust Magic, as Hanss had advised. After all, Maya knew she could trust Time, and she sensed that in its own way, Magic would be just as true as Time was. The complicating factor, both on Earth and on Elferterre, was Chaos, but Maya pushed that thought away as well.

In one of Maya's pockets was the green pouch with the lock and key, and Aiken and Orlaith were settled on top. The lioness was nestled in the other pocket, and beside her, in its box, the bee buzzed from time to time.

Will climbed onto the gyrocycle and started the engine. "Ready?"

He reached out a strong arm, and Maya used it to steady herself as she slid on behind him. "Ready."

Jay and Lexie were waiting on theirs, and Hanss had settled in the box behind them. Off they went down the road, away from the farm and away from Sheverre, who stood and watched until they were out of sight.

27: Over the Edge

They rode without incident until noon. Maya had successfully pushed the premonition to the back of her mind, and she thought about all the other things that had happened in this magical realm. As dangerous as Elferterre was, Maya would miss the crackle of Magic around her, the intense light, and the way everything stood out in sharp detail. She would miss Ehren and Tagen, who had taken them in without question. And finally, she would miss Myranda, the lavender witch. A part of Maya wanted to stay on Elferterre, learn more magic, and avoid Darkwood Forest altogether.

"Maybe when this is all over, I can come back for a visit," Maya murmured, knowing this was probably wishful thinking.

Will said, "I like it here, too. Maybe I can come back with you."

"Maybe," Maya replied doubtfully.

"Why not?" Will's voice was sharp.

Maya decided to take a practical approach. "Remember, we're from different times. You're eleven years older than I am. In my time, I'm nearly sixteen, and you're twenty-seven. That would be weird." Maya shook her head. "I can just imagine what my parents would say if I had a boyfriend who was twenty-seven. Especially my father. Man oh man, would he be mad."

"I said I'd wait. We belong together. You know we do. You could hear me across two universes. That has to mean something."

"It does. But, Will, think about it. You'd have to wait until you were nearly thirty before I was old enough. Even then, I'd only be eighteen. A lot can happen in that amount of time. You might fall in love with someone else. You might get married and have children. It might have already happened in my time."

"Do you think I would just forget you and go with someone else?" Will asked sharply. "After all that we've been through?"

"Andy did."

"Well, yeah. But in your time, he's old enough to be your father. I'm only eleven years older than you are. And I bet he didn't forget about you."

"No," Maya replied with a smile. "Andy didn't forget about me. He made it easy for me to meet him, even though he's now the president. He came to Bar Harbor for vacation. He invited Leah's father to his party, and my name was quickly added to the list."

"So there. He didn't forget, and neither will I."

Again, Maya felt as though she were sixteen going on forty. "Will, let's not make any promises. I've traveled enough to know that unexpected things can happen even though I can see. When we get back to New York, live your life. Don't wait for me."

Will didn't say anything, and his back was rigid, but Maya could tell he wasn't angry. Instead, it was because he didn't want to argue anymore. But Maya knew she had not changed his mind. Shaking her head, she squeezed Will's waist, and he leaned back into her.

Because of Lexie's bargaining skills, they still had a little money left, and they stopped at a roadside diner to have lunch. It was much like a diner on Earth, except no meat was served. But there were platters of fries and onion rings along with burgers made with something that tasted much like meat. Will and Jay liked the burgers enough to order two more when they had finished the first ones.

"Have room for dessert?" their server asked when they were finished. She was a petite elf with dark hair, and smiling, she looked at the empty dishes.

Lexie put a hand on her stomach. "No."

But Will and Jay overruled her. "Yes."

Pie and cake were ordered. "Ice cream?" the elf asked.

"What do you think?" Jay replied.

"Ice cream," the elf answered. "And more fizzy drinks?"

Jay gestured grandly around the table. "Another round of fizzy drinks for us all."

The elf laughed, but then the door opened, and four young elves, all male, strode into the diner.

Leaning over, the server said in a low voice. "Watch out for them. They don't like humans. It would be better for you to keep your voices down while you eat dessert."

She hurried away, and Maya, who sat facing the door, watched the elves survey the diner and make their way to an empty table not far from where the teenagers were sitting. The other humans in the diner lowered their voices, and even the elven customers warily regarded the four young elves. Maya sighed. She had seen their type on Earth and knew that like their human counterparts, these four elves were always looking for trouble.

"And I bet they find it," Will muttered.

"I bet they do," Maya replied.

"Play it cool," Lexie said, who now had a good view of them. One of the elves smirked at her, and Lexie ignored him.

"I'm always cool," Jay said.

Lexie nudged him in the ribs. "You are never cool."

"Oh, come on," Jay protested. "Look how everyone loves my music."

"All right," Lexie conceded. "Maybe you're a little cool."

The four elves began to talk loudly, dominating everyone's attention. Then one of them said something that Maya had been waiting for and dreading. "That tall blonde one's not too bad looking for a human. Hey, Blondie, come over here and say hi."

Lexie sat stiffly with a cold expression, but she didn't respond.

Maya said, "Let's skip dessert. Let's pay our bill and go."

"Why should we let them drive us out of the diner?" Will asked quietly, and Maya heard an undercurrent of anger in his voice.

Jay leaned forward. "Discretion is the better part of valor."

Maya frowned. "Actually, it's the better part of valor is discretion."

"Oh, my God!" Lexie exclaimed. "Whatever. Let's just get out of here."

Lexie got up and walked to the cash register. Maya, Will, and Jay followed her. With gleaming eyes, the four elves watched the four teenagers but didn't say anything.

Their server was by the cash register, and as the elf took their money, she said quietly, "Good decision." After making change, she handed them a white paper bag. "Dessert to go. I didn't pack ice cream, but our cakes and pies are tasty without it."

"Thank you." Maya took the bag.

"We're not all like that here in Norlander," the server said, her voice almost a whisper.

"I know," Maya replied.

Outside, Hanss was waiting in his box on Jay and Lexie's gyrocycle. "I saw those elves go in. I knew there would be trouble."

"Not too much trouble," Will said stiffly. "We left before there was a fight."

"Good," Hanss replied. "Those elves could beat you to a pulp. Don't think they couldn't."

Will patted his pocket. "I have my ball. It took down the imps. It could take elves down, too."

"Right," Hanss replied. "And then we'd have an elf patrol after us. And their gyrocycles are much faster than ours."

Will's jaw was clenched, but he didn't say anything as he helped Maya get on the gyrocycle. Soon they were on the road, and it took an hour for Will to relax. Maya didn't say anything, sensing it was better to let Will's anger dissipate on its own.

"It's not right the way the elves treat humans," Will finally said.

"No, it's not."

"When we get back, I'm going to talk to Pawel about it."

"It can't hurt."

When Will laughed, Maya realized how much like her Mémère she sounded, and she laughed, too.

The farther they drove away from Foretcour, the quieter the roads became until they only passed a vehicle now and then. Maya took in the crisp, beautiful countryside—how the green of the trees and plants seemed greener than they did on Earth, how the flowers were brighter, how the sky was an impossible blue. Riding on the gyrocycle brought the landscape close to her, and Maya let it fill her senses. Moving through the exquisite countryside, she lost track of time, and when they stopped at a turnout to eat their desserts, which were as tasty as the server had said they would be, it seemed that they had only been on the road a short time. But the sun was lower in the sky, and Maya figured it was late afternoon, which meant they had been traveling for several hours.

Will, Jay, and Lexie were quiet, too, and Maya could tell they felt the same way.

"This is quite a place," Jay finally said.

"I wonder if I could live here," Lexie murmured, looking out at the vast expanse of hills, trees, and rolling countryside.

"Humans aren't treated very well on Elferterre," Will reminded them, and the others agreed. Then, he, too, regarded the landscape. "But it is beautiful here."

By this time, they weren't far from Darkwood Forest. Arbor City, with The Trotting Horse and Myranda's cottage, was only about ten miles away. But the map directed them to go on a side road, which took them, in a roundabout way, to the vast field that surrounded the forest.

Jay and Will stopped the gyrocycles, and they all stared at the forest. With the dark evergreens lining the field, it looked like a fortress. Shivering, Maya thought about the ogres. She couldn't sense them waiting by the edge, but she knew they were there, patrolling the forest and looking for them.

"Why did I stick out my tongue at them?" Maya asked.

"It wouldn't matter," Hanss replied. "You tricked them out of their meal, and no matter what you did you would be on their bad side."

"You're probably right," Maya said. "But still."

"Can we take these gyroscopes in the woods?" Will asked.

"For a while," Hanss answered. "We left the woods in such a hurry that you probably don't remember, but the path to the portal is too narrow and overgrown for the gyrocycles. There are some elves that go back and forth, but not regularly, and the portals are picky about whom they let through. Few creatures of the forest bother with the portals, and this means the paths are not worn with use."

"That's a relief," Lexie replied. "Or else we'd have ogres running the streets of New York City."

"That definitely would not be good," Jay said.

"We'll go as far as we can." Will took a deep breath. "Are we ready?"

"Ready," Jay answered.

"Ready," Maya and Lexie said at the same time.

Hanss yowled.

Will and Jay started the engines, and the gyrocycles rolled through the golden fields, shimmering in the sun, then to the shaded strip by the forest. Soon they were in Darkwood Forest, surrounded by tall trees and the crackling of even more magic.

Hanss was right. The path was broad enough for the gyrocycles, and as they rode, Maya scanned the woods for ogres. They weren't nearby, but she could feel their relentless energy, and Maya knew they weren't far away. The gyrocycles were fairly quiet, making a faint whirring sound as they moved along, and there was only a slight crunching of leaves and needles on the pathway.

Maya sent her thoughts to the others. "If we don't talk out loud, maybe the ogres won't hear us, and we can slip right past them."

"Maybe," came the replies, and a watchful, uneasy silence settled over them.

As the gyrocycles rolled quietly down the path, Maya heard the cries of various animals. She could feel they were being watched, and with the exception of Hanss, Maya knew that she, Will, Lexie, and Jay didn't belong in the forest. Some one of those creatures was bound to alert the ogres that human intruders had entered the forest. It was only a matter of time.

But when the attack came, they were all surprised, even Hanss. They had come to a fork in the road, and a small group of ogres jumped out of the woods onto the path to the right. Will and Jay revved the engines and shot down the path to the left, even though it was the wrong way to go. With a yell, the ogres loped behind them, and Will and Jay drove faster. Terrified, Maya gripped Will's waist, but his concentration was on the path, on getting away from the

ogres. The map was beeping in distress as they went farther and farther away from the portal that would take them back to New York
City.

They came to another fork and another group of ogres and
went down another wrong path. Maya felt sick as she realized what
the ogres were doing, herding them like deer through the woods to
someplace where there would be no escape. The forest was filled
with the hunting cries of the ogres, and the sound enveloped them
from three sides, pushing them on. There was only one way to go—
forward—and Maya knew that they wouldn't be able to get back to
the portal they had taken from New York City.

"Is there another portal nearby?" Maya desperately asked the
map.

The map flashed its answer. There was one nearby, up ahead. If
they could go fast enough, they could outrun the ogres and use that
portal.

"But where will it take us?" asked Will. "And to what time?"

"I don't know," Maya replied. "But we don't have a choice.
Drive as fast as you can, Will. Drive!"

Will didn't argue. He pushed the speed to the point where it
seemed as though the gyrocycle was going to spin out of control and
wipe out. Maya's heart was beating loud and fast, and she heard
Lexie screech in terror as they went around a corner and nearly top-
pled over. But the ogres' cries were getting fainter and fainter, and for
a moment Maya actually felt hopeful. They were going to outrun
their pursuers. The portal would take them to a different time and a
different place, but they would be safe from the ogres.

Maya peered over Will's shoulder to look at the map, and she saw
they weren't far away. The path was getting narrower and narrower
until they were clogged with roots and large rocks, and the gyrocycles
couldn't go any farther. It seemed to Maya, as they got off the gyrocycles and headed down the path, that some of the rocks looked as
though they were freshly laid. This slowed down the teenagers and the
cat as they carefully picked their way around the rocks.

But the portal was not far away, and Maya didn't want to think
about why those rocks were there. Will had grabbed the map, and

the blinking light indicated that the location of the other portal was tantalizingly near to where they were. It was up ahead. Not far, not far. Getting closer.

Maya thought triumphantly, "We're going to make it! So take that, ogres."

They had come to the edge of a deep ravine, and they picked their way even more cautiously along the path. Maya glanced to her left, and her stomach lurched. She could hardly see the bottom of the ravine, and she had no idea how high up they were.

"Too high," Maya thought uneasily. One wrong step was all it would take to send them hurtling over the edge.

"Let's move off the path," Will suggested. "We can come at the portal from another angle." Will pointed to a rock wall that loomed just ahead of them. "The map says it's right there."

"Good idea," said Lexie, her voice choked and subdued.

But when the teenagers and Hanss looked into the woods, they stopped. Big shadowy creatures stepped forward, and there was no way to get around them. The teenagers were surrounded by five ogres, and more were thundering through the forest, coming their way.

Lexie screamed, and Maya choked back a sob as she realized that the ogres had wanted them to think that they were getting away. The plan all along had been to force the teenagers to the edge of this ravine, where another group of ogres would be waiting.

Novok stepped forward, and he scowled at Maya. "You think you're so smart, don't you? Well, there are no sprites to help you here, you little freak." He turned to the others. "Kill them right now. They'll still be fresh enough when we roast them tonight."

Maya took a deep breath. Various scenarios came to her, and she saw that there was only one way—the vision that she had had in the premonition the day before. Swallowing in sorrow, Maya removed the bee from her pocket, where it had been waiting all along for this event. With her free hand, she reached into her other pocket and took out the pouch with the web-encased lock and key. Orlaith scuttled up Maya's hand, across her arm, and onto her shoulder, where she clung tight. Aiken crawled out and flew beside the spider. Moving toward the edge of the ravine, Maya slipped her finger under the edge of the bee's box.

Maya called, "Novok, come and get me, you stupid ogre!"

As Novok roared in anger, Maya gave the pouch to Lexie, who was standing right next to her.

"Maya, no," Lexie whispered, but she took the pouch and hurriedly put it in her pocket.

Ignoring Lexie, Maya cried, "Will, throw the ball!"

In a flash, the ball was out of his pocket, and it clunked against the ogres' heads. It didn't knock them unconscious, but it did stop them from charging. All but one. Novok, undeterred by the ball, raced with murderous rage toward Maya.

"Go!" Maya screamed to the others as Novok grabbed one of her arms. She released the bee, and it went straight for Novok's face, stinging him on the lip, where the poison would go into his mouth and run down his throat, closing it so he couldn't breathe.

Now Lexie was sobbing, but she and Jay grabbed Will's arm and hauled him toward the rock wall. "No!" he yelled, twisting to get away. But Will was no match for both Lexie and Jay. Hanss rushed to the rock wall and said, "Open, please, and then stay closed, no matter how many times the kids ask you to open." A shimmering outline appeared, and Jay and Lexie pulled the struggling Will through the portal.

Blinking back tears, Maya watched as they disappeared through the portal. Novok began to choke, and for a moment Maya was hopeful. Maybe the premonition had been wrong, and she could get away after all. Magic swirled around her, giving her confidence, but then another force struck Maya, and it was a force she had felt before—Chaos. Magic and Chaos wrestled each other for control of the moment, and Maya was thrown off balance. Novok felt it, too, and glaring maliciously, the ogre tightened his grip on her arm. As Novok fell backward, he pulled Maya with him.

Tumbling over the edge of the ravine, they fell down, down, down.

www.ingramcontent.com/pod-product-compliance
Lightning Source LLC
Chambersburg PA
CBHW031944110726
47902CB00001B/289